Blood and Fire

MARCUS ALEXANDER

PUFFIN

PUFFIN BOOKS

Published by the Penguin Group
Penguin Books Ltd, 80 Strand, London WC2R ORL, England
Penguin Group (USA) Inc., 375 Hudson Street, New York, New York 10014, USA
Penguin Group (Canada), 90 Eglinton Avenue East, Suite 700, Toronto, Ontario, Canada M4P 2Y3
(a division of Pearson Penguin Canada Inc.)
Penguin Ireland, 25 St Stephen's Green, Dublin 2, Ireland (a division of Penguin Books Ltd)
Penguin Group (Australia), 707 Collins Street, Melbourne, Victoria 3008, Australia
(a division of Pearson Australia Group Pty Ltd)
Penguin Books India Pvt Ltd, 11 Community Centre, Panchsheel Park, New Delhi – 110 017, India
Penguin Group (NZ), 67 Apollo Drive, Rosedale, Auckland 0632, New Zealand
(a division of Pearson New Zealand Ltd)
Penguin Books (South Africa) (Pty) Ltd, Block D, Rosebank Office Park, 181 Jan Smuts Avenue,
Parktown North, Gauteng 2193, South Africa

Penguin Books Ltd, Registered Offices: 80 Strand, London WC2R ORL, England

puffinbooks.com

First published 2014
001

Text and character illustrations copyright © Marcus Alexander, 2014
Internal illustrations by Zul Fadhli Kamarrudin
Toning by Muhammad Fariz Zulkifli
Map by David Atkinson
All rights reserved

The moral right of the author and illustrators has been asserted

Typeset in 10.5/15.5pt Sabon by Palimpsest Book Production Ltd, Falkirk, Stirlingshire
Printed in Great Britain by Clays Ltd, St Ives plc

British Library Cataloguing in Publication Data
A CIP catalogue record for this book is available from the British Library

ISBN: 978-0-141-33979-5

www.greenpenguin.co.uk

Oh, my Sweet Adrenalin Days!
It's the looooooooooongest Shout-Out ever!!
For my paaaaaarty peeps: Marisa, Veronica, Macalicious,
Leafy, Dee, Nui, Nat, Dalal, Gavin & Seanie-Boy,
you rooooock (for real!)
For my boarding brothers & sisters: Pea, Fat Tone,
Darren, David, Emma & Caroline
For my gym brethren: Dara, Steve, Saaina, Ilan, Maria,
Luke, Obie, Marc, Valentino, Hose, Anna, Gabby,
Shelley, Eddie-ninja, Kim, Phoebe, Adam, Erol, Rashid,
Basil, Silje, Helen, Frank, Dan, Rocky, Alex, Alfie,
Katherine, Chris, Nikhol, Daniel, Akos, Alex, Felix,
Andrei, Ryan, Zoe, Poyaaaa, Simon, Alex, Ash, K,
Kay, Toni, Adrian & Danny
For my polymath dudes of zen: Dan, Vanessa & Joey
(you guys are too inspiring!)
For my homegrown peoples: Tommy, Daniel, David,
Gautam, Dylan, Kelly, Abi, Christiane, Anette, Bernie,
Tolu, Dionne, Andrea & Cheeky Ruth, Rusty, Gabbie,
Ellie, Tommy, Paula, Monica, Kitch, Claire, Richard,
Emma, Charlotte, Lyria, Kate, Paul, Darren, Kenye,
Simon, Riff-Rafia, Anjali, Goksel, Cress, Laurie, D,
Richard, Rohini, Allyson, Seasalt, Alex, Larissa, Scarlet,
Su-Yin, Sarai, Raj, Andy, Kerry, Ed, Khadine, Claudette,
Ant, Jonny, Les Pieroux, Larissa, Anne, Jada, Veronica,
Kiko, the Four-L's, Alice, Helen, Tracy, Nisha & Veronica
For my PK peeps: John, Naomi, Andy, Yao, Abdu,
Ronnie, Shi, Blaine, Alex & James
For the writers that I aspire to be like: Chris, Andy,
Adisa & Dillon

For my talented dancers: Shelley, Maria, G, Matthew, Sabrina & Theoharis
For my dare-all-wins self-employed peoples: Pi-Joe, Lisa, Boyarde, Pi-Neung, Tim & Julie (y'all braver than most!)
For those across the pond: Jeff, Jeff & Ana
& always for A, J & Sheenie x
Thank you all. You've bettered my life
& fired my imagination.
Let's party.
Marcus x

Contents

1

Rude Awakenings

An insistent hand shook Charlie's shoulder.

Roused from her dreams, she opened her eyes to find Marsila Keeper leaning over her. For some reason the woman had chosen not to remove the ribbon of yesterday's red warpaint from across her eyes. 'What is it, Marsila?'

'Lady Dridif has summoned us. Get up, get dressed and meet me outside in the corridor.'

As tired as Charlie was, it wasn't hard to guess what the leader of the Jade Circle wished to discuss.

The pendant.

''K,' mumbled Charlie. Covering a yawn, she sat up and swung her legs out of bed.

'Good. Be outside in five,' instructed Marsila before heading out the door.

With only a limited time in which to prepare, Charlie staggered around the room desperately trying to tidy her messy blonde hair into some semblance of a topknot while also searching for fresh water with which to fill the washbasin. This was not, after all, Charlie's usual room of residence. Yesterday's battle for Sylvaris had left the city war-torn and in a state of near ruin. Safe dwellings were in short supply, which was why Lady Dridif had insisted that Charlie and her companions spend the night in the Jade Tower.

As she went through the automatic motions of washing and dressing, she mulled over recent events.

Since being forced from London to the realm of Bellania, Charlie had discovered many secrets, the most important of which was that her parents, missing since she was seven, had been captured by Bane, lord of the Stoman people. The relief of finally knowing that they were still alive and had not intentionally abandoned her had been tempered when she was informed that her parents had been placed in Bane's Tapestry. It was a gruesome fate that left them displayed, like trophies, in an amber-like substance that kept them neither alive nor dead, but in a state of suspended animation.

And ever since Charlie had learned this, Bane had continued to be a deep and bloody wound in her side. He was a festering malady that would not heal. It was his actions that had caused all the spite and misery in her world and until he was dethroned from his seat of power he would continue to rip and tear at Charlie's life, never allowing her the chance to recover, never allowing her the chance to mend her family. She paused to pull a bitter face as she tugged on her boots. 'Stupid giant,' she muttered. The thought of him instantly soured her mood. 'I'm going to rip that hood off his head and stuff it in his ears if it's the last thing I do.'

Suddenly furious, she clenched her hands into tight fists.

Monstrously cruel and infinitely ambitious, Bane had set his sights on conquering all of Bellania. And while her parents, as Keepers of the Realms, had been among the first to fall, countless others had suffered too.

Bane had united all the Stoman tribes beneath him, then raised three of the largest armies that Bellania had ever seen. Certain of his superiority, he had promptly waged war against all the free lands. He had also prevented the mighty dragons, known as the Winged Ones, from returning from their seven-year cycle of absence. And without the possibility of the Winged Ones returning to restore balance Bane had been free to pursue his dreams of power.

It was a time of blood, chaos and war.

Two of Bane's armies had conquered the twin cities of Alavis and Alacorn, defeating the Human forces and bringing their land under Stoman control. And while everyone was focused on the events in Alavis and Alacorn, the largest of Bane's armies, known as the 'First', had snuck across the Great Plains to strike against the Treman capital, Sylvaris.

The Treman army had been torn to shreds and the city nearly destroyed. Charlie's triumphant return with her own dark army had saved what was left of the city and defeated Bane's First. But it had come at a cost: the gargoyle-like soldiers that she controlled had eventually been crushed, leaving the city defenceless.

'And Bane's still got two more armies . . .' said Charlie out loud, finishing the thoughts rippling through her head.

Hoping that this was a problem the Jade Circle would be able to deal with, she slipped her arms into a black jacket, checked her hair in the large mirror hanging slightly crookedly on the wall, then hastened out the door.

She found Marsila seated on a bench. The woman sheathed the knife she had been using to clean her nails, then uncoiled upward in an elegant tangle of long limbs and dark clothing. Everything she wore, from the reinforced boots to the tight Trellisweave trousers and the long-sleeved Skysilk shirt, gave the strong indication that she was prepared for action, perhaps even thirsted for it. And if the clothes weren't message enough, the many knives strapped to her person underlined her deadly potential. Which was odd, thought Charlie, because when you looked past all the knives and warpaint to the person beneath you could see that this green-eyed, black-haired Keeper was beautiful. But after Charlie's turbulent experiences in Bellania she had swiftly learned to look past someone's appearance and to judge them only by their actions. Having fought by Marsila's side in the battle to save Sylvaris, she knew the Keeper was one of the few people she could trust.

'Good,' said Marsila once she had checked that Charlie was indeed fully dressed and ready to move. 'Let's go and see what task Lady Dridif has in store for us.'

Far to the south, Jensen too was waking from his slumber. But unlike Charlie, he was sleeping rough. The sky was his roof and the hard ground his mattress. A blanket provided some warmth and a thin bedroll gave some cushioning but that was his only measure of comfort. Yet he was one of the lucky ones; others amongst his party had a harder time of it. Those without bedrolls had to make do with layers of leaves and hay as a means of insulating themselves from the cold.

It was a rough and ready approach to wilderness survival.

What had made the night even harder to endure was the

Marsila Keeper

lack of a campfire. They were in hostile territory and could not risk the luxury of light or heat.

Sighing unhappily, Jensen threw back his blanket, pushed himself upright and threaded his feet into his sandals. Raising his arms overhead, he stretched and did his best to unlock his stiff muscles. Like many of his race, Jensen was short and wiry; his skin was green and he had a fondness for wearing olive- and tan-coloured clothing. Again like many of the Tremen, his hair was tied up into a perky topknot that bobbed above his head, a brightly coloured feather threaded through it, and his long earlobes were pierced with wooden hoops. He stopped stretching when his back gave a satisfactory 'pop', paused briefly to check his topknot was in place, lifted the sword loaned to him as a poor substitute for the Thornsword he had left buried in Fo Fum's side, then staggered through the pre-dawn darkness to greet one of the sentries.

'Sweet Sap, but I'd give a prince's ransom for a cup of coffee and a toasty set of slippers,' said Jensen.

The sentry grinned at that. 'Well, we all know ya can afford a prince's ransom. However, us lowly soldiers have ta be resourceful when it comes ta staying warm.' Reaching into his tunic, he pulled free a small flask. 'Try dis. Old family recipe.'

Jensen pulled off the cap and peered inside. 'Has that got any of me Moreish powder in it?'

'No, dis is a man's drink! Me grandpa used ta call it his "sunshine shuffle".'

Jensen's brow furrowed. 'Shouldn't that be "moonshine shuffle"?'

'Nope. A swig of dis will make ya feel as though the sun is coming up, not going down!'

Unable to resist the man's good humour, Jensen took a pull on the flask. A slow smile blossomed across his lips as he felt its effects.

'Good stuff indeed. Yer grandpa obviously knew wot he was talking about.'

The sentry shared Jensen's quiet chuckle.

'How has yer watch been?'

'Quiet,' answered the sentry. 'And I'm hoping it stays that way.'

The first ray of sunshine broke the horizon, casting back the darkness and bringing with it a welcome promise of warmth.

Jensen grinned at the synchronicity of the moment. 'Did yer grandpa really call that stuff sunshine shuffle or do ya just have a great sense of timing?'

The sentry, like many of his profession, was enjoying the banter. He was about to reply when a flicker of movement caught his eye.

A shadow had failed to disappear with the rising of the sun. Noting the look of horror in the man's eyes, Jensen drew his sword.

Sensing that it had been spotted, the Shade hissed in annoyance. The sibilant sound was repeated from other shadowy nooks and crannies as its brethren shared its anger.

'Blight me Leaf!' snarled the sentry. Flowing from where he sat, he too drew his sword.

'Ambush! Ambush! Up arms!'

2

Debris and Hangovers

The Stoman guards couldn't quite fathom the meaning of their task. Nor did they enjoy it, but they knew better than to question their lord's demands. So, ignoring the stink and enduring the back-breaking work, all seven of them continued to pull the rubble from the ruined pit until they found what they were looking for.

It was not a pretty sight. The two great beasts lay in a festering mass of shattered wings and torn, slimy flesh. Picking the least damaged, the guards grabbed the corpse by the tail and heaved it to the top of the pit. They hauled it along dank corridors, grunting and cursing as they went. After a long toil they reached better decorated parts of the palace; here too they continued to lug their catch along. Past alcoves that held jewels and treasures, beneath archways decorated with captured weapons and brushing past gorgeous tapestries, they did not slow, nor did they think twice when forced to pull their leaking load across rare and precious carpets, ruining them with stains that would never wash out.

Sweating heavily, they approached their final destination. The Throne Room.

Men-at-arms swung open the spiked doors. Tufts of mist,

the soft hiss of hidden Shades and an oppressive atmosphere dribbled from between the doors to lap around their feet. Swallowing their fear, they adjusted their grip and hauled the dead monster after them.

Rows of footmen and guards armed with huge axes turned to stare as they trudged into the centre of the room but the Stomen ignored these sentinels; they only had eyes for the giant brooding upon the infamous Devouring Throne.

'My lor–' coughed one and had to start again as fear clenched his throat. 'My lord, as you commanded . . . the Wyrm.'

Slowly Bane's head lifted. His face could not be seen beneath the thick shadow of his hood, but when his voice rumbled across the Throne Room it carried a merciless tone of command. 'Good. You have done . . . well.'

Bane unfolded himself from his throne and thudded down the dais. Looming over the guards, he studied the broken Wyrm. Pleased with what he saw, he grasped the corpse by the tail and strode off, trailing the Wyrm behind him as easily as a child dragging a stuffed toy.

'Crowman,' boomed Bane. 'Follow me. It is time to test the merit of your idea.'

The guards watched with open mouths as their lord marched to the rear of the Throne Room and disappeared into a tunnel. The Wyrm was a huge beast, terrifying even in death, yet it looked like a puppy next to the craggy frame of their master.

Their expressions of wonder turned to fear as a flock of birds whirled down from the ceiling in a spiralling mass of inky wings. Just before the birds sped into the tunnel the

Stoman warrior

guards thought they saw the wings merge and take the shape of a man.

A tall, skinny man.

Fear rising to new heights, the guards hastened from the room as fast as protocol would allow.

It was apparent that the Jade Tower had not escaped the battle for Sylvaris unscathed. The stairs that Charlie and Marsila descended bore signs of structural damage. Cracks marred the stairwell wall and entire stretches of banister were missing; these had been temporarily replaced with spans of knotted rope to be used less as a handrail and more as a safety measure to prevent anyone plummeting over the side.

At odds with the damage were the signs of merriment that lay discarded in unexpected places. Charlie saw bright masquerade masks hanging from statues, pieces of clothing strewn on the floor, half-empty bottles of liquor lying in corners and plates of partially eaten food left in alcoves.

Patches of memory from last night floated to the surface of Charlie's sleep-befuddled brain. Yesterday's battle had been fierce (and unlike anything she had ever experienced or indeed ever wished to experience again), but in true Treman fashion the populace of Sylvaris had celebrated their victory in flamboyant style. There had been a parade and street party of almost epic proportions. Charlie rubbed at the bags beneath her eyes and couldn't help but grin as she recalled singing badly and off-key with Kelko as they stumbled from an impromptu game of K'Changa to join a group of councillors dancing on one of Sylvaris's sweeping bridges.

Charlie blinked. The celebration had been as intense as the battle earlier in the day had been brutal. Sylvaris and its people were exceptional. But why, she thought to herself, had she been woken so early? She couldn't have had more than three hours sleep. Glancing through a narrow window, she could see that the sun had yet to break the horizon and stars still glimmered in the sky. Tired as she was, a buzz of excitement began to fill her. Perhaps Dridif would have some news for her; news that could potentially bring her one step closer to freeing her parents.

Before she could ask any questions Marsila led her into a wide hallway at the end of which large doors had been left ajar, allowing a sliver of view through to the Jade Circle. Disturbingly, she could see councillors arguing and shouting.

Charlie turned questioningly to her companion.

'I have no idea what is going on,' muttered Marsila. 'But I intend to find out.'

She strode forward only to be stopped by a guard.

'Marsila and Charlie Keeper,' he said. 'Lady Dridif asks that ya join her in her study.'

A particularly loud barrage of protests echoed up the hallway. 'We're doomed, I tell ya! Doomed! Curse the luck of –'

The meaty sound of someone being slapped brought a sudden and uncomfortable silence.

The guard hunched his shoulders, unhappy with the tense situation he found himself in. Tonight was no night to be guarding the Jade Circle.

'Please go and see Lady Dridif. Now.' With a snap of his fingers, he indicated that the other guards should close the council doors. He led Marsila and Charlie to a discreet exit that led to a different part of the tower. 'Two floors up, third door on the right.'

Charlie and Marsila exchanged a look but followed his directions.

Reaching Lady Dridif's study, Marsila rapped her knuckles on the door.

'Enter!'

Lady Dridif's study had not changed since Charlie's first visit several weeks ago. A large fireplace occupied one wall, and along another was a huge map of Bellania. The third wall was covered by bookshelves and the fourth was one enormous window that, when the sun rose, would reveal the cityscape of Sylvaris and beneath that the rolling canopy of Deepforest. For now, it lay dark and foreboding.

Lady Dridif, the Jade Circle's leader, stood by her desk. Small as she was, the old Treman lady emanated strength and leadership. Like all Tremen, she had green skin and large earlobes, but instead of wooden ornaments she wore jade and turquoise, a sign of her devotion to her role as First Speaker of the Jade Circle. 'Come in, the pair of ya, and sit down.' She pointed to four seats arranged on the other side of her desk, two of which were already occupied by Charlie's friends Kelko and E'Jaaz.

Kelko was one of Charlie's closest and most loyal companions. The fat Treman was usually jolly and good-natured but this morning he looked a little the worse for wear. His stomach hung lower than normal and his topknot was in a state of disarray. He held a mug of steaming coffee in his hand, medicine to treat the worst excesses of last night's victory party. His long face brightened as Charlie took the seat next to him.

'Morning, blossom,' he said. Leaning closer, he gave a conspiratorial nudge and whispered, 'Best victory parade ever!'

E'Jaaz, a Human and a Keeper, sat in the other chair. E'Jaaz looked as dashing as ever. His long hair was pulled back by a braid of blue silk and the tattoos across his cheeks writhed each time he smiled. Once again his choice of shirt, black waistcoat and baggy trousers tucked into sturdy boots gave him the appearance of a roguish adventurer. He flashed Charlie a welcoming grin. Unlike Kelko he appeared none the worse for a long night of drinking and dancing.

'I apologize for calling a meeting at this early hour but I have news. Dark news.' Dridif's face grew harder and her hands curled into fists. 'Bane's Second and Third armies have pulled out from the twin cities of Alavis and Alacorn, leaving only the lightest of forces behind.'

'Well, surely that's good news?' said Marsila. 'If the Stoman presence is light, there might be an opportunity for us to retake the cities.'

'Yer've misread Bane's reasons for pulling his armies from Alavis and Alacorn,' said Dridif. 'They are not retreating. They are advancing.'

'Advancing where?' asked Kelko.

'I'd have thought that was obvious,' retorted Dridif. 'They are coming here ta Sylvaris. Bane's First started the task of hammering us inta the ground and the Second and Third are coming ta finish the job.'

3

Dark Paths

Mr Crow found the sound of Bane's measured footsteps both intimidating and reassuring. The contradictory feelings did not rest easily with him, but nonetheless it was true. The tunnel through which they walked was beyond gloomy and horribly claustrophobic. The thud of his master's footsteps only added to Crow's unease. Being so close to the Stoman Lord was never pleasant, but to be here, in the darkness with no other company, put a pressure upon his miserly soul.

Nonetheless, as they came upon another junction and Bane unerringly took the path to the left, the skinny lawyer made very sure to stay close. It would not do to be lost down here; he had seen the shadows move and heard sibilant noises, not to mention inhaling some vile scents that wafted out of concealed pits, hinting of things dead and rotting. So as much as Bane intimidated him, he was very careful to keep up and take some comfort from the *thud-thud-thud* of his footsteps. As long as he heard those he knew that he would, for the time being, remain safe.

Scraping his massive shoulders past the tunnel's exit, Bane stomped his way into a huge cavern and, using a dried river-bed as a subterranean highway, descended deeper into the surprisingly warm guts of the earth. Blind monsters, mutated beasts and ravenous creatures scuttled towards them, but sensing the power hidden beneath Bane's cowl they quickly retreated or froze into submissive poses.

Onward and deeper the two progressed. Past ancient statues sculpted by forgotten hands, over bridges spanning black waters that rippled with slow tides and crocodilian predators, through tunnels and twisting mazes they trod until they reached a cavern of silence. Cut into the cavern's far wall was an archway that hung over an empty door frame. At the top of the arch two glaring eyes had been carved into the rock. Uncaring and unheeding, Bane marched towards this. Bowing his head to dip beneath the archway, he made his way inside. Mr Crow, however, paused to look up with horror at the carving, and flinched. He recognized the eyes scowling down at him, and remembered only too well what lay inside. The change from Human to Crowman had not been easy and Bane's dark god had not been gentle in the process. It was an unpleasant experience that he never wanted to repeat, not for all the money in the world, which, for this greedy lawyer, was certainly saying something. Holding fast to his diminishing courage, he scampered beneath the archway and into the space beyond.

It was just as the lawyer remembered it: a seemingly endless room with walls that stretched into the distance. Streams of lava bubbled down the walls to feed a river of magma far below. Rising from this was the bridge that he and Bane stood upon; it too disappeared into the distance to meet the horizon. Waves of shimmering heat rose from the magma, bringing with it the stench of sulphur and burnt metal.

While this room held terrible memories for Crow, it held no fear for Bane. Throwing the Wyrm's corpse to the ground, he pulled free the mighty hammer that rested upon a mantlepiece and struck the gong that hung from the ceiling. The peal of sound crashed around the room, echoing and reverberating before dwindling to nothing.

A star appeared in the distance. It grew as it sped down the bridge towards them, stopping only a few metres away to bob and sway above the surface of the bridge like some misplaced comet. The flaming globe was dauntingly large, yet for all its mass it gave off no heat. Instead, it seemed to emanate an intense cold as if something inside were sucking at the life of all that surrounded it. Mr Crow nearly vomited when the long diamond-shaped head appeared from the gaseous depths; it was crisp and blackened, with no nose or mouth, just two unusually large eyes that glowed and never seemed to blink. Two reptilian hands snaked out of the light to paw and grasp at the air. Other than that there was very little to see; the god's body, if indeed there was one, was hidden by the flickering flames.

Bane bent one knee and briefly bowed his head. 'My god.'

'What is it you desire?' came an insectile voice that originated not from the glowing ball of light but from within Bane and Crow's heads.

'I would ask a boon, my god,' said Bane. 'I wish for an army like none other.'

'And how should we shape this army?' asked the god.

Bane snapped his fingers at the lawyer and urged him forward. But memories of his last experience with the god swamped Mr Crow's mind and numbed his legs. A growl of anger from his master quickly overcame this and, striding forward on stiff legs, he stared with ill-concealed fear at Bane's god as it loomed over him.

'Ca-can you make creatures like this?' He pointed with a shaking finger towards the Wyrm.

'We can,' said the god. 'But that is not what you want, is it?'

'No. Can you make them better? Bigger and out of stone?'

'All things are possible. But I need more than words. I need an image, an idea to work with.'

'What . . . like a drawing?' asked Crow. He squealed as he felt Bane's huge fingers round his waist.

'No,' rumbled Bane, 'not a drawing . . . My god needs a mind that is rich with imagination and ideas. Your mind.'

'No!' screamed Mr Crow as Bane forced him towards his god's pawing fingers. 'No! Not again! Not ag–'

And just like last time, Bane settled down to watch the show and take some measure of delight in hearing the screams.

A glum mood filled the study.

Charlie looked as though the ground had been ripped from beneath her feet. It was a look that Kelko shared and, to some extent, Marsila too.

E'Jaaz Keeper, in contrast to the others, remained unflappable. He let loose a grim chuckle. 'And there I was thinking that after our recent hardships and efforts we had won ourselves a brief reprieve. No holiday for us, then? Looks

Dark god

like I'll have to cancel my trip to the Scented Mountains.'

'How long do we have?' asked Marsila, ignoring E'Jaaz's attempt at nonchalance.

'Two days,' said Dridif, 'three at the most. Of course, it will take longer for Bane's siege engines and heavy wagons but we can certainly expect the light infantry, Shades and Rhinospiders ta arrive within that two- ta three-day estimate.'

The two older Keepers and Kelko shared unhappy looks. Such news was an unwelcome blow. Charlie could not believe it. What could they possibly hope to achieve in two or three days? What could possibly stop the Stoman armies? An unpleasant medley of emotions washed through her: nausea, hopelessness and a prickly simmering of impotent anger. As the sensations grew stronger an image of a shadow-wreathed giant looming over her parents appeared in her mind's-eye. 'Bane,' she growled.

Her companions looked at her askance. Charlie blushed. She hadn't meant to say that out loud.

'Wot was that?' asked Lady Dridif.

'Bane,' repeated Charlie when she realized that her friends expected her to share her thoughts. 'He's the spider at the centre of the web. If we can't defeat his minions or his armies, why don't we focus on him? There's three of us Keepers . . . three has to be enough to take him down, right? Once he's out of the picture, surely everything else becomes easier to manage?'

Kelko began to answer her but was shushed by Dridif's raised hand. The Jade councillor twisted in her seat to fix Charlie's eyes with her own. 'Forgive my blunt honesty,

Charlie, but it is too early in the morning and we have too many pressing matters ta spend hours debating the subject so I will offer ya some words of wisdom as ta why such a thing is not possible. First, Bane is too powerful even for three Keepers. If ya thought fighting Fo Fum was hard, allow me ta assure ya that Bane is a tougher opponent. Tougher by several levels of magnitude. Second, politics will work against us. If Bane is assassinated without crushing the clockwork of his government we risk a power vacuum that could be filled by another shadowy figure. Mr Crow perhaps? Or one of his generals? Wot if someone else takes up the rudder and navigates his armies towards us? We would be back at square one. No, if we wish ta ensure the safety of the realm and of Sylvaris we must approach dis problem from a different angle.'

'So wot are we going ta do?' muttered Kelko.

'We stick with our original goal. We *must* free the Winged Ones. Only they are strong enough ta crush Bane and broker peace across the land. And ta that end we must discuss how we, or rather ya Keepers, will use the pendant.'

Charlie's brain raced.

She was well aware that her pendant could be used to release the Winged Ones. However, Charlie did not have the pendant with her. It had been given to her best friend, Nibbler, a young and cheeky Winged One who had managed to escape from the Winged Realm before Bane had had it sealed.

Nibbler and her other close friends Jensen the Willow and Crumble Shard had, at the height of yesterday's battle, been sent via a Keeper's Portal as an advance party to scout the countryside near the Winged Mount. They had been given the task of finding the place known as the Serpent's Tail. This mysterious location was thought to hide a secret Gateway to which the pendant was the key. Bane had blocked the main Gateway to the Winged Realm but, anticipating this, the Winged Ones had had the foresight to put in place a secondary Gateway, a hidden path that could only be opened with the pendant originally entrusted to Charlie's parents. With her parents imprisoned in Bane's Tapestry, the burden of finding it had fallen upon Charlie's shoulders.

So Dridif must want Charlie to help find the Gateway. A flutter of excitement coursed through her at the thought of she and Kelko being reunited with their friends. It was the only blessing to arrive with the otherwise terrible news. She looked up to find Dridif staring at her.

'Hold yer horses, Charlie,' said Dridif.

'What?' Charlie fidgeted in her chair. She could tell that Dridif had been reading her like an open book. 'How do you do that? Know what I'm thinking before I say anything?'

The old lady harrumphed. 'Ya don't get ta me age or reach me position in the Jade Circle without learning a thing or two. Charlie, I'm sorry ta tell ya dis but I'm splitting ya from yer friends.'

Charlie groaned. Could things get any worse?

4

Outnumbered

The Shades rushed through the camp, slashing and biting at the Tremen unfortunate enough to still be tangled in their blankets and bedding. Their hunting shrieks mingled with the Tremen's cries of shock.

The cacophony of noise was deafening. The slaughter horrible. And still the sun shone as bright and cheery as on any other day, illuminating the scene clearly, allowing the horror to unfold with crystal clarity.

'Up! Get up!' screamed Jensen, determined to be heard over the din. 'Sword and axe! Ta arms and defend yerselves!'

Slamming his sword to the front, he parried a frenzied attack, then buried his weapon to the hilt in the shuddering flesh of his adversary. He wrenched his blade free and brought it up in time to slice another Shade nearly in two.

Feeling cold breath on his shoulders and the scrabble of claws on his back, he hastily spun round.

FFFFZZZZKKKRR!

There was a blinding flash of blue and a tortured shriek of agony.

Nibbler growled and pawed at the smoking remains of

Jensen's would-be killer before flashing his friend a wry smile.

'Better watch that back of yours,' he said, flapping his wings so he could rear and kick at the air. 'I can't be everywhere at once!' And as if to prove his point he let loose another chain of lightning at two Shades attempting to sneak up on Jensen.

'Me thanks!' Jensen allowed himself a second to smile but his expression faltered as he saw a group of Tremen and Crumble Shard, Charlie's Stoman friend, about to be overwhelmed by a shrieking, hissing pack of Shades. Out of the corner of his eye he saw another wave of Shades rushing into the camp. 'Sweet Sap, Nibbler, sort out that mess!' He pointed towards the group of Shades around Crumble Shard. 'I'll attend ta the rest. Go!'

Nibbler burst forward, a shower of sparks dancing around his feet as his talons scraped the ground. Jensen, with his sword at the ready, raced off in the other direction.

'Are we Tremen or goats?' he screamed at the dazed and shell-shocked Tremen. 'Carry the attack back at them!'

Hearing the weight of authority behind his words, the Tremen regained their senses. With a bellow of rage, they grasped weapons and swiftly closed ranks to form a shield wall. Shafts of lightning spat from behind the group as Nibbler harassed the remaining Shades.

'Ha! Ya black-livered lumps of fat!' cried an enraged Treman. 'Come at us now if ya dare! Come at us –'

His cry faltered as the sun rose even higher to reveal a long line of Stoman soldiers around their camp. Spear points and hooked axes glinted nastily in the dawn light.

'Oh, Sweet Sap,' muttered the previously enraged Treman, a look of horror on his face. 'We're for it now.'

The Stomen were not only far larger than the Tremen, they also outnumbered them.

But that was not the end of the bad news.

The ranks of the Stomen parted smoothly to reveal a party of Stonesingers garbed in ornate armour. Green flames of power flickered around their shoulders and danced down their arms. The Stonesingers stamped forward, chanting nastily. Hands raised, they gestured at the ground. With a rumble, the stone snapped apart in a zigzagging fissure that snaked towards the Tremen, forcing them to jump aside.

Still singing, the Stonesingers pointed towards the fissure and began to call something forth.

A creak followed a low-pitched groan. The sound snapped and reverberated through the chilly dawn air.

An arm of epic proportions punched up from the fissure. It snaked from side to side with poor grace until its branch-like fingers found purchase on a nearby boulder. Tensing, the arm pulled the rest of its body free from the soil and slowly but with great determination stood upright.

A behemoth.

It took a juddering step forward and slammed a wagon-sized foot down amongst the crowded Tremen.

Not all were quick enough to jump out of the way.

'Jensen!' shouted Nibbler. 'What are we going to –'

'Pull back!' hollered Jensen by way of answer. What choice did they have? 'Pull back!'

But they couldn't. More Shades had arrived and, dancing between them on delicate, skittish legs, were Rhinospiders.

Stomen armed with lances and tasselled spears rode their mounts with negligent ease. Their eyes viewed the gathered Tremen with contemptuous scorn.

'Going somewhere, you green-skinned monkeys?' sneered a rider. 'What's it going to be, squished beneath the behemoth's feet or fed whimpering and crying to my steed?'

The Tremen, threatened on all sides, were herded into a narrow defensive position. Tired, and with many carrying fearsome wounds, they moaned in dismay.

Luck was not with them today.

'Surrender!' cried a Treman, unable to face being devoured by a Rhinospider. 'We surrender!'

The Stomen laughed at that.

With Stonesong flashing around them, the Stonesingers urged the behemoth on. They watched with grim satisfaction as it raised its foot again. It paused, readjusted its aim and brought it crushing down. Pressed and hemmed in, the Tremen had even less space to jump aside than before.

Those who survived cried in terror.

With an awful juddering motion, the behemoth slowly raised its foot once more.

Growling furiously, Jensen raised his weapon. 'If we die, we die as Tremen, not as sheep! Up! Up and at them!'

'No!' shouted Nibbler. 'No! You'll die –'

'We'll die anyway!' snarled Jensen. Riding a wave of anger, he shook his sword. 'Who'll join me? Who'll show these dark-hearted curs that we know how ta die as free men?'

Nibbler stared at the Tremen in disbelief. His gaze took in the masks of rage and hopelessness and horror worn by the diminutive Tremen. He also caught the grim expressions of the Stomen, noticed their sneering lips, their uncaring eyes and looks of derision. As he breathed in he tasted the scent of fear, of blood and the indescribable smell of dread.

Something clicked inside his head like a switch being thrown. And without conscious thought he ripped the pendant from round his neck and waved it overhead.

But in the press and panic of the crowd and beneath the shadow of the behemoth's foot he realized he wouldn't be spotted.

He had to do something about that.

Spitting out bolt after bolt of lightning and gusting wave after wave of flames, he danced back on his rear legs and waved the pendant from side to side.

'THE PENDANT!' he screamed. His voice cut through the bedlam and sliced through the jigsaw muttering of fear and panic so that even the Stoman riders bobbing back and forth on bloated Rhinospiders heard him. 'I HAVE THE PENDANT! I HAVE IT! AND IT'S HERE FOR THE TAKING!'

A wave of interest was kindled amongst the Stomen. Who hadn't heard of the magical pendant wanted by all and coveted most dearly by their Lord Bane?

The Stonesingers' song faltered.

The Rhinospiders' dancing legs slowed.

Even the Shades ceased their endless twitch and snarl to stare at the pendant glittering in the crisp sunlight.

'YOU WANT IT? COME AND GET IT!'

Spreading his wings, Nibbler shot into the air. As he hurtled beneath the behemoth's foot he spiralled once, twice round its leg, then in a final wave of flame and lightning that was certain to grab the Stomen's attention he flew off. Banking low, he hovered over a nearby spire of rock and, dancing back and forth in the air, waited.

Teasing his enemy.

Taunting their hearts with what lay in his grasp.

The Stomen stared at his silhouette. Looks were exchanged, dry lips were licked. A ripple of motion shuddered through their force and without any commands being uttered they gave an almighty roar and burst into motion.

Howling, hissing and screaming, they chased after the Winged One and the pendant.

5
Loyalties

Charlie rubbed at her eyes. She was irritated and far from happy. 'Why do you have to split us up?'

'I'm not breaking ya up outta spite but outta necessity. I don't need ta tell ya that after yesterday's events me resources are limited and now I must split them even further.' Lady Dridif paused to pull a sour face. 'Freeing the Winged Ones is our most urgent goal. But with Bane's two armies rapidly approaching I must also devise a way ta defend me city. That is two cans of worms I must attend ta and only a few good men and women ta rely upon. Which is why I'm sending ya three Keepers ta the Winged Mount. Ya *will* find this Serpent's Tail and ya *will* free the Winged Ones.' Dridif paused to fix Marsila, E'Jaaz and Charlie with an unflinching stare. 'However, with me generals butchered and me army reduced from tens of thousands ta hundreds I'm presented with a problem of no small measure. I must harvest the few surviving seeds of talent that remain ta aid the defence of me city. Kelko, ya will stay here –'

'I'm not leaving Charlie,' protested Kelko. 'Not again and not when she needs me.'

'Loyalty is ta be commended,' said Dridif. 'But ya're needed here.'

'But wot about Charlie?' insisted Kelko. 'Ya're sending her inta lands held by the enemy. We know that Bane has garrisoned Shades –'

'Enough, Kelko,' insisted Dridif.

But Kelko, unabashed, continued: '– Stomen warriors and Stonesingers at the Winged Mount. There'll be behemoths too and wot about Rhinospiders?'

'I said enough!' snapped Dridif. She slammed her hand on the table and though she was a slight woman the desk shivered beneath her fist.

Silence fell across the room.

'They are Keepers!' said Dridif. In a quieter but no less fierce voice she continued. 'Keepers have and forever will be charged with dangerous tasks. It is their duty ta ensure peace and the sovereignty of the realms. It has been dis way through the ages and so it will remain for the foreseeable future. Ya know dis and they know it.' Kelko opened his mouth to bluster a reply but Dridif held up her hand. 'As young as she is, Charlie has proved her worth. Marsila and E'Jaaz have also done so countless times before. Knowing dis, I will not hesitate in sending them ta the lion's den. And as for ya, Kelko of the Fat Oak, well, I intend for ya ta stay here and lead our defences. Ya're ta be Sylvaris's first general.'

Kelko's mouth twitched and only after a few hesitant attempts did he find his voice. 'Ya wot?' he croaked.

'Ya heard me . . . *general*.'

'Bu-but why?' said Kelko. 'I mean . . . me?'

'Ya really need me ta answer that?' Taking a second look

Lady Dridif

at Kelko's dazed expression, Dridif sighed. Perhaps she would have to provide an answer. 'Who escaped the Soul Mines of Zhartoum and raced across the Great Plains ta warn Sylvaris of Bane's intended attack?'

'Kelko did,' said Marsila.

'Yes, he did. And when the battle lines faltered, who was the first ta take a step forward and face the enemy?'

'Kelko,' repeated Marsila.

'And when all the generals had been slaughtered and our lines were being overrun, who was the last ta leave?'

'Kelko,' said Marsila for the third time.

'And there ya have it, Kelko of the Fat Oak. Yer name is worth yer weight in gold.'

'A truly heavy name,' said E'Jaaz. 'And one that is uttered on the streets of Sylvaris with fondness and respect.'

Marsila nodded in agreement.

But Kelko's face had turned pale. 'Even if I don't agree with yer wisdom in picking me and as much as I appreciate the honour, how can ya ask me ta leave Charlie when we all know she'll be in danger?'

'Kelko . . .' began Charlie but was silenced by Dridif.

'Kelko, ya must accept that we face the end of days. Risks must be taken. If we do not take them, then all is lost. Literally. If we cannot take a stand Bane will wipe us from the face of Bellania. Sylvaris will be cast in shadow, our people will be enslaved – and with Bane's twisted taste for flesh we both know that Treman children will end up in his cook pot. Now Charlie will go and find dis Serpent's Tail and ya will manage the defences of Sylvaris. We need ya, Kelko of the Fat Oak. Ya will give our people new heart.'

Kelko released a sigh but he stood straighter and his chin lifted. 'End of days, huh? All right, I'll play at being general and at least while I'm here I'll know that Marsila and E'Jaaz Keeper will be by Charlie's side. Ya will keep her safe, won't ya?'

'Of course,' said E'Jaaz.

Marsila scowled at the other Keeper. 'Don't lie to the man. Kelko, you know we can't promise that. Anything could happen – loss of life, loss of limbs, capture, torture or death – but, as Keepers, we promise to do our utmost to keep Charlie in one piece.'

'Kelko of the Fat Oak,' said E'Jaaz solemnly, 'I promise you that I will die before allowing Charlie to be taken from my side.'

Kelko blinked in astonishment. 'Well, if that's the case I'll feel slightly better about allowing Charlie ta go with ya. And at least I know that rascal Jensen will be there ta keep an eye on the lot of ya.'

'No, he won't,' said Dridif. 'Jensen the Willow will be returning ta Sylvaris too. I need his rather special talents.'

'Wot?' asked Kelko. 'Why?'

'Money,' said Dridif with a shrug. 'War is a costly business and we need money as much as we need blades and warriors. Maybe more so. Money buys medical care, military supplies, food and clothing. It can influence the minds of those not yet swayed by Bane's fist, it can buy the vote of the freetowns in the deep south and be used ta bribe the barbarians of the icy north. Money is and will continue ta be an essential part of our fight for freedom And for that I need Jensen.'

'What position do you intend him to hold?' asked Marsila.

'Chancellor,' said Dridif.

'Me a general? And Jensen a chancellor?' Kelko swallowed in disbelief. 'Times really have changed.'

'That they have,' agreed Dridif. 'Now ta work. Let us discuss how these three Keepers are ta operate when they travel ta the Winged Mount.'

6

Messages and Tall Tails

The Shade scampered into the fortified temple that had once belonged to the Winged Ones but had since been requisitioned by the Stomen. Speeding past shackled slaves and between the legs of warriors, it slithered down corridors and round corners until it reached a large circular door that bore carvings of swallows and hawks. It squeezed its boneless body through the gap between frame and door, and eased itself into the candlelit room beyond.

The Stonesinger ceased his chanting and allowed the flicker of power to diminish from around his fists. 'What do you have for me?'

The Shade passed on its message.

'Interesting,' said the Stonesinger.

He rose from his reclining position and strode towards the oval patch of exposed rock that lay in the centre of the mosaic floor. Singing softly, he summoned his power. With gestures and sweeping motions of his hands, he caused arcane-looking words to rise from the ground. Once he was happy with the message he increased the volume of his song and the glow of flame that surrounded his fists. He lifted his hands overhead, shifting stances, then punched them downward.

A shade

SHHKMPF!

The raised words disappeared into the ground.

'It is done,' said the Stonesinger.

Message delivered, the Shade disappeared back beneath the door.

Hundreds of miles away in a chamber that lay beneath the Western Mountains, another Stonesinger stood next to a similar-looking patch of rock. When he heard the sliding of stone upon stone he ceased his quiet contemplations to study the raised symbols that had appeared. Once he was confident he had memorized the words he left the chamber and hastened towards the Throne Room.

'The lord has departed to confer with his god,' said the man-at-arms who guarded the door.

'Then allow me to pass my message to one of the generals.'

'Hello, sonny,' drawled a voice. 'We'll hear what you've got to say.'

The Stonesinger turned to find a pale-faced Treman looking expectantly up at him. The Treman's arms were crossed, two sword hilts jutted over his shoulders and running down his face was an impressive scar.

'What makes you think –' began the Stonesinger, only to stop when a heavy hand clapped down on his shoulder. The hand belonged to a powerful Stoman who was naked other than sandals, loincloth and a necklace made from teeth. A quiver hung from his belt and a longbow was strung over his shoulder.

'Don't think,' growled the near-naked Stoman, 'just talk.'

The Stonesinger froze as he felt something cold slide partly up his nostril. Moving just his eyes, he looked down to find the angry-looking Treman with one of his swords in hand, its tip the cold needle he felt in his nose.

'We're the Delightful Brothers,' said Stix, 'and if you don't want to look like you had an accident while picking your nose you'd better deliver us your message. We'll make sure it gets passed on to your lord.'

Fearing more for his nose than for his reputation, the Stonesinger politely, very politely, informed the Delightful

Brothers of the events unfolding near the Winged Mount.

'Pendant?' said Stix.

'Winged One?' said Stones.

Smiles, like unholy flowers, blossomed on the brothers' faces.

'Sounds like we've just found a job that would suit our talents,' said Stix.

Grinning wickedly, the Delightful Brothers sent the Stone-singer packing, then headed into the Throne Room.

'So if no one's heard of this Serpent's Tail,' said Marsila, 'how are we going to find it?'

'I've studied the maps and none of them, old and new alike, have any mention of a Serpent's Tail,' said Dridif. 'Or at least none near the Winged Mount. The only mention of a Serpent's Tail is in the lands far ta the west.'

'Is that worth looking into?' queried E'Jaaz.

'No,' mused Dridif. 'That far away from the Winged Mount makes it nothing more than a red herring. We need ta be precise about dis. The dark god told Charlie that the Serpent's Tail could be found within the shadow of the Winged Mount so that is where we must concentrate our efforts. I would guess that we're looking for a geographical location that *looks* like a serpent's tail.'

Dridif gestured for her guests to join her by the large map that filled the wall of her study.

The three Keepers and Kelko moved closer.

'You do realize that the Winged Mount is huge?' said Marsila. She pointed at its location. 'That's going to cast one heck of a large shadow and, as the sun moves, that shadow is going to travel across a lot of ground. We could be talking about an area that is tens of square miles. That's an incredible amount of distance in which to find something.'

Dridif remained silent. This was not news to her.

'Like looking for a needle in a haystack,' said Kelko.

Charlie groaned inwardly. With time so short they couldn't afford to treat this like some sort of fairy-tale treasure quest.

'But surely the Winged Ones would have left some sign?' said E'Jaaz. 'Some indicator as to where the Gateway must be? To leave us with nothing more than a hinted location is too vague. Even for them.'

'I think it was intended ta be vague,' said Dridif. 'The Winged Ones wouldn't have wanted the information ta be easily revealed if the pendant fell inta the wrong hands.'

'So we're really going to be combing through miles and miles of enemy territory hunting for something that looks like a snake's tail?' grumbled E'Jaaz. 'I'm betting that you guys are all thinking this Serpent's Tail is a crag, a funny-shaped hill or cliff. Am I right?' There was a round of sheepish nods. 'Well, what happens if it's not something as large or as obvious as a cliff? What if we're looking for something small? I'm guessing that we don't have the leisure of taking months to find this tail either?'

'No, ya most certainly do not have months!' snapped Dridif, irritated that once again he was trying to make light of the matter. 'Ya have days, three at most, before people start dying. Time is of the essence!'

'Is there any chance we should be looking for Serpents' Tails? As in plural?' suggested Charlie. 'I mean, the god did say "Serpent's Tail" but that's spoken word, right? Phonetically speaking, serpents' and serpent's sound the same but when you write them down they mean two different things. So maybe we could be looking for a series of hills or even, I don't know, old trees that resemble a bunch of snakes' tails?'

'Now that's a good point,' said Kelko. 'Dridif, have ya heard of anything that might sound like –'

'No, I have not,' retorted Dridif. 'And before we go down that route or ya decide ta spend the entire day debating wot this Serpent's Tail may or may not look like . . . well, just forget it. Wot we need is eyes on the ground! Which means enough talking and more action. Charlie, E'Jaaz and Marsila, ya will travel ta the Winged Mount. Once there ya will make sure that scoundrel Jensen the Willow returns here.'

'What about Crumble Shard and Nibbler?' asked Charlie.

'Nibbler will of course stay with ya. This Crumble Shard . . . I remember him. He seems like a nice enough lad but he is not my concern. He may stay or return as ya see fit. Just bear in mind that where ya go might not be safe for civilians. Now any last words?'

'If we free the Winged Ones,' said E'Jaaz, 'will you throw us another celebration parade?'

'E'Jaaz! I warn ya not ta push yer luck!'

'Oh, by my Blessed Will,' muttered the man. 'You risk life, good looks and liberty to keep Bellania safe and what thanks do you get?'

'E'Jaaz . . .' said Dridif. Her voice grew hard.

The roguish Keeper grinned back disarmingly at the older lady.

'Oh, save me,' grumbled Dridif. 'I've better things ta do than listen ta yer foppish provocations. Right, ya all know wot ya're supposed ta do so get on with it. No, not ya, Kelko, remain here. As my newest and latest general ya and I have things ta discuss.'

Realizing that they were dismissed, Marsila, E'Jaaz and Charlie rose.

'Hey!' protested Kelko. 'Aren't ya forgetting something?'

Turning, Charlie found herself wrapped in his tight embrace.

'Ya go get those Winged Ones, Charlie,' said Kelko. 'And make sure ya come back in one piece.'

7
Wings

Something had changed. The endless bridge still stretched into the distance, the slow waterfalls of magma continued to stream down the walls and the shimmering waves of heat rose from below, bringing with them the oppressive stink of sulphur. But the atmosphere had changed from merely daunting to something sickly and otherworldly. Odd shadows flickered over the ceiling and the bridge, shadows that had no cause to be there. And interspersed between the blast of the heat and the stink of the sulphur came chill gusts of wind and the unpleasant tang of brine and maritime rot.

Nothing was as it should be and the cause was obvious. Bane's dark god.

It loomed over the bridge in its globe of light like a sickened comet. Bobbing and swaying from side to side, it gathered its power, preparing itself for the task ahead. The flames around it flickered and its long, insectile fingers shivered and shook. Abruptly it slowed its movements. Spreading its hands wide like a conductor before an orchestra, it paused, then, with an odd lurch, it gusted into ghastly motion.

Bane watched with interest as his god worked. Mr Crow, however, could not bear to look. Instead he studied his hands, turning them this way and that. He should have been concerned that after his last run-in with Charlie and her pet dragon his flesh was still translucent. But he wasn't. He had already pushed that particular worry to the back of his mind. What he focused on now was how his brain hurt. This was his second visit to Bane's god and each time it had done *something* to the insides of his head.

'Not a good thing,' he said to himself. 'No, not a good thing at all.'

Shivering, he tried to push the memory of the god's cold embrace to the back of his mind too. But it was getting harder and harder to do. His head was already heavy with dark things and he was running out of space to store them.

'Not good,' he repeated. Clenching his hands into fists, he summoned an image of that brat, Charlie Keeper. The rage she provoked always helped to clear his head. 'You're going to pay, little filly, you're going to pay. Oh yes, for all that poor Crow has had to endure.'

A cricking, cracking, clattering sound drove him from his thoughts. Against his better judgement he looked. Two eggs were rising from the fabric of the bridge. As the god splayed its hands over them they grew and changed, bulging as if being pushed from the inside, stretching and elongating into long worm-like shapes. With a final creak, the eggshells shattered and the *things* inside bulged outward. The beasts opened their maws with a wet *shloop-shloop* sound and shook wings that were still wet with ichor. Reaching out, the god placed its hands on then *in* the beasts. White light flared and once it had diminished the two *things* were far, far bigger than before.

Bane the giant, wrapped in bandages and shadow, moved forward to better study the creatures.

'Good,' he growled, 'but, my god, I would ask that you make the next bigger.'

'Your desire,' said the god, 'I shall so grant.'

'An army of these,' said Bane.

'An army,' confirmed the god.

'Crowman, I must return to my Throne Room. Stay here and ensure my wishes are fulfilled.'

'Stay h-here?' squawked the lawyer. 'By myself?'

'You will have company soon enough,' snapped Bane.

'B-but –'

'Am I not making myself clear?'

Mr Crow trembled as he tried to stare into the dark depths of Bane's cowl.

'Yes, lord . . . I will stay.'

Bane grunted. Gesturing for his two newest servants to follow him, he thumped his way off the endless bridge, leaving the lawyer to snivel while his god began to work on his army.

The glory of flight filled him.

The wind thrummed beneath his outspread wings, sunlight tickled his shoulders with welcome warmth and the sense of weightlessness washed away the last traces of sleep.

Nibbler felt as though he could spend his life riding the thermals. Up here was where he belonged.

But he couldn't. At least, not yet.

He stared at the pendant clasped in his talons. It looked like a cross between an acorn and an egg, and for an object that everyone was fighting over it was distinctly underwhelming. Nondescript as it was, it seemed out of place in his grasp and he knew it would only look right when it was returned to Charlie's neck. An image of his friend chuckled through his thoughts; he pictured her with her wild hair spilling out of its topknot and with that cheeky smile splashed across her face.

He almost grinned at the memory until it was swiftly replaced by a much darker image of the last time he had seen Charlie: no longer laughing, her leg bearing the scar from Darkmount's treachery and the glimmer of darkness in her eyes.

How did she fare? Had she survived the battle? Or was it still rampaging, with her caught up in its tides, trying desperately to fulfil her role as a Keeper?

Unbidden, a growl escaped his lips and then a name: 'Bane.'

Shaking his head to clear his thoughts, Nibbler banked and wheeled in the sky. Bane had a lot to answer for but the giant was far away and he had more pressing concerns. Such as keeping the Stoman soldiers, Shades and Stonesingers away from Jensen, Crumble and the other Tremen.

Scanning the landscape, he spotted the enemy far below.

He grunted in annoyance. He had allowed himself to fly too far, too high. The Stomen, realizing they wouldn't be able to catch him, had slowed. Some were pointing to where the Tremen had last been seen; perhaps they were of a mind to give up the chase and return for easier prey. Nibbler couldn't allow that; he *had* to keep them focused on the prize. On the pendant.

Collapsing his wings, he stuck out his neck, straightened his tail and fell into a plummeting dive.

The wind whistled past his ears. Driven by anger and the need to keep the Tremen alive, an unknown and unspoken instinct rose inside him, perhaps some genetic predisposition or evolutionary adaptation from aeons of being a predator. Whatever it was, it urged him to raise his shoulder blades – *just so* – and to angle his wing tips – *like this*. Suddenly, with his body flared in this new position, the wind began to scream as it rushed around his wings and over the ridges and gnarls of his thick skin.

Like a warning siren or klaxon from yesteryear.

Grinning in astonishment, he clenched his muscles tighter, perfecting the pose until the wind *howled* around him.

The shocked Stomen stopped to point up at the skies. Up at the winged form that fell towards them, bringing with it a menacing sound of terror.

Feeling more alive than ever before, Nibbler opened his mouth and let loose a crack of electricity.

Lightning to match his new-found thunder.

8

Words of Warning

Gloomy thoughts filled Charlie's head as she plodded up the stairs after the other two Keepers. Once again fate seemed to be stacking the odds against her. Saving Sylvaris from Bane's First had been hard enough and that was when she'd had an army of her own at her back. The idea that the city she loved would have to face another two of Bane's armies seemed like a cruel trick. Nor was she too thrilled about their deadline. Could they really be expected to find and free the Winged Ones in three days?

The stress of the burden caused her stomach to churn. There was so much going on, so many tangled threads, that she feared her own desire might get lost amongst all the others. She *would* fight for Bellania, she *would* do all in her power for her friends and Sylvaris, but she also had to free her parents from Bane's Tapestry. *She had to*. Clenching her fingers into fists, she looked up at the two Keepers ahead of her. They were as different from each other as chalk from cheese; Marsila with her headstrong disposition was a sharp contrast to E'Jaaz and his happy-go-lucky ways. *But at least*, thought Charlie, *they're real Keepers*. Perhaps she could afford to relax a bit, knowing they would take the lead. She might only be a Keeper-in-training and her grasp on the Will and the Way might not be complete but they were professionals. Charlie hoped their experience and knowledge would give them the edge they needed.

As they reached the top of the stairs and entered the Keepers' Room of Travel a sense of comradeship settled over the group.

'There's no need to form a Triad for this,' said Marsila. 'At least, not yet. E'Jaaz will open the Portal to the Winged Mount, but before that, Charlie, one last word.'

Aware that she was intended to give them her full attention, Charlie straightened her back.

'Charlie,' continued Marsila, 'you have done well to get so far. Truly. You have done your parents proud, you have done us, as Keepers, proud. But you're still a child –'

'Don't patronize her,' rebuked E'Jaaz. 'She's fourteen. Call her what she is.'

'A teenager, then. Either way, you're inexperienced and . . .' Marsila suddenly sighed. 'Ah, forget it. I don't think there's much point in doing the *we're adults and you're just a kid* talk. Not after everything you've been through and not after hearing how you handled Lady Narcissa's treachery. Just remember, you're working with us now. That makes you part of a team and any mistakes you make can have consequences for E'Jaaz and myself. Got it?'

'Got it,' said Charlie, glad that someone was finally judging her not at face value but on the value of her accomplishments.

'Thank you,' said Marsila. 'One other thing: we have less than three days to find the Serpent's Tail, open the Gateway and see the return of the Winged Ones. Three days. So that means we're going to have to move how?'

'Fast?' suggested Charlie.

'And . . .?'

'Erm . . . really quick?'

'Hard, Charlie. We're going to have to move hard and fast. Repeat it back to me.'

'Hard and fast?'

Marsila rolled her eyes. 'I don't want to hear a question. I want to hear certainty. I want to hear determination. Sylvaris depends upon us. Bellania depends upon us. Lives hang in the balance. So tell me how we're going to move when we get to the Winged Mount?'

'Hard and fast.'

'Say it again.'

Not really enjoying it but realizing what was expected of her, Charlie pushed her concerns aside and grasped her Will. When she spoke next her eyes glittered with determination. 'HARD AND FAST.'

Happy that she had impressed upon Charlie the seriousness of the situation and the need for swift action, Marsila relented. 'Good. Let's get to it, then.'

Seeing that they were ready, E'Jaaz embraced his Will and with a flourish of his golden fists tore open a crackling Portal. Summer warmth, the welcome glow of sunlight and the scents of persimmon, pomegranate and lotus wafted into the room. Charlie closed her eyes and smiled; it was moments like this that made her glad to be a Keeper. Breathing deeply, she opened her eyes to stare through the Portal to the land beyond.

Her first impression was of a wind-eroded landscape full of canyons, rounded boulders and sandstone spires in soft shades of red, yellow and brown. As she looked longer she noticed splashes of green and signs of lush life amongst the wilderness. There were strange gnarled trees with emerald-coloured leaves, corkscrewed cacti with purple thorns and, growing in the shade, an abundance of ferns. Dragonflies and humminghawks flitted from flower to flower and long-necked shirasheer (which Charlie considered to be a cross between a sheep and a giraffe) grazed in the distance.

But all of this came second to the Winged Mount. It towered over everything, eclipsing the landscape with its magnificence. Its base was wide but sloped upward to form a spiralling trunk that ended in a top-heavy peak which scraped the turquoise sky.

Looking at it, Charlie was struck by two thoughts: first, that the Winged Mount had to be the epitome of a fairy-tale mountain; and second, that there couldn't be anything natural about it. She'd had enough geography classes to know that mountains like this couldn't exist. It should be surrounded by others, just as Everest was buoyed up by the Himalayas.

'Magic,' she whispered with a contented smile.

Marsila sniffed. 'There's no such thing as magic. As a Keeper you should know that –'

'Look,' retorted Charlie, 'you might want to tell me there's no such thing as "magic" and that the Will and the Way is a science but if I want to use the word I will. And that,' she thrust a finger towards the mount, 'is magical in every sense of the word.'

Marsila shook her head and tutted. E'Jaaz, however, covered a grin.

Before she could put forward her argument, something caught Charlie's eye. 'What's that?' She pointed towards a building on the Winged Mount's lower slope. Distance made it hard to pick out details but it looked like a sprawling affair.

'The Embassy of the Winds. It used to be the complex that hosted the Winged Ones' Gateway,' answered E'Jaaz. 'It was a place of joy, feasts and dancing, but it's been over-run by Bane's soldiers and now it's a home for Stonesingers. They're garrisoned there to ensure that the Gateway to the Winged Realm remains sealed.'

'Oh,' said Charlie. 'So do you –'

'Hang on,' interrupted Marsila. She frowned slightly as she pondered the view. 'You've opened the Portal in the wrong place. Didn't we drop the Tremen off further to the north-east?'

E'Jaaz stroked his chin. Realizing she was right, he sealed the Portal with a swirl of his hands. With a look of concen-tration on his face, he opened another.

This time E'Jaaz had got it right but something was wildly wrong. The stony clearing to which the Portal led was littered with discarded bags, shattered weapons and sticky pools of congealed blood which had turned black in the heat of the sun.

Of the Tremen there was no sign.

'What the jabber is going on?' growled Marsila. Summon-ing her Will, she prepared for the worst.

Bane sat upon his Devouring Throne and listened to the two brothers speak. They offered to kill the Hatchling and retrieve the pendant, and when he raised some questions they answered each with assured confidence. Bane liked what he heard, liked what the two seemed capable of achieving.

'And so it shall be,' he said. 'Go then, to the Winged Mount, be my voice, be my blade, and see this task done.'

The Delightful Brothers' yellow eyes flashed with nasty triumph. Certain of their path and of their abilities, they made to leave the Throne Room.

'You depart too soon,' said Bane, the deep baritone of his voice rumbling around them, hinting at gifts not yet given. 'And without suitable weapons for bringing down a Hatchling from the sky.'

The Delightful Brothers paused.

They watched as Bane gestured something forward . . . then smiled when they saw what emerged from the shadows. There were two of the things. One winged monstrosity for each brother.

Bane rose from his throne. Lifting his arms, he began to chant, and when his arms blazed with power he pointed aloft and tore the ceiling apart to reveal the chasm that led to distant sky.

'Go!' commanded Bane. 'Go and prove to me your worth! Go and do not return until you have the pendant and blood drips from your fists! Go!'

Teeth gleaming, eyes blazing, the Delightful Brothers ran to the stone Wyrms and clambered aboard. As the beasts began to lift off from the floor their wings buzzed and their tails whipped from side to side. Gathering speed, they spun around the room, past the dais and between the columns that supported the ceiling. Scales rasping, teeth clashing, they drove themselves towards frenzy. With a last whirr of their wings and a final flick of their tails, they surged up the chasm and into the stormy heavens.

Beneath his cowl Bane smiled as he watched his latest creations disappear. If those two beasts were mere prototypes he was eager to see what his new army would be capable of.

9

New Horizons

E'Jaaz and Marsila sprang through the Portal. Their hands were aglow with contained Will. Their eyes danced this way and that, checking everywhere for signs of ambush.

Charlie, however, held her heart in her mouth. Stuck on the wrong side of the Portal, she couldn't stop staring at the sticky pools of congealed blood. *What if some of that blood is Jensen's?* she thought to herself. *Or Crumble's? Or Nibbler's?* There was no way she could deal with the death of another close friend. Azariah's death had cut her far too deeply. She couldn't carry another scar like that with her. Jensen and Nibbler's faces in particular flashed through her mind and a sudden sense of dread clutched at her.

'Get a grip,' she muttered to herself, 'and get on with the job.'

Sensing Marsila and E'Jaaz's impatience, she hastened through the Portal.

'You OK?' asked E'Jaaz.

'Yeah, I'm good,' she lied. She did her best to imitate their professionalism but she felt inadequate next to their casual ability to endure the sight of so much blood. Trying not to think of her friends, she straightened her shoulders and summoned her Will.

As she looked around for signs or clues to the Tremen's whereabouts she noticed Marsila studying her.

'Good girl,' said the fierce-looking woman and nodded in approval. 'Such scenes can be shocking, and the sight of blood can be an easy distraction. But as Keepers we must learn not to allow first impressions to cloud our judgement. Tell me, what can you deduce from this scene?'

Charlie wasn't sure she was ready for a quiz but, having learned to endure similar teachings from Azariah, she decided to play along.

'That there was a fight . . . and that for all the blood there are no bodies.'

'Which tells you what?'

'That whoever took part had time to remove their dead and wounded?'

'Good. And what can you tell from the blood? Do you know whose it is?'

'. . . No?'

'That is correct. You cannot. It is impossible to tell if it belongs to friend or foe, man or beast, so worrying about it or the welfare of your friends is a needless and pointless action,' said Marsila. 'It is, in fact, wasted emotion and wasted energy. Let us instead concentrate on the task at hand and save fears for your friends until we are presented with real proof for concern.'

Marsila waited for a response from Charlie but the girl was busy thinking.

'Do you understand?' urged Marsila.

'Yes. Yes, I do,' said Charlie. 'Stay focused and keep moving. Hard and fast, I've got it.' But understanding the lesson didn't make it any easier to put aside her worries. Wary of Marsila's scrutinizing eyes, she hid her true emotions by turning to scour the countryside.

'The Tremen went this way,' said E'Jaaz, who had wandered ahead to better study the muddied footprints. 'And it looks like their antagonists went that way.' He paused to purse his lips in wonder. 'Seems like they were in a rush too. I don't get it. From what I can read from the tracks, the Stomen had the upper hand. They were winning, so what do you think got them so riled up? What could have given them cause to leave?'

'I'm not sure but I have a feeling we won't like the answer. E'Jaaz, take point and lead the way. Charlie and I will watch the rear.'

E'Jaaz led them at a jog. Following the scuffed marks of the Tremen was not difficult by any means and it didn't take them long to find where they had gone.

A ruined temple squeezed between a craggy rock face and a slow-moving stream.

Serene and seemingly peaceful, it lay in a decrepit state of decay. Trees grew around the building and in places actually sprawled over the roof; thick roots crept down the walls before disappearing into the mossy soil. Ancient carvings of both Winged Ones and Bellanians peeked from beneath a thick coating of ivy and orchids.

To Charlie's eyes the building was remarkable, the very embodiment of long-lost and forgotten temples. It was the sort of place one would read about in dusty magazines or find sketched in crumbling history books. But her gaze didn't linger long as her attention was drawn to the Tremen gathered inside the ruins. There was a flurry of movement as people realized they had visitors.

'Make way! Make way!' cried a voice.

A familiar figure pushed his way clear of the throng.

Charlie's heart skipped a beat when she found that her worst fears had been ungrounded.

If his huge smile was anything to go by, Jensen was alive and well.

'Me little Hippotomi! I knew ya'd come!'

Inner turmoil subsiding, Charlie hastened over to greet her friend. Jensen pulled her into a quick hug, then held her at arm's length so he could better examine her.

'Ya look tired, lass. Everything OK? How did the battle fare at Sylvaris? Did we beat –'

'Jensen of the Willow,' said Marsila, interrupting his questions, 'I know you have much to ask but time is of the essence. More than you could ever believe. We need to know what happened to you and we need to know what you have learned about the lie of the land.'

'But –' began Charlie, only to be cut off by a look from Marsila. She swallowed her sense of disappointment. 'All right, hard and fast. I've got it.'

Jensen looked from Charlie to Marsila and back again. Sensing the Keepers' combined need for urgency, he straightened up and began to recount the story of their ambush.

10

A Hasty Reunion

The three Keepers and Jensen had moved inside the temple.

While Jensen told his tale, Charlie discreetly took note of her surroundings. Dappled sunlight and a warm breeze floated through the temple. The building was as romantic and beautiful on the inside as it was on the outside. Carvings graced the walls and ancient mosaics added splendour to the floor.

But all was not pretty and peaceful.

Groans of pain and whispers of dismay filled the air.

Walking wounded held bandaged arms or hobbled around on makeshift crutches. The seriously hurt lay on the floor awaiting treatment from the two Treman healers and Crumble Shard, whose stonesinging abilities allowed him to mend broken bones.

Charlie paused in her scrutiny of the temple to momentarily study her friend. Although Crumble was far slimmer than an adult Stoman he nonetheless towered over the Tremen and the thick, gnarled skin that ran down his muscular back was in sharp contrast to the green skin of his smaller compatriots. The soft sound of his chanted Stonesong was welcome in this unhappy moment and had a calming quality that settled the nerves of the more traumatized Tremen.

Continuing her inspection, she noticed that the dead had been placed with as much respect and reverence as possible in a line along the length of a wall. Their still bodies were shrouded with blankets. Charlie did her best not to count the fallen but a small voice in her head couldn't help but tally the cost.

Seventeen.

A raised voice snapped her attention back to the present.

'He did what?' Marsila nearly choked.

Jensen repeated the story. 'He waved the pendant over his head and flew off. The Stomen charged after him and ever since he's been leading them away from us. One of the sentries reported seeing flashes of lightning half an hour ago so we know he's still going strong.'

Marsila clapped her hand to her forehead and moaned.

'What is it?' asked Charlie.

'How could he have been so stupid?' said Marsila. 'Does he know what he's done?'

'Yeah,' said Jensen, quick to defend the young Winged One. 'He stopped the Stomen from slaughtering us is wot he did.'

'What's the problem?' asked Charlie, confused as to why Marsila appeared upset.

'Is it not obvious? No? Then let me spell it out for you. Revealing the pendant might have brought short-term gains but it has muddied the waters and decreased our chances of success. When Bane hears of the pendant's appearance this close to the Winged Mount he will send all the forces that he can spare to crush us! You know our task was diffi-cult to begin with, so imagine how much harder it will be when the countryside is boiling with Stomen and Stonesingers. Our element of surprise is well and truly over.'

An uncomfortable silence settled across the group.

E'Jaaz was the first to break it by clapping a companionable hand upon Jensen's shoulder. 'Not everything is bleak. Sylvaris still stands. Come, let us gather your people and prepare for your return.' Leading the Treman aside, he added, 'You should know that Lady Dridif has made Kelko a general and she wishes you to become chancellor.'

Crumble arrived, blocking Charlie's view with his lanky frame and preventing her from hearing Jensen's reaction to that particular titbit of news.

'Charlie, I know we're in a rush but please come with me. I've got something to show you.'

Distracted, Charlie allowed herself to be led past the crowd of Tremen to the far side of the temple. There she found a beautiful image of a Winged One crafted with such skill that it looked like it might come to life and fly off. One of its forelegs was held upright with talons splayed as though waiting to receive something.

'Why did you want to show me this?' asked Charlie.

'Here,' said Crumble. Leaning closer, he pointed at a small hole lying above the Winged One's outstretched palm. 'Look at this – it's a socket. I'm not sure but I think your pendant would fit perfectly.'

'Like a keyhole,' muttered Charlie thoughtfully. She stuck her finger into the pendant-shaped depression. 'Do you think this could be the hidden Gateway to the Winged Realm? Could we really be that lucky?'

'I'm not sure.' Crumble shrugged. 'I just thought I should

point this out. Although it would be nice if something turned out to be easy for a change.'

They shared a grin at the thought.

'Charlie!' called Marsila, shattering their moment. 'We're ready!'

'What? But I thought –' stammered Charlie. 'I haven't had a chance to talk to –'

E'Jaaz appeared by her side. 'I'm sorry, Charlie – you too, Crumble – but we cannot afford the time. We must form a Triad and send these Tremen home.'

His hands rippled with unfocused Will.

As Marsila took up a stance next to him her hands too blossomed with golden light.

Both Keepers had expectant looks on their faces.

Charlie stared at Jensen and Crumble in shock. She hadn't had a chance to even greet them properly, let alone ask how they had fared since she'd seen them last. She had so many questions to ask. She had to –

'Charlie, we must form a Triad.' Marsila's insistent words sheared through her thoughts. 'We must do it now before –'

'Shades!' yelled a Treman. Pushing his way into the temple, he staggered up to the Keepers. 'They've returned!'

A muttering of fear arose. The gathered Tremen were in no shape for another confrontation.

'Charlie,' said E'Jaaz, 'we can afford no more losses. Forget your goodbyes and form a Triad now!'

There was no other option. Charlie did as he asked.

With the glow of Will surrounding the three of them, E'Jaaz tore open a broad Portal that led to the Jade Tower.

'Go!' he roared to the Tremen. 'Run!'

The Tremen needed no further encouragement. Grabbing their fallen and aiding the wounded, they pushed and staggered into the safety of the Jade Tower. As they did so the ground in the temple began to rock and groan as a behemoth *thud-thudded* its way towards them. The hissing of Shades grew closer, as too did the chant of Stonesong.

'Charlie!' cried Jensen. 'Whatever happens, I want ya ta promise me –'

'Jensen!' yelled E'Jaaz. 'There's no time! Go! You're needed in Sylvaris! You too, Crumble Shard. Both of you go!'

'Charlie, promise me –'

The behemoth's fist burst through a wall, showering the Keepers with dust and debris.

'Jensen! You're endangering us all!' screamed Marsila. 'We'll look after Charlie. Just go!'

Distraught, Jensen grabbed Crumble and together they jumped through the Portal.

It winked shut.

As the behemoth's hand began to lunge and scrabble around in search of prey, Marsila looked to E'Jaaz with the calm of leadership in her eyes.

'Get us out of here. Two miles north will do.'

He nodded and at his gesture another Portal appeared. They jumped through, leaving the behemoth's massive hand to clench impotently inside the empty temple chamber.

11
A New Direction

E'Jaaz's Portal deposited them closer to the Winged Mount. Once they were clear it slid shut with a brief twinkle that outshone the morning sun.

'Close one,' remarked E'Jaaz.

'Very,' agreed Marsila.

Together they turned to survey their environment.

The landscape was much the same as it had been at their jump-off point: rock spires, gnarled trees and a profusion of cacti amongst a background of red and brown boulders. Charlie, her mind in turmoil, raised her hands to shield her eyes from the sun's glare and stared in suspicion at a building peeking above a depression in the land. For a second she thought it was the temple they had just evacuated, but once her brain kicked into gear she grunted in annoyance. It wasn't. The absence of Shades and behemoth should have been clues enough. *I've got to keep my head screwed on*, she thought to herself. *There's too much at stake for me to act like a fool.*

Maybe it was coincidental, maybe not, but both Marsila and E'Jaaz chose that moment to turn and inspect her.

'I see you're a lady who likes to cut it close to the line but, Charlie, I've got to tell you, I'm far too young to be collecting grey hairs,' said E'Jaaz. 'Maybe next time you could be a touch faster with grabbing hold of your Will?'

Charlie blushed at that. She hoped it was the end of the matter but Marsila wanted to add her two cents too.

'What did I say to you back in the Jade Tower?'

Charlie resisted the urge to cram her fist into her mouth. 'I'm part of a team?'

'Yes . . . and?'

Charlie gritted her teeth. 'Mistakes have consequences.'

'Yes, they do,' growled Marsila, 'and yours almost cost a lot of lives. If I or E'Jaaz ask for something, you do it, and do it without hesitation. Particularly when it comes to forming a Triad or opening a Portal. Do you remember what else I said back in the Jade Tower?'

'Er . . .'

'I said that I wouldn't do the *we're adults and you're just a kid* talk. It's a decision I suspect will come back to haunt me.' Marsila's eyes pierced into Charlie's own. 'Please . . . do not let us down again.'

Another uncomfortable silence, of which recently there seemed to have been far too many, settled across the group. Charlie, already unhappy that she hadn't had the chance to speak to her friends for what might well be the last time, began to really comprehend the situation she was in. Beneath this layer of irritability she could also sense the ticking of an internal clock that counted down the hours Sylvaris had left. It was not a welcome sensation; for her, responsibility had never been an easy burden. And the knowledge that Bane would be likely to send more troops to this region only added to her sense of unease.

'So how to proceed?' mused E'Jaaz. He craned his neck back to peer at the Winged Mount's summit. 'That's going to cast one heck of a shadow. I can tell that finding this Serpent's Tail is going to be a lot of fun. Yessiree. A. Whole. Lot. Of. Fun.'

'I'd suggest –' began Marsila but was cut off by Charlie's sudden words.

'We have to go back.'

The two adult Keepers shared a telling look. E'Jaaz tried a diplomatic approach. 'I know leaving friends behind isn't always easy, but at times like this moving forward is the only option.'

'That's not what I mean,' retorted Charlie.

Marsila grumphed in annoyance. 'We're *not* going back to Sylvaris just so you can say a proper goodbye to your friends.'

'Wait! Let me explain myself.'

'Charlie,' said E'Jaaz, 'Marsila's right. We have to –'

'Will you hang on a second!' protested Charlie. 'Look, I might not have formed a Triad quick enough for you guys earlier but that doesn't mean I don't have a brain! Please listen to me. Crumble found some sort of a socket for the pendant back at the first temple. I think it could be the Gateway.'

Startled, E'Jaaz and Marsila shared yet another look.

'And stop doing that!' complained Charlie. 'I hate it when people do that *look* in front of me. I'm not deaf, I'm not stupid and, yes, I might make mistakes from time to time but please stop those,' she put on a voice, '*she's just a kid* glances.'

Surprisingly, it was Marsila who melted first. 'I'm sorry, Charlie,' she said. 'Old habits,' she added with a shrug. 'Please tell me more about this "socket". What makes you think it might be the Gateway?'

'Well, I'm not a hundred per cent sure it's the Gateway but there was this really lifelike carving of a Winged One and where its talons were outstretched there was a hole that looked like it fitted the pendant. I mean, what else can it be? A socket for the pendant, a Winged One and an outstretched hand . . . it's got to be something, right?'

'What about the Serpent's Tail?' asked E'Jaaz. 'Did you see anything that resembled that?'

'Er . . . no. But surely it's worth checking out, isn't it?'

'Could be. Marsila?'

'I can't believe we'll be lucky enough to score this Serpent's Tail first go,' said Marsila. 'But, yes, it's worth looking into. However, first things first. Let's get hold of our wayward Hatchling and the pendant before we go trooping off anywhere else.'

'Agreed,' said E'Jaaz. 'We need a vantage point of some sort . . . How about that?' He pointed to a series of ripples in the land that rose to become a ridge.

'That'll do,' said Marsila. 'Let's go.'

The two Keepers took off at a jog. Charlie hastened after them but it was surprisingly hard work; the lack of sleep and the punishment that her body had endured over the last week had taken their toll. Gritting her teeth, she forced herself to keep up and even though she choked on the dust kicked up by Marsila and E'Jaaz's feet she succeeded in keeping pace all the way to the top of the ridge.

'Does someone want to tell me,' she puffed, 'why we didn't just cut a Portal up here?' She paused to look at them suspiciously. 'Please tell me this wasn't a character-building activity?'

'Opening Portals drains your energy,' said E'Jaaz.

'And jogging doesn't?'

'Ha! Now I see why Jensen likes to call you his Hippotomi,' chuckled E'Jaaz. 'I'm not sure how far Azariah got with your Keeper's education but using your Will drains your energy at a deeper level than normal physical activity does. And seeing that we don't know how long it's going to take us to find this Serpent's Tail –'

'Better be less than three days,' muttered Marsila.

'– Or what manner of obstacles we might come up against, it makes sense to save our Will for when we really need it. Imagine how embarrassing it would be if we finally reached the Serpent's Tail only to find we didn't have the strength to open the Gateway. They'd be telling jokes at our expense for millennia to come.'

'Here,' said Marsila. Taking pity on Charlie, she passed over a small water flask. 'Stay hydrated.'

As Charlie took a welcome swig of the water she caught a flash of lightning in the distance. 'There! That's him, isn't it?'

The Keepers studied the small speck that wheeled and dived in the sky. Every once in a while it would let loose a barrage of flame or lightning. Oddly enough they could hear the distant rumble of thunder although it was a relatively cloudless day.

'What do you think?' said E'Jaaz. 'Portal or flare?'

Charlie wasn't certain what he was suggesting but after a thoughtful pause Marsila replied, 'I think he's moving too fast for him to notice a Portal. Let's go with a flare.'

Both Keepers summoned their Will. A little slow on the uptake but rapidly learning what was expected of her, Charlie followed suit.

'So we've stopped jogging and we're going full splurge with the Will?'

'Time and place, Charlie,' said E'Jaaz. 'Time and place.'

E'Jaaz raised his hands overhead, pushing a pillar of golden flames several metres into the air. Marsila did the same thing. Charlie hesitantly copied them.

Marsila grinned at her young companion. Even with the warpaint on her face the smile transformed her, making her seem younger and more carefree. 'I've always loved doing this.' She pushed her pillar of flame into E'Jaaz's. The two columns of Will rose even higher and twisted round each other like lengths of spun sugar. 'Your turn, Charlie!'

As Charlie's contribution merged with the others', the pillar suddenly erupted. Spearing upward, it spat great sparks into the sky. The hair on top of her head began to move and, staring up at what she had created, Charlie's mouth dropped open.

For long seconds the three admired the spectacle, then one by one they dropped their hands.

Charlie didn't need to ask whether or not Nibbler had seen it. As she shaded her eyes from the sun she saw the black dot veer from its path. Righting itself, it sped towards them. Bit by bit the speck grew until they could distinguish spread wings, then the detail of each limb, and finally the

young Winged One drew close enough for them to see the
look of delight on his face.

Collapsing his wings, he landed in a cloud of dust.

'Charlie!' He rushed
over and batted his
head beneath
her arm so he
could better
nuzzle her.
'Did you
see me?
With the
lightning? And
did you hear
me do the
thunder? Did
you?'

'Good to see
you too!' laughed Charlie. Grinning as
madly as her winged friend, she hugged him back.

'Sorry to interrupt,' said E'Jaaz, 'but after that flare
Nibbler won't be the only one coming. So before the Stomen
stumble upon us, let us attend to business. Do you have the
pendant?'

Nibbler held it aloft.

A sudden shout gave them cause to turn. A score of
Rhinospiders had crested a nearby set of stone spires. Their
riders pointed enthusiastically up at the Keepers. Spears held
aloft, they urged their mounts forward.

Remarkably, E'Jaaz and Marsila appeared unperturbed.

'Destination?' enquired E'Jaaz. 'I suggest we return to the temple to study Charlie's socket.'

'Agreed,' said Marsila. Opening a Portal, she stepped through.

Charlie and Nibbler smirked as they realized that the Rhinospiders would never reach them in time. Unable to resist, the two waved and flung rude gestures at the approaching enemy before scampering through the Portal, leaving the enraged Stomen behind.

12

Temples

The Shade sidled into the Throne Room and slithered up to Bane's side.

'Lord, the Stonesingers report that Keepers have been seen near the Winged Mount.'

Bane's fingers curled but did not quite form a fist. They were well and truly in the end game and this would seem to be the Keepers' final gambit. He would counter their move and crush them. Once and for all.

'I want reinforcements dispatched to the Winged Mount. Send messages to Alavis and Alacorn, to the Stubborn Citadel, to the Lowland Slump, to the Great Plains garrison and to the Chiming Ground. Inform every commander that they are to send three divisions each to the Embassy of the Winds.'

The Shade made to leave but stopped when Bane's hand caught it by the scruff of the neck. It tensed beneath his grasp.

'Tell them speed is of the essence. Tell them all that I want those Keepers skinned and salted and their heads delivered to me before the last Sylvarisian tower burns. Understood?'

'Yes, lord.'

Bane released the Shade.

'Then see it done,' he said.

'What do you think?' asked E'Jaaz.

Their small group stood several hundred metres distant from the temple.

'Looks clear,' said Marsila. 'Let's go take a look at this socket.'

They approached the building with caution. There was an abundance of footprints but no other sign of Shades or behemoth. With no prey or easy targets the Stomen had presumably left the immediate area. But, unwilling to take any chances, Marsila sidled up to the temple and slowly poked her head through a ruined wall. Satisfied that they were indeed alone, she eased her way inside, the others following.

'Here,' said Charlie, and pointed at the carving. 'Think I should try the pendant?'

'Go for it,' said E'Jaaz.

Charlie pushed her pendant into the socket.

It was a perfect fit.

'Isn't something supposed to happen?' asked Charlie.

'Focus your Will and try opening it as you would any other Gateway,' instructed E'Jaaz.

Licking her lips, Charlie rolled up her sleeves and called on her Will. Flames danced across her fingertips and cast odd shadows on the ceiling.

'All right, here goes . . .'

She directed her Will at the pendant.

They noticed the smell first. It was a tangy mix of peach and campfire smoke. Then there was a hum, like the noise of a speeding elevator but stretched out as though coming from a great distance.

Deciding that more power was needed, Charlie dug a little deeper.

The pendant suddenly blazed with the luminance of a small sun. A wind picked up and all the carvings in the temple, including that of the Winged One, appeared to writhe and move. An outline of a large circular door appeared on the wall, its edges glowing with the same intensity as the pendant.

The wind grew stronger, as did the smell, and the noise increased until it sounded like a jumbo jet was screaming overhead.

Just as it seemed to reach a peak there came an odd clunking noise. The light flickered off, the smell of peach and woodsmoke diminished and the elevator-like noise fluttered to silence.

'Wh-what?' stuttered Charlie. She looked at her hands in astonishment; they still glowed with power. 'What happened?'

'I'm not sure,' said Marsila. She went to the wall and stroked her finger along its surface. The outline of the door had vanished. 'It's bit of a mystery and that's for sure.'

'It *is* a Gateway,' said E'Jaaz. 'We all saw the door.'

'Perhaps it's the wrong one,' said Nibbler with a shrug. 'Perhaps we should try the others. Maybe the pendant will work in one of them.'

'Others?' Marsila looked startled. 'What others?'

'Well, the other temples,' said Nibbler. 'I've seen lots of

them – they're all over the place. They've probably got Gateways in all of them.'

'Wait. Wait just a minute.' Marsila pinched the bridge of her nose. 'You're saying that not only is there a multitude of temples in the vicinity but that each has a Gateway?'

'I'm not sure about the Gateways but the temples certainly look the same. At least they do when you fly overhead. And if they look the same doesn't it make sense for them all to have a Gateway?'

'How many temples did you see?' asked Marsila.

'Um . . . I don't know. A lot?'

'Give me a number, Nibbler,' insisted Marsila. 'If you can't be precise I'll settle for a guess.'

'Er, fifty? Sixty? Though I think there were more on the other side of the Winged Mount too.'

Marsila shook her head. 'That will teach me to get my hopes up. Part of me really thought we had struck gold with this find . . . I should have known better. Fifty to sixty temples and maybe a Gateway in each? That does not bode well for us.'

Charlie, who had felt an initial surge of success upon seeing the glowing Gateway, was hit by a wave of disappointment. 'Wait, let me try again. Maybe I did something wrong.'

'No,' said E'Jaaz. 'You did it right. Before we expend any more energy on this I think it would be wise to verify Nibbler's theory. We need to find out if there are indeed more hidden Gateways in the other temples. If there are then we'll have to come up with a strategy for finding the right one.'

'Let us put this theory to the test,' said Marsila. 'And let us be quick about it.'

13

A Study of Shadows

Marsila's Portal led them just shy of the ridge that they had used previously to signal to Nibbler.

Once satisfied that the Rhinospiders and their riders had vacated the area, they jogged to the nearby temple that Charlie had previously mistaken for the one used by the Tremen. Here too Marsila urged caution and only entered the building when she was certain it was vacant.

Inside they found another gloriously carved Winged One and, even though its design and posture were slightly different from the first, it too contained a socket.

'Shall I just go for it?' asked Charlie.

Getting a nod of affirmation from Marsila, she repeated her earlier attempt.

Gold light, the scent of peach and burnt wood and the peculiar elevator noise filled the room but just when it seemed as though the Gateway would open, it shut down once again.

After the flicker of light, dwindling sound and last remnant of scent had fled the room, the three Keepers paused to take stock.

'So the Hatchling was right,' said E'Jaaz. 'A keyhole for the pendant and a hidden Gateway in each temple.'

'I don't get it,' said Charlie. 'I thought the pendant was supposed to open the Winged Ones' Gateways? Why hasn't it worked on any of these?'

'Needle in a haystack,' said E'Jaaz.

'Come again?' said Nibbler, puzzled by his cryptic words.

E'Jaaz chuckled wryly. 'Ah, sorry, Nibbler. The idea's only just come to mind but after working with your elders in the past I've got a good grasp of how they think. Particularly when they're trying to be crafty. If you want to keep something hidden but someone has perhaps managed to get their hands on the key, what better way to keep that thing safe than by hiding it even further, like a needle in a haystack? Think about it – if the pendant was to fall into the wrong hands it'd make it that much harder to find the right Gateway if the thief had to sift through a hundred lures to find the right door.'

'But we're not thieves!' protested Charlie. 'We're *supposed* to open the Gateway. Why make it harder for us?'

'I don't think it was made intentionally hard for us. From what I can gather, your parents were given all the information needed to find the right Gateway. With them missing, it falls upon us to muddle through with an incomplete picture.'

'Do you really mean that?' asked Charlie. 'That the Winged Ones hid the real Gateway in a load of fake ones?'

'Sure,' said E'Jaaz. 'What else could it be?'

'So, uh, Gateway or decoy, it still means we've got to find the right temple for the pendant, doesn't it?' stated Charlie.

'Which poses a bit of problem,' said Marsila. 'You said you saw fifty to sixty temples, Nibbler?'

'Yes,' agreed Nibbler, 'and maybe the same again on the other side.'

Marsila sucked on her lip as she digested that number. 'Checking a hundred and twenty buildings to find the right Gateway is going to be an issue. This really is like looking for that proverbial needle. If we consider the time it will take and factor in the likely increase of Stoman activity . . . well, the odds do not look favourable. Not at all. Charlie?'

'Yes, Marsila?'

'Lady Dridif informed me that you learned of this Serpent's Tail not only from a dark god but also from a Stone Bishop.'

'That's right. Edge Darkmount,' said Charlie. Mentioning his name caused her to grit her teeth. The despicable way he had betrayed her was something Charlie would never forget. 'He said there was writing on the pendant, a bit like Braille which we have on Earth, that he called Hydraic script. He told me about the Serpent's Tail after reading it but it was his dark god who told me where the actual location was.'

'I can read Hydraic script,' said Marsila.

Charlie and E'Jaaz blinked in astonishment at that admission.

Marsila caught their shared look. 'What? You think I spend all my days running around adventuring and looking for fights? Pfft. I'd be a poor Keeper if I did not exercise my mind as well as my body.'

'Er . . . how many languages do you know?' asked E'Jaaz, clearly intrigued.

'Six fluently and I can read a further two that are classed

as "dead languages" and no longer used. Then I can muddle my way through another three, but far less elegantly than any of the others.'

Again Charlie and E'Jaaz shared a look of shock. They'd had no idea that behind Marsila's tough countenance lay a scholarly mind.

'Any more questions?' She ignored the fact that both Charlie and E'Jaaz obviously wanted to quiz her further. 'No?' She pretended not to see E'Jaaz's raised hand. 'Good, then I think it would be prudent for me to double-check that we have all the knowledge at our disposal.'

'Sure,' said Charlie, who could see the wisdom in that. Pulling the pendant over her head, she passed it to the Keeper.

Marsila closed her eyes and lightly ran her fingers in a spiralling motion across its surface, reading the delicate bumps with her fingertips. She recited the message that was written across it.

'*Should Fate bar our return and darkness cover the skies use this shard to unseal the veiled Gateway. Search for us in the shadow of our mount. Find us in the Serpent's Tail. From Wings on high seeking prey . . .*'

'Seeking prey . . . what? Why'd you stop?' asked E'Jaaz.

'I didn't stop,' said Marsila. 'That's all it says. It just ends like that. I think there were two or three more words but they've worn off. Here, look for yourselves.'

Leaning close, the others peered to see where Marsila's fingers were indicating. She showed them the faded patch on the pendant's surface. It was a subtle sign of wear and tear that had not affected the pendant's overall appearance but had had a drastic effect on its hidden message.

'What do you think the missing words hinted at?' asked Nibbler.

Marsila shrugged. 'I don't know. The rest is quite straightforward. The shard to unseal the hidden Gateway is the pendant. "Our mount" means the Winged Mount. As to what "from Wings on high seeking prey" could mean . . . well, we can't know. Not with the original script missing. E'Jaaz, can you think of any Winged sayings that might illuminate that passage for us?'

'From Wings on high seeking prey?' muttered E'Jaaz. 'No. Nothing springs to mind.'

'Nibbler? Any ideas?' asked Marsila.

'Uh . . . no.'

'So we've got an unfinished clue and I don't think there's any way we can uncover the lost words, so we're still stuck up the creek without a paddle.' Marsila sighed. 'All right, people, if you've any ideas –' she paused to fix Nibbler with a weighty look – 'any intelligent ideas that is, then let's hear them.'

E'Jaaz cleared his throat. 'Finding the keyhole for the pendant was a stroke of luck and I'm sure that will have saved us a lot of time. But think back to the dark god's words – *the Serpent's Tail lies within the Winged Mount's shadow* – and what we've learned from the pendant itself: *search for us in the shadow of our mount* and *find us in the Serpent's Tail*. It sounds like we're very much on the right trail, but so far we've found no hint of this tail. I think that's what we should be looking for: a temple that has or is close to something that resembles a serpent's tail.'

'How about if we split up?' suggested Charlie. 'Couldn't we cover more ground that way? If we split we could check all the temples in a quarter of the time.'

Marsila shook her head. 'There's only one pendant. And splitting our forces while the Stomen hunt for us is not a bright idea.'

'Do you think the Serpent's Tail could be a carving inside one of the temples?' asked Nibbler. 'Maybe we have to look inside each one till we find a sign?'

'And what about the last line on the pendant with the missing words?' added Charlie. '*From Wings on high seeking* something something. That could be an important clue.'

'More than likely,' admitted E'Jaaz, 'but our dice hasn't landed the way we would have liked and with luck being what it is . . . well, we work with what we've been given. Two out of three lines is better than none.'

'How can you give up on the third line?' asked Charlie in disbelief. 'It could be essential!'

Marsila looked at her like she was a complete novice. E'Jaaz, quick to keep the peace, jumped in with an explanation. 'Charlie,' he said, 'out here, in the middle of a mission, we only have limited resources and a limited time span in which to work. In an ideal situation we'd have experts looking at the pendant, researching it and studying it to see if there was any way to recover its lost secrets, but –'

'But there isn't,' said Charlie, finishing his line. She wasn't happy about it but she could see his point. Hoping to avoid looking like a rank amateur, she swallowed any further protests and nodded. 'OK, I get it.'

'I don't like this either,' said Marsila. 'There are too many unknowns. The Serpent's Tail could be anything: a building, a spire of rock, a statue, a carving . . . it could even be something foolish like a dead snake nailed to a tree.' Looking far from happy, she crossed her arms. 'We cannot afford to fail and we cannot afford to be anything other than certain. We have no choice but to take the pendant to each temple and try each Gateway.'

'Check each temple?' said Charlie. 'That's going to take days!'

'Then we had better get started,' growled Marsila.

'Wait,' said E'Jaaz. 'I think I can cut our workload. Come.'

They followed him outside and at his urging turned to face the Winged Mount.

'We think that the Gateway is going to be in one of these temples. That's a given, correct?'

The others nodded in agreement.

'And although we don't know what or where the Serpent's Tail is we can at least be confident that it lies in the Winged Mount's shadow. So logically it becomes merely a matter of checking not all the temples but only those found in shadow.' Picking a branch from off the floor, he used it to scratch a diagram into the ground. 'This is the Winged Mount.' He sketched a circle. 'And this is where we stand.' He marked a cross to the north-east of the circle. Reaching for a dried twig, he stabbed it into the centre of the circle hard enough for it to stand upright. The twig cast a shadow that fell to the south. 'As the sun rises in the east and sets in the west we can expect the shadow to fall from here –' he marked a spot – 'to here.' He marked another. 'And at this time of year we can expect to get, say, this length of shadow –' he carved a wavy line around one side of the circle – 'which means we need to be looking for temples in this area only.'

For the first time that Charlie could remember, Marsila gave E'Jaaz an appraising look. 'So we only need to check the temples on the southern face. You've cut our workload in half – I'm actually impressed.'

'Does that mean I get a kiss?'

'Don't push it,' snapped Marsila.

'I'll settle for that dance you owe me.'

'Idiot . . . I tell you what, if you find us the right temple I'll consider giving you a dance. A short one.'

Charlie wanted to grin, but she couldn't stop looking at the diagram of the Winged Mount and its play of shadow. Something about it felt wrong. 'I don't get it. I've seen Dridif's maps and I know we're in the northern hemisphere and I know it's summer . . . so shouldn't the southern face be getting the most sun?'

'That would be right for the realm of Earth,' agreed E'Jaaz. 'But not for Bellania.'

'Uh . . . really? So how does that work, then?'

'Yeah,' said Nibbler, adding his interest. 'I'd like to know too.'

'It normally takes an apprentice Keeper three years of education to decipher the mysteries of this realm, but you're a bright girl, Charlie, and I'm sure it wouldn't be too hard for a Hatchling to pick up. I think you'd get the hang of it in a couple of years,' said E'Jaaz.

'We're in bit of a rush. Can't you just give us the layman's terminology?'

'Sure,' said E'Jaaz. 'You're taught that Earth is a globe

and it orbits Sol giving it different plays of shadow on the northern and southern hemispheres. Well, when it comes to Bellania, think of it not as a globe but more as a cylinder turned partially inside out.'

Nibbler went slightly cross-eyed and Charlie kneaded her head.

'That doesn't help,' said Charlie.

'In that case, let's save this conversation until we've got more time to –' The shriek of approaching predators cut E'Jaaz short.

The group turned to see a wave of Shades crest a nearby slope. Squealing and mewling, they raced closer.

'This is starting to get bothersome,' muttered Marsila. Hands bright with Will, she ripped open a Portal and jumped through. The others hastily followed suit.

14

Up the Ante

As soon as the Portal irised shut behind them, Marsila spun round.

'Right, this is it. They're not playing around so neither should we. We need a game plan and we need one now. We cannot afford to get bogged down with fighting, so swift movement is going to be the key to our strategy. Portal in, check our target, then Portal out before the enemy have a chance to close in. E'Jaaz, what's your suggestion for tackling the problem of the temples?'

'We need to know the lie of the land and the location of each temple. I think we should put Nibbler to good use and get him to reconnoitre.'

'What does *recon knighter* mean?' asked Nibbler with a suspicious look.

'It means to scout ahead,' explained E'Jaaz.

'Oh. I can do that. No problem.'

Happy that Nibbler was willing to do his part, E'Jaaz continued. 'I think it best not to spread ourselves too far afield. Let's cut our search area into sectors. Once Nibbler has identified the temples in a sector we go in and mark off all the incorrect Gateways before moving on to the next. Sound good?'

'Sounds good,' said Marsila. 'The Stomen are still a problem. I don't doubt that we will stumble across some from time to time; it's inevitable. But to prevent them from getting wind of our strategy or tracking us I think it best to check non-sequential sectors. Any questions?'

There were none.

Marsila pulled one of Dridif's maps from a pocket. Unfolding it, she showed it to Nibbler. 'We're here,' she identified their location. 'I want you to search this area, then meet us here.' Her finger moved across the map. 'Once you regroup with us you can mark the temples. Got it?'

'Yup,' said Nibbler. 'Should I go now?'

'No, I want you to stay here and regale us with witty stories and tall tales of adventure. Really, we have all the time in the world.'

'Er . . . I'll go now, then.'

'Please do.'

With a hop and a flap, he beat his way into the skies.

'He's descending,' said Charlie. She stood with her eyes shielded from the sun so she could better track Nibbler.

'Good,' said Marsila.

E'Jaaz opened a Portal and together they stepped through.

Nibbler landed seconds later. Trotting over to Marsila's side, he pointed at the map. 'Here, here, here and here.'

Marsila pencilled crosses on the map. 'Then there were three more here, here and . . . here.'

'Seven?' said E'Jaaz with surprise. 'That's more than I had expected for this sector. If the other regions are similar that's going to give us a total of ninety temples. More than our original estimate. That's not good.'

'Good or not, we're sticking with this plan,' stated Marsila.

A squad of Stomen broke cover from where they had been lurking. Shouting and bellowing blood-curdling war cries, they raced towards the small group.

But having grown used to similar occurrences, the Keepers ignored the threat. They knew they had long seconds to spare before the enemy could be on them.

'This temple first,' said Marsila. She held the map up so the others could see. 'Triad up and let's go.'

The three joined forces to open a Portal and stepped through.

As the Portal winked shut, something whistled through to bury itself in the dirt between E'Jaaz's feet.

A spear.

Its head was wickedly barbed and the end of the staff quivered with unspent momentum.

Charlie looked at it in shock.

'That could have put a crimp in my stride,' admitted E'Jaaz.

Marsila didn't look too thrilled either. 'We must not grow careless. We'd better take steps to ensure our next departure goes more smoothly.'

With grim faces they headed towards the temple.

Once again Charlie repeated the process of awakening the concealed doorway. Unfortunately it was another failure.

'Cheer up, Charlie,' said E'Jaaz. 'With every dead end, the chances of our finding the Gateway increase.'

'Huh?'

E'Jaaz chuckled. 'Supposing there's a hundred temples that we have to check . . .' Marsila spluttered and E'Jaaz shrugged in response. 'I know we estimated ninety but I'm using a round number of a hundred to better illuminate my point. So when we started, the chances of us getting it right were one in a hundred. We've checked three Gateways so theoretically there's only ninety-seven left –'

'There'd better not be ninety-seven,' muttered Marsila.

'Which means that our chances have increased to one in ninety-seven,' continued E'Jaaz with a bright smile. 'Always look for the golden lining.'

'Enough chit-chat,' said Marsila. 'Let's go cross another temple off our list and see if we can't increase our chances some more.'

15
Shared Stories

Eight temples later, Charlie was a wreck.

They'd had three close encounters with Stomen and one fraught episode where a Shade had nearly succeeded in jumping through the Portal with them.

'I'm knackered,' said Charlie. Reaching for her lower back, she tried to knead her taut muscles in the hope that they would unknot. Having to use her Will to constantly open Portals and try Gateways was draining.

'Yeah, you don't look so good,' admitted Nibbler. He peered at the dark shadows under Charlie's eyes.

E'Jaaz nudged Marsila. 'I think a break might be in order.'

'Not yet,' argued Marsila. 'We've only covered eleven temples. We need to do more. We must. At best Sylvaris has sixty hours left before Bane's armies commence hostilities, at worst forty-eight hours.'

E'Jaaz frowned. 'What? Do you think we should continue through the night? With the multitude of Shades nearby I don't think that's wise. Facing a pack of the dark brethren in the daylight is one thing but facing them at night while we're exhausted is a different matter.'

'We have an hour or two of sunlight left,' countered Marsila. 'I'm for pushing on while we can. I would be happier crossing another four temples off our list before calling it a night.'

'Hey,' said Charlie. The thought of Sylvaris in peril was heavy in her mind and she crossed her fingers in the hope that Kelko and Jensen were safe. 'I'm not for stopping either. Let's keep rolling.'

'All right,' said E'Jaaz. 'Let's go. Just try to avoid overdoing it. We're going to need your Will in good shape for the next couple of days.'

They managed to visit another three temples before the light started to wane and E'Jaaz insisted that they stop.

'We'll do better in the morning when we're fresh,' he reasoned. 'And I would consider it safer to make camp now and take what rest we can rather than risking greater fatigue and the potential of making a fatal error next time we encounter Shades.'

Marsila thinned her lips but could not help agreeing with him. As much as she felt the pressure of their impending deadline, it made no sense to blunder blindly ahead.

'OK. But we're up and ready to move with first light. Agreed?'

'Agreed.'

'Nibbler,' continued Marsila, 'we cannot afford the Will required to return us to Sylvaris so we'll need a place of refuge for the night. Did you see anywhere that would suit as a campsite? It needs to be somewhere safe and secure from prying eyes.'

'I saw a couple of islands,' said Nibbler. 'They weren't

anything big and the river that surrounded them wasn't particularly wide, but would they do?'

'Sounds possible,' said Marsila. She unfolded their map. 'Show me where.'

Nibbler gave her the location and after a brief conference with E'Jaaz it was decided. Summoning their Will, they cut a Portal and leaped through.

Nibbler's description was correct. The islands weren't big and the river that ran on either side wasn't wide, but it looked deep and very fast. Crossing it by foot would not be easy.

'This will do,' said E'Jaaz. 'Let's make the best of it.'

After her travels across Bellania Charlie had grown proficient at pitching camp, but tonight's experience was something different. They were in hostile territory and being hunted, so above all they had to be discreet. Marsila and E'Jaaz were required to put their remarkable wilderness training and survival skills to full use.

As Marsila worked, she talked about staying out of sight and making sure that no smoke or light was visible. In a remarkably short time (with Nibbler and Charlie's aid) she had created a series of bedding piles hidden behind a bluff and dug what she called an 'Alavisian firepit'. To Charlie's eyes it looked like little more than two pits dug into the ground that met at the bottom; one side held firewood, the other supplied a source of ventilation. She did, however, have to admit to being impressed when the campfire emitted no smoke and, as the flames were below ground, they were impossible to see from more than a metre away. And yet for all the 'low profiling', as Marsila liked to call it, the campsite felt remarkably cosy.

And just as they were about to ask where E'Jaaz had disappeared to, he sauntered back into their camp with three fish, cleaned and wrapped in herbs, and a handful of bulbous roots that he called jerritots (which he promised would taste like 'fluffy marshmallow and butterlime' once they were cooked).

'Is camping always like this with you guys?' asked Nibbler.

'I wish,' chuckled E'Jaaz. 'Six years ago I was fulfilling a commission for one of the Ice Chieftains and I failed to check if the cave I was overnighting in was vacant. A giant skunk-bear took offence at me intruding (or maybe it was an interest in the pie I was cooking) and chased me out into the snowdrifts. I spent the rest of the night clapping my hands and stomping my feet to keep warm and bemoaning the loss of my meal. And the year before that I was running away from one of the Hilat Tribal Kings and even though I made my camp far enough away to avoid detection I made the mistake of going to sleep right on one of the lizardmam-moths' migration paths. I'd only gone to sleep for a minute or two before the ground started shaking. In the few seconds it took me to realize that it wasn't an earthquake I nearly got trampled by a horde of wandering lizardmammoths.'

'And why were you running away from one of the Hilat Tribal Kings?' asked Marsila.

'There was a slight misunderstanding after I was caught dancing with one of his daughters.'

Marsila snorted. 'Why am I not surprised?'

Unabashed, E'Jaaz gave her a wry smile. 'And what about you, dangerous lady? Any camping endeavours to share with us?'

'I nearly got caught during one of my first missions for the Winged Ones. I was exhausted and didn't have enough Will left to escape through a Portal so I avoided being captured by hiding neck deep in a stinking swamp. The place smelt so bad that no one came near and I was left in peace for the night. I even caught some sleep.'

Charlie and Nibbler stared at her in awe.

'And then there was the time I had to sneak into the Lachi Temple in Tibet to copy one of their maps for the Folded Realm –'

'Tibet?' said Charlie, interrupting Marsila's flow. 'On Earth?'

'That's right. Don't forget we operate in the realm of Earth too. With your family's house, that's something you should know.'

'But . . . Tibet?'

'Of course Tibet. Do you want me to finish the story or do you want to talk about Earth?'

'Finish the story!' said Nibbler and gave Charlie a look that said in no uncertain terms that he expected her to stay quiet, at least until Marsila and E'Jaaz had finished their awesome stories about camping.

'I needed to sneak into the Lachi Temple,' continued Marsila, 'but the monks had shielded the region to prevent the use of Portals so I had to go in by foot. The Temple was at the top of a mountain so I had no choice but to climb. It took me three days and two nights. And each night I spent in a tent that hung from the side of the mountain with nothing beneath it but icy air and a three-thousand-metre drop to the rocks below.'

'Wow!' exhaled Nibbler. 'That's amazing! Charlie, do you think we'll have stories to tell like that when we're older?'

'We've got stories already. And if we want to get any older we're going to have to stop that chump Bane first.'

'Good point,' admitted E'Jaaz. 'But talk of Bane can wait. Let us eat, get what rest we can and continue our task upon the morrow.'

Kneeling down to better reach their campfire, he began to prepare their dinner. Their meal was good and after the fatigue of the day it was a welcome relief. The conversation was pleasant too, but this was not a camp like those Charlie had enjoyed when she had first met the Tremen; this was the end of a day that was heavy with purpose. And knowing that tomorrow would be just as fraught and just as hard, the group soon put an end to idle chat and retired to their beds.

16

Screams in the Night

E'Jaaz roused Charlie from her dreams.

'Your watch,' he said. 'I saw a squad of soldiers march up the far riverbank an hour ago but other than that it's been quiet. Keep an eye out for an hour and a half, then wake Nibbler for his turn.'

He flashed her a reassuring smile, unfurled his blankets and was asleep in a matter of moments.

Charlie pushed her way past the few shrubs and trees that shielded their camp. She found a vantage point at one end of the island that allowed her to see both sides of the river. Stifling a yawn, she slid her back down a tree trunk and tried to make herself comfortable.

Aware of how tired she really was, she paused to consider her position. 'Maybe comfortable isn't such a good idea,' she said to herself.

She didn't doubt that it would be easy to fall asleep sitting up. Just thinking about it seemed tempting. Sighing, she stood, found a couple of rough pebbles, then resumed her seat with the uncomfortable pillow of stones beneath her.

'Oh yes, good times,' whispered Charlie with a disbelieving shake of her head. 'If only my friends could see me now. Sitting on stones to keep myself awake.'

Looking out, she noted that the landscape seemed different at night. Very different. The boulders and rock spires, splendid to look at in the daylight, now seemed cruel and forbidding. Half glimpsed in the gloom, the spires looked like hooked claws, and her imagination couldn't help but conjure up images of Rhinospiders, with their thin legs and fat, bloated bodies, hidden behind boulders, just waiting for the right moment to sneak on to their island.

After that, it didn't take long for her mind to switch to darker, more menacing enemies. The nasty faces of Stix and Stones, the Delightful Brothers, flashed before her eyes. She couldn't forget how twisted they had seemed from the first moment she had met them. Her unpleasant stay in the Ivory Tower with the two of them as her captors had cemented her opinion of them as bitter, vengeful pieces of work. Their hatred for her had grown all the more when she had accidentally killed Lady Narcissa, their treacherous mother, while saving Jensen's life.

Then there was Mr Crow, the deceitful, greedy lawyer who had always had his eye on her house and the wealth it contained. Wealth that he felt, by rights, should belong to him. Charlie had never understood how his crooked mind worked but somewhere along the line his longing for her family's wealth and misplaced sense of ownership had caused him to develop an intense hatred for her. She knew that he also blamed her for his arrival in Bellania, into Bane and his dark god.

Crowning them all, of course, was Bane. She hated him

for all that he had done and that he intended to do. Deciphering his feelings for her was a little harder. She wasn't sure if he thought of her as anything more than an annoying bug. Whatever his opinion, she knew that in order to secure his grasp on the realm he required her death.

And no matter how you add it up, mused Charlie to herself, *that's a lot of powerful enemies with grudges against me*. In an attempt to dispel her jittery thoughts, she grabbed a stick and started drawing marks in the dirt. Fourteen for the temples they had already checked on the southern side of the Winged Mount and another seventy-six (to make a total of ninety) so she could work on the maths required to calculate their chances of success. E'Jaaz's earlier explanation of their odds had really struck a chord. And added to this medley of thoughts spinning through her mind was that unfinished clue on the pendant.

She was just in the process of scratching another mark when she heard a shriek echo out from across the darkness. It was a cross between a lion's rasping cough and the screech of a coyote.

There was a rustle behind her. Flustered, she tried to spin round but after sitting on the pebbles her legs had gone numb. When she did manage to face the surprised faces of Marsila and E'Jaaz she did so on her hands and knees. Nibbler joined them a moment later.

'What was that?' he asked.

'I don't know,' said Charlie. 'I didn't see it.'

The shriek came again. Haunting and eerie, the sound caused the hairs to stand on all three Keepers' arms. Nibbler's ears flickered in alarm.

Again came the challenging cry and again, each shriek more fearsome than the one before.

Then another voice arose to join the first, shattering the night with a chorus of strident screams, hoots and caustic whistles.

'There's two of them,' said E'Jaaz. 'Whatever they are.'

'They sound familiar,' said Charlie. 'Almost like Wyrms but not quite . . .'

'That's not a Wyrm cry that I'm familiar with,' said Marsila. 'Sounds too big.'

'And too hungry,' added Nibbler.

Charlie shivered as she heard the cry come again.

'Well, no use worrying over something that can't be seen,' said E'Jaaz. 'We'll deal with it in the morning.'

Charlie couldn't believe it when she saw him head back towards camp. How could he be so calm? Who could bear to sleep while some unseen predator rampaged in the nearby darkness?

The haunting shrieks came again but quieter as though receding into the distance.

'They're going away, but I'll extinguish the fire,' said Marsila. 'Until we know what we're dealing with there's no need to risk being seen. Wake me if they come closer.'

Charlie did a double take as Marsila too returned to bed.

'G'night, Charlie,' said Nibbler.

'What? You're going to sleep as well?' said Charlie in disbelief. 'With those things out there? Am I the only sane one here?'

'Well, like Marsila said, they're going away. Besides, if I'm getting up soon to cover the last shift it kinda makes sense that I get what sleep I can. Night, Charlie.'

There was a rustle as Nibbler pushed his way back through the brush.

Alone, Charlie looked out into the darkness. Her heart pitter-pattered as the night continued to be broken by spine-chilling hoots, whistles and chattering wails of unseen monsters.

Like two spiteful teenagers, Stix and Stones dismounted from their rides and swaggered through the Embassy of the Winds. Guards thought to stop and question them but after seeing the two arrive on their stone-like beasts they pretended to look elsewhere as the Delightful Brothers passed by.

'Where's your boss?' said Stix with a sneer to a large Stoman.

'Who's asking?'

'His replacement,' Stix replied with a nasty grin.

The soldier's first instinct was to smack the Treman but after looking twice he changed his mind. 'Down the corridor, left at the junction, knock on the door with the shield and wing carvings.'

Stix and Stones sauntered off. When they reached the door they didn't bother to knock.

The impressive Stonesinger seated behind the desk half rose from his seat. 'Who the –' He paused then slowly sat down. 'I've heard of you two. The Delightful Brothers, right? What do you want?'

'Travel, fame and the opportunity to hunt,' said Stones with an idle shrug.

The Stonesinger growled, 'I'm not playing games. What do you want *here* in my garrison?'

'Your job,' said Stones. He allowed a menacing smile to appear on his face.

'My job,' said the Stonesinger through gritted teeth, 'is not up for grabs!'

'We thought you'd say that,' said Stix. 'If we were polite we might mention that your lord sent us here and that we're taking over with his permission . . . but we're not polite and we don't do nice. So what are you going to do about it?'

The Stonesinger sprang from his chair with a snarl on his face.

Once it was all over, the Delightful Brothers mulled over the three-dimensional map of the area that rose from the floor.

'What do you think those little flags mean?' Stix asked his brother.

'I'm not sure. Let's find out.' He tugged the door open and bellowed, 'Captain!'

There was a moment's quiet, then the sound of running feet.

'Sir?' said the Stoman and snapped a salute as soon as he entered. His composure faltered when he noticed the blood, then his fallen commander and the Delightful Brothers watching him with cold eyes.

'We're in charge,' spat Stix in a voice so full of poison and hate that the captain flinched. 'Your lord, Bane, sent us. So we're here. And we're in control. Problem?'

The captain was quick to grasp the new state of affairs. 'No problem, sir. What do you need?'

'We want information on the Keepers and the pendant,' said Stones. 'What do these flags indicate?'

The captain carefully made his way into the room to stand next to the map. 'They're indicators of conflict, sir. Each shows where we spotted or clashed with the Keepers.'

'What are these buildings?' asked Stix.

'The old temples, sir. We've had a lot of skirmishes around those.'

'You don't say,' drawled Stix. 'All right, laddie, these are our commands . . .'

17

Red Eyes and More Coffee

Before the pre-dawn light banished the stars, E'Jaaz and Marsila rose from their beds like clockwork machines.

Marsila bent to stir Charlie but found her wide awake, her eyes bloodshot and the dark circles beneath larger than ever before.

'Couldn't sleep, huh?'

'No! And I don't understand how you guys managed with those whatever-they-ares out there,' grumbled Charlie. 'How could anyone sleep with all that howling?'

'You need to learn to switch off that mind of yours,' said Marsila. 'Idle thoughts, wild fears and useless speculation will keep anyone awake. Even the Maoli Masters know better than to waste an opportunity for sleep; they save their philosophy for the light of day.'

'I'd like to see these Mooli Masters switch their minds off when there's great blooming big monsters screaming for their blood in the middle of the night.'

'Maoli,' corrected Marsila. 'Not Mooli.'

'Bleuuurgh,' groaned Charlie and rubbed furiously at her eyes. 'Maoli, Mooli, Mooing, whatever. I'd just like to get a decent night's sleep for once.'

'Our moonlight visitors do seem to have withdrawn,' said E'Jaaz. 'Perhaps these hidden beasties are nocturnal? If luck is with us we'll discover the right Gateway and be on our way before we ever put a face to our mysterious monsters.'

Marsila snorted. 'Have you ever known our luck to be that good? No, the chances are we'll come face to face with our unseen predators before the day is done.'

'Hey, guys!' said Nibbler, returning from his watch with a cheerful grin. 'I heard you were up and . . . Whoa!' He did a double take when he saw Charlie's bloodshot eyes and messy hair. Even by Charlie's standards this was reaching new lows. 'What happened to you?'

'I don't want to talk about it,' muttered Charlie. 'All I want is some hot food . . . and maybe the chance to find out if black coffee really works.'

'Well . . . you might be in luck,' said E'Jaaz. 'With our beasties absent for the moment I'm sure we can rekindle the campfire and a fresh brew of coffee would be in all our interests.' He paused to peer at her bloodshot eyes. 'Although, to be honest, in your condition I think a little dragonsblood wouldn't go amiss.'

Marsila snorted in derision. 'Fool's request. There won't be any dragonsblood until the Winged Ones return.'

'What's dragonsblood?' asked Charlie.

'Winged Ones' blood,' replied Marsila.

'What, literally?'

'Literally,' acknowledged Marsila.

Charlie's mouth wobbled as her mind chased itself in circles trying to consider all the implications. 'Haaaaang on a minute,' she suddenly protested. 'Everyone stares at me like a fool each time I say "dragon" instead of Winged One but how come it's OK for you to say "dragonsblood"?'

'It's an ancient word that survives from the time before the Great Cataclysm,' explained Marsila. 'When the realms of Earth and Bellania split, the Humans on that side continued to call Winged Ones by the local name of dragons but here we address them with their chosen honorific of Winged Ones. Dragonsblood is one of the few exceptions to the rule.'

Charlie was too tired to grumble about the inconsistencies of that. She was, however, puzzled as to the benefits of drinking a Winged One's blood. 'So, uh, what does dragonsblood do?'

'Yeah,' added Nibbler, just as intrigued as his friend.

'It's a restorative,' explained Marsila. 'As Keepers, we share the same genetic traits as Winged Ones – indeed, all our powers come from the ancient mingling of our bloodlines.'

'Er . . . I've never got that bit,' said Charlie. 'How can Keepers and Winged Ones share the same genes?'

'That's a long conversation,' said Marsila. 'And something we don't have time for. Charlie, I'm well aware that your education as a Keeper is lacking but until this war is over that's something we won't be able to address. For now, please just take my word for it. But back to dragonsblood. As Keepers, our bodies and powers are in tune with those of the Winged Ones. In times of need, be our wounds too great or our Will too weak, we can restore ourselves with the blood of the Winged Ones. It is, however, a double-edged gift. There can be side effects and the receiving of it is always painful. I don't really know why E'Jaaz bothered to mention it as without the Winged Ones present it's not something that's available to us.'

'Er, hello? Someone forgetting something?' said Nibbler. He made a show of patting his body as though checking for something that he might have misplaced. 'Wings? Wings? Ah yes, I still have wings so I'm guessing that would make me . . . a Winged One! So roll up, roll up! Dragonsblood if you need it! Going today at a bargain price of two barrels of Larva-Larva fruit for a cup of dragonsblood!'

'Ew! Nibbler!' protested Charlie. 'That's gross. I'm not going to drink your blood! Do you think I'm a vampire?'

'Well, E'Jaaz did say it might help your fatigue,' said Nibbler. He twisted his head to one side to better expose his neck. 'Are you sure you don't want a little –' he made some horrendous sucking noises – 'a little nibble?'

'Nibbler!' protested Charlie.

'Oh, my Sweet Heavens,' snorted E'Jaaz. 'It's too early for this kind of pandemonium. Nibbler, you're still too small to be offering your blood. When you've fully grown into your wings you'll have enough to spare. But until then let's stick with the traditional fare of coffee and food, and save gnawing on Nibbler's neck for another day, shall we?'

Hearing no words of protest, he lit the fire, heated some rations and then rummaged through his pack to pull out one of the smallest and oddest-looking kettles Charlie had ever seen. He added some ground coffee and water to the kettle, then settled back, humming gently.

The four of them sat in a companionable silence as the aroma of roasted food and fresh coffee wafted across their small campsite.

Marsila waited for everyone to enjoy a mouthful of food and a sip of coffee before pulling the map out. 'This is going to be a working breakfast, people. We have a lot of ground to cover and a clock that is fast running out. We need to discuss our search pattern for the remaining temples, how we're going to tackle the issue of the Shade and Stoman attacks, and how we're going to proceed when we come face to face with our howling friends from last night.'

'You really think we're going to bump into those beasties?' asked E'Jaaz.

Marsila didn't bother to reply; she just gave him a look.

'So beasties it is,' acknowledged E'Jaaz with a grimace. 'Monsters aside, I think we should continue to follow yesterday's procedure for checking the temples. Maybe make the sectors smaller and jump around a bit more to keep the Stomen guessing.'

'What about the . . .' said Charlie, hesitating, '. . . the you-know-whats?'

'Monsters?' said E'Jaaz. 'We wait until we see them before making any judgement. If they prove to be as big and as bad as they sound I think it would be wise for us to bail as soon as they appear.'

'You mean run?' asked Charlie.

'Sure. We've got enough on our plate already. I don't want to add "confront and slay howling monsters" to our to-do list.'

'Agreed,' said Marsila. 'Now if everyone's finished, let's get to it.' She paused to stare at Charlie's bedraggled condition. 'On second thoughts, Charlie, go down to the river and see if you can't wash some of that sleep away. E'Jaaz will have another coffee waiting for you when you return. Nibbler, go keep her company.'

Ten minutes later, with hair tidied and another strong coffee inside her, Charlie appeared somewhat presentable. More importantly, the shadows beneath her eyes had receded and, although not a bundle of enthusiasm, she had managed to shake off the worst effects of last night's dismal lack of sleep.

'You look better, Charlie,' grinned E'Jaaz. 'More human and less like the walking dead.'

'Braaaaaaaaaaaaaains,' began Nibbler, who had a penchant for doing zombie sound effects, but was quickly cut short by Marsila.

'Stop that!' She pointed at the map. 'We'll search this area first. Triad up and let's get our game face on.'

With a wave of golden light, they opened a Portal and disappeared to start their hunt anew.

18

The Chancellor

The chamber of the Jade Circle had been converted into a war room that bustled with activity. Maps hung from walls, blackboards had been erected to mark the flow of supplies and couriers, and messengers had taken up stations around the perimeter ready to carry notes, commands and letters.

Jensen, in his new position as chancellor, was seated at the Jade Table. He had been up till late and it showed. His eyes were red and the large stack of coffee mugs gave a good indication of the hours he had been keeping. He double-checked the letter he was working on, scribbled his signature on the parchment, sealed it with a generous blob of wax, then passed it to the waiting messenger.

'Get it there as fast as possible,' he said.

The messenger nodded and hastened from the room. As he left another arrived and placed a scrawled note in Jensen's waiting hands. Jensen frowned as he read, cursed and threw it over his shoulder to join a rising pile of discarded letters.

Hearing his sigh, Lady Dridif raised an eyebrow. 'Wot news?'

'The Tribe of the Painted Lady agreed ta the blood price but it will take them two days ta reach us. And two days –'

'Could be a day too late,' Dridif finished his sentence. Jensen nodded grimly.

'Wot about the others?' asked Dridif.

'The Barbarians of the north are sending all the men and women who can hold a blade but it will take them three days ta arrive. The archers from the freetowns of the south will be here tomorrow but they are only nine hundred in number . . .'

'Ya want ta say that things don't look good, do ya not, Jensen the Willow?'

Jensen knew better than to answer that question but his lips did tug downward to form a small grimace.

'Well,' continued Dridif, 'things have been bad ever since Bane rose ta power. Perhaps things will get worse but we are no strangers ta dis; we are Sylvarisians and we will do wot needs ta be done. Come fire, famine or plague we will press on. So, Jensen . . .'

'Yes, ma'am?'

'Keep writing.'

'Yes, ma'am.'

Hiding his frustration and doing his best to put on a brave face in front of the other councillors, Jensen put quill to parchment and began writing a new missive addressed to the people of Quicktide Bay offering them one hundred thousand florins from his rapidly diminishing wealth plus favourable trade agreements should they come to aid Sylvaris in its time of need.

Stix and Stones sat astride their mounts and watched the flow of reinforcements as they streamed in from distant garrisons. They were predominantly Shades and Rhino-spiders but the brothers were confident that Stoman soldiers, although moving more slowly than their shadowy and faster counterparts, would arrive later in the day.

'That's a lot of manpower,' muttered Stones.

Stix flashed him a grin. They usually only worked with each other but Stix was excited by the idea of command. Ordering thousands of soldiers around wasn't something they got to do every day.

Stones stroked his chin as he contemplated the numbers. 'There are too many to house in the Embassy of the Winds,' he muttered.

'No matter,' said Stix. Twisting in his saddle, he pointed his finger at a nearby Stonesinger. 'You, come here.'

The Stonesinger didn't enjoy being bossed around but he knew better than to complain to someone riding a stone monster. 'Yes?' he grunted.

'We need somewhere else to garrison all these men. Suggestions?'

'There's a large temple on the southern face,' he said after some thought. 'It's not as large as the Embassy of the Winds but it's big enough to hold a thousand men and has room to stable Rhinospiders too.'

'What do you think?' Stix asked his brother.

'It'll do,' replied Stones. 'And it'll make it easier to distrib-ute our forces around the perimeter of the mountain.'

Stix turned to the Stonesinger. 'See it done.'

The Stonesinger nodded before departing.

'Brother,' Stix raised his eyes to the heavens, 'shall we?'

Stones grinned. 'By the Seven Hells, yes!'

Cackling like two twisted children, they took to the skies on their beasts of stone.

19

Howly-Howly Monsters

'Crack my Realm!' growled E'Jaaz as he turned aside a pack of Shades with a wave of Will. He ducked to allow Nibbler to spit a jet of flame over his shoulder, then spun round to deflect a blow from a club-wielding Stoman that was intended for Marsila's head. Locked in a battle with two Stonesingers, Marsila simply didn't have the resources to defend herself from all sides.

'Hurry it up, Charlie!' shouted Nibbler. 'It's getting a little tense in here!'

Charlie, her back to the action, was concentrating on the wall in front of her. The pendant, held tight in the socket, lost its glow and the last traces of a Gateway diminished as she relinquished her Will.

'It's another dud!' she retorted. 'Let's go to the next –'

'No!' cried Marsila. 'Take us back to the campsite. We need to re-evaluate our plans.'

Pressed on all sides by frothing adversaries, Charlie couldn't afford to ask the reason why. She simply tore open a Portal and threw herself through. The others followed in a more controlled fashion. Will and lightning blazing, they stepped backwards, keeping the enemy at bay.

Once they were through, Charlie slammed the Portal shut.

'Eight temples!' spat Marsila in sudden fury. 'Eight in four hours! It's not good enough. Not good enough at all.'

The day had not progressed smoothly. They had encountered resistance from the very first temple they had visited and it was a pattern that had repeated itself as they fought to investigate each and every prospective Gateway. Stoman soldiers had been waiting at one, Shades at another, Rhino-spiders at the third, and at times – like the last temple – they had been confronted by all three.

'We must move faster,' continued Marsila, 'and be more efficient.'

'How?' asked Charlie, who was every bit as frustrated with their progress. She could practically feel the tick-ticking of time passing them by. 'How can we move faster when we have to deal with that lot at every place we stop?'

'We forget the aggressive defence and switch to passive. We form a shield at each temple.'

E'Jaaz spluttered. 'At *each* temple? That's going to drain us and drain us fast. I don't know about that, Marsila. Perhaps we should stick with what we've been doing already?'

'No. We have to speed things up and this is the only way,' said Marsila in an unyielding voice.

'What's a shield?' asked Charlie.

'A barrier of Will,' explained Marsila. 'If we throw a wall of Will around us nothing short of a behemoth or a cadre of Stonesingers will get through. With a shield in place we can spend less time fighting and more time crossing Gateways off our list.'

Charlie looked slightly confused. She couldn't quite get her head round the idea of a shield of pure Will.

'You've done this before,' said E'Jaaz. 'Lady Dridif told us you blocked the top of Narcissa's Ivory Tower with a wall of Will. A shield is the same thing but with the three of us we'll be able to project it around us like a sphere.'

'Oh . . . so what's the problem, then?' said Charlie. 'If it's as simple —'

'What Marsila is neglecting to mention is that holding a shield for an extended period of time is fatiguing. More so if people are pressing against it. Sure, holding one for thirty minutes or so is no hardship, but for hours on end? Against non-stop attacks?'

'What choice do we have?' asked Marsila. 'If you've got a better suggestion I'm all for it.'

There was silence.

'So shield it is,' said Marsila with a grim nod. 'Let's get it on.'

'Whoa!' protested Charlie. 'Hold up. I know you're all awesome at being Keepers but I'm still new to this game, so before we go rampaging off can someone please explain how I make this shield? It won't be a good look if your sides of this shield are up but mine is down.'

'Uh . . . sorry, Charlie,' began E'Jaaz with a sheepish look. 'Perhaps we should have explained a little better. You don't have to worry too much about the technique. So long as you maintain your part of the Triad, Marsila and I can tap into your Will to fuel the shield. Just concentrate on testing the Gateways and we'll worry about keeping the Stomen off your back.'

Charlie paused for a second. Part of her mind was distracted by the beauty of the landscape and the wonder of the Winged Mount rearing overhead. With its unusual, top-heavy peak, it really was a marvel. Oddly enough, something about its shape cried out to her.

'Now why does that look so weird?' she muttered.

'Excuse me?' asked E'Jaaz. 'I didn't quite catch that.'

'From Wings on high seeking prey . . .' whispered Charlie.

'Charlie?'

Charlie blinked. Snapping out of her thoughts, she returned her attention to the present. 'Never mind. If you guys think you can handle this shield, and if you think it'll speed the process up, I'm more than game. So like Marsila said . . . let's get it on.'

Summoning her Will, she held it out and waited for the other two to merge theirs.

'Don't you guys think it's weird that we haven't bumped into those howly-howly monsters from last night yet?' asked Nibbler. He stared accusingly at the landscape as though it were guilty of holding back the surprise.

Marsila slapped her forehead and stared at Nibbler in disbelief. 'You had to go and say something like that, didn't you?'

'What?' protested Nibbler.

'As if times weren't tough enough, you had to go and jinx us.'

'Huh?' said Nibbler. He still wasn't following her line of thought. 'How'd I jinx us?'

'By mentioning those things. Everyone knows that if you talk about something the chances of it coming true are much more likely. It's like saying, "Oh, it doesn't look like it's going to rain today," only for it to pour five minutes later.'

Muttering to herself about the foolishness of Hatchlings and how 'howly-howly monsters' was an idiotic name, she tore open a Portal and stalked through. The others scrambled after.

20

Menacing Skies

The shield glimmered.

Every time a Stoman pounded against it with clenched fists or a Shade slashed at it with extended claws, it resounded with a noise that was reminiscent of a dropped bouncy ball.

BOOOOOING-BOING!

Charlie felt slightly dazed. It was a bit like being inside a golden bubble, only this was a bubble that wouldn't pop or break, no matter how hard the Stomen attacked it.

'Stay focused, Charlie,' insisted Marsila. 'We're doing well but you've got to keep your mind on the job.'

Charlie pushed her thoughts aside and forced her Will upon the pendant secured in the keyhole.

Thirteen. They'd cleared another thirteen Gateways in the space of two hours. Much faster than their earlier eight but the cost was higher too. All three Keepers were feeling the strain. The dark circles beneath Charlie's eyes had reappeared, sweat beaded across Marsila's brow and E'Jaaz's fine clothes were starting to appear rumpled. Maintaining a shield of Will against the Stomen's non-stop attacks was no easy feat.

As Charlie continued to funnel her Will into the pendant

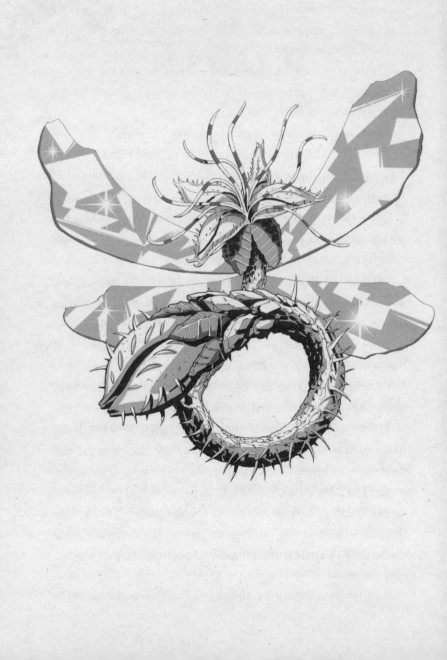

the familiar outline of a door and the sound of a screaming jumbo jet receded. It was another failure.

'All right,' said Marsila, 'we've cleared this sector – let's move on to the next.'

Dashing through a Portal, they made a swift retreat.

As they reappeared in a different region they hastily took cover between a scattering of rock spires.

'You want me to do my thing?' asked Nibbler.

'If you would, my rascally Hatchling,' said E'Jaaz. 'Make haste too, otherwise Marsila will scold both of us with her beautiful but rather fiery tongue.'

Marsila scowled at that. Nibbler, deciding that now would be a bad time to dawdle, beat his way into the air with great flaps of his wings. The three Keepers watched him depart with envy. Each of them would have given almost anything to enjoy the freedom of the sky and a chance of relief from the constant pressure of maintaining a Triad.

'At least we are progressing,' began Marsila. 'We checked fourteen Gateways yesterday and twenty-one today. That's thirty-five in total. And with each additional Gateway our chances of stumbling across the right one increases. If we maintain this pace we might even –'

A sudden trumpet blast shattered the calm.

Another trumpet joined the first, then another, until it seemed that countless instruments tore the air with their strident alarm.

'Oh, for the Sacred Realms!' cursed Marsila. 'What now?'

Fearing an attack, they checked the surrounding land-scape and the skies above them, but relaxed as they spotted

Nibbler gliding calmly overhead. For now, everything remained peaceful and free of threats.

'Well, it's obviously a warning or signal of some sort,' mused E'Jaaz. 'But for whom?'

An unpleasant shriek, deep and filled with fury, cut across the klaxon call of the trumpets. It was answered by a second howling voice.

'Oh no . . .' sighed Charlie. 'That can't be good.'

A titanic form lurched over the side of the Winged Mount and hurled itself up into the sky. Seconds later, another joined it. With a flash of dragonfly wings and glistening scales, the two beasts corkscrewed up into the air. Their long maggot-like bodies were packed with muscle and their tails, lashing from side to side, were covered with barbed spikes.

'Are . . . are those Wyrms?' asked E'Jaaz in a disbelieving voice.

'If they are, they're like none I have ever seen before,' muttered Marsila. 'Look at them. They're huge!'

They stared with wide eyes and slack mouths at these *things*, these new predators that coiled and writhed through the sky and whistled and barked in gluttonous delight.

'What do you think it would take to stop something that big?' asked E'Jaaz. '*Could* you stop something that big?'

'I don't know, but you can bet we're about to find out,' said Marsila with a grimace.

'Oh, my gosh! Oh, my gosh! Nibbler!' screamed Charlie as she saw the two things speed towards her friend. 'Nibbler, look out! LOOK OUT!'

She almost thought he hadn't heard but at the very last moment he managed to wheel aside, leaving the beasts to claw and bite upon empty air. Then, in an act of what seemed like madness, he spun through the air in a tight figure of eight until it was he that was chasing them. Lips peeled back in a fierce grin, he unleashed a massive jet of flame that lit the sky with a burst of red.

KKRR-WHUMPF!

The trumpets fell silent.

The rushing wind and the crackle of flame were the only things to be heard. Nibbler, certain of victory, hovered motionless in the air waiting for his opponents to plummet, flaming, to the earth.

The beasts, screaming furiously and still very much alive, burst through the cloud of smoke, trailing embers and half-spent flame behind them. Enraged and flying far faster than before, they gave chase. They hooted and bellowed as they pursued Nibbler up and down in an endlessly elaborate game of aerial cat and mouse. The sky soon seemed a ruined mess of fire, black smoke and twisting, clawing bodies. But for all the chaos and power being unleashed in the heavens, it swiftly grew apparent that this was a fight Nibbler could not hope to win.

'Open a Portal,' said Charlie.

'To where?' asked Marsila.

'Anywhere! It doesn't matter where, we just have to make sure it's big enough for Nibbler to fly through.'

'OK,' said Marsila, sensing what Charlie had in mind. 'Triad up, but let me take the lead.' Grunting with the effort, she tore open a rift. After a moment's pause she allowed the diameter to shrink. Charlie gave her a sharp look. 'We don't want it so large that those things can fly through too,' explained Marsila.

She hastened through to the other side. E'Jaaz joined her.

'What are you doing?' asked Charlie. 'What about Nibbler?'

'Charlie, you don't want to be on that side of the Portal when we shut it. We want those things over there and Nibbler and us over here!'

Feeling stupid, but still craning her neck round to keep an eye on her friend, Charlie stumbled through the Portal.

'He hasn't seen us,' said E'Jaaz with a frown.

'Form a flare,' instructed Marsila.

'And hold open a Portal that size?' spluttered E'Jaaz. 'Are you trying to make this as difficult as possible?'

'So make it a mini flare!' snapped Marsila. 'Just get it done.'

E'Jaaz pushed a small column of his Will back through the Portal. Charlie followed suit. Marsila, jaw tensed with effort, joined hers to theirs. The flare exploded into a fountain of golden sparks. The dogfight in the air stuttered to a halt. Nibbler, quick to take advantage of the moment, pulled his wings in tight and, with the wind shrieking about him, plummeted earthward. Moments later the beasts gave chase but Nibbler, moving so fast that he actually blurred, took the lead and shot through the Portal.

'Close it!' commanded Marsila. Her eyes grew wide as the two beasts drew closer. Their mouths gaped open horribly, allowing the three Keepers to see right into their disgusting gullets. Shriek after terrible shriek flew from their maws, so strong, so loud and powerful that the Keepers flinched. Fighting to maintain a grip on their Will, they forced the Portal shut.

21

Clipped Wings

As the Portal closed, Charlie had a last fleeting impression of brutal teeth and lolling tongues. Oddly enough, she was certain she caught a glimpse of something or someone hunched upon a saddle.

Groaning, she rubbed her eyes and shook her head in an attempt to rid her ears of the ringing caused by the beasts' shrieks.

'There!' said E'Jaaz and pointed back towards the Winged Mount.

They could see, now miles away, the two things writhing through the air.

'Down,' instructed Marsila. 'Keep yourselves low to the ground. I doubt they'll be able to see us from such a distance but I think it wise not to make it any easier for them to find us.'

They turned to watch Nibbler who, having bled off his great speed, was now able to return safely to earth. Looking slightly shell-shocked, he trotted towards them with one wing held outstretched.

'Erm . . .' he muttered, 'does one of you guys want to pull this out?'

They all stared at the barbaric-looking arrow sticking through the membrane of his wing. Charlie was horrified.

'Does it hurt?' she asked.

'It's weird but no, no it doesn't.' He reached over to pinch his wing. 'It's just, y'know, skin. I think it would hurt a lot more if it had hit muscle or bone.'

Charlie's brow furrowed as she examined the arrow. There was something familiar about it. Careful not to damage her friend any further, she pulled it out as smoothly as possible. 'I've seen these before . . .'

'Yes,' acknowledged Nibbler. 'You have. Both of them were there, they were riding those things.'

'Seen who before?' asked Marsila. 'Who was riding those –'

'Stix and Stones, the Delightful Brothers,' growled Charlie. 'Right?'

'Right,' said Nibbler.

'Oh, those low-down, spiteful, sour-faced chumps,' began Charlie, then added, 'I knew it. I just knew it! There's no way they were ever going to disappear. Not after what I did to their mother. Argh, and look at them now! Riding those . . . those . . . what were they?'

'I'm not sure,' said E'Jaaz. 'I've never seen things like that before but I can't help thinking that they look like Wyrms.'

'Just like Wyrms but bigger and certainly meaner,' said Marsila.

'And what was with those spikes on their tails?' asked Charlie. 'It's like someone took the Wyrms and put them into some evil genius's laboratory, stuck some bolts through their necks, added some heavy stitching and made them more . . .'

'Efficient?' suggested E'Jaaz.

'I was going to say stupidly scary,' said Charlie. 'But efficient works.'

'They were made from stone,' said Nibbler.

'Rubbish!' snorted Marsila. 'There's no way something made from stone could fly. Certainly not something that big.'

'I'm telling you,' insisted Nibbler, 'they were made from stone! You didn't see them up close – I did. Their scales looked like they had been carved from basalt and their flesh looked rocky and their wings seemed to be made from some sort of crystal. Besides, each time I hit them with flame it just bounced off.'

'It's that power-hungry fool Bane,' grumbled Charlie. 'This is his work. I mean, come on, just think about it. The real Wyrms were thought to be extinct and we know who sent those, right? And for these weird stone-mutant-Wyrm-things to appear with Stix and Stones on their backs? It's got to be Bane's doing. It's got to be.'

'Why didn't you use your lightning on them, Nibbler?' asked E'Jaaz.

Nibbler opened his mouth but nothing came out; he was clearly embarrassed that he had not thought of that. After a while he shut it, then tried again. 'Erm . . . I'm not sure. I panicked, I guess.'

'Well, try it next time and if that doesn't work aim for the Delightful Brothers. I'm sure that'll slow them down.'

'Young Hatchling,' said Marsila, 'did you note all the temples in this sector before those things came?'

'Er, yes,' said Nibbler.

'Good. Mark them on the map.'

While he did so Marsila stared, thin-lipped, at the distant beasts and slowly shook her head. 'These new arrivals will make our task more complicated. We all know what we have to do and we all know how we've got to do it, but does anyone have any ideas on how to counter this additional problem? If they attack us while we're in a temple we're going to be in a world of trouble.'

There was a thoughtful silence and much rubbing of chins but no answers were offered. Charlie, who normally found it easy to think outside the box, was at a loss for words. After hours of hard work her muscles were laden with lactic acid, her limbs felt heavy and a throbbing headache robbed her of the ability to be creative. Grumbling at her own failures, she crossed her arms and stared grimly at Stix and Stones's new rides.

'How about I distract them while you three continue checking the temples?' suggested Nibbler.

'What do you mean by distracting them?' asked Charlie. She had a sinking feeling that he was about to put himself in harm's way again.

'Fly circles around them and hit them with lightning when they get too close.'

'What? Nibbler, you just got an arrow stuck in your wing and you want to go back for more! Even for you that's crazy.'

He was about to retort but E'Jaaz got a word in first. 'How is your wing?'

Nibbler spread it so they could all admire the hole. 'OK,' he admitted. 'I think it just looks worse than it is.'

'If we sewed it up, do you think you'd be able to fly?'

'I think I can fly now,' said Nibbler and flapped his wings to prove his point. Even with the small hole in it, his wing looked none the worse.

'Whoa, hold on!' protested Charlie. 'You can't seriously be thinking about sending Nibbler back out there? Those two blooming big monsters almost yammed him up!'

'Ah, Charlie, we're all taking risks,' said E'Jaaz with an apologetic grimace. 'It doesn't matter if we're up in the air or down in the temples; there's danger everywhere. If Nibbler can keep some of the heat off us and allow us to continue checking Gateways off the list, then it makes sense.'

'But we've got a shield of Will to protect us,' argued Charlie. 'Nibbler's got nothing and I don't know about you but I'd rather face the Shades and Stonesingers than those . . . those . . .'

'Stowyrms?' suggested Marsila.

There came a rumble of agreement from E'Jaaz and Nibbler, who approved of the name.

'– than those Stowyrms,' concluded Charlie.

'I'll be fine, Charlie,' said Nibbler. 'I won't be fighting them, just annoying them, and we all know I'm good at that. If they look like they're going to come for you I'll spit lightning at them and fly circles around them.'

Charlie pursed her lips.

'Really, Charlie, don't worry. I'll be OK and I promise not to do anything stupid.'

Charlie was not convinced, particularly when he promised not to do anything stupid, which almost guaranteed that he'd wind up in trouble. Just as she was about to protest,

Lady Dridif's words came to mind: *the end of days*. And if she was honest with herself, it really was the end of this world as she knew it. If Bellania was to regain its freedom, if Bane was to be defeated and if she was ever to see her parents again, then risks had to be taken. Not just by her but by her friends too. For this to work, everyone would have to contribute.

'All right, just don't –'

'I won't, Charlie. Don't worry.' Nibbler grinned cheekily. 'Well, don't worry too much. Rest assured, I'd hate to be Stowyrm food, so you can be certain I'll be flying as fast as I can.'

'Right,' said Marsila, 'enough chit-chat.' She pointed at the map. 'Hatchling, if we get into trouble or need you in a hurry we'll throw another flare, but if not we'll meet you back here when we're done.' She rummaged through a small pouch until she found thread and needle. 'But before you're done, let me sew you up. We don't want that hole to get any larger.'

Nibbler suffered through her ministrations but once she was done he appraised his wing with a little smile. 'Thanks, Marsila, that looks great.'

'You're welcome. Now off with you.' As Nibbler beat his way into the air, she turned to E'Jaaz and Charlie. 'Ready?'

Torrents of golden Will gushed from the three Keepers' hands. A Portal blossomed open and with grim looks of determination they jumped through.

22

Challenges Given, Challenges Met

Shoulders bunching, wings flaring, Nibbler corkscrewed up into the sky. He knew that rage should be filling him, that the sight of these alien interlopers riding above the Winged Mount, the hereditary home of his people, should be fuelling a terrible anger. To his shock, what he felt instead was a savage joy.

Grinning madly, he realized that he relished the chance to test himself, to prove that he was the better flyer and that *he*, not *they*, belonged in these skies. With talons flexing in and out of their sheaths and with his heart pounding so loudly that he could hear the pulse of his blood over the rushing wind, he drew nearer, ever nearer to his unsuspecting foes.

Their attention seemed to be fixed on the ground below and just as Nibbler was beginning to think that he would be able to close in on them unawares, Stones swivelled in his saddle to fix Nibbler with his menacing yellow eyes. Screaming something to his brother, he freed his bow, unsheathed an arrow, then sighted, pulled and released in one smooth motion.

Nibbler turned the arrow to ash, just as he had at Lady Narcissa's tower many days ago, then (completely forgetting his promise not to get into trouble) he was there, within striking distance of the Stowyrms. Breathing deep, he tensed, flexed some internal muscles and unleashed a sparkling torrent of lightning that scorched and crackled along the side of Stones's ride. The Stowyrm screeched. Desperate to distance itself from the jagged forks of electricity, it rolled and dived, and Stones was nearly flung from his saddle. Only by grabbing hold of the reins did he manage to prevent himself from plummeting to his doom.

Nibbler grinned, then yelped in alarm as he was drenched in shadow. Carried away by his success, he had failed to notice that Stix had manoeuvred his Stowyrm overhead. As Nibbler desperately wheeled aside he caught a whirlwind glimpse of dragonfly wings, a flash of dark scales and Stix's pale face twisted into a grimace of hatred. Then they were past and Nibbler lost some altitude as he was buffeted by the beast's wake. Righting himself, he felt something whirr past his face. He turned, shocked to see that not only had Stones regained both his seat and his composure and let loose with his bow again, but that his steed was almost upon him. As he forced himself into a high-G manoeuvre he could see that his recent barrage of lightning had failed to do any real damage. The flank of Stones's Stowyrm sported a long line of white scarring, but that was it – no gaping hole, no smoking ruin.

Nibbler grunted in annoyance.

Completing a series of tight loops, he sped past Stones and his Stowyrm only to be forced aside as Stix rose to cut him off. Nibbler's earlier bravado swiftly evaporated and as the two brothers started to gain the upper hand he began to regret his cocky lack of respect for the flying beasts. He had thought himself capable of besting them but the truth was they were simply too strong, too large. Maybe he could take on one but not both.

Muttering to himself, he tried to create some distance. If he could widen the gap, then perhaps he could pursue his original intention of merely antagonizing them to the point where they forgot about Charlie and the other Keepers.

His ears pricked up as he caught the strident sound of a distant horn. Risking a glance over his shoulder, he was surprised to see that he was alone in the skies.

The Delightful Brothers and their brutal steeds, heeding the call of the horn, had disappeared.

The temple was much the same as the others and, true to form, it came with a variety of enemies. This time it was Shades and Stoman soldiers.

Hissing and snarling, the Shades had rushed forward to envelop the Keepers' shield of Will with a fleshy wall of darkness. Just before they cut off the last remnants of light Charlie thought she saw a soldier raise a bugle to his lips.

Her suspicions were confirmed when a blaring horn rang out.

'Forget about that,' said Marsila, 'and test the Gateway. Quickly now!'

Charlie pushed the pendant into the keyhole and funnelled her Will into it. As the Gateway began to scream and the wall began to glow, the nightmare details of the Shades' features were revealed through the golden shield. Charlie shuddered as she saw their glaring eyes, long fingers and rubber-like flesh pressed against the bubble of Will. It was a sight she would never forget.

As the Gateway began to dull and the screaming noise receded she could once again hear the blare of the soldier's horn. She opened her mouth to inform Marsila that she was done when the mass of Shades abruptly disappeared. The return of bright daylight was blinding.

'What's going on?' growled Marsila.

E'Jaaz looked to Charlie. 'Have you –'

The far side of the temple exploded. Great slabs of masonry cracked and slammed against their shield. Snarling and gnashing, the two Stowyrms forced themselves into the building, their huge teeth tearing at structural supports and crushing blocks of stone into fragments. Upon their backs rode the Delightful Brothers. Stix held a sword in one hand, reins in the other. Stones, somehow managing to steer his mount with just his knees, raised his great bow.

TH-DUNK!

A heavily barbed arrow ricocheted off the Keepers' shield and buried itself in the wall.

At this range the Delightful Brothers could easily be seen. Looks of obscene enjoyment were plastered across their faces; Stix's facial scar was noticeably flushed and Stones's lips were peeled back in a mockery of a smile.

Scrabbling through the wreckage of the temple, they drew nearer. The three Keepers, stunned by the sudden turn in events, were momentarily frozen. Darting forward like a striking snake, Stix's Stowyrm brought its teeth down on the Keepers' bubble of Will.

KKRICKKA-KRACK!

Even though it succeeded in forcing one of its sabre-like teeth through the shield (it came perilously close to E'Jaaz's head), the barrier held.

'We're getting out of here!' screamed Marsila.

Hands aglow, she tried to open a Portal but the Stowyrm shook its head from side to side like a dog worrying at a particularly tough piece of meat. The bubble of Will was flung around, causing the Keepers inside to lose their footing. As the Stowyrm tried to get a better grip on the shield's shiny surface it opened its mouth a touch wider only for the bubble of Will to slip from its grasp and ricochet through a hole in the wall. Bouncing down an incline, it rebounded off a rock spire and crashed through a thicket of golden-leaved trees before finally coming to rest. Dazed and bruised, the Keepers tried to pull themselves upright.

'You brat!' bellowed one of the Delightful Brothers as he and his mount wriggled through the wreckage of the temple.

'Think you could get away from us?' shouted the other as his Stowyrm joined his brother's.

E'Jaaz was the first to regain his feet and tried to help Marsila and Charlie up, but he had a sinking feeling it would be too late.

Then there was a rumble of thunder. A fork of lightning spat down from the heavens and grounded itself in one of the Stowyrms. The power of the strike lifted Stones clear from his saddle and deposited him several metres away. Seconds later Nibbler streaked by; the wind from his passing caused the Stowyrms to rear and fluster.

'Get us out of here,' groaned Marsila. She held her left wrist gingerly with her right hand.

Charlie opened a Portal and they limped through. They held its shimmering circumference open only long enough for Nibbler to join them before allowing it to ripple shut, leaving the frothing, hate-filled faces of Stix and Stones behind.

23

Shadow Play

Marsila hissed as E'Jaaz examined her wrist.

'It's not broken,' he declared. 'Just badly sprained. We could do with a Treman healer.'

'Well, we're not going to get one out here,' muttered Marsila. 'Just wrap it tightly.'

E'Jaaz rummaged through his backpack. Pulling his blanket free, he cut a long strip from its fabric then went to work binding Marsila's hand and forearm.

'Some ice would slow the swelling,' he murmured.

'While we're wishing for the impossible,' said Marsila with an unexpected grin, 'a long bath and a cocktail or two wouldn't go amiss.'

'Are you going to be all right?' asked Charlie.

'So long as you don't ask me to punch anyone with my left hand I should be fine.' Marsila nodded her thanks to E'Jaaz, then experimentally flexed her wrist. 'Good enough.' She heaved herself upright. 'So that didn't go quite as well as we'd hoped. Nibbler, I take it your tactic of distracting them didn't work as you'd planned?'

'I – er . . . no. No, it didn't. If I had enough time maybe I could take one of them down, but both of them together? I don't think so.'

'How'd it go with the lightning?' asked E'Jaaz.

'Well, it definitely hurts them,' admitted Nibbler, 'but no permanent damage. They veer off for a bit but come right back for more.'

'And distracting them didn't work,' said Marsila.

'Actually, it did, but only until they heard the trumpet. Then they didn't hang around. As much as I annoy them, I think they want to stop you more than they want to fight me.'

There was silence as each member of the group pondered their options. Charlie, looking towards the Winged Mount, was once again struck by the odd shape of the peculiar mountain. Something about it seemed to call to her but the thought swirling inside her head failed to form, proving as elusive and as annoying as a word stuck on the tip of her tongue. As she stared, cock-eyed, at it she mulled over the words on her pendant. *From Wings on high seeking prey* . . . For some reason her brain kept repeating that line as an endless litany that whispered incessantly in the sleep-fogged corners of her mind.

'– listening to me, Charlie?' asked Marsila.

'Huh?'

Marsila sighed. 'I said that we should take out the Stoman bugler before entering the next temple. That way they won't be able to signal to the Delightful Brothers.'

'Bugler?'

'The soldier with the horn or trumpet.' Marsila paused to scrutinize Charlie. 'Are you OK?'

'Uh, wait. Let's forget about the bugler . . . I think . . .'

Charlie tried to rally her thoughts and spur her tired tongue into motion. 'Do you think that the shadow of the Winged Mount . . .?'

Growing irritated, Marsila opened her mouth to berate Charlie and tell her to focus on the job at hand but E'Jaaz held up a calming hand. 'Hang on, Marsila, let's hear this.'

'I – I think . . .' Charlie paused to sort through her muddled thoughts. Only once she had reached a moment of clarity and was absolutely sure she had indeed untangled the riddle that had been haunting her did she open her mouth. She spoke quietly but with a certain confidence. 'I think the shadow might be the Serpent's Tail.'

'Mighty General.'

'Yer Chancellorness.'

As weary and stressed as they were, the two friends shared a smile.

'How'd the speech go?' asked Jensen.

'Terrible,' replied Kelko with an anguished shudder. 'I made a real muddle of it.'

'But everyone cheered. We heard it all, even from inside the Jade Tower.'

'Yeah, they did.' Kelko paused to look down at his big stomach. 'I'm still not sure why. I'm no hero and I'm definitely not a general.'

'Well, ya might not have much experience in the general department,' admitted Jensen, 'but I think ya do OK in the hero department.'

Kelko the Fat Oak

Kelko blushed. Keen to change the subject, he asked, 'So wot do ya have for me? Yer message was quite mysterious.'

'I've got a little something ta show ya.'

'It's not yer Moreish powder, is it?'

'I'm happy ta say it's something even better than that. Come on, let's take a little mosey.'

Intrigued, Kelko followed his friend deeper into the Jade Tower, down several flights of stairs and into a small store-room. The room was bare other than a cloth-covered table.

'I've been bemoaning the loss of me Thornsword,' said Jensen. 'And with times being wot they are I asked the foot-men to scour the tower in the hope that they'd find me some Thornwood so I could shape meself a new blade.'

'And did they find any?'

'No,' admitted Jensen. 'But they found some of dis.'

He whipped the cloth away from the table to reveal –

'Bramblewood!' breathed Kelko in awe.

'Aye,' said Jensen. 'Bramblewood. Two spans of it.'

The Tremen paused to appreciate the two lengths of timber upon the table. The wood was a deep dark green that was only a few shades away from being black. Gnarly-looking purple thorns rose from the wood with the jagged-ness of shark's teeth. Bizarrely, when Kelko carefully threaded his thumb between the large thorns to stroke the wood, it released a strong scent of chilli and lime.

'There's enough here for –' began Kelko.

'Yes,' said Jensen, finishing his friend's sentence, 'enough for a Bramblesword *and* a Brambleaxe.'

'What?' said Marsila in astonishment. She stared at the Winged Mount in confusion. 'How? It doesn't look anything like a tail!'

'I know,' admitted Charlie. 'But I've been staring at it all day and something about the shape of it kept nibbling at my mind. Here, look at this –' she squeezed her hands together and interlocked her fingers – 'my hands don't look like anything, do they? But when you look down at my shadow a bunny rabbit appears.'

The two Keepers looked from Charlie's hands to the shadow on the ground.

'That doesn't look like any rabbit I've seen before,' said E'Jaaz.

Nibbler cocked his head to the side to better study the results. 'Maybe rabbit after it's been chopped up and thrown in the cook pot?'

Charlie resisted the impulse to groan. 'All right, so I'm not any good at shadow puppets! But do you get my point? An object might look like one thing but can still have a shadow that looks like something else entirely.'

Finding some sense in Charlie's muddled explanation, Marsila let her previous irritability dissolve in a long sigh. She turned to study the mountain, willing to give this new idea some consideration. After a pause (and ignoring the continued dogfight between Nibbler and the Stowyrms) she added, 'I understand the principle but I still don't see it. I don't think that a mountain shaped like that could cast the shadow of a serpent.'

'I think it only works at midday,' said Charlie, 'when the sun is directly overhead.'

Marsila and E'Jaaz pondered this some more.

'All right,' said Marsila, conceding the point, 'it's worth checking out. Any thoughts, people?'

'Hang on,' said E'Jaaz. 'Charlie, how did this idea come to you?'

'Er . . . perspective,' she said with a shrug. 'I kept thinking about that line with the missing words on the pendant.'

'*From Wings on high seeking* something something?' queried E'Jaaz.

'Yes, that bit,' said Charlie. 'I was trying to think about it from a Winged One's point of view. It must have said "From Wings on high seeking prey running below", or maybe "seeking prey scampering beneath", or something like that. I mean, if all the Winged Ones are like Nibbler, then they like their food . . . a lot. And big flying predators must be used to looking down when searching for prey. Which got me to thinking that maybe that's what the pendant was hinting at. That we should look for the Serpent's Tail as a Winged One would when flying. So I tried to imagine how things might look from up in the air.'

'Huh,' muttered Nibbler, 'now why didn't I think of that? Charlie, you're all kinds of awesome.'

A grin of admiration appeared on E'Jaaz's face. 'Thinking from different angles even while we've spent the day fighting from one temple to the next? Well done, Charlie, you'll make a better Keeper than me, that's for sure.'

Marsila snorted. 'Even a goatherd could make a better Keeper than you.' Realizing how that sounded, she added, 'Not to take anything away from you, Charlie. Well done indeed. You've proved yourself time and time again so let it be said that I'm glad to have you by my side today.'

'Thanks,' said Charlie with a big smile. A compliment from this tough lady meant a lot.

'Anyway, enough of these sweet nothings,' added Marsila. 'Let's focus on the problem at hand.'

They all studied the Winged Mount.

'I think we're just going to have to travel up there and take a look for ourselves,' said Marsila after a moment of contemplation.

'Um . . . I know I'm still new to our profession,' said Charlie, 'but couldn't we just open a Portal over the mountain and move it around until we find what we're looking for?'

'Nice idea but it wouldn't work,' said E'Jaaz. 'At least, not today.'

'Why not?'

'We're too tired, Charlie. It's one thing holding a Portal open long enough to jump through but you're talking about holding one open for minutes, maybe tens of minutes.'

'We held one open long enough for the army of gargorillas to travel through.'

'That we did, Charlie, and it was awesome! But that was when we were fresh. Look at us now: we're all fatigued and the bags beneath your eyes look like they're big enough for a travelling salesman to store his wares in. If we do what Marsila suggests we only have to hold a Portal for a couple of seconds each way. It's a more efficient use of our energy.'

'So are we agreed?' asked Marsila.

'Aye.'

'Yes.'

'Good,' said Marsila. 'Then let's get on with it.'

24

The Serpent's Tail

'Just keep them as far away from the Winged Mount as you can,' said E'Jaaz.

'No problem,' said Nibbler. But instead of flying off he hesitated. 'Er, is there any chance of some food? All this lightning and acrobatics is giving me an appetite.'

Right on cue, his stomach rumbled.

E'Jaaz rummaged through his pockets and pulled out some strips of jerky. Nibbler gobbled them up, then looked wistfully at his other pockets.

'Hatchling, you certainly live up to your nickname,' chuckled E'Jaaz. 'Do your part of this task and we'll see about plugging that hole in your belly later.'

'Steak would be good, or roast haunch,' suggested Nibbler.

'We're in the middle of the wilderness,' said E'Jaaz.

'OK, rabbit, then.'

'What? You cheeky monkey! Do you really think I've got time to catch you rabbit while all of this is going on?' E'Jaaz shook his head from side to side. 'If you're that hungry you can catch your dinner yourself.'

Nibbler's stomach growled again. 'I can't help being hungry,' he protested. 'It's these growing pains.'

'I know who else is becoming a growing pain,' muttered E'Jaaz and wriggled his eyebrows but his mischievous words went right over the young dragon's head. 'I tell you what, you keep the Delightful Brothers distracted and I'll see what I can rummage up later. Deal?'

Realizing he wasn't going to find a better offer this side of Sylvaris, Nibbler pounced on it. 'Deal!' Grinning at some internal fantasy image of roast venison and barbecued quail, he spread his wings. 'See you later, Charlie!'

They watched him take to the air.

'Our turn,' said Marsila. 'Grab your Will and Triad up.'

The three of them turned to face the Winged Mount. Strange and wonderful, the beautiful mountain pulled the eye with a beguiling gravity. Behind it, the sun rose high in the sky but had yet to reach its zenith.

Marsila peeled open a Portal and together they jumped through.

The wind hit them first in a billowing non-stop gust that was stronger and fresher and certainly more cutting than any seaside breeze.

The cold came next. The frigid, near sub-zero conditions came as a shock to their systems after the warmth of the rocky land below.

Last to surprise them was the air itself, which was thin and lacking in oxygen. They quickly found themselves gasping and panting.

'We can't risk staying up here too long,' said Marsila. 'Altitude sickness will be a real concern. Charlie, if you start to feel too lightheaded tell me and we will return.'

Charlie didn't feel lightheaded; what she did feel was the

onset of a crushing headache. However, there was at least some good news: the cold and rushing wind had swept away the worst effects of her fatigue. Smiling, she nodded to show she understood, then pointed at E'Jaaz in shock.

Blood was dripping from his nose.

Seeing them stare, he wiped his face, then studied his red fingers with a remarkable lack of surprise. He shrugged. 'It happens when I don't get a chance to acclimatize. Still, if I pass out, Marsila, you will give me the kiss of life, won't you?'

'Idiot,' said Marsila. 'If you didn't get a dance from me in Sylvaris what do you think the chances are of me giving you any sort of kiss? Now stop blathering and let's go take a look at this shadow.'

The Portal had delivered them so that they were facing the mountain's peak. Someone had made a cairn of rounded stones to mark the summit and tied to this were old flags that flapped endlessly in the wind. As Charlie turned to look the other way, a little 'Oh' of wonder escaped her lips. Even E'Jaaz and Marsila, well travelled as they were, found themselves smiling in delight.

The view was breathtaking.

The land, rumpled and creased like a blanket, stretched as far as the eye could see. The yellows, browns and reds of the countryside surrounding the Winged Mount merged on one side with the greens and greys of distant grasslands while in the other direction they ebbed into a land that glittered and sparkled most peculiarly in the sunlight.

'What's that?' asked Charlie, pointing at the strange new land off to her right.

'The Chiming Ground,' said Marsila.

'The Chiming Ground?' Charlie whispered the words to herself in an effort to get used to its name. 'Why does it glimmer like that?'

She thought she might get a mundane answer, perhaps something along the lines of salt reflecting the light, or perhaps that it was trapped moisture refracting the sun's rays, but what she really hoped to hear was that it would be something fantastical. Something that would reflect the wonder of Bellania.

She was not disappointed.

'You've seen the stone trees and crystal flowers of the Stomen?' asked Marsila.

Charlie nodded. She had indeed seen gorgeous rock gardens when she travelled with Crumble Shard through the lands beneath the Slumbering Hills.

'Well, the Chiming Ground,' continued Marsila, 'was once thought to be a dull, featureless plain. It is said that the great Stoman poets of old were displeased with its lack of grace. And so, determined to change that and create a land of beauty, they and their lineage spent the next hundred years singing and calling forth forests of stone trees and great swathes of crystal flowers until they were able to flourish and reproduce by itself. What we can see from up here is merely a faint glimmer of what it's really like. When you're actually there and walking beneath the stone boughs of Shima Trees and between the petals of Weeping Herald Plants the majesty of the place hits you. Charlie, you would not believe the sights! There are bushes with leaves of blue crystal, ferns made from moonstone, orchids spun from maw-sit-sit and flytraps crafted from obsidian. And when it rains the droplets of water chime against this amazing forest, causing the whole landscape to sing. Of course, you won't get a Treman to admit that there is any place more beautiful than Deepforest, but before the rise of Bane the Chiming Ground used to be one of my most treasured travel destinations. Now it's no longer safe to visit.'

'Why not?' asked Charlie.

'It is where Bane breeds his Shades.'

'What?' Charlie spluttered. She couldn't imagine Shades growing in a place full of crystal and light. 'That doesn't make sense.'

'Of course it does,' said Marsila. 'What better place for darkness and terror to be born than in a place of beauty and light? Besides,' she added with a grim look, 'I think that marring a place of wonder with a dark blight suits Bane's twisted way of thinking. Either that or he decided to ruin the place I love the most as a personal slight. He seems to really dislike Keepers so I wouldn't put that past him. He's a miserable excuse for a man and the sooner we rid Bellania of his curse the better. And to that end let us pursue our purpose in coming to this peak.'

She pointed towards a perilous gap in the peak which would provide them with a suitable vantage point. She strode forward, then scrambled the last few metres on her hands and knees until her head was literally hanging over the side of the drop. Grabbing hold of their courage, Charlie and E'Jaaz squirmed their way forward to join the fearless lady.

Charlie gulped. Looking down from this angle was very challenging.

'There's our shadow,' said Marsila and pointed.

The Winged Mount was an unusually shaped peak but its shadow was even more so. The Keepers studied it with interest.

'Well,' said Charlie after some thought, 'it does have an odd trunk that *could* be a tail and that blob at the end *could* be the pointy bit of the tail . . . but you really have to want to see it.'

'And you have to squint a bit too,' admitted E'Jaaz, who cranked his head from side to side to better make out the shape.

But Marsila did not want to play along. Fuelled by her need to save Sylvaris, consumed by her duty as a Keeper and weighed down with the knowledge that time was ever passing by, she scowled and gripped the ground with white-knuckled hands.

'Squint?' she growled. 'Want to see it? We can't waste time with this – we dare not!'

She was in the process of pushing herself upright when E'Jaaz rested a hand between her shoulder blades.

'Wait,' he urged. 'I still think this idea has merit. Let us wait a moment longer.'

'Wait?' said Marsila. 'Wait for what? No matter how long we wait that shadow is not going to miraculously transform into a tail. It's not going to –'

'Hold on, Marsila.' He pointed up to the glowing orb of the sun. 'It's not yet midday. I think it would be worth our while to wait until then.'

Marsila narrowed her eyes.

E'Jaaz felt compelled to defend his reasoning. 'As the sun

travels, the shadow will move – perhaps it'll change a bit. And besides, you and I both know how much the Winged Ones like to be symbolic.'

'S-s-symbolic?' stuttered Charlie, so cold now that her teeth were chattering.

'They like symbolic measurements: half moons, full moons, eclipses, equinoxes. All that good stuff. So hanging on until midday when the sun reaches its zenith might be prudent.'

'How long is that going to be, E'Jaaz?'

He glanced up at the sky. 'Half an hour?'

Marsila didn't look pleased at the notion of sitting still for so long but she relented and instead of complaining she pulled one of her knives from its sheath and started sharpening it.

And so they waited. They spent the time admiring the magnificent landscape, trying to name the spires of distant cities and commentating on Nibbler's antics as he continued to harass the Stowyrms with occasional forks of lightning and outrageous aerial manoeuvres. Every now and then they would get to their feet and jog on the spot in an attempt to warm themselves and all the while they were keeping an eye on the shadow.

Slowly, painfully slowly, the shadow began to move in an arc, tracing its way from west to east like the action of a sundial. As the shadow moved it crept across the folds of the land, drenching all that it covered in cool shade. But for all its slow movement, its shape did not noticeably change. As it grew closer to midday E'Jaaz continued to check the sun's position in the hope that they'd got something wrong, but it seemed that they hadn't.

Charlie had a sinking feeling in her gut. She had been so sure she was right. She had really thought this was going to be it, that the Serpent's Tail would be revealed and they could finally release the Winged Ones and that everything would work out.

'Should have known better,' she whispered to herself. 'Fairy tales are for suckers.'

The wind lifted her bitter words and what should have remained private ended up reaching Marsila's ears.

'You're right, Charlie. Fairy tales are for suckers. The world is a tough place, and if you want to succeed in something you have to work hard to make it happen. But you *are* a worker, you're determined and you always do your best. So maybe your hunch was wrong this time but you tried your hardest and, more importantly, you tried to look at the problem from a different angle and for that I salute you.'

Charlie blinked. She had not expected such words of kindness from a lady who chose to wear warpaint and who gnashed her teeth at the slightest delay. For the first time in her life Charlie was struck by the rather adult concept that people could have hidden depths and that beneath Marsila's tough exterior there were other layers of her personality just waiting to be discovered.

Unaware of the insights unfolding inside Charlie's head, Marsila continued. 'So tell me, Charlie, what do we do if one idea doesn't work out the way we'd hoped?'

'Try another one?' suggested Charlie.

'Too right we do. So let's not give up now. Let's get down there and try –'

Marsila's eyes suddenly grew wide. Charlie's pendant was glowing.

'Hey, take a look!' called E'Jaaz. 'Something's happening.'

Charlie and Marsila turned to look at where E'Jaaz was indicating. His outstretched finger pointed not at the shadow but rather at the fabric of the mountaintop. It was changing. Parts of it were becoming translucent, allowing the sunlight to travel through it. Startled, they looked down at their feet to discover that all of a sudden they seemed to be standing on nothing.

'Bleurgh,' said Charlie as she found herself fighting vertigo.

Crouching, she reached beneath her feet and was reassured when her hands touched something. It felt like glass. Feeling it helped settle her stomach. Kneeling down, she could see through the floor to the rest of the mountain. It was an odd change but also quite a subtle one. Not all of the mountain had become translucent; in fact, it looked like only a small portion of it had and that the changes had merely altered its outline a little.

Some sixth sense caused her to stare at the shadow below. The subtle changes of the mountain had had a drastic effect on what she saw.

'The Serpent's Tail!' said Charlie. A smile of delight broke across her face.

E'Jaaz and Marsila spun round.

'Well, I'll be . . .' said E'Jaaz. 'Those sneaky Winged Ones.'

'They tampered with a whole mountain just to tweak a shadow,' said Marsila in something that was part statement, part expression of disbelief.

The shadow weaved like a child's drawing of a slithering snake's tail and ended in an arrowhead.

And in the middle of this arrowhead was a large temple. Oddly, the building seemed to ripple with motion although shadow and distance made it impossible to decipher any detail.

E'Jaaz squirmed to one side so he could pull a compact telescope from his pocket. Holding it to his eye, he took stock of the temple.

'Crack my Realm,' he cursed.

'What? What is it?' asked Charlie.

E'Jaaz silently passed her the telescope.

'Oh, you've got to be kidding me,' said Charlie when she looked through the lens.

The temple was heaving with Stoman soldiers, Shades, Rhinospiders and Stonesingers.

25

Hummingbird

'A garrison?' cursed Marsila. 'They chose the very temple we need to visit as a place to garrison their troops? What kind of luck is that? Pfft!'

Growling with barely constrained rage, she flung a stone at the offending temple and watched miserably as it plummeted towards the earth. Fortunately it fell short of its mark and none of the Stomen seemed to notice.

E'Jaaz and Charlie joined her in staring at their goal. They too had long faces and even though they had both wrapped themselves in their travel blankets the cold and altitude were grinding them down and adding to the misery of the moment. E'Jaaz's nose had started bleeding again and Charlie's headache had grown to the point where it felt as though her skull was being bludgeoned by a sledgehammer.

'Let's get out of here,' suggested E'Jaaz. 'We've seen all that we need to and staying up here isn't doing us any favours.'

'Agreed,' growled Marsila. Disappointment and anger were still very evident upon her face. 'Triad up.'

Charlie gasped as she felt her Will lurch, proving difficult to hold. By the look of concentration on E'Jaaz's face, he too appeared to momentarily struggle. Wiping blood from his nose, he dug a little deeper, then held up glowing hands to merge his Will with Marsila's. They looked at her expectantly.

'It's – er . . . it's . . .' began Charlie, still struggling. She was shocked to realize that beneath her headache and beneath the cold she was more fatigued than ever before.

'Don't worry,' said Marsila, 'I've got it.'

Grunting, she tore open a Portal by herself. It wasn't big by any means but was far larger than E'Jaaz or Charlie would have managed by themselves. It seemed that at present Marsila was the strongest of the three.

The Portal led back to their campsite on the small island. The return to lower altitude and the warmth of midday sun felt like a blessing. Shedding their blankets and loosening collars, all three of them slumped around the Alavisian fire-pit.

'More problems,' said Marsila. 'And fewer options.' She looked to E'Jaaz. 'You know my style. I like to tackle problems head on but it's plain to see that we don't have the strength to force our way into such a mess. You're the devious one, how would you go about getting into that temple in one piece?'

'Well, I wouldn't have chosen the word "devious" to describe my finer qualities,' said E'Jaaz. He tried to muster a dashing smile but the look was spoiled somewhat by the dried blood crusting his upper lip. 'I like to think that I'm more of a mischievous man than a devious man.'

'Well, that's a shame,' retorted Marsila, 'because what we need right now is a devious individual to find a way to sneak us inside.'

An uncomfortable silence settled across the campsite. Sleepiness was not only making them irritable but making it hard for them to see a way round their problems. Charlie was suffering worse than either of the other two. Having finally reached her limit, her eyes were drooping and her head kept bobbing forward as sleep tried to overcome her.

'The Hummingbird Strategy,' said E'Jaaz after a few moments of thought.

'What was that?' asked Marsila. 'The Hummingbird Strategy? Sounds like something used in a board game.'

'It is,' admitted E'Jaaz, 'but it's also a strategy that can be used in espionage, economics and warfare. The legendary general Kirack the Breaker used the Hummingbird –'

'We don't have time for history lessons!' snapped Marsila. 'Stop warbling and get to the meat of the matter.'

'All right,' said E'Jaaz. 'The Hummingbird Strategy was developed after a monk, studying the ways of nature, saw how a hummingbird managed to tease bees away from their hive with deceptive offerings of flowers and while the beehive was left relatively unguarded the hummingbird would swoop in to steal the honey.'

'I'm going to disregard what I know of honeybees and pretend that what you just said made sense –'

'All stories become embellished with the passing of time,' murmured E'Jaaz with a roguish shrug.

'– and assume that you're using this analogy with some kind of intelligent intent. I'm also going to assume that we're to take the role of the hummingbird and that the temple garrison will be the beehive.'

'Bees and honey,' slurred Charlie as her head lolled

forward once again. Snapping awake with a grunt, she sat up straighter and tried to pretend that she hadn't just fallen asleep.

'What,' continued Marsila, 'are you intending we use as the bait to lure out the Stomen? I'm assuming it's not going to be flowers?'

'I'm intending to use ourselves as bait. But to do so successfully we're going to have to wait until darkness.'

'You know we can't afford to wait until dark,' protested Marsila. 'Sylvaris needs us now.'

'I know they need us. The whole of Bellania needs us, but we are forced to work with the tools we have at hand –' E'Jaaz raised his eyebrows in Charlie's direction – 'and our tools at hand are a little sleepy at the moment.'

'Hey, I heard that!' said Charlie, but the other two ignored her.

'All of us are tired,' continued E'Jaaz, 'and we both know that it will take us several days of rest to fully recover. Pressing on now would be a foolish, possibly fatal mistake. What I strongly suggest we do is take the hours of daylight we have left to rest and recoup what strength we can, then take action tonight when we can better put the Hummingbird Strategy to use.'

'But why darkness?' insisted Marsila.

'So we can entice the Stomen with the correct bait,' explained E'Jaaz. 'I appreciate that you are keen to press on but unless you have a better option I would counsel that we go with a ruse that lessens the number of foes we have to face.'

'And you think this will keep the Delightful Brothers off our backs?'

'Sweet Realms, I sincerely hope so,' said E'Jaaz. 'Even if we do recover a glimmer of strength by tonight there's no way we could face their Stowyrms.'

Something about that last sentence plucked at Charlie's mind . . . something about the Stowyrms. 'Nibbler!' she said and stood bolt upright, only to sway sleepily from side to side. 'We forgot to get Nibbler back!'

'You,' said Marsila, 'are not going anywhere. If you try to do anything in that state you'll probably cause more mischief than good. Stay here and I'll go and fetch that scoundrel of a Hatchling.'

'I'll come with you,' said E'Jaaz.

'Pfft,' said Marsila, 'you're in almost as bad a shape as Charlie. No, you stay here, keep an eye on our sleepy Keeper, and I'll be back in a minute.'

Muttering to herself, Marsila created a Portal and disappeared through it.

Charlie rubbed at her eyes, then tried to focus on E'Jaaz. It wasn't easy as everything seemed to be blurred.

'Is she always so . . .'

'Determined?' suggested E'Jaaz.

'. . . tough,' finished Charlie.

'Yes,' said E'Jaaz after some thought. 'Yes, she is. She's known for it. Famous for it, in fact. They say she wasn't always that way but her past is marred by tragedy. Her twin sister was killed by a Shade when she was a young teenager, near your age in fact.'

'Really?' said Charlie. Her heart gave a lurch. Ever since her parents had been taken from her she knew what that kind of loss felt like. It had been one of her driving forces;

it had shaped her, in fact. Made her stronger, harder . . . and, truth be told, it had made her a touch darker too.

'Really,' confirmed E'Jaaz. 'It changed her from a bright and happy girl to the tough cookie that we know and love today. Sound like anyone familiar?'

He smiled and chucked a fake punch to Charlie's chin. She grinned back at him.

'No matter how hard the task, Marsila always gets the job done. I realize she can seem a bit harsh but you need to know that she's counted amongst the best of us. Next to your parents, she and Azariah were the Keepers that the Jade Circle relied on the most. And as dangerous as she is, I'd do almost anything to get that dance with her. Tough and beautiful ladies like Marsila truly are one in a million, wouldn't you say, Charlie?'

Expecting a response but getting none, he turned round to find that Charlie's head was bowing forward again, her chin nearly touching her chest.

The rumble of her snoring soon filled their small campsite.

26

The Last Dinner

The scent of grilled fish woke Charlie. Grinding her knuckles into the corners of her eyes, she let loose a yawn that would have shamed a hippopotamus and staggered upright.

'Wheurffag'wan?' She shut her mouth, swallowed and tried again. 'What's going on?' She looked up at the darkening sky in shock. 'How long have I been asleep?'

'Long enough for us to wonder whether you've got some kind of demon stuck in your throat or if you had to practise really hard to become so talented at snoring,' said E'Jaaz.

Charlie was too concerned over lost time to scowl at his attempt at humour.

'We let you sleep as long as we could,' said Marsila. 'More than any of us; you needed it the most.' Seeing that Charlie was starting to blush, she added, 'Don't worry, we all took turns to catch a nap so don't beat yourself up over it.'

'What about Sylvaris?' asked Charlie. 'Have we left it too late?'

'Time is still pressing,' admitted Marsila, 'but we believe that waiting for darkness was the right move to make.'

Feeling something prod her shoulder, she turned round to find Nibbler trying to grin at her while simultaneously swallowing a large haunch of meat. Held towards her in one of his paws was a plate spilling over with cooked fish, more jerritots and a salad of golden leaves. The aroma wafting off it was enough to set Charlie's stomach growling.

'And we caught plenty of rabbit too,' said Nibbler once he had managed to swallow his mouthful.

'You're OK?' asked Charlie. 'You didn't have any trouble with Stix and Stones?'

'Not really,' said Nibbler. 'They were getting used to the lightning and the flame and I thought maybe they were bored, so to keep them occupied I started throwing dung at them and calling them names. Stix got so annoyed I thought he was going to burst all the blood vessels in his face.'

'Dung?' said Charlie, once her brain had digested the image of Nibbler catcalling at the Delightful Brothers and throwing muck at them from above. 'Where did you get dung from? And do I really want to know the answer to that?'

'Well, I thought about slinging mud at them from the river but when I came down I scared off a load of long-necked shirasheer. They left a lot of dung about . . . and it really smelt.'

'Please,' began Charlie, 'please tell me you didn't pick it up with the same paws that just held my dinner?'

'Uh? Oh no! Eeuck, I wouldn't use my paws to pick up shirasheer poop. I kinda scooped it up with those wide Hooble leaves, which was great because I could carry a lot. Which made it really hard for Stix and Stones to dodge it all.' He grinned at the memory. 'And of course I washed my paws before dinner too.'

Unable to stop herself, Charlie felt her mouth tug into a grin, which in turn grew into a chuckle. 'Ah, Nibbler, you always know how to make me smile! My life would be slow and dull if you weren't around.'

She suddenly realized that not only was she able to laugh again but that her sleep had done her a world of good. There was no doubting that she was still deeply tired but her spirit had recovered and she felt far stronger than at any period over the last two days.

'So,' she said between mouthfuls, 'what's the plan? Weren't we discussing something about a kingfisher?'

E'Jaaz and Marsila looked puzzled.

'Oh!' snorted E'Jaaz once he had deciphered her wayward words. 'You mean a hummingbird!'

Charlie blinked, then recovered quickly enough to hide her embarrassment. 'Kingfisher, hummingbird, they're practically the same, right?' There was silence around the campfire. 'Er, OK, maybe they're not. Um . . . so there *was* some mention of a hummingbird?'

Always the gentleman, E'Jaaz ignored her blunder. 'Yes, the Hummingbird Strategy is the ruse we will use on the Stomen when night falls. We have to clear that temple of as many of the enemy as possible. The fewer we have to face the better, and the Hummingbird Strategy will aid us towards that end.'

'Sooo . . . what *is* this Hummingbird Strategy?' asked Charlie. 'It sounds all sorts of mysterious, but what exactly are we going to do?'

'The Stomen and the Delightful Brothers know we've been checking the temples. They have, after all, done their best to block us all day long. So we're going to amplify their impression of us.'

'How?'

'We're going to lure them with decoys. If we open Portals to as many temples as possible in as little time as possible it should rile them no end. And to make sure we grab their attention, we're going to let loose a flare in each temple. If we do this well enough, they'll have to divide their forces if they intend to cover each location. And the more Stomen we divert from the garrison, the fewer we'll have to deal with.'

Marsila stirred. 'I don't like it that we've allowed so much time to slip through our fingers. And I don't like to think that Sylvaris might be fighting the enemy while we wait here but I agree with E'Jaaz. I think this ploy brings us the best chance of success.'

Charlie dusted off her lap and stood tall. She was as ready as she was ever going to be. 'So what are we waiting for? Let's get on with it.'

'Er, not yet, Charlie,' said E'Jaaz (and he was decent enough to hide his smile behind his hand). 'It's not yet fully dark so let's take this opportunity to rest and eat while we can.'

'Oh,' said Charlie. Feeling a bit silly, she sat back down.

'If it means anything,' said E'Jaaz, 'I like your enthusiasm. Very invigorating.'

Charlie blushed a little harder.

'Stop teasing her, E'Jaaz,' said Marsila. 'And refill her plate. Eat up, Charlie. We don't know when we'll next have a chance to rest, so enjoy the moment if you can – it only gets harder from this point on.'

27

Beacons of Light

E'Jaaz opened a Portal and together the three Keepers and Nibbler peered through it. It revealed a night-time landscape, dark and shadowy, and only thinly illuminated by the crescent moon and starry sky. The temples, however, were lit by torchlight and the reflected glow of enemy campfire.

'Hmm,' mused Marsila. 'I think another Portal would be better. Try somewhere a little higher up the Winged Mount to see if that gives us a better vantage point.'

E'Jaaz nodded. Closing the first, he opened another.

'Better?' he asked.

'Much,' agreed Marsila.

Their small group passed through the Portal on to the sloping side of the Winged Mount. The wind at this higher altitude was stronger and the temperature cooler but what it offered in return was a better view of the temples below along with the added privacy and security they would need to carry out their plan. *And at least*, thought Charlie to herself, *it's nowhere near as cold as it was at the very peak.*

'Set the screen up over there,' said Marsila.

Together they pulled the bundles of wicker and branches

that they had gathered through the Portal and assembled them to make a screen. It was a rough affair but the best they could manage with a limited supply of resources. They plugged what gaps they could and covered the thinner parts of the screen with their blankets and bedrolls. Then, in a final act of crude engineering, they lashed additional guide ropes to the frame and weighed the base with the few boulders that were close to hand. When they had finished they were presented with a screen that although ugly to the eye would at least shield the glow of their Will from the land below.

Or, in any case, that was the theory.

'Good enough,' said Marsila. 'That'll have to do.'

Charlie eyed their creation with some misgivings. It appeared quite patchy and at this height they were very exposed to anyone looking up from below.

'Do you think it'll really block all our light?' she asked.

'Probably not,' said Marsila with a shrug. 'But we've done the best we can and there's nothing else for it but to press on. E'Jaaz, are you ready?'

'To roll the dice? Always.'

Marsila turned to Nibbler. 'Hatchling?'

'I'm ready.'

'Charlie?'

Charlie felt a flutter of nervousness but she swallowed the emotion. 'One thing's been bothering me. If we do open the Gateway won't all those Stomen be able to get into the Winged Realm? Won't that be a problem?'

Marsila and E'Jaaz chuckled.

'No, Charlie, that won't be a problem,' explained E'Jaaz,

clearly appreciating the opportunity for a laugh in this otherwise sombre moment. 'Any Stomen stupid enough to jump in after us are going to get their eyebrows burned off.'

'And their weapons turned into slag,' added Marsila. 'The Winged Ones can manage all of those soldiers and Shades and more without breaking a sweat. All we have to worry about is getting that Gateway open. Any more questions or are you good?'

'I'm good,' said Charlie, glad to put the last of her doubts aside. 'Let's get this done.'

'All right, people,' said Marsila. 'Triad up.'

Standing behind the screen, they summoned their Wills. Marsila placed the map on the floor in front of her and as an afterthought weighed down its corners with pebbles. Giving it a moment's study, she grunted once she was certain she had committed what was required to memory.

'First temple coming up,' she said.

She wove her hands in a figure of eight and tore open the first Portal.

'Flare,' said Marsila, and punched a pillar of Will directly into the temple beyond.

Charlie and E'Jaaz copied the motion. The temple erupted in a kaleidoscope of light, filling it to the brim before bursting through windows and doors out into the night.

'I can see it!' shouted Nibbler, who was standing to one side of the screen and now hopping up and down in excitement. 'I can see it, it's awesome! It's making the walls of the temple glow.' Putting E'Jaaz's telescope to his eye, he squinted at the distant building. 'And the Stomen are going nuts too. Oh, it's great. It's working!'

'Very well,' said Marsila in a calm voice at odds with Nibbler's. 'One temple down. Time for the next.'

She closed the Portal, only to re-open one a second later into a similar-looking building.

'Flare,' she instructed.

Charlie and E'Jaaz complied so that this temple too seemed to burst with golden light.

'Awesome,' said Nibbler, his eye still pressed firmly against the telescope. Unable to control his excitement, his tail began to swish from side to side.

'Next,' said Marsila.

They shattered the calm of the third building with their flare.

'Good, let's move on,' said Marsila.

Building a rhythm, the three Keepers began to pick up speed. Their Portals opened into temple after temple and at each they sent a spluttering, sparking wave of Will flaring through. Sometimes they would open into an empty room and at others they would disturb slumbering Stomen or basking Shades. These would scream and shout as the unexpected bursts of light took them by surprise. After a while the bedlam in the temples grew to the point where, even when there was no Portal open, they could hear the faint curse and panicked scream of the distant enemy reaching them from afar like the sound of waves.

Marsila, unable to contain herself, actually grinned. 'It sounds like the first part of our plan has gained momentum. Time to press on with the next and push our foes while they're still reeling.'

She opened another Portal and this time jumped into it,

landing in another temple. The others joined her. With fists blazing, they ran through the temple, then leaped out of the windows and doors to land amongst the enemy who were loitering outside around a campfire. They pummelled and kicked the surprised soldiers, knocking them from their feet. Nibbler unleashed gusts of flame and Charlie, flowing from K'Changa stance to stance, darted here and there, dropping foes as fast as she could.

'Enough!' said Marsila after less than a minute had passed.

The group of companions retreated into the temple, leaving the Stomen dazed and confused. Tearing a fresh Portal open, they dived through to land in yet another temple. Surrounded by haloes of Will and wrapped in grim determination, they ghosted from location to location, harassing and striking the enemy. And as cries and shouts of alarm continued to ring around the land Charlie and her companions began to grin in triumph.

They could feel the cogs in the wheel of their plan turning. Momentum building, they pressed onward.

28

Winged Delight

'They what?' cursed Stones.

'They're everywhere!' cried the panicked solider. 'They pop out of the air and rip our formations to shreds! They're unstoppable, they're –'

Stones's fist smashed into the soldier, sending him flying across the length of the courtyard. 'Idiot,' rumbled Stones. 'We have no time for warriors who cry in the heat of battle.'

Stix looked every bit as displeased as his brother. He snapped his fingers at one of the men guarding the great doors. 'Remove that,' he pointed at the unconscious soldier, 'and send for someone else. Someone who can report without crying like a little girl.'

The guards dragged away the snoring soldier. Moments later a Shade appeared. Hugging the shadows, it cautiously made its way towards the Delightful Brothers.

'Report,' snapped Stix.

'My brethren have received mixed information,' hissed the Shade. It remained in the shadows and was careful to avoid getting too close to Stix and Stones (proving that it was wiser than their previous visitor). 'In the last hour, between thirty and forty of the Winged Ones' temples have been struck but details are haphazard at best. Some have reported seeing only the glimmer of the Keepers' Will, others give claim to seeing entire buildings shining with light. Rumours and tall tales aside, there has been definite contact with Keepers. Intelligence is not clear or precise regarding the numbers involved but we believe there are between five and eleven Keepers involved in these attacks. We have not yet been able to pin them down.'

'Why not?' rumbled Stones.

'Their tactics have changed. It is they who now ambush us. They strike quickly and melt away before we can bring our full weight of numbers to bear.'

'You cannot corner them inside the temples?' asked Stones. 'Can you not over- whelm them while they are constrained by walls and hem them in?'

'That tactic worked before but not any more.' The Shade bristled with agitation. 'They move dif- ferently. Swiftly and with purpose. They no longer use their Will to shield themselves. No longer do they stay in one place. They are like quicksilver. Fast. Dangerous.'

Stix looked to his brother.

'Eleven Keepers,' he said. 'Does that sound likely?'

'No, it doesn't,' said Stones. 'I think it's just the original three playing games with us.'

'Hmmm, my thoughts too, brother.' Stix looked at the Shade. 'You. Show us which temples have been hit.'

Hissing, the Shade unhappily made its way into the light to stand beside a Stonesinger's three-dimensional map. Doing its best to keep one eye on the brothers, it began to mark locations on the map.

'Huh,' snorted Stones as he watched the Shade work. 'They still keep to the southern border of the Winged Mount.'

'That they do,' remarked Stix. 'Nonetheless, it would be wise, would it not, brother, to congregate our forces around all of the temples? North and south?'

'Of course,' agreed Stones. 'North and south it is. You!' His thick finger pointed at a guard. 'Send messages to the captains that they are to distribute a further two squads to all temples within a two-mile circumference of the Winged Mount. I want a Stonesinger at each temple too.'

'Yessir!'

'Wait!' roared Stones. 'I have not finished yet. I want a further four divisions of equal strength standing ready at the four compass points. Instruct them to be ready to move fast. When we finally corner our visitors they will be the anvil that we crush the Keepers against.'

The unfortunate guard mustered the courage to ask a question. 'And, er, sir? The hammer will be . . .?'

Stix and Stones stared at him with unflinching yellow eyes.

'Us, of course,' said Stix and bared his teeth in a feral smile.

'Go,' said Stones. 'See it done.'

'Yes, sir.' The guard disappeared through the door.

'Why would you send my brethren to the north?' asked the Shade from the safety of the shadows. 'It is clear the Keepers seek something in the south. Why not squeeze all our might where we know they are going to be? Our lord would not be pleased if he thought you were making foolish mistakes.'

'*Your* lord took us into his employ on the merit of our accomplishments,' growled Stones. 'Foolish we are not.'

'Only a fool would think to look in the direction that the enemy wants us to,' said Stix. 'A wise hunter knows to spread his net far and wide.'

'We know that the Keepers are growing desperate,' said

Stones, adding the weight of his words to his brother's. 'They still have not found what they require otherwise they would be long gone by now. It is just as obvious that this wave of attacks is a ruse to divert our attention.'

'How do you know that?' asked the Shade. It had moved through the shadows so that its voice now came from a different part of the room. 'How can you be so sure?'

'Because it is exactly what we would do if our positions were reversed,' said Stix. 'So until we know precisely where they aim to be we will watch and cover all the options. And besides, little shadow, what are you worried about? We have more than enough manpower to cover all the temples.'

'More than enough,' said Stones. Darting forward, he plunged his hand into the darkness, then pulled it free to reveal the Shade wriggling and writhing at the end of his arm. He stared menacingly at it with his cat's eyes until it settled into a submissive stillness. 'Tell your brothers and sisters to do as they are told. Tell them that when it comes to catching and skinning a Keeper, no one knows how to do it better than a Delightful Brother.'

Stix came to stand by his side. They watched as the Shade, cowed, slunk from the room.

'To the skies?' said Stones.

'To the skies!' agreed Stix with a predator's grin.

They strutted through the Embassy of the Winds, and out into a poorly lit courtyard. Large *things*, half seen, half hidden, coiled restlessly in the shadows. As the Delightful Brothers drew near, the sound of scales rasping against the courtyard's walls grew. So too did the clicks, hoots and whistles of the waiting beasts.

Grinning like two wicked children given presents that they did not deserve, Stix and Stones headed towards the shadows that hid their impatient mounts. They clambered into their saddles and, gripping the reins, shouted, 'Hup! Hup!'

Arching their backs and unsheathing their wings, the two Stowyrms burst into the sky. In a blur of dragonfly wings and gnashing teeth, they writhed their way higher and higher into the moonlit night. The only thing left in their wake was a stirring of wind and the echo of Stix and Stones's unpleasant laughter.

29

One Last Push

Even though they were back on the chilly slopes of the Winged Mount, sweat coursed off the three Keepers. For the last hour they had worked tirelessly. They had opened countless Portals, jumped through dozens of temples and ambushed scores of Stoman soldiers. And after all their hard work they sported new injuries: a dark bruise coloured Charlie's jaw, a line of blood from a near miss ran across E'Jaaz's cheek and Marsila favoured her right wrist after further damage to her already injured left. Nibbler, however, seemed as spry as ever and had had the good luck to avoid all injury.

'Think we've done enough?' asked E'Jaaz.

'With the number of Stomen at that last temple? Yes, I certainly think so,' said Marsila with a smile still bright on her face. 'Let's take a look, shall we?'

She moved round in front of the screen, then crouched down, swung her legs out and sat herself right on the edge of the precipice. The others, still buzzing from their last encounter, quickly joined her. Together they looked out across the night-time landscape.

It was aglow with thousands of lights. There were

hundreds of campfires and a multitude of flickering torches
held in the hands of the enemy. From where they sat, up on
the Winged Mount, it was like watching a swarm of fireflies.

'Wow,' breathed Charlie. 'That's a lot of Stomen.'

'Let's have a closer look through that looking 'scope of
yours, E'Jaaz,' said Marsila.

E'Jaaz passed it over and Marsila pressed it to her eye.

'Hmmm . . . I'd say that we've succeeded in our task.
Here, take a look.' She passed the telescope to Charlie.

Charlie peered at the large temple that was their goal. It
was easy to pick out. Bedecked with lanterns and illuminated
by great fires, it was like an island of light amidst a sea of
darkness. Large carvings of Winged Ones, far bigger than
those at the other temples, graced the exterior walls. It still
rippled with activity – Charlie could see ranks of organized
Stomen and Rhinospiders congregated around the building
like spokes gravitating towards a central hub – but it was
evident that it was far less populated than it had been in the
daytime. Far, far less.

Looking at it, Charlie felt a mixture of emotions. There was
no denying that she was excited. All their hard work over the
past couple of days had led them to this. The Winged Ones'
Gateway lay in the temple below and if Charlie could open
it then all her ambitions would be realized: peace in Bellania,
the end of Bane and the return of her parents. But beneath
this heady wave of excitement coiled an uneasy sense of
doubt and worry. Could they make it? Would this really
work? What happened if something went wrong? Everything
she cared about depended on their success. The more Charlie thought about it, the more her doubts grew. Scowling

angrily, not at the Stomen below but rather at herself, she forced her pre-fight nerves aside and did her best to ignore them.

'How are we going to do this?' asked Nibbler. 'Are we going to charge in like we did at the other temples?'

'No!' said E'Jaaz. 'Definitely not. With the amount of manpower still down there we want to sneak our way in and avoid fighting until the last minute. If we can pull this off without having to fight for every inch I'll be a happy man. Marsila?'

'I agree.'

'Charlie?' asked E'Jaaz.

'Uh, yes,' she said. 'I'm always in favour of being sneaky.'

E'Jaaz looked back at Nibbler. 'Hatchling, got any concerns about going in quietly?'

'No. I like sneaky as much as the next man.'

'Glad to hear that,' said E'Jaaz. 'Now let's put our heads together and find a way into that temple.'

30

Last-minute Plans

Kelko marched through Deepforest. Sic Boy, the big beast of a dog, ghosted ahead of him, blazing the way. The border, where forest met Great Plains, was his goal. At his side, spread out in a long ribbon, were lines of soldiers, predominantly Tremen but there were also squads of Humans and Stomen. The arms and armour were mismatched. There were the spiked bark suits of the Shoud'iar Tremen, the polished wood plate armour of the Eastern Tremen, the stone shields of the renegade Stomen and the polished-blue chain-mail of the Alavisian and Alacornian Humans who had survived and managed to flee the conquest of their native lands. There were wooden swords crafted by treesinging, stone maces and warhammers crafted by stonesinging, and mundane weapons created through forging and blacksmithing. But as mismatched as the soldiers looked they were made uniform by the colour they wore: the turquoise of the Jade Circle.

Kelko grunted and hefted the Brambleaxe that rested in his grip. Glancing down, he could not help but admire the cruel-looking weapon. Double-headed, its two half-moon blades caught the light and spearing between these was a huge thorn that did service as a central spike. Living up to its name, a wealth of smaller but equally sharp thorns erupted from its main shaft. Truly, it was a thing of beauty. Just as truly, it was a thing of barbaric viciousness and part of Kelko was ashamed to carry it. He was not a man of war and hated the fact that he would be forced to act like a butcher before the day was done.

Gritting his teeth, he swallowed and forced saliva down his parched throat. Then he pushed past the last line of trees to stand at the edge of the Great Plains. The advisors that Lady Dridif had loaned him took up positions on either side. Shielding his eyes from the setting sun, he squinted westward.

He noted the deep trenches that his people had dug, and beyond those the great fields of Tanglewire, Mollybush and Strangleweed that the Treesingers had grown in the hope of slowing the Stoman advance. And beyond those lay the grasslands of the Great Plains, rising in shallow rolling hills like a green sea that swept all the way to the horizon.

But of their enemy there was no sight.

'Where are they?' growled Kelko. He didn't mean to snarl the question but the anxious wait was almost more than he could bear. Sic Boy *groofed* a bark, not dissimilar to his owner's growl of frustration.

'They're coming, m'lord,' said one of his advisors.

'We've got the say-so of our scouts,' said another.

Far from happy, Kelko adjusted the grip on his weapon. His advisors looked askance when the knuckles on his hands popped and cracked. Realizing that he had been holding the Brambleaxe tighter than was necessary, he tried to relax, but failed. He had too much on his shoulders, too many people relying on him. Taking a deep breath, he tried to calm his mind. 'I wonder how Charlie is doing?' he whispered.

'Wot was that, m'lord?'

'Huh? Nothing,' muttered Kelko, thoughts of his blonde-haired Keeper friend filling his head. He hoped she was safe. Hoped that perhaps she had found this mysterious Winged Ones' Gateway and hoped that she would find a way not just to save the day, his city and his companions but to return in one piece. 'Stay safe, blossom. Stay safe.'

'M'lord?'

'Wot?' snapped Kelko.

'Look ta the horizon.'

Raising his eyes, he noticed distant motion.

'Bane's armies,' he muttered.

They were many hours away and impossible to discern as anything more than a waving line but they were coming.

Time was running out.

Nibbler appeared from the darkness with an abrupt snap of spread wings. Landing lightly, he padded over to the Keepers.

'From what I saw there are two options. There's a gorge to the east that you could use or a large pile of boulders to the west.'

'Boulders,' said Marsila.

'Gorge,' said Charlie.

'If anything goes wrong there's more room to manoeuvre behind a stack of boulders than there is down a ravine,' reasoned Marsila.

'But less chance of anyone seeing our Portal if we open it beneath everyone's line of sight,' countered Charlie.

'The gorge sounds good,' agreed E'Jaaz.

Marsila gritted her teeth but conceded the point in favour of the majority. Finally decided, the three of them summoned their Will, opened a Portal and, Nibbler by their side, stepped through.

The ravine was a pit of darkness and with only a narrow band of stars overhead it took long seconds for their eyes to adjust. When they felt they could see clearly enough they pulled themselves hand over hand up the craggy side of the ravine to the top. There they slowly raised their heads until they could peer over the rim to the temple beyond.

Up close they could appreciate how much larger it was in comparison with the other temples they had visited. It was a majestic building and its walls, heavy with carvings and draped with curtains of ivy, were illuminated by a multitude of torches. Spying through its windows, they could see that the inside bustled with motion; Stomen and Stonesingers continued to stride in and out of the large doors and tethered in long lines down one wall were scores of Rhinospiders.

'Huh,' muttered E'Jaaz. 'Maybe we should go back to rattling a few more of the other temples.'

'It's too late for that,' retorted Marsila. 'If this is how many are left then this is how many we will deal with.'

'Well, I don't think there's any way we're just going to waltz in there,' said E'Jaaz. 'Not without getting caught.'

'Waltz?' said Marsila. 'Why does everything you suggest have to be dance-related?'

Ignoring the two of them and pushing her growing concerns aside, Charlie studied the building's layout.

'Let's just open a Portal and drop down on the roof,' said Charlie.

The others stopped muttering to stare at her.

'I like the idea,' said E'Jaaz. 'But it wouldn't work.'

'Or if it did,' continued Marsila, 'it would be courting disaster. What would happen if the Stowyrms or the Delightful Brothers flying overhead noticed the glimmer of the Portal? They'd be over here in a flash. No, let's try something else.'

'How about we go with the old knock 'em out and wear their armour trick?' said E'Jaaz.

'They're Stomen, E'Jaaz. If you wore their armour you'd look like a three-year-old trying on his mother's clothes. Look, we're just going to have to –'

'I liked Charlie's idea,' said Nibbler. 'Going in through

the roof would give you more time to look for the keyhole without being detected.'

'Maybe it would,' said Marsila, 'but we still have to deal with the problem of the Stowyrms seeing the light from our Portal.'

'So let me fly you in.'

There was a thoughtful silence.

'Do you really think you could lift E'Jaaz and me?' asked Marsila eventually.

'I don't think I'd be able to fly you there, but I think I could glide in with you one at a time. I've flown with Charlie before and that was for a good half an hour. You guys are heavier but if I don't have to carry you for long I don't think it would be a problem.'

Marsila looked at E'Jaaz but before she could say anything Charlie opened her mouth. 'What better option are we going to come up with? Let's do it.'

'All right,' said Marsila. 'We'll try it your way. Hatchling, how do you want to do this?'

'If we can head back up the slope of the Winged Mount a bit it'll give me enough altitude to glide down. And if we angle it right I can drop you guys off without stopping, which is great because less flapping means less noise and less noise means we're less likely to be caught.'

'You want us to walk back up the mountain?' asked E'Jaaz.

'Just a bit.'

'Seems like an awful lot of moving around going on here and not much action,' E'Jaaz grumbled.

'Well,' said Nibbler, 'if you want to head right into the temple, be my guest.'

'Nooooo, that's fine,' said E'Jaaz hastily.

Ducking back down into the gorge, they crossed to the other side, pulled themselves up and started the laborious process of hiking up the incline.

31

Talk of the Future

'I'm going to start with the heaviest first,' said Nibbler. 'So when I get tired at least my load gets lighter.'

'That would be me, then,' said E'Jaaz. He licked his lips and looked towards the temple. It seemed a long way down. 'Are you sure about this, Hatchling? You're not even halfway grown yet –'

Nibbler cut him short. 'There's only one way to find out, isn't there?'

He prodded E'Jaaz (who was clearly having second thoughts) in front of him, spread his wings wide, wrapped his forepaws round E'Jaaz's chest and dropped forward to disappear into the night.

There was a muffled squawk as E'Jaaz fought the urge to scream like a little girl. Then silence.

'Has he said anything about me?' asked Marsila.

The question startled Charlie. She turned to study Marsila's face but the woman avoided her gaze and instead looked out at the temple.

'I assume we're talking about E'Jaaz and not Nibbler?'

Marsila frowned at Charlie and resumed her study of the

temple. Finally she sighed and allowed her shoulders to sag. 'Yes, we're talking about E'Jaaz.'

'Ha!' snorted Charlie, then quickly clamped a hand over her mouth as Marsila gave her another look. Aware that it must have taken a lot for Marsila to even ask such a question, Charlie squashed the urge to tease her and, as ever, settled upon honesty. 'He said that you were dangerous . . . and beautiful. And that he would do almost anything to get that dance you promised him.'

'Huh. Imagine that. I expected to die in battle weeks ago but luck has been with us.' Marsila paused to study the stars. 'Who knows, I might even live to see the return of the Winged Ones. So maybe . . . maybe I'll take him up on his offer once we're back in Sylvaris and once this is over.' A girlish smile, so new but very much looking like it belonged, appeared briefly only to disappear seconds later like a flash of welcome sunshine obscured by storm clouds. 'This is to remain between us,' warned Marsila, 'at least for now. Dancing is for happier times. Right here, right now, I need my game face on.'

'Sure,' said Charlie. She was a little puzzled by Marsila's abrupt decision to confide in her. She wasn't sure what this sudden thawing of her tough exterior meant but knowing that she had a softer side made it easier to empathize with her. 'But I thought you didn't like E'Jaaz. You're always so quick to tell him off.'

'Ha! A man like E'Jaaz needs a good telling off now and again. It keeps his head from growing too large. As for liking him, well, whether I like him or not is irrelevant at a time when there is so much at stake.'

A gust of wind set their clothes rippling. Charlie, troubled by Marsila's earlier words asked, 'Did you really think you were going to die?'

'Of course. With the rise of Bane and the banishment of the Winged Ones I thought all hope was lost. And as the Stoman forces grew stronger I fully expected that my life would be taken in the defence of the realms.' Marsila looked Charlie right in the eye. 'As Keepers we live a blessed life but we are bound by our responsibility to the realms. And from time to time some of us are forced into situations that might require us to lay down our lives so that thousands more may live. When we first met upon that bridge in Sylvaris, I thought my time had come and that in order to defend those fleeing the blade of the enemy my life would be forfeit. But you arrived with words of strength and determination, and when you brought your dark army to crush Bane's First I found that weak flicker of hope rising in my chest once again. Now I no longer dream of death and darkness but find myself imagining a time when I can remove this paint of war and hatred from my face and relax and laugh once more.'

'I . . . I don't know how you can talk so calmly about giving up your life for others. I don't think I could.' Charlie swallowed a lump in her throat. 'As badly as I want to see Bane defeated, I don't want to die. Each time I've fought I've been angry and that's given me the strength to see things through, but when things are calm and quiet the idea of dying, no matter the reason, terrifies me. Does . . . does that make me a coward?'

Marsila chuckled. 'No, Charlie, that makes you Human. You're young and innocent and have long years of life lying ahead of you. Leave thoughts of death and dying to the adults.'

'Marsila, E'Jaaz told me you lost your sister when you were my age . . . Did that . . . I mean, is that why –'

'Why I'm as hard as I am today?' said the older woman, finishing Charlie's words with a bitter smile. 'In a word, yes. I won't bore you with the story of how it happened but I will tell you this: mistakes were made that day, mistakes that caused the shattering of my family and the loss of the sister I loved. If I had been more disciplined, if the members of my family and the Keepers around me had been more . . .' Marsila closed her eyes as though she was reliving the moments of that distant day. When she opened them they were hard and filled with certainty. 'Well, there's no need to point the finger of blame but I learned tough and valuable lessons that day, lessons that I will never, *never* forget. Just remember, Charlie, that no matter the burden, no matter the cost, we are Keepers and it is vital that we live up to the principle of our names. We must maintain the balance of the realms. We must keep the peace.'

Before they could continue their conversation there came a flutter of wings and Nibbler appeared out of the darkness.

'Charlie,' said Marsila, 'we'll talk later.'

Charlie nodded, then turned to her winged friend. 'How'd it go?'

'All riiiight,' said Nibbler. 'My shoulders aren't dislocated and I'm pretty sure E'Jaaz landed in one piece so I guess you could call it a successful trip. What about you, Marsila, are you ready?'

'Just don't drop me.'

'I'll take that as a yes, then.' Taking hold of Marsila, he flashed Charlie a grin. 'I'll be back in a moment.'

They disappeared into the gloom. Charlie couldn't help but notice that, unlike E'Jaaz, Marsila did not squawk. She smiled to herself at that.

32

The Calm Before the Storm

Left alone on the mountainside with her own thoughts, Charlie was pleasantly surprised to find that her doubts had subsided somewhat. Perhaps, after everything she had endured, she was finally getting used to the rollercoaster life of an adventurer. Either that or the discovery that Marsila might actually return E'Jaaz's guarded feelings was enough of a shock to keep her mind occupied.

Relaxing and savouring the faint scent of cloves on the cool breeze, Charlie tried to recall happier times with her parents. Memories came to her of autumn trips to the countryside and summer evenings spent with her family in London parks. She remembered the sound of her mother's laugh and the startling turquoise of her father's eyes, but time had robbed her of many details. No matter how she struggled she couldn't recollect what motorcycle her father used to ride or what her mother's favourite piece of music was. When she considered further she realized that many of her childhood memories were faint and hazy, and the more she tried to concentrate the more she found her mind kept getting stuck on the ugly times. Instead of happy details she remembered the first beating Mr Crow had given her; the day he sold all her parents' clothes and threw out their photo albums, the many times he'd failed to get her grandma the correctly labelled medicine; and, of course, the way furniture started slowly disappearing from all the hundreds upon hundreds of rooms in her house as well as how Mr Crow's suits and ties kept getting smarter as the house grew drabber. As her grandma had become sicker his lifestyle had grown more lavish.

The sudden flutter of Nibbler's wings shook her from her pensive thoughts.

'You all good, Charlie?'

'Good as I'm going to get,' she replied, glad to be distracted by his company. 'How'd the last drop-off go?'

'Less squawking and a better landing.'

They chuckled at that.

'So this is it,' said Charlie. 'The end at last.'

Nibbler smiled and threw a forepaw over her shoulder. Together they looked down at the temple. 'Are you ready for it?'

'Yes. Yes, I am.'

'Bet you never thought we'd end up here with the pendant.'

'Nibbler, I never thought any of this would happen to me. Not the Silent Duel with Constantina, not Edge Darkmount or the Patchwork Realm, and I never thought I'd ever witness a city burn.'

'But we've seen a lot, right? I mean, I know there's been bad things but we've travelled a lot, tried delicious foods, seen amazing sights and learned some awesome things.'

Thinking about it, Charlie had to admit that he was right.

'And made new friends too,' she added and elbowed Nibbler in the side.

'Yeah. That too.'

There was another comfortable silence. Charlie was forever grateful for the company of her friend. He was a salve for the turmoil that she kept hidden from sight. The stars twinkled overhead and the torches below continued to give the illusion of a firefly swarm.

Nibbler cleared his throat. 'I'm your boy, Charlie.'

'And I'm your girl,' she calmly replied.

'You've got my back and I've got yours.'

'Friends forever.'

The comfortable moment stretched and time effortlessly trickled by.

After a while Nibbler asked, 'Think they're wondering where we are?'

Charlie chuckled. 'Probably.'

'Want to go?'

'Yes. Let's end this. Once and for all.'

Nibbler wrapped his forearms round her, spread his wings wide and jumped. The soft sound of the wind whickering past them and the sense of gliding filled them. Charlie drank deep on the moment, the feel of the breeze on her cheek, the fresh scent of night air, the stars overhead and lights below.

Then they were there, flying silently over a troop of Stomen, whizzing past cracked pathways and ancient statues, over the carved walls to land between two of the roof's domes with a muffled flutter of collapsing wings.

'Psst!' hissed E'Jaaz. 'Over here.'

Hunkering down, they crawled through the shadows,

past rising bas-reliefs, and crept along the curve of one of the large domes to where E'Jaaz and Marsila were hiding. They all knelt down in a tight circle and put their heads together so they could talk in whispers.

'What kept you?' asked E'Jaaz.

'Sorry,' shrugged Nibbler. Not wanting to mention that he and Charlie had been hanging out, he fabricated a white lie. 'After carrying you two big lumps I had to rest my wings a bit. Have you guys checked out the temple?'

'We peeked inside the domes,' said E'Jaaz with a grin of delight. 'We've found the Gateway.'

Nervous but feeling more than a little excited, Charlie asked, 'Where?'

E'Jaaz pointed behind her. 'Beneath the big dome. Of course, it comes with problems but we expected that.'

'They've been using it as a temporary barracks,' explained Marsila. 'It's about two-thirds empty at the moment but they've rotated in some off-duty squads to catch some shut-eye. The carving with the keyhole is on the far wall from where we stand at the moment. But because life always likes to put two hurdles in the way where one would do, not only are there soldiers asleep right by the keyhole but there's also a cadre of Stonesingers in there too. Still, we're not going to mess around; we'll be using the same tactics as before. In as quick as possible, get over to the carving, raise our shield and hold tight until Charlie gets the Gateway open. And, for Sweet Realm's Sake, no matter what they throw at us we keep that shield up. Right, let's go wake those soldiers.'

Rising to her feet, she took off. E'Jaaz ghosted after her. Even knowing that it was coming, Charlie was shocked by the abruptness of their action. She had assumed there would be more talking, more of a chance to mentally prepare herself for this last push. Scrambling, she hastened to catch up with the other two Keepers.

Nibbler, also slightly unimpressed that there was no last-minute speech or a chance to wish everyone good luck, followed too. However, caught up in the excitement of the moment and totally oblivious to the dangers ahead, he was soon swishing his tail and lolling his tongue at the thought of one last spectacular battle.

33

Mosaics

Marsila tore back the ivy that covered the skylight vent in the roof, ripped the ancient and near-crumbling grille from off its mounts and, with a quick look over her shoulder to make sure everyone was still behind her, jumped through the opening. There was a faint flash of gold as she summoned her Will, then nothing.

'Ancient Keepers, grant us luck,' said E'Jaaz. 'Lots of luck.'

Then he too grabbed hold of the opening and disappeared into the chamber below.

Heart pounding in her chest, Charlie jumped feet first into the angled vent. Her heels scraped against the stonework and she picked up speed as she slid further forward. The light from below grew stronger, then the skylight's shaft came to an end, dropping her into free fall.

Charlie caught a quick glimpse of a round room, a mosaicked floor, lots of statues and an unhealthy number of Stomen rising from their neatly ordered beds with looks of anger on their faces and weapons in their fists. Seeing the floor rapidly rising towards her, Charlie grasped her Will and landed in an explosion of yellow flames.

Immediately a large and very spiky mace whipped through

the air towards her. Charlie's mouth formed an 'O' of surprise, her eyes grew wide . . . then instinct took over. Whipping her head beneath the mace and ignoring the swoosh of its passing, she tripped her assailant, somersaulted over a Stoman still attempting to rise from his bed, then started sprinting towards the other Keepers. On the wall behind them was a carving of a Winged One; its wings were spread wide and in its outstretched palm was a stylized version of a burning comet. Countersunk into this comet was the socket.

'Ooooof!'

All the air exploded out of Charlie's lungs as a fist landed in her gut. Distracted by the keyhole, she had failed to watch where she was going. Pain lanced through her and she struggled to stay upright.

'Brat!' snarled the Stonesinger. Purple lines of power crackled around his shoulders and arms. Punching her again and again, he knocked her to the floor and, raising a huge foot, slammed it down towards Charlie's head. There was a snarling whirlwind of claws and flames as Nibbler bore the Stonesinger to the ground. Lightning flashed, then the young dragon jumped upright, leaving what was left of his foe whimpering on the floor. He grabbed Charlie with one paw and dragged her towards the far wall, spitting flames and lightning whenever any of the Stomen got too close.

Gasping for breath and almost overcome with pain, Charlie tried to stop her feet drumming uselessly against the floor. She did her best to stand upright but her diaphragm was still clenched, making it hard for her lungs to work. As Nibbler continued to drag her along she heard more shouts,

Winged One

a clatter as something heavy was dropped, then a burst of golden light. Two pairs of strong hands took hold of her and hauled her upright.

'I know you're winded, Charlie,' shouted Marsila, 'but give us your Will. We have to Triad up!'

Charlie tried to stand on her own two feet but only succeeded in coughing up a small puddle of vomit.

'Come on, Charlie!' cried Marsila.

Slumping forward, Charlie held out her Will, then emptied the rest of her stomach's contents across the floor. As the others formed a Triad she felt a current of their shared strength wash through her. She forced her breathing into a more natural pattern and raised her head as E'Jaaz and Marsila wrapped the four of them inside a bubble of gold.

Angry lines of Stomen began to crowd around the Keepers,

screaming and yelling as they tried to force their way past the golden shield. Axes and barbed spears crashed impotently. Each time they struck the bubble of Will it would flare, make that odd bouncy-ball noise and deflect their weapons.

BRRRR-BBOING!

BBBOOOOOING!

At any other time the Keepers, safe in their shield, might have smirked but the venom displayed on the faces of their enemies, the overwhelming number of them, the seriousness of the situation and the acidic stink of Charlie's vomit all sobered them.

Their earlier confidence evaporated.

'Charlie, can you –' began E'Jaaz.

'I'm good,' gasped Charlie, cutting him short. 'I'm good,' she repeated even as her stomach clenched. 'Just give me a second.'

'We don't have a second!' yelled Marsila as she watched a Stoman raise a trumpet to his lips. Grabbing a knife from its sheath, she flung it through the shield, knocking the trumpet from his fingers. 'Get on with it!'

Furious with herself for being caught off guard, and only too aware that every second counted, Charlie spun round to better examine the carving's socket.

'It's too high and we need to get nearer!' she said.

As the four of them shuffled closer to the wall Charlie spotted an upturned stool lying just outside the circumference of their shield. She lunged for it, but an axe, intended for her outstretched hand, splintered it into pieces.

'Oh, for crying out loud!' groaned Charlie. She cast her

eyes around for something else to stand upon. But there was nothing else.

'Come on,' insisted Marsila. 'Hurry it up!'

Vexed, Charlie punched her hand through the shield, grabbed a helmetless soldier with her glowing hands, then snatched him forward to meet a crushing blow from her head. The Stoman's eyes rolled up and he collapsed in a heap. Charlie dragged him closer to the wall, then stepped on his back. Standing on her tiptoes she reached up to the keyhole but found that it was still out of reach.

Almost growling in frustration, Charlie repeated the process. She avoided the swish of a downthrust sword, grabbed its owner's cloak and yanked him in. Kicking him in the knee, then following that up with a series of elbows and punches, she flipped him over her hip to land on top of his comrade. She adjusted his senseless limbs, then clambered on top and reached out.

'Yes!' she exclaimed.

Tearing the pendant off from round her neck, she slapped it into the socket and funnelled her Will into the keyhole.

The pendant began to glow.

Stix and Stones rode the night skies. Wheeling and swooping, they patrolled the dim landscape below, keeping a watchful eye on the torchlit temples that gleamed in the darkness.

A trumpet sounded.

Stix cocked his head to one side to better detect its origin over the buzz of his Stowyrm's wings. He waved to his brother who, having heard it too, merely shrugged his indifference.

'Let us wait, brother!' yelled Stones, his voice loud enough to be heard over the rushing wind. 'The glimmer of Will shall be our signal. Patience!'

Stix grunted and tugged on the reins, causing his Stowyrm to bank to the side. This wasn't the first trumpet they had heard in the last hour and he doubted it would be the last. The soldiers, rattled and jumping at every little noise, were worse, in Stix's opinion, than a huddle of choirboys. And, even now, with no credible reports of the Keepers making an appearance, they still heard a trumpet or bugle call at almost every turn of the clock. He was tempted to fly down there and yank the trumpet from the sentry's lips and stick it in an unspeakable place.

Growling to himself and trying not to fidget with the hilts of his swords, he rose to ride beside his brother. Side by side, with a crescent moon shining overhead, the two flew their stone leviathans through faint wisps of cloud.

A soft glow appeared beneath them. At first neither noticed, but as the strident alarm of trumpets continued to howl and the glow grew to an other-worldly brightness, they wheeled their mounts in a barrel roll that left them facing the strange event below. The large southern temple that their troops were using as a temporary garrison was shining like a lighthouse beacon.

'Ha!' roared Stones. 'They show themselves! Brother, our time has come. Let's gut that little rabbit and her friends and hang their heads from our saddles!'

'Yes!' shouted Stix with feeling. Whipping a sword from his back, he held it overhead. 'For mother!'

'For mother!' echoed Stones.

They kicked their heels into their beasts' flanks and dived through the sky, hurling their screams of hate and vengeance before them.

34

The Gateway

'Comeoncomeoncomeoncomeon,' muttered Charlie in an impatient chant. Still standing atop the two unconscious Stomen, she jigged from side to side, urging the Gateway to hurry up and open.

It *felt* like the process was working but it was taking an unpleasantly long time.

The bright outline of the Gateway had appeared, the carvings on the walls were writhing and a strong wind had arisen, sucking clothes and bed sheets into a vortex and whipping them around the chamber in tight circles. That weird sound, so oddly reminiscent of a rising elevator, had also grown to near-epic proportions. Louder and louder it screamed, greater than they had experienced at any of the other temples, but still the Gateway had yet to open.

Outside their shield, only the cadre of Stonesingers remained. The Rhinospiders and soldiers had been forced out of the chamber by the power of the wind. The Stonesingers stood in a semicircle, facing the Keepers with hate-filled eyes. Their cloaks fluttered around them, flames of purple and green flared from their fists and, to counter the fierce wind, they had commanded the mosaic floor to rise up and wrap round their feet, securing them with anchors of stone. The chant of their Stonesong must have been loud but amidst all the bedlam and chaos it was almost impossible to hear it inside the shield. They could, however, see that the grim Stonesingers were gesturing for a behemoth to rise. With a lurch, the ground split apart and a terrible arm arose. The Stonesingers made hooking motions with their hands and the floor ripped further apart to reveal the monstrous shoulders and featureless head of their stone puppet.

'Why isn't this working?' shouted Charlie, loud enough to be heard over the rising scream of the Gateway.

'It *is* working!' yelled E'Jaaz. 'The Gateway is forming. Just keep at it!'

BRRAABOINGGG!

The bubble of Will skittered as the behemoth, not even clear of its pit yet, rolled around to slap them with a huge hand. With gritted teeth, Marsila and E'Jaaz fought to keep their shield in place.

'Hatchling!' yelled Marsila. 'A little help!'

A fork of lightning cracked into the behemoth's knee, causing it to stumble. Patches of Stonesong reached their ears as slowly, ponderously, the behemoth raised itself upright.

'The Stonesingers!' urged E'Jaaz. 'Not the behemoth!'

The shield shook as the behemoth delivered another blow. Cracks appeared in the fabric of their Will.

'Come on, Hatchling!'

Opening his jaws, Nibbler let loose. The Stonesingers wavered before his onslaught and, uncontrolled, the behemoth momentarily collapsed, its head and shoulder ripping a long furrow in the wall. But, far from finished, three of the Stonesingers pulled great slabs of rock from the ground and used these as barriers to block Nibbler's lightning, giving the others the freedom to return unhindered to their puppeteering. Groaning and creaking, the behemoth pulled itself upright again and resumed its bludgeoning attack on the Keepers' shield.

Dazed as she was, and fighting to maintain her balance upon her makeshift footstool, Charlie did her utmost to concentrate on the pendant and the socket. Sending out additional tendrils of Will to investigate the keyhole, she noticed that something felt slightly off. Much like a key in a real lock, it was as though it hadn't quite caught properly, as though not all of the lock's tumblers had engaged. In Charlie's mind it felt like the pendant needed a little more energy to overcome this obstacle.

'I need more Will!' she shouted.

'What?' roared E'Jaaz. He cupped hand to ear to better hear over the pandemonium.

'I need more –' Charlie staggered and nearly fell as the behemoth struck another glancing blow. 'I need more Will!'

'If we feed you more, the shield will weaken!' shouted E'Jaaz.

'I don't think the Gateway will open without it!' Charlie made stabbing gestures at the pendant to give her words additional emphasis.

They were drenched in shadow as the behemoth loomed overhead.

Groaning with effort, E'Jaaz leaned close to Marsila. 'What do you think?'

'I think we're stuck between a behemoth and a hard place!' retorted Marsila. 'But the odds have always been stacked against us. Give her the Will and let's see this done!'

E'Jaaz nodded. Allowing the amount that he fed to the shield to slacken, he transferred the excess to Charlie. The bubble of gold around them thinned and, as the behemoth struck, more cracks, larger than before, zig-zagged across its surface. Marsila and E'Jaaz stared in concern. With no other options left to them they began to lash whips of Will at the behemoth in the hope of slowing it down. Cracks of lightning and cascades of flame flew over their heads as Nibbler joined his efforts to theirs. The Stonesingers, aware that the end of this game was rapidly approaching, redoubled their efforts too. More rocks and craggy spears were flung at the Keepers' weakening shield, their voices – still barely heard over the tempest – grew slightly louder and the tempo of their Stonesong increased. The behemoth juddered faster, its bludgeoning blows fell with increasing frequency and the Stonesingers' purple and green flames of power rose higher and higher to twist and turn alarmingly in the wind's whistling vortex.

At the very epicentre of all this frenzied attention was Charlie. Lurching from side to side, she fought to retain her precarious perch on top of the two fallen Stomen. Nonetheless, she could feel herself growing more powerful as more Will was passed to her from the others. Her lips pulled back in a gesture that was more snarl than smile and, seizing the moment, she *twisted* the way her Will funnelled into the pendant. The change was instantaneous. The elevator noise deepened and mellowed until it sounded reminiscent of old trees groaning in the wind or ancient doorways creaking on their hinges. The outline of the Gateway throbbed with additional light and the wall contained within the Gateway's outline was depressed inwards.

'It's happening!' shrieked Charlie. Eyes wide in disbelief, she stared at the glowing Gateway. 'It's really happening!'

She reached towards the pendant with trembling fingers.

KRRR-KRACK!

The wall on the opposite side of the chamber burst apart. Huge slabs of rock smashed to the floor and one of the large circular doors toppled inwards to crash with a resounding boom. Snaking its way in with a gnashing of teeth and a flutter of wings was one of the great Stowyrms. Upon its back was Stones. Malevolent yellow eyes flashed murderously as he pulled his bow from his back and, in one smooth motion, strung an arrow and released it to spit across the room.

The shield shattered.

Charlie felt the hot whizz of something crack past her neck and an unbearable stab of pain in her hand. Her eyes sprang wide open and a half-formed scream of horror gurgled in her mouth. Stones's brutal arrow was quivering in the soft glowing fabric of the Gateway and where her little finger used to be was a gap and a disturbing splatter of blood.

Her blood.

She swallowed the remnants of her first scream. Drew a deep breath and prepared to unleash another scream. A scream worthy of the terror and pain that she felt. But a stern voice of authority reached her ears first.

'Focus, Charlie. Stay focused!' Marsila, eyes still facing forward on the enemies that threatened them, reached behind her to wrap her fingers reassuringly around Charlie's upper arm. 'No matter the burden, no matter the cost, we are Keepers! Open that Gateway!'

The monstrous crunch of the behemoth's footsteps shook them as, unhindered by the non-existent shield, it strode closer to loom over them.

There was a crackle of lightning as Nibbler continued to fight, a chant of Stonesong half heard over the shriek of the wind and the rumble of disturbed brickwork as Stones and the Stowyrm wriggled further through the wreckage of the wall.

But Charlie barely registered any of this. All she could focus on was the pain cramping up her arm and the shred of pink that used to be a part of her lying on the floor.

'Charlie!' shouted Marsila. 'Stop thinking like a child, act like a Keeper and for Realm's Sake open that Gateway!'

Marsila's words cut through Charlie's confusion and pain, shearing past the horror of losing a chunk of flesh to reach the knot of determination that lay hidden but ever present inside her chest. The ball of determination pulsed and throbbed and, fuelled by Marsila's words, flared into life. Adrenalin pumped through Charlie's heart. Matched by a rush of resolve, it shivered up her spine to sear its way into her brain.

Shunting her pain and shock aside, Charlie stood on her toes and slapped her mangled hand against the pendant. Blood mixed with her Will, changing it from its normal yellow to a golden red. Gritting her teeth and forcing all the remnants of her Will into the keyhole, she commanded it to open.

The pendant lurched beneath her hand and, with a final glimmer, the socket sank inwards. Bit by bit, the carving, the pendant and the wall surrounding it seemed to be sucked away to dwindle and vanish in an impossible twist of perspective. And where the wall had once been now stood a doorway, edged with a golden nimbus of light, and through this Gateway, so similar and yet so different from a normal Portal, was a breathtaking, fantastical view.

But before Charlie's dazed eyes and disbelieving mind could untwist the ethereal sight of what lay beyond, there came a crash of epic proportions. Whipping her head round, she stared up at the ceiling in time to see the great dome collapse.

Time slowed.

Charlie's jaw dropped open as Stix and his brutal Stowyrm squirmed through the cascading rubble. She caught a glimpse of flames reflected like shimmering jewels in the crystalline wings, a flash of scales, saw Stix's cat's eyes flared wide with triumph, then all she could see was the Stowyrm's mouth spread wider than should have been possible and row after row of glinting teeth.

Time sped up.

The Stowyrm's wings blurred, its spiked tail lashed and, with terrifying speed, it slammed slobbering and juddering on top of Marsila. Smacking its mouth shut, and with its momentum still unchecked, it careened into the behemoth, bounced off, then wriggled and writhed to stand side by side with its companion.

Of Marsila there was no sign other than a trail of glistening red liquid.

Charlie, E'Jaaz and Nibbler's movements stuttered to a silent standstill.

The Gateway, now open, fell silent. The tempest of violent winds at last spent, the detritus which had been caught up fluttered slowly to the floor. With the Triad broken, the remaining two Keepers' Will sputtered and vanished.

And in this sudden, awkward and horrific silence, the Delightful Brothers began to speak.

'Hello, little rabbit,' growled Stix. He fixed Charlie with an unwavering stare. 'Thought you could outrun us, did you? Thought you could scamper away after taking our mother from us? Well, you thought wrong!'

Stones held up his necklace and rattled it. 'Time to add your teeth to my collection. Time to pay!'

He drew back his bow and, taking advantage of his enemies' state of shock, smiled wickedly . . . and released.

The arrow spat through the air and Charlie, still devastated by the turn of events, stared dumbly as it sped towards her. There was a flicker of motion as E'Jaaz jumped in front of her.

THUNK!

The force of the arrow slammed E'Jaaz into Charlie. She moaned as she felt a stabbing pain in her leg. Looking down, she could see the arrow protruding from E'Jaaz's thigh and with a nauseous sense of alarm realized it had gone right through him to penetrate her own leg.

'Uuuuugh,' grunted E'Jaaz. Face white, he collapsed forward, and Charlie, snagged with him, struggled to bear his weight.

'Well, what do you know?' drawled Stix. 'Looks like you missed, my brother. Why don't you try again?'

'My pleasure,' smirked Stones. 'It's not every day that you get to turn a Keeper into a pincushion.'

'For mother!' said Stix.

'For mother,' agreed Stones. Pulling his bow back, he let loose another arrow.

Nibbler, his innocence now irretrievably vanished, woke from his stupor. With a growl of pure fury, he spat a jet of flame at the arrow, turning it to dust. He sent another crack of lightning towards the Delightful Brothers and, before they or their Stowyrms could react, grabbed both Keepers in his arms and jumped through the Winged Ones' Gateway.

35

Hotstepper

'Huh?' grunted Stones. Looking first at the Gateway, then at his brother, he slung his bow over his shoulder and dismounted. 'Imagine that.'

Stix also jumped down to join his brother. Ignoring the Stonesingers and their behemoth, they made their way to the edge of the glimmering Gateway. Together they stared through it and an expression very much like wonder fluttered across their devious faces.

A view of stars and galaxies and floating islands greeted their astonished eyes. The brothers gasped and for a while they thought they were being treated to the inner secrets of space. But it was not so. The prevailing colour of the infinite background was deep indigo, not black. And the waves of spiralling stars seemed to bob and sway like Chinese lanterns afloat on some mysterious and ethereal current. The floating islands, great slabs of land covered with swathes of greenery and forest, were clearly lit but there was no obvious source for this illumination.

'Now I've seen it all,' said Stix. 'The Realm of the Winged Ones.'

Slowly and carefully, they peered over the edge in the vain

hope of spotting their prey. But nothing could be seen, just an endless drop that lay between infinite layers of drifting islands.

'Think we should go down there and take a look?' suggested Stones.

'Maybe,' said Stix. He looked at their two Stowyrms. He didn't doubt they would be able to cope with the odd realm. It was, after all, a realm for flying beasts.

Suddenly a dark silhouette whistled past the Gateway. The wind of the unseen thing's passing buffeted the Delightful Brothers. Seconds later a roaring growl, equal to anything the Stowyrms could deliver, pounded into the chamber.

Eyes wide, mouths pinched shut, Stix and Stones slowly backed away.

'Maybe not,' admitted Stix. Turning to his brother, he added, 'I think that the time has come for us to consider our options.'

Charlie remembered a terrifying fall, a tangle of limbs as she plummeted with E'Jaaz in her arms and Nibbler grunting as he did his best to slow their descent. There had been a whirr of stars, a flash of odd islands floating on nothing, then a crack and snap of breaking tree limbs followed by a ripping sensation and a flare of agony as she and E'Jaaz were torn apart.

Then nothing.

It was the rasping pain in her butchered hand and the stab of agony in her leg that finally brought her back to consciousness. Opening her eyes, she tried to sit up, only to find Nibbler's paw pushing her back down. She lifted her head to see his other talon pressed firmly against the flesh of her leg, doing his best to stem the flow of blood.

She bit back the urge to moan or cry.

'Mars–' began Charlie but, unable to say the woman's name, fell silent. This wasn't a kid's story. There was no coming back from the dead. No miracles. Not here. Marsila was gone. Unable to look to the past and not yet ready to deal with the future, she instead concentrated on the present. 'E'Jaaz? Is he . . .?'

'He's OK,' said Nibbler. Then, realizing that wasn't quite the truth, added, 'for now.'

Charlie tried to sit up again only to be pushed down once more. 'Stay down, Charlie. You're bleeding too much.'

Shaking with pain, fear and disbelief, she scrunched her eyes shut. She raised her ruined hand and tried to dredge up what was left of her courage. But her eyes refused to open. It seemed that part of her didn't want to face the reality of her latest loss, of being mutilated. Biting the inside of her cheek, she pushed the weaker part of herself down and forced her eyes open.

Her hand was not a pleasant sight.

Half growling, half sobbing, she tried to make a fist but the motion was agonizing. She gave up and instead pushed her hands down to cover Nibbler's paw.

'I've got it,' she said and pushed Nibbler's talons away to put pressure against her wound. She twisted her head round and saw that they were in a lush and verdant forest. Not as magnificent as Deepforest but nonetheless she could feel the age and majesty of the place. The trees were heavy with moss, the floor soft with a blanket of old pine needles, the air rich with the scent of vanilla, juniper and cedar. Looking up, she noticed a tunnel of broken branches – the passage of their crash-landing into this forest – and through this she spied an unusual indigo sky, full of stars that seemed to wink and shine as though their attention was fixed solely on her.

She blinked and pushed the magnificence and wonder away, choosing instead to look around until she spotted E'Jaaz. He was lying on his back, one of his arms trapped beneath him at an unnatural angle, and the head of Stones's barbed arrow jutted from his leg.

'Go check on him, Nibbler.'

Concerned for Charlie's wellbeing, but also aware that things couldn't get much worse, he did as he was told. Padding over to E'Jaaz, he took a closer look at his wound.

'It's not bleeding much but I think the arrow broke his bone.' Nibbler switched his attention to the man's arm. 'And I think his shoulder is dislocated.'

'Is he conscious?'

Nibbler gently patted E'Jaaz's cheek. 'No.'

Ignoring Nibbler's earlier instructions, she sat up and, with a groan, applied more pressure to her wound. It hurt but she was reassured to see that the bleeding had slowed. It dawned on her that there was no one else to take charge so she took a slow steady breath, pushed her pain aside and focused her thoughts. Logic and faint memories of first-aid classes came to mind.

'His shoulder can wait. His leg should probably take priority.'

'Do you want me to pull the arrow out?' asked Nibbler dubiously.

'No! It's plugging the wound. If you pull it out it'll bleed all over the place. See if you can find something to splint his leg. Maybe tie something round the arrow to stop it wriggling and making it any worse.'

'And what about you?'

'I . . .' Charlie faltered. 'I'll have to make do with a tourniquet.'

Tugging the belt from round her waist wasn't easy as the motion caused the pain in her leg to flare and she nearly shrieked when she accidentally knocked her damaged hand. Sweating profusely, she pulled the belt tight round her thigh. But she wasn't thrilled when she looked at the results. Her leg still bled and her hand still dribbled a large amount of fluid.

'This isn't going to work, Charlie. I'll have to get help from –' Nibbler looked around – 'from somewhere. Just keep putting pressure on your leg and I'll be back as soon –'

The *snap-snap* of breaking wood made both of them jump.

'Stowyrms?' whispered Charlie in alarm.

Nibbler raised his hackles. Padding over as silently as he could, he crouched protectively over her. The cracking noise grew and with it the sound of swaying treetops. Then the steady *thump-thump* of heavy feet clumping through the forest loam.

Charlie grew tense. She grabbed hold of Nibbler with one white-knuckled hand, raised her other and summoned her Will. A faint flicker of golden flame fluttered across her remaining three fingers and thumb. It was pathetic, worse than the time she had been hung out to dry in the Stoman prison.

'Keepers?' called a rich, baritone voice. 'Keepers, are you there?'

Nibbler half-opened his mouth but was silenced by Charlie's hand on his muzzle. She slowly shook her head. After all her hard lessons and bitter betrayals, she would not allow them to fall prey to any strangers.

The thud of large feet grew. So too the noise of trees creaking and groaning as they were pushed aside. Then silence, broken seconds later by the sound of some serious sniffing. The movement resumed, growing closer and closer, then stopped.

'Greetings,' said the voice.

Charlie and Nibbler flinched.

There was another rumble of movement as several nearby trees were forced apart to reveal a dragon of huge proportions. Snaking its head forward on its long versatile neck, it stared at Charlie and Nibbler with mesmerizing green eyes.

'My name is Hotstepper.'

36

Dragonsblood

Stix and Stones eyed the Gateway with misgivings. It didn't take much imagination on their part to consider what could, at any moment, come snarling through.

'This is not a good position to be in,' said Stones after a period of contemplation.

Stix refrained from pointing out what an understatement that was. Instead he said, 'We need time to think.'

The Delightful Brothers stared at the array of Stoman forces circled around them. Power-wreathed Stonesingers, skittering Rhinospiders, grizzled soldiers, rustling Shades and a scattering of behemoths. Many more crowded outside to peer through the hole in the wall; others pressed themselves between the remaining doorways. Of all of those gathered, not one of them looked in any other direction than the Gateway. A current of some indefinable emotion rippled through the congregation.

Fear? Anger? Restlessness? Whatever it was, neither Stix nor Stones could decipher it. Nor did they care to. They were, after all, the most dangerous present and theoretically still in charge.

'Stonesingers,' growled Stones. 'Start sealing the Gateway.

The rest of you, pull back! This is now a hotspot and you will need room to manoeuvre! And someone get me the quartermaster; we're going to need siege bows dug out of storage.'

One of the sergeants, looking slightly flustered, called out, 'Sir, the Keepers got the quartermaster.'

'Well, you've just got yourself a promotion, then,' growled Stix.

Gesturing for his brother to follow him, he pushed his way through the crowd, clambered on to his Stowyrm and, once clear of the temple, took to the skies.

They didn't go far. The two Stowyrms flared their wings to land and perch amongst a grove of rock spires.

'What do you think?' asked Stix.

Stones snorted. 'I think things took a definite turn for the worse. I don't think Bane is going to be too happy and I don't think this part of the world is going to look too clever if the Winged Ones make an appearance.'

'I take it you've got no confidence in the Stonesingers plugging the Gateway?'

'It took them nine months to successfully block the Gateway at the Embassy of the Winds. Whatever this lot manage to achieve, it won't be enough to slow the Winged Ones down if they decide they want to return.'

'Why bother, then?'

'They're soldiers,' said Stones. 'They need to be kept busy.'

'You mean keep them too busy to realize the danger they're in.'

Stones shrugged. 'That too.'

Stix clenched his fists round the pommel of his saddle. 'I'm not happy with the idea that that whippersnapper of a Keeper still gets to breathe. Not after what she did to us, to mother. I want to rip the skin from her back and tear the hair from her scalp and weave them together to make a belt!' Furious, he punched his hand repeatedly into the scales of his Stowyrm. The great beast, affected more by its rider's mood than the ineffectual pounding on its rocky flesh, stirred unhappily.

'Well, we have made a start, my brother,' rumbled Stones. 'We have killed one of her mentors, crippled another and bloodied her body. And from the whispered rumours we overheard in the Western Mountains, Bellania has not been kind to Charlie Keeper. Mr Crow stole the lifeblood from her teacher, Azariah Keeper, the bishop Edge Darkmount snapped her leg and twisted her soul, and Fo Fum beat her body black and blue. The Patchwork Daemons chased her, Bane's First burned her home in Sylvaris and if we ever need cheering up all we need remember is that –'

'– Bane has her parents in his Tapestry,' said Stix, finishing his brother's words with a smirk. 'Ha! I bet that little rabbit is wishing she never left London.' Clapping his hands together, he looked up at the moon and the stars, and smiled. 'That list of hurt has lifted some of the burden upon my honour. So, brother, what to do with this situation. Do you think it worth our while to wait?'

'I think that things are only going to get worse, but we have our weapons, gold in our saddle and our steeds to ride. We are safe in the knowledge that if we need to disappear that option is available to us. But let us bide our time and see how events continue to unfold. What is that saying they have on Earth?'

'It's not over until the fat lady sings?'

'No, the other one.'

'It ain't over till it's over?'

'That's the one,' growled Stones. 'It ain't over till it's over.'

'Hello, little brother,' said Hotstepper. He leaned down and touched his muzzle to Nibbler's.

The pain in Charlie's leg, in her hand, in her heart, all were momentarily forgotten. Life had been merciless and cruel and she had long ago learned to push aside hopeless dreams and fantasies but *this* was the stuff of fairy tales. This new dragon, this adult Winged One called Hotstepper, was gigantic! His head dwarfed Nibbler's and even though the rest of his body was hidden amongst the trees Charlie could not help but appreciate how large and how powerful he seemed. And his scales! Burnished silver, with flecks of glittering blue and black. And his eyes! No iris, no whites, just a solid emerald green.

Aware that her mouth had been open for some time and that she was at risk of dribbling, she shut her jaw before she made a fool of herself.

The moment stretched . . . then Hotstepper swayed his huge head to stare at Charlie.

'The Keeper,' he said. He lifted an enormous paw and tenderly pulled back her torn trousers, then just as gently lifted her mangled hand. 'Wounded.' He caught sight of E'Jaaz's fallen form. 'Both of you.'

'Can you help?' asked Nibbler.

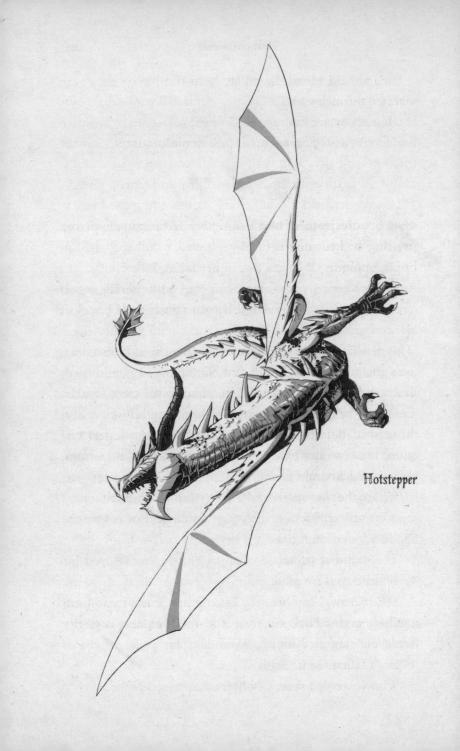

Hotstepper

'I can,' said Hotstepper. The deep rumble of his voice vibrated through Charlie's bones. 'But it will not be pretty or painless. They are Human and I'm not a Treman or Stoman healer.' He twisted his neck to look past the torn branches into the beguiling sky. 'And with the Gateway open we cannot afford the luxury of time. We must move and move swiftly.'

Hotstepper held a talon to his mouth and gusted out a small but precise jet of blue flame. He held his talon in place, twisting and turning it until it glowed a dull red, then a bright orange.

'Little Keeper, you have lost a lot of blood. We must quench the flow.' He paused before adding in a tone of apology, 'This will hurt.'

Charlie, not quite sure what was happening, stared at him. She had grown used to Nibbler and the splendour of Bellania, but being this close to a full-sized dragon was mesmerizing and the magic of the moment clouded her thoughts. That soon changed as Hotstepper pressed his talon, like a soldering iron, against the wound in her leg. Charlie shrieked and would have flailed about if Hotstepper hadn't reached down to grasp her with his other paw. The scent of grilled pork and a wisp of smoke wafted in the air. Charlie's stomach heaved. But it wasn't over yet.

'Your hand next,' said Hotstepper.

'Wait!' urged Nibbler. 'Wait! Can't we do anything else?'

'My sorrow, little brother, but we are in the middle of nowhere and we have far to go. Without healers present, battlefield surgery is all I can offer.'

'Do it,' moaned Charlie.

'What? Are you sure, Charlie?' stammered Nibbler.

Tears streaked down her face and she fought to hold back the sobs and the shivers of pain long enough to speak. 'Wh-what choice do we have?' she gasped. She offered up her hand. 'Ju-just do it be-before I change my mind.'

Hotstepper ground the tip of his glowing talon into Charlie's hand.

'Gaaaaaaaaargh!' gurgled Charlie, instantly regretting her bravado and lack of choices. The agony was relentless and even though the job was done it felt worse not better. Cramp clenched her muscles and her spine burned like it was on fire.

'Stand strong, little one,' murmured Hotstepper, 'for we are not done.'

Raising his other paw, he parted the flesh on his forearm. Blood, which glittered oddly, welled to the surface. He dripped this liquid gift over Charlie's leg and, ignoring her screams and the look of anguish on Nibbler's face, daubed some more over her blistered hand. Finally he tilted her head back to pour even more between her quivering lips. Her screams grew muffled and her eyes rolled back in her head. With a final shudder, she fell still and silent.

'What have you done?' cried Nibbler, aghast.

'What had to be done.'

Nibbler rushed over to cradle Charlie's head. 'Is . . . is she OK?'

'No,' snorted Hotstepper. 'She is missing a finger and has lost more blood than is wise. But at least we know she will survive and soon, very soon, she will grow strong once more. Now, let me attend to our other fallen friend.'

37

Torn Moon

'Wake up, Charlie,' said a voice. She felt a gentle pat on her cheeks. 'Wake up.'

She opened her eyes to find Nibbler crouching over her. A little bit puzzled as to where she was and how she'd got there, she sat up. As she put her hand to her brow a scattering of pine needles dropped to her lap. She stared at those for a moment, then studied her surroundings in confusion.

Everything came rushing back when she saw the ancient moss-covered trees. With a little 'Oh' of shock, she lifted her damaged hand and turned it this way and that. She was still missing a finger and her hand looked awkward but it was healed. There was no trace of blood, no scabs, only a fresh pink crinkling of scar tissue down the edge of her hand. Amazed, she lifted the flap of her trouser leg to examine the arrow wound. That too had healed, leaving another web of fresh scar tissue.

'Huh,' she grunted in wonder.

The image of Stix driving his Stowyrm into Marsila flashed before her eyes. So did the memory of Stones's arrow searing through her finger. She felt the stirring of rage but she pushed it down and tucked it away. With tasks to attend to she could not afford to get sidetracked by the past. Her friends and Sylvaris were relying on her. She would allow herself a chance to mull over her losses only when they were safe.

She started to say something to Nibbler but stopped. She was tired, there was no doubting that, and after all she had been through it didn't come as a great surprise. Her head still felt like it was wrapped in cotton wool but it had been that way ever since Marsila had woken her in the Jade Tower. What did surprise her was that she was no longer in pain. She did not ache, her leg didn't twitch and her hand didn't clench or spasm in agony. Remarkably, and for all that she had endured, she felt relatively OK.

'Charlie?' asked Nibbler. 'Is everything . . .?'

'OK,' finished Charlie. 'Yes, and . . . I'm not sure.' She tried to focus on *just* how she felt. 'Something's changed. I feel tired . . . but stronger. Does any of that make sense?'

Nibbler gave a start and a guilty look over his shoulder. 'Perhaps. I think we need to talk to Hotstepper about that.'

Charlie leaned to the side so she could look past her friend. Hotstepper was standing over E'Jaaz. The Keeper looked diminutive next to the muscular bulk of the adult dragon.

'Why's E'Jaaz tied to a pole?' asked Charlie.

Not only had the Keeper had his leg bound and splinted but his whole body had been wrapped round a large branch that had been stripped free of bark. He could almost have been mistaken for a martyred saint tied to a stake. A saint who had a barbaric-looking arrow jutting from his thigh.

'And why isn't he talking?' added Charlie as an after-thought.

'He is tied that way so I can better carry him in his weak-ened state,' said Hotstepper. 'His leg is indeed broken and I have not the skill to remove the arrow without risk of cutting an artery. So although I have stabilized him, we will keep him this way until we can get him the attention he requires. And now we have treated you and your friend we must hasten to tell the others that the way to Bellania has once more been opened.'

Thudding over to Charlie, he lifted her with ease and plopped her between his shoulder blades.

'Think you can hold on?' he asked.

Still bemused and not truly awake, Charlie looked at the armoured ridges and large horny scales that lay along his spine. She gripped some of them experimentally and wrig-gled her bum until she found a more comfortable perch. 'Er, yes. I think I can hold on. Why, what did you have in mind?'

Hotstepper twisted his neck round so he could stare at her with his amazing eyes. An expression of amusement fluttered across his face. 'I forgot how entertaining it is to be around young Keepers, particularly young Keepers drunk on Winged Ones' blood. Ha! What do you think I had in mind, little Keeper, other than flight?'

With a hop and a bound, he reached E'Jaaz's side. He grasped each end of the branch between his forelegs, crouched low, then sprang upward. Bursting above the tree-line, he opened his wings and with rapid flaps beat his way into the indigo sky.

Charlie peered about with bleary eyes, still feeling dazed

and sensing that something unusual was happening inside her body. Nibbler, wings spread wide, stared back at her while he flew by Hotstepper's side.

'Charlie,' he called, 'whatever you do, just hold on, OK? It's – erm . . . a long fall.'

Unable to stop herself, and ignoring the tiny voice of sanity screaming distantly inside her head, she leaned over so she could peer beneath Hotstepper's broad wings. She could see E'Jaaz lying quite peacefully on his wooden pole. His hair waved in the wind and his eyes remained closed. Beneath him she could see the graceful rise and fall of the forest's canopy. And even though she was flying relatively high, everything seemed quite all right until, with an abrupt suddenness, the forest ended and became a nothingness; just a long, empty fall into a bottomless sky. Then just as suddenly as the forest had ended, another fantasy landscape appeared beneath them. It was a forest too, but laden with different types of trees and hung on a stretch of land that was even lower in the sky than the first. Below this, Charlie caught sight of another floating landscape of sand dunes and boulders, then beyond that one of mountain ranges and another seemingly full of waves that spilled endlessly over the side in misty waterfalls. And as Charlie craned her neck back to look, above them she saw the jagged bottom of more islands floating overhead.

A hundred thoughts surged through her brain. How could there be breathable air in space? And how could the sky be indigo and not black like real space? And where did all the water go when it fell from the watery island? And what replenished it? And why did everything seem drenched in sunshine when there was no sun?

The more she thought, the more questions came to mind. Just as she was about to open her mouth to see if Hotstepper would help ease her curiosity, a wave of fatigue washed over her. Still feeling odd, both inside and out, she leaned forward, wrapped her arms round Hotstepper's neck and fell into a deep sleep.

'Islands!' shouted Charlie, snapping her eyes open and leaping to her feet in one jerky motion.

'Oh!' she added when she saw that she was surrounded by a group of dragons each as big as or bigger than Hotstepper. Then, 'Oops,' when she realized that all of them had been startled by her abrupt change from a horizontal to vertical position. Feeling like a complete idiot, she tried to cover both her blushing cheeks with her hands. Her eyes drifted over the group of Winged Ones and she froze when she caught sight of the majestic vista.

A mountain of gold reared above the heads of the dragons. Not a pile of money or stacked ingots but a *real* mountain made of gold. And where the mountain ended the indigo, star-clad sky started. But it was not an empty sky. It was filled with an endless array of those strange floating islands. The ones directly behind the golden mountain seemed huge, magnificent and completely impossible. The ones further back dwindled with perspective until those furthest away were lost amongst the stars. There were islands of ice, of sand, of jungle and of crashing waves. There were islands too that seemed to disobey the laws of imagination.

Some glowed with odd strobing lights, some writhed with a strange motion and some seemed to flicker in and out of sight as though they were caught half in and half out of the fabric of this incredible realm.

'Charlie Keeper?'

Charlie jumped. Flicking her eyes back to firmer ground, she saw that Hotstepper had moved close. Nibbler stood beside him, staring at the other Winged Ones with an expression of dazed wonder.

'Er, yes?'

Hotstepper pulled his lips into a wide smile. 'Welcome back to the land of the living.'

'Thanks, I . . . Wait. I wasn't snoring earlier, was I? When I was out cold?'

Hotstepper didn't reply but his smile grew even wider.

'Oh no,' whispered Charlie. Here she was in the heart of magic and fantasy, in a realm spun from myth and dreams, and not only had she been sleeping in front of her hosts but she had been snoring too. In front of dragons! She resisted the urge to slap her forehead and stood straighter in an effort to retain some scrap of dignity.

Hotstepper chuckled. 'No matter, Charlie. I think that much can be forgiven of the person who opened the Gateway to Bellania. Come, follow me. I must introduce you to our Elder.'

Still feeling like a fool and very much aware that she was blushing worse than any beetroot, Charlie trailed after Hotstepper. He led her across the circle, in front of all the others, to stand in front of the largest of all the Winged Ones.

'Torn Moon, I bring you Charlie of the Keepers. Charlie of the Keepers, you stand before she who leads us, Torn Moon.'

Charlie stared up at the leader of the Winged Ones. Torn Moon's imposing size and musculature was intimidating and, standing so close, Charlie was only too aware of how easy it would be for this creature to squish her into the ground. Torn Moon's scales were predominantly charcoal black though bursts of bright green, red and orange showed in the hollow beneath her folded wings and across the arch of her chest. But it was her eyes that drew all the attention. It was like looking into liquid gold.

Charlie felt her mouth go dry.

Torn Moon brought her head close to Charlie's. Daunted, the young girl had to fight not to take a step back. The Winged One's lips peeled open to reveal row upon row of spear-like teeth.

'You are the get of Elias and Mya of the Keepers, are you not?'

'G-g-get?' stammered Charlie.

'Hush, child, I will not eat you.'

A rumble of laughter came from the other Winged Ones.

'Get,' repeated Torn Moon. 'Child of their loins, offspring, flesh of their flesh, daughter.'

'Y-yes,' said Charlie, still struggling to get a grip.

'Then I bid you welcome. Doubly welcome for showing us the way back to Bellania.'

'Ah . . . you're welcome. My parents are trapped . . .' began Charlie but found it difficult to continue. Just how did one go about asking dragons for help?

Torn Moon tut-tutted. 'While you slumbered my young

son told me of all that has unfolded in our realm of Bellania. We know of Bane and the broken peace and the taking of Keepers and this "tapestry" that holds your sire and mother. Rest assured that we will rectify all the errors made in our absence. Preparations are being made and in short span we will return to our favoured land.'

It took a while for Charlie to decipher Torn Moon's archaic patterns of speech. 'You knew all of this already?'

'We surmised that it was the wretch Bane who had barred our return but details and news of events were hidden from us. It was our newest and most recently returned child who gifted us with knowledge of what has happened during the long years of our absence.'

Charlie scrunched her forehead. Something wasn't adding up. 'Son? There were other Winged Ones in Bellania?'

Another rumble of laughter came from the congregated dragons. Torn Moon lifted a paw to point at –

'Nibbler? Nibbler is your son? He's royalty?'

The rumble grew to become a roar of hilarity.

Torn Moon's lips quivered. Rearing her head back, she too joined in the laughter. After a while she lifted a paw, calling for some measure of quiet.

'No, Charlie of the Keepers, you misread the meaning of my words. I am Elder of the Winged Ones. Queen of all. All before you are my children. This young Hatchling who you call Nibbler is but one of my brood.'

Charlie's face, only just recovered from blushing, started anew. 'You . . . *all* the Winged Ones came from you?'

This time it took longer for Torn Moon to stop the laughter.

'Charlie of the Keepers, you are truly refreshing. As much as I would like to linger and listen to your unusual ability to misinterpret words I have a battle to prepare for.'

A weathered and aged Winged One who had been studying Charlie throughout her conversation pushed his way through the crowd and leaned close to mutter something to Torn Moon. Once finished, the two paused to look at the young Keeper.

Feeling nervous beneath their combined gaze, Charlie said, 'What?'

'Last Laugh says there is a hole in your soul,' said Torn Moon. She leaned closer to stare at her Human visitor. 'I think there is truth to his words. You carry your suffering like rusted chains round your ankles.'

'Chains?' Charlie looked down at her ankles but saw nothing. Feeling confused, she added, 'Hole?'

'Yes,' said the Winged One called Last Laugh. 'You are young but your soul is old. And as strong as it is, it is incomplete.' He looked to Torn Moon. 'Send her to the Hunger.'

'Hunger?' said Charlie, now twice as confused but also alarmed at what these magnificent creatures thought might be missing from her soul. 'Incomplete?'

'I agree,' said Torn Moon. 'Hotstepper, take our visitor to speak with the Hunger. Charlie of the Keepers, the Hunger will have wisdom for your ears. We will talk when you return.'

Realizing that she had been dismissed, but feeling no less confused, she allowed Hotstepper to lead her and Nibbler away from the gathering of Winged Ones.

38

The Winged Realm

'Can we stop a minute?' asked Nibbler.

'What troubles you, little brother?' enquired Hotstepper.

'Where are you taking Charlie?'

Charlie, also wanting to know the answer, looked to Hotstepper.

'To see the Hunger.'

'Yes, we got that bit . . .' said Nibbler, 'but what is "the Hunger"?'

Hotstepper grinned. 'Not a *what* but a *who*. The Hunger is the eldest of the eldest, the oldest and wisest of us all. It would seem that Torn Moon and Last Laugh think that Charlie of the Keepers could benefit from his –' Hotstepper made a show of coughing – 'words of wisdom.'

'Why did you cough like that?' asked Charlie. She was alarmed enough by the thought that the Winged Ones believed there was something lacking in her (and the idea that her soul might have a 'hole' in it was not the sort of thing she ever wanted to hear). For Hotstepper to cough, no matter how wryly, did not bode well for her current state of mind.

Sensing her alarm, Hotstepper smiled. 'I do not exaggerate when I say that the Hunger is the oldest of us all. And although his mind is sharp he has a fondness for playing with the definition of "wisdom".'

Nibbler looked back towards the gathering of Winged Ones. 'So this is going to be one of those *wise master teaches student valuable life lesson* moments, right?'

Hotstepper looked from Nibbler to Charlie and back again with a bemused look. 'Little brother, you have been away from the fold for too long. Either that or Charlie of the Keepers has spoiled you with her ways, for I know of no other Winged One that talks like you.'

'But is it?' insisted Nibbler. 'It's just a talk, right? I mean, Charlie's not going to be under any pressure, is she?'

'She will be fine, little brother.'

Nibbler looked back again at the gathering of dragons, longing in his eyes. 'Charlie . . . if it's all right with you, I'd like to stay here a bit. I want to get to know . . . well, y'know.'

It dawned on Charlie that although she thought of Nibbler as family he was finally in the midst of his own kind. And while an irrational part of her feared to lose him, and as much as she didn't want to travel through this strange realm without a friendly face, she hurriedly pushed her self-ish thoughts down and summoned a weak smile. She would, for now, go on alone.

'There's no way I could ever say no to you, Nibbler.'

The smile on his face caused her heart to lurch.

'You're the best, Charlie!'

With one last grin he bounded off.

Hotstepper picked her up and placed her back between his shoulders. 'He will be fine, Charlie of the Keepers, and so will you.'

Bunching his legs beneath him, Hotstepper sprinted towards the edge of the island and leaped into space. Wings spread wide, he carried the two of them towards distant islands.

'So,' began Charlie, 'now can you tell me what it was that you did to me?'

'Did to you?' queried Hotstepper.

'You've done something to me, I'm sure of it. I feel weird, like there's some kind of electricity playing just beneath my skin, and I keep getting hot and cold flushes. I remember you healing me and then . . .'

'Ah,' said Hotstepper, realizing what his guest was talking about. 'It is the blood, Charlie of the Keepers, that is making you feel this way. My blood. I'm sorry it makes you feel uncomfortable but it's a side effect all mortals feel when they take the gift.'

'Gift?'

'Aye, it is a gift. A gift of life. You were not in a good way, Charlie of the Keepers. With the amount of blood that had seeped from your flesh you would not have been able to recover, at least not for a long time. Blood, Winged Ones' blood, brings many gifts: healing, energy and unfortunately pain. But it was a necessary gift and it is what has allowed you to regain your feet so quickly after suffering such severe injuries. But Winged Ones' blood is not meant for mortals. The side effects that you feel are the price you pay for the healing and power that it brings.'

'Uh . . .' began Charlie, but wasn't too sure what to say or if indeed there was any proper response upon learning that you had taken dragonsblood. '. . . Thank you?'

'You are most welcome, Charlie of the Keepers.'

Feeling the need to clear the air, Charlie asked, 'What is this place?' She spread her arms wide to encompass all the floating islands. Hotstepper, looking ahead, didn't see the gesture but nonetheless caught the gist of her question.

'Our home,' he replied simply.

'I know that . . . but how can a place like this exist?'

'Are you sure you want me to tell you?' asked Hotstepper. 'Would it not be more enjoyable to simply live with the mystery of it?'

'Er . . . no,' replied Charlie, quite certain that her curiosity would never be able to endure an unsolved mystery like this. 'I think I'd really, really like to know more.'

She felt his muscles ripple beneath her thighs as he chuckled. Fortunately, she was too preoccupied by all the sights to question why he and the other dragons seemed to find everything she said so funny.

'We were not the first to call this realm our home, neither are we the only race that lives here, but none can question our right to dwell here. What better place for a Winged One than a realm of endless sky?'

Charlie had to agree with him.

'All that you can see,' continued Hotstepper, 'all of that which we call home, is the net which surrounds all other realms. You are familiar with the Great Cataclysm that broke the first land into the separate realms of Earth and Bellania?'

'Well, I wouldn't say I'm familiar with it,' said Charlie. 'But I've heard about it.'

'The Cataclysm was not a tidy event. Not all the bits and

pieces from the original land fitted easily into either realm. Some were lost, some were hidden and other parts, unable to resist the tidal pull of universal gravity, ended here.'

He pointed towards a distant island, craggy and covered with trees and mist. 'That is part of the original land.' He pointed in a different direction to a scrap of rock made tiny by perspective. 'So too is that.'

'What about the other islands?'

Hotstepper continued pointing. 'That is part of the Siren's Realm, that from the Silken Lands, those two from L'Layla; the land over there with the blue glow contains part of the Sixteenth Hell and its neighbour with the snow-capped mountains was once part of the Thrice Spun Realm. All of these have a history and all came to rest here once they were torn from their original realm.'

Charlie's mouth began to water at the thought of being able to endlessly adventure across all of these scraps of realms. It would be island hopping like none other!

As they flew beneath a particularly large stretch of land she was treated to another sight.

'What's that?' she asked, pointing towards a bright spear of light.

'The true Gateway to Bellania. When we first learned it had been sealed and when it grew apparent that the pendant had been lost we were left with scant option other than to try and burn our way past Bane's seal.'

Drawing closer Charlie could see that the great beam's source of light was twelve Winged Ones, each of which was breathing a non-stop stream of flame into a concave mirror placed in front of them, which in turn redirected their energies to join the others' to become one mighty lance of flame. It was clearly striking something but the target was hidden behind a great splatter of white fire.

A Winged One landed amidst the twelve and after a brief communication the twelve stopped their endeavour and took flight. They passed beneath Hotstepper and headed in the direction that he and Charlie had come from.

'Word of your arrival and tale of the hidden Gateway's opening spreads. My people fly to Torn Moon to discuss Bellania's fate.'

Looking around, Charlie noted spread wings near and distant, all heading in the same direction.

'If you have so many realms to choose from, what makes Bellania so special to you? I mean, don't get me wrong, I know I love the place, but why do you?'

'It is our ancestral home.'

'Huh? Hang on a minute, I thought before the Great Cataclysm Earth and Bellania used to be the same place.'

'They did,' agreed Hotstepper.

'So how come you go to Bellania and not Earth? If they both used to be the same place then surely they're both your ancestral homes?'

'They are,' admitted Hotstepper, 'but the Cataclysm altered more than the geography of the two realms; it affected the laws that govern them too. While the Tremen can treesing and the Stomen can stonesing in Bellania they cannot do so in the realm of Earth. The same can be said of the technology of Earth. What works there does not fare so well in the realm of Bellania.'

'Oh, so that explains . . .'

'Explains what?' prompted Hotstepper.

'Well, I know it sounds stupid but ever since I arrived in Bellania I've always wondered why someone hasn't tried to conquer the realm with guns and tanks and stuff like that.' Realizing she appeared a little reckless, she hastened to add, 'I know that's a bloodthirsty thing to say but the thought kept popping up in my head. I mean, if there's someone like Mr Crow who came over from Earth it's not too difficult imagining people like him trying to gain power with guns.'

'It has been tried before,' said Hotstepper. 'Several times, in fact. I'm not familiar with this "tank" that you talk of but we have seen cannons and muskets. A general from your land learned of the Gateways that led from Earth to Bellania. Greedy and foolish, he killed the Keeper family who guarded it and forced his way into Bellania with an army at his back.'

'What happened?' asked Charlie, eyes wide.

'They formed up in pretty lines, uniforms crisp and glittering in the sunlight with cannons and muskets at the ready. The general strutted around like a vainglorious rooster and when we appeared on the horizon he ordered his men to fire.' Hotstepper chuckled at the memory. 'There was a lot of sizzle and a little bit of smoke but no explosion. The look on their faces was priceless.'

'What happened next?'

'We ate them.'

'What?' croaked Charlie.

'We ate them,' repeated Hotstepper.

'But-but you can't do that!' stuttered Charlie.

'Why ever not?'

'Because you're dragons,' said Charlie, momentarily

forgetting to call them Winged Ones. 'You're supposed to be wise and honourable and . . . and . . .'

'Wisdom and honour *are* amongst our traits,' said Hotstepper. 'But sometimes a lesson must be taught to those who would try to oppress others. Do not mistake my people for ravenous beasts driven only by our hunger, for clearly we are not. We are *peacekeepers* and peace and balance are what we revere above all else. However, once in a while foolish people must be eaten in order to maintain that balance.'

'Er . . . please don't tell me that Winged Ones eat Keepers too?'

'What? No!'

Not necessarily feeling any safer, Charlie added, 'Not even once in a while?'

'No! Never. The Keepers and the Winged Ones are kin. We share a common ancestry. To eat a Keeper would be like eating your own family. A disgusting thought.'

Hearing that, Charlie relaxed slightly, although she was of course still confused as to how Keepers and Winged Ones could be related.

'What about Tremen and Stomen and other Humans?' she asked. 'Do you eat them too?'

'I can see this idea does not rest easily with you. Charlie of the Keepers, allow me to reassure you that we only ever eat those who deserve the punishment and that we only do so when an example must be made. Only the most cruel and most twisted are torn by our teeth. Besides, Humans, Tremen and Stomen don't taste that good and they take a terrible time to digest. Believe me, Charlie of the Keepers, a Winged One with stomach cramps is never a pleasant sight.'

As horrified as she was, Charlie couldn't help but smile a little at that.

'Of course, taste and indigestion aside, there is someone who we aim to dine upon soon.'

'Who?'

'Bane.'

Charlie nodded quite contentedly at that thought. There was no doubt that eating anyone was morally wrong but she was prepared, just this once, to put morals aside for the person who had stolen her parents and brought war and terror to the realm of Bellania.

Sitting back, she relaxed and watched the stars and islands drift by.

39

Rumbling Hunger

'How much longer will this take?' asked Charlie.

'Not long,' said Hotstepper, but sensing her disquiet, he enquired, 'What's the rush?'

'I don't know if Nibbler told you but Sylvaris is –'

'Ah . . . Sylvaris, the Jewel of Deepforest. We know the plight that Sylvaris is in but we must gather our numbers before storming back to Bellania. Our little brother has told us how Bane's armies have grown and how the Stonesingers have been swayed from the path of peace. But rush we must not. My people are scattered and it will take long hours to gather enough wings to crush Bane's rebellion. Time enough for you and me to reach the Hunger's Isle and return.'

Doing her best to put thoughts of Sylvaris aside, Charlie stared at a distant swathe of clouds and twinkling stars. She lost track of her thoughts for a few moments until Hotstepper suddenly fell into a shallow dive, ducking his neck and pulling his wings in. Their destination was a strip of land that looked like it had been ripped from a tropical beach. There were stretches of sand studded with palm trees and ivy-covered boulders bordered crystal-clear waters. As they grew closer they could see brightly coloured fish in the water and the ruins and toppled columns of ancient buildings.

Hotstepper landed in a cloud of disturbed sand. A flock of bright orange birds, shocked by their arrival, took flight in a chorus of trills and tweets.

'Get down, Charlie of the Keepers,' said Hotstepper.

She slid to the ground. The sand beneath her shoes was so fine that it squeaked when she moved, the air smelt fresh and the island was wonderfully warm. She gazed around, hoping to catch sight of their mysterious host, but other than the palm trees, boulders and ruins there was not much to see. There were a few hills towards the hub of the island and Charlie could see a large cave at the base of one. Perhaps, she thought to herself, they would find this ancient Winged One there. After all, what better place to find an old dragon than in a big cave?

'Should we start –'

'Did you bring me something to eat?' boomed a big voice.

Charlie jumped and likely would have fallen if she hadn't lurched into Hotstepper's flank. Realizing that the question was perhaps directed at her, she said, 'Ah . . . no. No, we didn't.' She looked around and even overhead but could find no body to match the booming voice.

'What?' snorted the voice. 'You came to meet the Rumbling Hunger and brought no food? What kind of mortal makes a foolish error like that?'

There was a creak, then a groan and with a shocking abruptness a large patch of boulders moved. Charlie yelped and backed once more into Hotstepper's side, then watched with eerie fascination as the boulders stood up and turned round to reveal that they were, in fact, a Winged One.

Bemused, Charlie rubbed at her eyes.

It was a dragon like no other. He was as large as Torn Moon but so old that his muscles and scales had taken on a craggy appearance. And even though he stood right in front of her, his scales, which were the colour of burnt umber and bronze, almost seemed to blend into the fabric of the ruins, making it easy to appreciate why she had at first mistaken him for a part of the landscape.

The Winged One's huge head and soft brown eyes grew close as he leaned down to inspect his guest.

'So you mean to tell me that you didn't even bring a snack?' said the Winged One.

Realizing that Hotstepper wasn't going to come to the rescue, Charlie said, 'Er . . . sorry, no.'

'Foolish mortals,' grumbled the Winged One. 'And as for you,' he prodded Hotstepper's chest, 'you certainly should have known better.'

'Forgive me, eldest,' said Hotstepper and gave a brief bow of deference.

The Winged One snorted again, then started to amble off. He paused to look back over his shoulder. 'Well, are you coming or not?'

'Who, me?' asked Charlie.

'No, I'm talking to all the other visitors who decided that today was a good day to drop by without bringing a gift.' He rolled his eyes when Charlie hesitated. 'Yes, I'm talking to you. The Human girl with the scruffy hair. Yes, you. Come on, let's go and see if I can curb my hunger with some snacks, otherwise I might grow so hungry that I decide to eat you.'

Having only just heard how Hotstepper had a history of

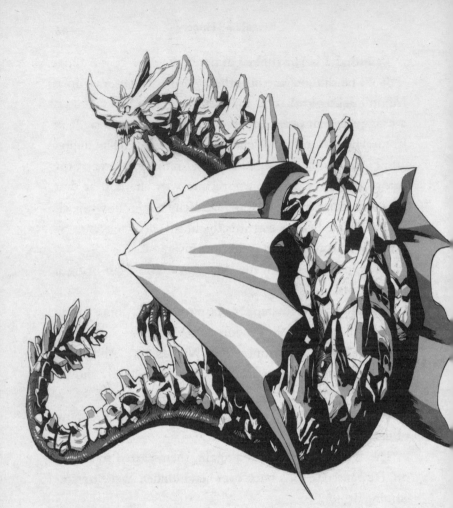

Rumbling Hunger

eating criminals, Charlie faltered. She couldn't work out if this strange Winged One was being serious or not, nor was she too sure how safe he was. He certainly looked strange and from the way his stomach kept rumbling it was obvious that he was hungry.

'Go on,' said Hotstepper, and he gave her a gentle nudge. 'You'll be safe enough. Just listen to his words and do all that he asks of you.'

Charlie hesitantly made her way over to her host.

'And you,' said the Winged One, looking at Hotstepper, 'can wait here. And next time you visit make sure you bring something tasty with you.'

Without checking to see if Charlie was following, the Winged One headed towards the hills.

40

Wisdom

'Sooooo,' began Charlie, 'should I tell you why I was brought here?'

'Ssssh!' said the Winged One.

Crouched by the water's edge, he watched with intense interest as a large, brightly coloured fish swam lazily back and forth.

'Er . . .' began Charlie but fell silent.

She wasn't sure what she had been expecting but it certainly wasn't this. The large dragon had ignored her for the last ten minutes. She knew that he was considered wise so she figured this was supposed to be a test of some sort . . . The only trouble was that she had no idea what sort of test it was or what she was supposed to do.

There was a flash of movement as the Winged One hauled the fish from the waters, threw it into the air, caught it with a *click* of his teeth and swallowed it whole, all in one smooth motion.

'Yummm,' said the Winged One with a contented smile. 'Nothing like a little Fluttercarp to ease the wait between lunch and afternoon teatime. So, my little wayward Human, what did you say your name was?'

'Charlie Keeper, er . . . sir.'

'Pfft. None of these foolish manners,' protested the Winged One. 'I'm definitely not a "sir". Call me Rumbling Hunger or if you must shorten my name "Hunger" will do. So tell me, little Charlie, what did you hope to get out of this visit to my wonderful island of fish and coconuts?'

'Um . . . I'm not sure,' admitted Charlie. 'Torn Moon and Last Laugh said there was a hole in my soul and that you would know how to fix it.'

'Is that what they said?'

'Yes, sir. I mean, yes, Hunger.'

'And why do you think they sent you to see me? Do you suppose they thought that learning how to fish for Fluttercarp would help this hole in your soul?'

Charlie fidgeted. She knew he was teasing her but his size, obvious age and unusual behaviour were making her feel flustered. 'I guess they sent me to see you because you're wise?'

Hunger rolled his eyes. Seeing the flash of another Fluttercarp, he turned his attention back to the lake. 'Wise, huh?' he said with a distracted air. 'Do you meet many wise people, Charlie?'

Sensing that this was a weighted question, Charlie gave it some thought. Images of Azariah and Lady Dridif came to mind. 'I think I've met some wise people.'

There was a splash and a curse as Hunger stabbed his paw into the water only to miss the prize. The Fluttercarp spun away, then returned in slow teasing circles just out of Hunger's reach. 'And what,' said Hunger, pulling his wet paw from the lake and shaking it dry with a look of displeasure, 'do you think makes a person wise?'

'I don't know,' said Charlie. 'Age?'

There was a growl as Hunger tried and missed yet again. 'Age? Pah! I've met plenty of old farts who somehow managed to stumble through life without a thimble of wisdom to share between them. Do you have any other ideas as to what might constitute wisdom?'

Charlie gave it some thought. 'Intelligence?'

'Intelligence? Rubbish! I've met many great mathematicians and inventors who were able to solve great riddles and problems but failed in almost every other aspect of their daily lives. Drat!' he cursed as he nearly fell in the lake. The Fluttercarp, clearly feeling that the dragon was no threat, continued to swim nearby.

'OK, experience, then.'

'Experience shmerience! I have met many famous adventurers who have seen and lived a lot but still blunder in every direction that they go.'

Feeling slightly let down by her first impression of Rumbling Hunger and feeling the prickle of impatience, Charlie crossed her arms. 'Well, if you don't think age or intelligence makes you wise, what does?'

She stared challengingly at the soggy-armed Winged One.

'Ah,' he said with a coy look of amusement on his face. 'And here I was beginning to think that you would never ask. *Wisdom is understanding the lessons learned from past mistakes.*' Keeping his eyes pinned to Charlie's, he reached out, slapped a nearby palm tree, caught one of the coconuts as it fell to earth and, with a powerful flick of his wrist, sent it slamming into the waters of the lake. The stunned Fluttercarp bobbed to the surface. Grinning wickedly, Hunger broke eye contact with Charlie to reach out and hold his catch aloft. The Fluttercarp woke and started to flap nervously in his grasp. Hunger gently tilted it back into the water. 'I'll eat that one later.'

Quickly realizing there was a lot more to Rumbling Hunger than met the eye, Charlie chose to keep her mouth shut.

'And the reason,' continued Hunger, 'why the others of my kind consider me wise is not because of my age.' He held a leg aloft so Charlie could appreciate how old and worn his scales were. 'Nor is it because of my intelligence.' He burned a series of arcane symbols into the riverbank. 'And neither is it because of my experience.' He extinguished the flames with a lazy sweep of his tail. 'The reason why I am considered wise, young Charlie, is because I have made so many mistakes in my life.'

'Huh?' said Charlie. This was not the explanation she had been expecting.

'Ha!' chuckled Hunger. 'Does that come as a surprise? Then let me confuse you even more. I am two thousand seven hundred and eighty-three years old. And in that time I have led and lost eleven major battles, I've been fleeced and cheated thirty-five times, and I'm sorry to say I've managed, at some time or another, to break half the bones in my body. In my travels I have been lost and forced to fly the wilderness of the Shifting Realm for twenty-one years; more than that, I was tricked by the Daemon Kindred and imprisoned in the Eleventh Hell for a hundred and three years! I have been deceived, betrayed and left for dead more times than I care to count. The tales that I could tell you, young Charlie, would shrivel your ears and cause your heart to clench.'

Caught by the cadence of his voice and the rhythm of his words, Charlie, unable to stop herself even if she wanted to, asked, 'And they still consider you wise?'

'That they do, young Charlie. And they consider me wise because I have learned the lessons that life's hard experiences have taught me.' Moving close, he leaned over her, drenching her in his shadow and fixing her with his brown eyes. 'You should never be afraid to make a mistake. Neither should you allow fear or loss to quench the fire of your heart. And it is plain as the light of day, little Charlie, that life's lessons have quenched the fire in your heart.'

'What? But . . . but that's not true!'

'Is it not? Hold up your hand.'

Charlie did as she was told. The ruined edge of her hand, with its missing finger, stared accusingly back at her. Looking up, she saw Hunger looking at her through the gaps in her fingers.

'Your flesh has been damaged and yet you seem quite meek about it.'

'That's not –'

'Meek is what you have become,' insisted Hunger, ignoring her objection. 'That scar on your leg is not the only one you carry, is it? Your leg was broken recently, was it not? By your enemies?'

Charlie's eyes widened and, unbidden, her hand stretched down to touch her leg. How could he have known that Edge Darkmount had broken it?

'And what about your heart? Even a blind man could tell that it has been broken time and time again.'

Charlie faltered beneath the strength of his gaze and took a step back. Hunger relentlessly followed.

'Your face carries the shadows of past betrayals and your eyes are haunted by the pain you've endured.'

Charlie stumbled as she tried to take another step, only to fall backwards and land on her backside. Images of Mr Crow, Bane, Lady Narcissa, the Delightful Brothers, Edge Darkmount, Lallinda the Daemon Queen and more flew before her eyes. And ever in the background hung the ghostly images of her parents and her grandma.

'Yes,' growled Hunger. His eyes blazed as he loomed over her. 'All that and more you carry with you. But where is the anger? Where is the sorrow? WHERE?' he roared.

Terrified by the abrupt change in Hunger, she scuttled backwards until she was sitting in the waters of the lake. She thought about swimming off, or even using her Will, but instead she found herself growing very still. 'It's gone,' she admitted. She thought back to her fight with Fo Fum and the battle of Sylvaris. 'I used to be full of anger and rage but I let it go.'

'And that's where you went wrong,' said Hunger in a softer voice. 'You didn't just give up your anger, you gave up everything else.' Picking her up, he gently deposited her on the bank so she could start to dry off. 'Even though you keep losing,' he pointed to the gap of her missing finger, 'and even though you continue to endure more and more pain,' he touched the fresh scar on her leg, 'you do not allow yourself the opportunity to feel. You, Charlie Keeper, have not understood the lessons of your experiences.'

41

Verraverry Berry

'I've learned enough to make sure I'm not betrayed again by strangers.'

'A good lesson learned,' admitted Hunger, 'but not enough. Not enough by far. All that you seem to have learned, little Charlie, is that you don't want to be hurt again. But pain and hardship are part of life. You should not be scared about what life brings your way, rather you should embrace it.'

'What are you saying?' asked Charlie.

'I'm saying that after being surrounded by darkness and after *becoming* the darkness and after learning to live without it, you are now still afraid to live. I'm saying that although you plod on and have not strayed from your path you have given up on life.'

'What? That's not true!'

'Isn't it?' asked Hunger. His eyes burned into hers.

Unable to stand his gaze, Charlie looked aside. 'I . . .' she began but found she could not get the words started. *Is he right?* she thought. Were there some grains of truth hidden in his words? Looking inward, Charlie tried to study herself . . . and found herself uncertain.

'When was the last time you cried?' asked Hunger softly.

Charlie held her mangled hand aloft.

'Did you cry for yourself or out of pain from your wound?'

Charlie slowly lowered her hand. 'Pain,' she admitted.

'I sense you lost someone recently. No?'

The image of Stix's Stowyrm slamming into Marsila played itself over and over in her mind. 'Yes.'

'And did you cry for them?'

'I, uh . . . no. Marsila was an amazing person but we weren't that close. I only knew her for four days.'

'But she left an impression upon you?'

'Yes.'

'So how did you feel after her passing?'

'Numb?' answered Charlie. She was surprised by just how true that was.

'And how do you feel now? Answer me truthfully, child.'

'Numb,' repeated Charlie.

'You feel numb because you have locked part of yourself off from the rest of the world.'

Charlie opened her mouth to protest but found that words failed her.

'It is apparent to all that you have suffered and suffered greatly. Even these old eyes can see that you have endured more than any man or woman should in a lifetime, let alone a child like yourself.'

'I'm not a child,' snapped Charlie, 'I'm fourteen!' As soon as she said the words she regretted them.

'Perhaps,' acknowledged Hunger. 'But what does that make you to a Winged One enjoying his third millennium? A child you are in flesh and mind, and so you shall remain until you release your fears.'

Charlie scrunched her eyes shut and balled her hands into fists. 'And how,' she growled, 'do you suggest I do that? Bane has my parents! And everywhere I look, everywhere I've been, lies a trail of death and deceit!'

'Charlie Keeper?'

'Yes?'

'I have no idea how you should go about accepting your fears.'

'What?' choked Charlie. This was the last response she had expected to hear.

The sound of Hunger's rich laughter echoed off the hills and shivered across the lake, sending the Fluttercarp diving nervously for the depths.

'But I thought you were supposed to be a wise dragon?'

'Winged One,' corrected Hunger.

'Wise Winged One, whatever,' shrugged Charlie. 'I thought you were supposed to solve all my problems!'

Hunger laughed again. 'Wise I may be, young Charlie, but I cannot do everything for you. However, if you want to hear something wise, how about this: the shepherd can lead his flock to the waters but he cannot make them drink.'

'What is that supposed to mean?'

'It means, Charlie, that although I can tell you that you should lose your fears and learn to embrace life once again it is up to you, not me, to work out how to do that.'

'Oh,' said Charlie. None of this had gone how she'd thought it would. Surely there was more to hanging out with a wise dragon than this?

As if reading her thoughts, Hunger said, 'Let me help you,

Charlie. Although I might not be able to open your heart, allow me to tell you a story.'

'What kind of story?'

'A wise man's story,' said Hunger with a cheeky smile.

Charlie, unable to help herself, mirrored his expression.

'Once upon a time a young monk was walking through a forest. So deep was he in thought that he failed to notice the Shade that was stalking him. When the Shade finally broke cover and pounced, the young monk managed to jump aside. Panicked, and fearing for his life, he ran as fast as he could. Past tree after tree he ran, the Shade hissing and snapping at his ankles. The forest soon ended and the young monk found himself running towards a cliff. Knowing that if he stopped to face the Shade without a weapon or shield he would die, he instead decided to risk everything and jumped. As he fell he caught hold of a slender Verraverry bush. With a long fall below and a howling Shade above, the young monk held on. After all, what choice did he have? But as young and as slender as the monk was, his weight soon began to pull the bush from the cliff. And to make matters worse, a second Shade appeared at the foot of the cliff. Screeching and spitting, it looked up at him while the Shade above stared down. As the bush continued to pull itself free the young monk noticed a single Verraverry berry hanging from its stalk. Holding on to the loosening plant with one hand, he plucked the berry with the other and ate it. It was the most delicious thing he had ever tasted. Its flavour was so ripe, so majestic, it was like none other and the taste of it seemed to dance across his tongue.'

Hunger fell silent and Charlie waited for him to continue but he seemed to have finished.

'What? Is that it? What happened to the monk?'

'He fell to his death and his body was mauled by the Shades.'

Disgusted, Charlie crossed her arms. 'What kind of fable was that? That sucked!'

'Yes,' said Hunger with a roll of his eyes, 'it is very apparent that you missed its moral.'

'All right, then, explain it to me.'

'The Shades represent the obstacles and bad things that happen in our life. They are inevitable and are to be expected. The Verraverry berry represents the pleasures and joys of life. Fleeting and rare they are, to be enjoyed whenever possible. Death awaits all of us and there are many Shades that lie in wait along the path of life but, no matter what, Verraverry berries are always to be enjoyed for without them life is hollow.'

Previously unimpressed, Charlie felt a spark of *something* ignite in the dark recesses of her mind. There was something in Hunger's words that plucked at the fabric of her being. And although she didn't quite comprehend what it was, she did realize that it was something worth pursuing.

'Are you saying I should ignore the bad things in life and concentrate on the good?'

'No,' Hunger snorted in a very un-wisely manner. 'What I'm saying is that life has a tendency to deliver bad things our way. Expect this, flow with this and always do your utmost to overcome these unwelcome obstacles. But, most importantly, do not allow these dark things to take over

your life. Ride them if you will but always remember to
reach out to grasp the good things that come your way. It
is these, not the darkness, that should shape your life.'

Charlie remained silent while she digested his words.
Looking back to how the darkness had consumed her previously, she asked, 'What about anger?'

'What about it?'

'Well, is that something I should be avoiding too? When
these . . . things started happening to me, all I felt was anger.
A lot of anger. I let it consume me to the point where I
became as bad –' she paused to correct herself – '*badder*
than the people who tried to stop me.'

'What happened to this darkness that you invited in?'

'I gave it up,' said Charlie. 'I didn't think it was getting
me anywhere so I let it go.'

'It is good to allow darkness to pass,' said Hunger. 'But
not to the point where you cease to allow yourself to feel.
Am I right in suggesting that you feel a lot of responsibility
for those around you? And that you suffer from guilt when
you cannot stop the world crumbling and those around you
falling?'

'Yes,' whispered Charlie.

Hunger's eyes softened. 'Responsibility and sorrow are
good. These are not Human or Treman or Stoman sensations
but sensations that all sentient beings feel. But better than
all of this is balance – and balance, young Charlie, is the one
thing you are missing.'

Something clutched at Charlie's heart.

Hunger reached out and tilted her head back up until she
was staring into his eyes. 'Would it surprise you if I said that

anger is as good for you as sorrow? Anger is a powerful emotion and used correctly it can be a force that can be governed for good. When I feel anger I use it. I guide it and ride it and use its energy to overcome difficult tasks. Anger can be used not only as a destructive tool but as a tool to build. Many are the times in my life when if I had not been angered I would not have had the will to carry on. Remember this, Charlie: all emotions have a use and are not to be avoided. Even pain and hurt and fear and loss can be endured and used for the greater good.'

Hunger's stomach rumbled. It was a prodigious sound and caused Charlie's eyes to widen in disbelief.

'Ha!' chuckled Hunger. 'Enough with these words! I think the time has come for less talking and more eating. Come, let us get some food and see what that whippersnapper of a Winged One has been up to while we've been chatting.'

'Are you calling Hotstepper a whippersnapper?' asked Charlie incredulously.

'Young Charlie, when you fly past your second millennium and reach your third you'd better believe that everyone else becomes a whippersnapper. Now let's go and see if that Hotflubber has managed to get me some food.'

'Hotstepper,' corrected Charlie.

'Whatever,' retorted Hunger.

42

Fluttercarp

'I have brought you some food, eldest,' said Hotstepper with a bow of his head.

Charlie and Hunger looked at the three fat fish laid out in a line.

'Those are Fluttercarp,' said Hunger.

'Yes, eldest.'

'And where, Hotflubber, did you get these? Was it from some distant isle? Some other realm?'

'No, eldest, I got them from yonder pond.'

Charlie and Hunger turned to look at the pond behind them.

'You mean to tell me you got me Fluttercarp from my own isle?'

'Er . . . yes, eldest.'

'Listen, junior. Getting Fluttercarp from my own isle is not what I call "getting me some food". It is what I would call "getting me food from my own pantry". And, junior, let me tell you, I'm not so old that I cannot collect Fluttercarp from my own isle. It would have been nice if, while Charlie and I were hard at work, you had gone and caught something that was not readily available from my own pantry.

Like Skyelk or Tuberworm or even Cloudkudu.'

'I'm sorry, eldest. I will remember this for next time I visit.' Hotstepper bowed low. As he did so, he rolled his eyes at Charlie.

'I saw that!' said Hunger. Reaching out, he idly cuffed Hotstepper round the back of the head. 'Ah, the youth of today. Did you see that, Charlie? When I was a lad at least I had the good manners to come up with a convincing lie if I was ever caught pinching food from someone's pantry.'

'I didn't pinch them, eldest.'

'No?' said Hunger. 'Were you "borrowing" them, then? Did you plan on putting them back?' He prodded the fish. They didn't move. 'Well, Hotflubber, do you think they'll miraculously come back to life if you put them back in the pond? No? Well, in that case I call it pinching and not borrowing.'

'I'm sorry, eldest.'

'And stop calling me that!'

'Well, stop calling me Hotflubber!' retorted Hotstepper.

'It's the name your mother gave you on your Namingday.'

'She sneezed!' protested Hotstepper. 'Everyone knows that.'

'Sure.'

'Wait,' said Charlie. 'You're Torn Moon's son?'

'What's she going on about?' asked Hunger.

'Er . . . she thinks Torn Moon is everyone's mother.'

'What? She thinks all the Winged Ones came from Torn Moon?'

'Yes.'

The two chuckled at that.

'What?' protested Charlie. 'She said all the Winged Ones were her children.'

Hunger and Hotstepper shared another laugh.

'Little Charlie, "mother" and "children" are honorary titles. Let me assure you that Torn Moon *did not* give birth to all the Winged Ones. This young whippersnapper, Hotflubber –'

'Hotstepper,' corrected the younger Winged One.

'– is the son of my great-granddaughter. And so he should know better than to call me "eldest" when "Grandpoppa" would be more appropriate.'

'I'll call you that when you stop calling me Hotflubber.'

'It's what your mother wanted.' Ignoring Hotstepper's look of outrage, he turned to Charlie. 'So I guess you'll be expecting a chance to Fight the Flame before you go?'

'Wait. "Fight the Flame"?' queried Charlie. 'What's that?'

'Oh, so you've never heard of it?' said Hunger. 'In that case, let's not bother. You won't be missing out on anything.'

'No, wait!' protested Charlie who, having at first dreaded her journey to meet 'the Hunger', was surprised to find that she was very much enjoying herself. 'What *is* Fight the Flame?'

'It is a chance for a mortal to spar with a Winged One,' explained Hotstepper.

'Hey!' said Hunger. 'Who's the wise one here? I'll do the explanations, if you don't mind. Young Charlie, Fight the Flame does indeed present the opportunity for a Keeper to spar with one of my kind.'

'What does "spar" mean?'

'It means to pretend fight.'

'Oh.'

'From the way you carry yourself I can see that you have had some training in K'Changa.'

'A bit,' agreed Charlie, who was in two minds as to whether 'pretend fighting' was cool or not.

'So you'll be wanting to Fight the Flame, then.'

'Er . . . OK,' said Charlie. 'So how do we do this? How do you pretend fight?'

'Oh, easy. You promise not to use your Will and we promise not to burn your legs off.'

'Ah . . .' Charlie couldn't find a suitable response to that. Nor could she appreciate how someone her size was supposed to fight a Winged One as large as Hunger. Pretend fight or otherwise, he was as big as three double-decker buses squished together. Perhaps his age would slow him down?

'Don't look at me, little Charlie. I'm too old to be jumping around.' Hunger pointed behind her. 'You'll be Fighting the Flame with junior.'

Looking round, Charlie caught a blur of movement. She staggered backwards and only narrowly missed being squashed by Hotstepper's fist.

BAAAMM!

The Winged One's paw pounded into the ground, sending a wave of sand up into the air. Horrified by his speed and power, Charlie scampered backwards.

'W-wait!' she protested but was forced to cartwheel aside as Hotstepper, pulling his fist from the ground, rushed after her.

'There's no waiting in Fight the Flame!' called Hunger.

Behind Hotstepper's blurring form Charlie could see that the wise dragon was settling down to watch the fight.

'Grrrrr!' growled Hotstepper. His teeth snapped shut inches from Charlie's head.

Feeling the blood drain from her face, Charlie hastened to get some distance between herself and the maddened Winged One. But that was not an easy task. As he charged forward he slammed paw after paw into the ground, doing his utmost to turn her into a pancake.

'You call this pretend fighting?' shrieked Charlie.

'Still got both your eyebrows?' called Hunger. He casually plopped one of the Fluttercarp into his cavernous mouth. 'Feet still connected to the ends of your legs? Yes? Then stop complaining. You'll know Hotflubber means business when he rips your spinal column out of your back!'

The intentional misuse of his name seemed to further enrage Hotstepper. With growls and huffs he pursued Charlie up and down boulders, between palm trees and through the shallows. Fluttercarp swam away and terrified birds took to the skies. Alternating between talon-blows and tail-swipes, he relentlessly chased the young Keeper back and forth.

'This is Fight the Flame,' called Hunger, 'not kiss-chase! Fight back, little Charlie, or Hotflubber is going to feel like a sissy!' Chuckling, he threw another fish into the air and caught it between his jaws with a satisfied smack of his lips.

'Fight back?' squawked Charlie as Hotstepper's tail shattered the boulder she had just been standing on. 'How am I supposed to fight a dragon without my Will?'

'Winged One!' corrected Hunger.

'Fight back?' repeated Charlie, more to herself than as a

question for the two crazy Winged Ones. 'Yeah, right.' Dodging a particularly vicious swipe of razor-sharp talons that left a palm tree hanging at a tilt, Charlie held up her hands and called, 'Time out! Time out!'

But Hotstepper didn't listen. Relentless and apparently merciless, he continued to pursue her.

'Time out?' said Hunger around another mouthful of fish. 'There's no such thing as a time out. Come on, young Keeper, show us your spirit!'

Close to fear and growing very concerned for her safety, Charlie flipped into a series of handsprings and back tucks, doing her utmost to earn herself a little breathing room, only to find when she finally stopped that Hotstepper was already there. He sent her flying with a flick from one of his talons.

'Oomph!' Charlie staggered to her feet. She was shocked to look down and find a rip in her shirt. 'All right,' she muttered to herself, 'this is going beyond a joke.' She reached for her Will only to be slapped by a wave of water kicked up by Hotstepper's tail. Her concentration broke. Trying again, she was flummoxed when a dismembered Fluttercarp's tail smacked her in the face. She looked up, distraught, to see Hunger waving the rest of the fish at her from afar.

'No Will, remember?' he called.

She tried to shout something but was knocked off her feet as Hotstepper charged past.

'I bet the thought of fighting Bane has crossed your mind once or twice,' hollered Hunger. 'But you can bet a foe as powerful as Bane would be harder to defeat and even less inclined to allow you to use your Will.' He paused to swallow the last of the Fluttercarp. 'If I were you I would start being resourceful and find a different way to fight junior. Time to start thinking outside the box!'

Charlie growled to herself. Leaping over Hotstepper's paw, she rolled twice across the ground and scampered behind a boulder. Why did supposedly 'wise' people always find the need to sound so cheerful when it was obvious she was in a world of danger?

The boulder she was crouched behind disappeared into a cloud of dust as Hotstepper pounded it with his fist. Spurred into sudden decision, Charlie jumped to her feet and chose to run towards Hotstepper instead of away.

'I'll show you what to do with your box!' snapped Charlie. This time she ducked beneath Hotstepper's teeth and kicked him as hard as she could in the leg. She whimpered in pain; it felt like she had kicked a concrete bollard. 'Not a good move,' she groaned and somersaulted to the side as Hotstepper tried to use the same leg to trample her into the sand.

Jumping over his tail, she ran up it, along his spine and punched him in the back of his head.

'YESSSS!' roared Hunger and punched his own fist into the air. 'Great! Keep going, young Charlie, keep going! And remember to enjoy the moment!'

'Enjoy it?' squeaked Charlie as Hotstepper dislodged her with a flick of his neck. It was obvious he had felt her blow as much as an elephant would feel the bite of a mosquito. 'How am I supposed to enjoy this?'

'Do you not feel alive?' roared Hunger. 'Do you not feel adrenalin rampaging through your veins? Does not everything seem clearer?'

As Charlie did her best to survive she was shocked to find that Hunger's words rang true. She *did* feel more alive. Her sight was razor sharp, her senses of smell and taste and sound were heightened. And even though her fingers trembled with adrenalin, she could not deny the effect it had upon her.

'Remember the Verraverry berries,' cried Hunger. 'How many people can say they fought a Winged One? How many can say they Fought the Flame?'

Shocked to find she was not only relaxing and moving with more fluidity but that a smile had appeared on her lips, Charlie had to acknowledge that perhaps the old Winged One was not as crazy as she had thought.

She began to land more and more blows upon Hotstepper and even though he managed to knock her from her feet and land some blows of his own (that came scarily close to breaking her) she began to feel a blossoming of determination rise from the depths of her soul. It was time to *really* think outside of the box.

She slid beneath Hotstepper's talon, then pulled herself up his wing, dodged a swat of his paw and used his neck to springboard towards a palm tree. Grabbing a coconut in passing, she rolled, snatched a handful of sand and flung it in Hotstepper's eyes. Then she launched the coconut into the air, followed it through with a flash kick and watched with satisfaction as it flew not towards Hotstepper's head but towards Hunger's.

The old dragon snagged it out of the air with a look of delight. 'Bravo, young Charlie, bravo! Now that's what I would call a Verraverry moment!'

43

Indigo Sky

'The time for you to return draws near,' said Hunger. 'But before you depart, one last word of –'

'Wisdom?' suggested Charlie.

'Insight,' finished Hunger with a dry drawl.

'Is this going to be something serious or are you going to try and crack a final joke at my expense?'

'No, little Charlie, I'm quite certain you can crack enough jokes at your expense without my aid. What I wanted to give you was some advice.'

'Oh. Sorry.'

'May I?'

'May you what?'

'Give you that advice?'

'Uh, yes. Please do.'

'You are a Keeper. You share the same genetic history as the Winged Ones –'

'Er . . .'

'Young Charlie, is it really necessary for you to interrupt me with *ers* and *ahs*?'

'I'm sorry but it's the whole genetic thing,' explained

Charlie. 'I don't understand how Humans and Winged Ones can share DNA. Isn't that a bit weird?'

'Yes, it would be weird if all Humans shared our genetic traits. But they don't. Only Keepers do.' Hunger held up a paw to forestall any further interruptions from Charlie. 'When the Great Cataclysm occurred and our ancestral land was split it became very apparent that we would need guardians to watch it in our absence. We created the Keepers by introducing our flesh and blood to Humans. At first the Will was weak in the families that we chose but after several generations of merging the first wave of true Keepers arose. And unlike the Tremen and Stomen, who can only manifest their skills in the realm of Bellania, the Keepers were able to move freely and with power between the two realms. This is how Keepers came to be. Now does that satisfy your craving for knowledge or do you still feel the need to open your mouth and interrupt me some more?'

'Um . . . sorry,' began Charlie with a bashful squirm of her shoulders. 'Just one more thing – I still don't understand how Winged Ones passed their DNA to us. I know I always get told off for saying this . . . but was it magic?'

Hunger's mouth creased into a soft smile. 'Perhaps it was a magic of sorts, young Charlie, perhaps it was.'

'Will I ever see some magic?' asked Charlie, her eyes wide with wonder.

'Ah . . . from what I can gather of the ill that has happened to Bellania in our absence, the need might come to renew the line of Keepers. If the need does arise then yes, Charlie, you will have your chance to witness something that you might consider "magic". Now enough distractions. The time

for your return is close and –' there came a deep rumble
from his stomach – 'it is more than apparent that I must eat,
so allow me to speak without further interruptions.'

Charlie nodded to show she was prepared to keep her
mouth shut.

'You are a Keeper. You share the same genetic history as
the Winged Ones and so we share the same traits of heart,
mind and spirit. Knowing this, the one thing you must never
forget is that no matter what emotions you feel – be it love,
loss, rage or pain – be aware that these are only temporary.
Yes, I have urged you to use these, to embrace and enjoy
them as best you can, but bear in mind they will only carry
you so far. You will need something other than pure feeling
to get you to your final destination.'

Even though he had asked her to remain quiet Charlie
couldn't help but whisper, 'What?'

'Determination.' As he said the word the muscles in his
jaws tensed and something seemed to flash in his eyes. 'Determination is what separates us from the weak and the
incompetent. It is what drives us and pushes us. No matter if
our muscles, if love tears at our heart or if our mind is awash
with rage, determination will carry us through. So fill yourself
with determination, wrap it round you like armour against
the folly of failure and suck it into your body to use as fuel
for your soul, and always, always remember, young Keeper,
that so long as you have the Will you will find the Way.' Eyes
dimming, Hunger shook himself like a beast shedding water
from its back. 'Right. That's my share of wisdom for the day.
Time for you to go, Charlie.'

'You're not coming?'

'Pfft, no!' snorted Hunger. 'I'm too old to be gallivanting around Bellania and playing at war. No, I will leave such tasks to those with more ambition and less hunger in their belly. But do not worry: though I may not be with you in body at least be heartened to know that I'm with you in spirit.'

'That's not quite the same,' grumbled Charlie.

Hunger laughed. 'No, you're right. It isn't, is it? It's a poor excuse that old folks like to use on the young. Well, the truth of the matter is, I have seen more than enough war and I like to think I have earned my right to relax and enjoy my dotage in peace. So while I act like an old bum and dream of plates piled high with roast venison and dripping with waterfalls of gravy, be reassured that my boy Hotstepper here will be accompanying you back to Bellania.' He stretched out a talon to gently stroke Charlie's chin. 'Goodbye, young Charlie. I very much look forward to our next meeting.'

Hotstepper picked her up and plonked her between his wings. Grinning, he looked at the old Winged One. 'So it's "Hotstepper" now, is it?'

'A slip of the tongue,' protested Hunger. 'I meant Hotflubber.'

'Sure you did, Grandpoppa.' Chuckling in delight, he leaped off the edge of the island and spread his wings wide.

'Goodbye,' called Charlie and waved.

Hunger returned the gesture, then went in search of something other than Fluttercarp to eat.

'So what now?' asked Charlie as the two of them flew through the indigo skies, soaring above and beneath a long line of islands.

'We return to Torn Moon's isle, check that enough of my kind have gathered, then fly through the Serpent's Tail Gateway and show Bane the folly of his ways.'

'As simple as that?' said Charlie.

'Simplicity is always best,' confirmed Hotstepper. 'It leaves less opportunity for things to go wrong.'

Both of them turned to watch the inhabitants of the island on their left as they floated by, a crowd of purple- and pink-tinged crabs that waved their claws at them.

'Did he tell you about all his failures and mistakes?' asked Hotstepper.

'Yes,' said Charlie, 'he did.' She paused before asking, 'Was he really imprisoned by the Daemon Kindred for a hundred and three years?'

'He was,' said Hotstepper.

'And did he really lose eleven battles?'

'He did. Does this make you think less of him?'

'What? No! How could it?' Charlie was horrified to even consider the idea that Hunger could be seen in a poor light. 'I think I've messed up enough in the past few weeks. Give me a couple more years and I might start catching up with him.'

Hotstepper chuckled at that. 'It is good you think this way because there is more to him than meets the eye. As much as he likes to boast about his mistakes, his successes outweigh them all. He discovered the hidden realm of the Tram'Win, brought peace to the three warring tribes of the Gliara and, even though he lost eleven battles, he won two extended campaigns and prevented seven bitter feuds between Tremen and Stomen from growing into all-out war. He has built great buildings and bridges, created famous pieces of art and taught kings and queens the importance of diplomacy . . .'

'Wow,' breathed Charlie who, having seen enough pain and war to last her ten lifetimes, could not help but be impressed by Hunger's achievements.

'. . . And most recently he created the pendant to be used as a failsafe should Bane grow too powerful in our absence. It was Rumbling Hunger who gave the pendant to your parents.'

Charlie lurched forward in panic. 'I forgot to mention the pendant! It disappeared when –'

'Don't worry,' chuckled Hotstepper.

'Don't I need it?'

'What for? You've opened the Gateway and that was its only purpose.'

'I can't believe I didn't think to mention it before now –'

'Charlie of the Keepers, you have fulfilled all your duties as a Keeper. So why not relax and let us take care of our part of the bargain? We *will* restore balance to Bellania. We *will* see Bane torn from his Devouring Throne.'

'And my parents?'

'We will see them safe too.'

And with those simple words Charlie finally relaxed. 'So I've done it,' she whispered to herself. 'I've finally done it. I'm going to see my parents again.'

Hotstepper, whose hearing was better than Charlie appreciated, smiled when he heard her words.

44

The Golden Mountain

'Look!' said Hotstepper.

Charlie roused from her daydreams and sat up so she could better peer over Hotstepper's head. The isle with the golden mountain was nearly obscured behind a mass of fluttering wings. Only the very tip of the mountain rising above the cloud of flying Winged Ones could be seen.

'Is that –?'

'Yes!' chuckled Hotstepper. 'My people have answered the call. Come, we had best join them before they depart.'

As Hotstepper glided in, Charlie gazed at the gathered dragons with awe and a strong sense of satisfaction. They were the sword that would defeat Bane's hold on Bellania. It was these magnificent beasts that would make her dreams come true.

'Promise kept!' called a Winged One as she caught sight of Charlie on Hotstepper's back.

'Promise kept!' cried a Winged One with silver scales.

'Promise kept!' cried another.

The cry followed them as Hotstepper flew deeper.

'What does that mean?' asked Charlie.

'They're saluting you!' replied Hotstepper.

'Why?'

'Because you opened the way back to Bellania.'

'But why are they saying "promise kept"?'

Delighted by her naivety, Hotstepper laughed yet again. 'Because you held true to your role as a Keeper. You've done your part in keeping the realms safe.'

'Oh,' said Charlie.

'"Oh"?' Hotstepper found that hilarious. 'Is that all you can say? After reuniting our realms and allowing us to return to our chosen land? "Oh." Ha! Charlie of the Keepers, you are a jester!'

He flared his wings and landed amidst the crowd. Torn Moon, standing head and shoulders above the others, paused mid-conversation with several of her subjects so she could address Charlie.

'How fared your visit to the Hunger?'

'It, er . . . went well,' replied Charlie once she had knocked her brain into a gear suitable for deciphering Torn Moon's antiquated way of speaking.

'And your soul?'

Charlie put hand to chest. 'I'm not too sure about my soul . . . but I feel better.'

'Then I am glad.'

Last Laugh, standing by her side, gave Charlie a congratulatory nod.

'Elder, do we have enough Wings?' asked Hotstepper.

'We do,' said Torn Moon. 'We fly soon.'

Giving both Charlie and Hotstepper one final glance, she returned to conferring with her subjects.

'Wait, what about –' began Charlie, but she was cut short

by Hotstepper. Craning his neck round, he gave her a kind but warning look of gentle admonishment.

'Sshh. Charlie of the Keepers, do not forget that you stand in the presence of our Queen.' He began to push his way back through the crowd. 'We owe you our thanks and I'm sure that Torn Moon will always be willing to grant you counsel but you must not forget this is a time of war. Do not embarrass her by interrupting her in front of her captains.'

Charlie blushed. Hotstepper had a point. She couldn't imagine a general or prime minister on Earth taking the time to talk to a fourteen-year-old while holding a council of war. However, manners or not, she still had questions that needed answering.

'What about Sylvaris?' she asked Hotstepper. 'Will you guys save it?'

'Once Torn Moon has formed a bridgehead and secured our point of entry back to Bellania it would be safe to assume that Sylvaris will be our first port of call.'

Driven by her worry for Kelko and Jensen, Charlie felt the need to press for confirmation. 'Is that a promise?'

'I'm sorry, Charlie of the Keepers, but I cannot give you any certainties. Neither can I tell you what Torn Moon intends. But calm your fears for we are Winged Ones and we return to Bellania with the sole intent of righting the balance.'

'MY CHILDREN!' roared Torn Moon. Her mighty voice cut through the sound of the crowd. 'OUR NUMBERS HAVE SWOLLEN AND WE FIND OURSELVES READY! SPREAD YOUR WINGS AND LET US RIDE THE WINDS! TO BELLANIA AND SUN-FILLED SKIES!'

Torn Moon

Snapping open her wings, she leaped upward. The thousands of Winged Ones that had gathered on the island bellowed their approval. One by one they too opened their wings and beat their way up into the indigo skies. Charlie, eyes wide with wonder, stared at the mass of dragons rising to form a great ribbon of bodies that corkscrewed through the air. She caught glimpses of beating wings, blazing eyes and scales that glittered with reflected starlight. Before she could admire the view any further Hotstepper cried, 'Hold tight!' and with a lurch he raced to the edge of the isle. Flinging himself into the abyss, he peeled his wings open and with confident flaps rose into the sky to join his brethren.

Caught in the moment, Charlie gripped Hotstepper's shoulders with hands that tremored with excitement. Never in her wildest dreams did she ever think she would witness a moment like this.

'Whoooooooooo!' cried a familiar voice. 'Whoop-whoop! Charlie!'

She felt a rush of exhilaration flutter in her stomach as she turned to find Nibbler flying beside them. His mouth was open wide and he was practically slobbering with excitement.

'Isn't this the best?' he hollered. Looping around Hotstepper, he waved enthusiastically at her. 'How'd it go with the wise one? Do you feel cunning and awesome?'

'It was great!' admitted Charlie as she too, buoyed up by his enthusiasm and the magic of the moment, finally felt herself start to relax. 'Where's E'Jaaz?'

Nibbler pointed to a distant arc of Winged Ones. One of them carried the Keeper in a sling that dangled beneath its feet.

'Is he OK?' asked Charlie.

'He's still unconscious,' answered Nibbler, 'but Last Laugh said he'd be fine. We just have to get him to the healers when we're back in Sylvaris.'

And as simply as that Charlie knew that although things were out of her control everything was going to be OK. E'Jaaz was alive and could be healed and although Sylvaris was in trouble it would soon be saved. And once those loose ends had been taken care of it would not take that much more to dethrone Bane and see the return of her parents.

After all, she thought to herself, what could stop an army of dragons?

Looking at the great mass of wings flapping around her, Charlie allowed herself a small smile of success.

45

The Return

Charlie could see the shimmering outline of the Gateway. It hung in an empty patch of the indigo sky, its golden lining looking very out of place amidst the backdrop of the Winged Realm. Charlie squinted as she stared ahead. It looked different from when she had last seen it. The reason soon struck her: its entrance had been blocked.

Before she could point this out to Hotstepper and make him aware that Stonesingers had somehow blocked the way, a squad of six Winged Ones flew past. Beneath them hung a long shape held in place by strong tethers. Charlie blinked in astonishment when she finally worked out what the massive object was. A battering ram made of gold, its head carved to resemble that of a growling dragon.

The six overtook Torn Moon and the rest of the army. Picking up speed, they dived towards the Gateway and released their load, leaving the battering ram to fly at its target. There was a flash of white light, then a crack of concussion followed by a cloud of dust that dissipated to reveal shafts of Bellanian sunlight piercing the realm of the Winged Ones.

With a roar, Torn Moon and her cohorts spiralled towards

the Gateway. Tucking their wings tight to their flanks, they streamed through. Almost immediately there came the flicker of flung flames and the roar of angered giants that Charlie quickly recognized as the Winged Ones' battle cry.

'Are you ready?' called Hotstepper.

'Like you wouldn't believe!' answered Charlie. 'Let's get this done!'

Growling with anticipation, Hotstepper beat his wings twice more, then pulled them tight to join the others diving towards the Gateway. Charlie heard the whistle of wind as it screamed past her ears and saw the glint of exposed teeth as other Winged Ones flew by her side, then she was through. She caught a glimpse of the broken architecture and toppled carvings that used to be part of the old temple, followed by a whirr of blue as she and Hotstepper pulled out of their trajectory to fling themselves up into the bright skies.

Gazing around her, Charlie could see Winged Ones cavorting through the sky, relishing the opportunity to feel the wind beneath their wings and the warmth of the sun on their backs. Then, one by one, they began to drop down to earth with flames erupting from their mouths and vengeance flickering from their eyes.

The Delightful Brothers, up on the Winged Mount, were watching the temple from a safe vantage point. Both held telescopes to their eyes and had been waiting patiently for events to unfold.

When they saw the Winged Ones' golden battering ram

burst through the temple's dome they knew it had started. The ram sent great slabs of stonework and masonry flying before continuing, momentum unchecked, to fly out of sight like some glittering missile. Flame came next, great billowing torrents of it, that gushed past the remaining temple walls to crackle and spit before dissipating in curdles of black smoke.

There were some cracks and pops as superheated rock shattered, then a distant roar arose that grew and grew until the very ground shivered in protest. A dark shadow spat from the temple, then another and another until a seemingly endless stream of growling black silhouettes cascaded from the ruins. With the motion of unfurling fans the shadows spread wings wide to reveal themselves as Bellania's missing Winged Ones. Scales of blue and green, silver and gold, blood red and sunburst yellow glittered and glimmered in the sky.

'Huurrgh,' muttered Stix in distaste as he continued to press his eye to his 'scope.

A keening moan of disbelief filtered from the Stoman forces as they realized the true might of what they faced. Those with quicker minds than their fellows started running straight away. When those slower on the uptake noticed their comrades fleeing, they too joined the race, until a great flood of retreating Stomen could be seen scurrying from the temple like termites evacuating a besieged mound.

Stones let his telescope drop to his saddle so he could better watch the wider play of events.

'I'd forgotten how big they are,' Stones muttered. He gestured with his chin to the Stoman forces shrieking and wailing as they fled the Winged Ones' onslaught. 'Think they'll be able to bring any of the Winged Ones down?'

'Maybe some of the Stonesingers will manage one or two,' growled Stix. 'Then again, maybe not.'

As he said this there came a flurry of activity from one of the crags that circled the ruined temple. The soldiers positioned there, unwilling or perhaps unable to flee, had chosen to stand their ground. Stix and Stones could not hear the twang of siege bows but they could see that they shook and jumped as their teams fired the huge engines. Two great bodies fell from the skies like kites cut loose from their strings, to smash gracelessly into the ground. A third Winged One joined the other two as a behemoth, urged on by Stonesingers, flung a rock into the sky.

But there was no further opportunity to attack as the Winged Ones' reaction was swift. Bellowing in anger at the loss of their brethren, the dragons tore down from the sky to unleash a rain of fire that blanketed the soldiers and set the siege bows alight. The behemoth, unaffected by the flames, was torn limb from limb as three Winged Ones descended to rend it with tooth and nail.

'Seen enough?' Stones asked his brother.

'I have.' Stix folded his telescope away and stored it in one of his saddlebags. 'What do you think?'

'I think the balance of power has swayed.' Stones stared disdainfully at the soldiers. 'That lot down there don't stand a chance.'

'Think Bane is finished?'

'Not yet. You don't reach that level of power and dominance by being a pushover. I think that even though these beasties have returned to Bellania, Bane could yet win the day.'

'So you want to stick with this path?'

Stones nodded thoughtfully. 'For the time being, yes. If Bane ends up on top we'll receive a big slice of the pie.'

'You don't think he'll be angry with us for failing to prevent the Winged Ones from returning?'

'Maybe,' said Stones, 'but at the moment he's going to need all the help he can get. Which means there's plenty of time to get ourselves into his good books again. Back to the Western Mountains?'

'Back to the Western Mountains,' agreed Stix. However, he paused a moment before urging his Stowyrm down the other side of the Winged Mount and stared at the Winged Ones with a measured eye. 'I'd really like to try our hand against one of those. See if we can't take one or two of them down.'

Stones looked at the hundreds and hundreds of Winged Ones wheeling and circling overhead. 'I think we'll get our chance and we'll get it soon – but, brother, now is not the time.'

'Later, then,' growled Stix.

'Later,' agreed Stones.

46

First Taste of Victory

And as simple as that, it was over. The Winged Ones ruled the skies over the Winged Mount and the Stoman garrison had been –

'Defeated!' chuckled Nibbler. 'Well, I say defeated but really I mean smashed, crushed and smushed! Now that's what I call a day of pure awesomeness!'

'Stick your tongue back in, little brother,' said Hotstepper with an indulgent smile. 'Excitement, particularly on a day like this, is perfectly understandable but a touch of decorum would not go amiss.'

'So what's next?' asked Charlie.

'I think,' said Hotstepper, looking at the group of elders who surrounded his queen, 'we are about to find out.'

The three of them watched Torn Moon confer with several of her captains. Five of them nodded their heads, then took to the skies with their companies streaming after. Three of the captains headed off with their crews in tow to secure the Embassy of the Winds while the remaining two returned to the ruins of the temple to watch over the Serpent's Tail Gateway.

'WINGS UP!' bellowed Torn Moon. 'WE FLY TO SYLVARIS!'

Thousands of wings unfurled all at the same time with a noise that Charlie would never grow tired of hearing. She watched as they leaped into the air and allowed themselves to be carried by the winds up the length of the Winged Mount and past its peak, then whipping once, twice, three times around the vortex that played at the summit, they broke off and headed north-east at incredible speed.

'Grab hold of your Will!' instructed Hotstepper. 'At the altitude we will be flying at you're going to need it!'

Muscles bunching, he tore open his wings and hurled himself up the Winged Mount. The wind caught at his body and propelled him forward. The crags and cliffs of the mountain rushed beneath him, then they were skimming over the snowline, whipping past the flag-lined summit and up into the crisp freedom of the sky. He rode the tempest that lashed above the peak, spiralling even higher, until they were buffeted by a thunderous crosswind. Roaring with delight, Hotstepper held his wings straight and allowed himself to be caught by the current. Muscles snapped with tension as he shot forward and even though Charlie had wrapped herself in Will the winds tore at her hair and tugged tears from her eyes. Holding on as tightly as she could, she pulled herself forward and wrapped her arms round Hotstepper's neck.

The thrum and rumble of the wind grew, as did the shake and tremor in Hotstepper's muscles, and just as it seemed to reach a crescendo it abruptly ceased. The sudden silence and slackening of force were shocking.

'Ha!' said Hotstepper gleefully. 'I've missed that! Too long have we been away from the skies of Bellania.'

'Wh-what happened?' gasped Charlie as she struggled against the cold.

'Equilibrium,' said Hotstepper. 'We're flying as fast as the wind. The hard part is done and now we get to enjoy the ride.'

'C-c-cold,' stammered Charlie.

'Still got hold of your Will?'

'Y-y-yes.'

'Shield yourself.'

Charlie did as she was told.

'No-not working,' she said. 'St-still cold.'

Hotstepper risked craning his head round to check that Charlie had indeed shielded herself. Seeing the glimmer of gold surrounding her, he smiled in relief.

'Don't panic,' he warned. He turned his head back to face the way they were travelling and allowed a trickle of flame to ease from his mouth. It flickered and fluttered down his neck, danced off his scales and breezed across Charlie's shield. The effects were instantaneous.

'Haaaaa . . . toastie,' she sighed.

Relaxing, she peered over the side to see Nibbler flying below. His eyes were narrowed into slits and a look of incredulous joy was plastered over the rest of his face. Beneath her friend lay the curve of the land. She could see the grasslands of the Great Plains, the grandeur of its greenery broken by the occasional river; to her left she could just about make out the rise and fall of the Western Mountains; and off to her right lay a seemingly endless land and the faint glimmer of a distant sea.

'Beautiful,' whispered Charlie. Rising up in her seat to peer past Hotstepper's head, she could see the army of Winged Ones gliding effortlessly on the jet stream. Beneath their furled talons Charlie could make out the distant smear that was Deepforest, its greenery turned a bluish-grey by the blur of distance. 'How long will it take us to get to Sylvaris?'

'Three hours.'

'What? Really?'

'Yes.'

'Wow . . . er, how can we get there so quickly? It took Nibbler days.'

'The skytides are a powerful tool for those who know their location,' said Hotstepper. He glanced at Nibbler, now flying slightly ahead of them. 'My guess is our little brother missed that part of his education but by the size of his smile I would say he is enjoying the ride.'

Charlie too, could not deny that she was enjoying every moment of their flight. With her Will and Hotstepper's flames flickering around her, she wrapped her arms once more about the dragon's muscular neck and watched the world pass by.

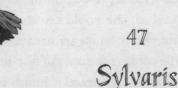

47

Sylvaris

There were shouts of anger from the Winged Ones as they saw the pillars of smoke rising over Deepforest.

'Oh no,' whispered Charlie.

Her stomach lurched as she realized that all her worst fears might have come true. Hoping against hope, she bobbed from side to side, trying to find the source of the smoke. She had to know if it was Deepforest burning or the city itself. She *had* to know.

'Stop lurching around,' instructed Hotstepper.

'But –'

'I know, Charlie of the Keepers, I know. But your wriggling around is not making flying any easier. Just hold still for now.'

'But what if it's the city that's burning?' said Charlie, thoughts of Jensen and Kelko first and foremost in her mind.

'If it is, then we will remedy the situation when we arrive.'

Charlie bit her lip. She had placed all her faith in the Winged Ones and their ability to save the day but had she been fooling herself? Could anyone really turn the tide of war? Thoughts of using her Will to Portal ahead came to mind but before she could pursue the idea she was interrupted.

'DOWN!' commanded Torn Moon, her voice snapping like a whip.

Tucking their wings in, wave after wave of Winged Ones left the jet stream and plummeted downward in a stomach-churning free fall. Charlie, knowing Hotstepper was about to follow suit, gripped tight with her knees and wrapped her arms securely round his neck. But as mentally prepared as she was she still shrieked as he fell into a steep dive and Deepforest, no longer below, instead rose up like a wall in front of them.

They fell for long, long minutes, then one by one the Winged Ones slowly pulled themselves out of their dive to fly over the gold- and green-coloured forest canopy. Ahead of them lay great billows of smoke that obscured their view. Charlie only had moments to study the land before they were amidst the dark clouds of ash. She coughed as she inhaled, the acrid scent scalding her throat, then they were through the worst of it and gliding over Sylvaris.

The city had been devastated.

Again.

Fresh fires smouldered, their glow giving buildings a hellish appearance. Towers that had survived the first battle had toppled and the few that still stood looked worn and battered. Bridges had tumbled, leaving little more than twisted stubs and splinters behind. Marketplaces lay ruined and K'Changa playing fields were scorched. Looking beyond this, Charlie was heart-stricken to see huge swathes of Deepforest blackened and crumpled and devoid of life.

But she could see that Tremen still moved on the floating boulevards and walkways and that Sylvaris, although bloodied, remained free. Her hopes soared, then swiftly fell as a bank of smoke drifted aside to reveal the Stoman army with its endless rows of soldiers and Shades that stretched from the forest's edge all the way back to the horizon. Charlie saw the crackle of power writhing amongst groups of Stone-singers and looming out of the crowd like titans of old were juddering behemoths. And all that stood between these and Sylvaris was a thin line of struggling Treman soldiers doing everything in their power to hold back the tide.

Hotstepper's sudden growl was so loud, so strong, that Charlie felt it in her bones. Other dragons began to snarl and shout, their angered voices booming across the sky. And before Charlie could question what was happening, the Winged Ones descended over the battlefield.

Kelko stared angrily at the line of flailing soldiers. He knew they were fighting a doomed battle just as he knew that his beloved city, broken as it was, was likely to be burned to the ground by day's end. His hands curled round the haft of his Brambleaxe. All he wanted to do was get into that line and join his fellows in their fierce fight to hold back the Stomen.

But he couldn't, could he? He was Sylvaris's general and Lady Dridif had been more than curt when instructing him to lead from the back and not from the front. A good general used his mind and wits to lead, not brawn, she'd said. But Kelko knew he wasn't a real general. He preferred to work with emotion and instinct rather than cold wit. He'd done his best for the people of Sylvaris but really it had been the advisors that Dridif had loaned him who had devised the strategies. And now, with all commands given, he was expected to stand back here and watch like a useless figurehead.

'Ah, Blight me Leaf,' he muttered. Turning, he addressed the three grizzled (and rather old) advisors who stood by his side. 'Right, lads, I appreciate yer help but I think the time for playing generals is over. We've done the best we could but it's time ta get in there and show those fool Stomen that we don't give up easy. Now don't try and stop me –'

'We won't,' said one.

'Eh?' said Kelko. 'Ya won't?'

'Nope,' replied the one on his left. Pulling his sword from its scabbard, he eyed the battle line with a crazed glint in his eye.

'Time for giving orders is long past,' said the third. 'Now let's get bloody.'

Snarling, the three advisors raised their weapons and ran to join their comrades. Kelko stared foolishly after them, pausing to regain his composure. With a glance over his shoulder, he took one last look at his beloved Deepforest, then fixed his eyes upon the enemy.

He saw the Shades slash at his countrymen with talons of shadow.

He saw Rhinospiders scuttle over fallen bodies and watched as their riders plunged spears into flesh.

He saw Stonesingers urge behemoths to rise and stamp their feet, killing all beneath and rocking the very ground with their might.

He saw siege weapons fling burning rocks into the forest canopy.

Behemoth

He saw –

'I've seen enough,' he growled. 'MORE THAN ENOUGH!'

Wrapping himself in anger and rage, he slapped his helmet over his head, readjusted his grip upon his Brambleaxe, sprinted forward and slammed shoulder first into the struggling mass of soldiers.

'Burn me forest?' he bellowed.

He smashed a Stoman's sword in two.

'Destroy me city?' he screamed.

He kicked a Shade with his armoured boot.

'Kill me people?'

He swung his Brambleaxe, knocking a Stoman from his feet.

He opened his mouth to say something but a red mist descended across his vision and a fresh wave of rage burst from his heart. Snarling and gnashing his teeth, Kelko began to *really* move. He lashed out with feet, axe blade, haft and fist, pummelling his way forward. Deep into the Stoman ranks he went, dropping all that came before him like wheat before a sickle. Deeper and deeper he strode, the line of Tremen pushing with him until at last he could move no further. The weight of the seemingly endless Stomen stopped him in his tracks. Crowded from the front and crowded from behind, he had nowhere else to go. He found his face pressed close to a Stoman's. They snarled at each other but, unable to raise their weapons, they had to settle for wrestling with words of hate.

'Green-skinned, leaf-loving pig!' spat the Stoman.

'Shut it, chump!' retorted Kelko. Fuming, he turned to his compatriots and shouted, 'Sylvaris!'

'Sylvaris!' echoed the Treman to his left.

'Sylvaris,' whispered the dying Treman to his right.

'SYLVARIS!' bellowed Kelko as loudly as he could.

The shout was repeated by all the Tremen. Groaning and moaning, muscles close to bursting, they took a step forward, forcing the Stomen back.

Kelko grinned into the face of his angered adversary.

'We might be smaller than you,' he said, 'but we're *tougher*!'

'SYLVARIS!' he shouted again and as his comrades repeated the word he tried to take another step forward.

But the Stomen didn't budge. Their front lines had been pushed back as far as possible and as the Stoman lines behind pressed forward an impasse formed.

'You can't beat us,' spat the Stoman soldier. 'You can't! We are as endless as the ocean's waves and you but a sinking ship that we will smash against the shore. Listen to us!'

A fresh peal of Stonesong rose over the Stoman ranks. The chant grew and grew and the Stonesingers were only too happy to gorge themselves on the additional power.

'Do you hear?' said the Stoman. 'That is the sound of your demise, little man.'

The soil beneath their feet rocked then bulged upward. The two forces were split apart as great mounds arose. Shouting in horror, the Tremen pulled back. The air remained thick with the sound of Stonesong and the many Stonesingers harvesting the song continued to point flaming fists towards the ground.

Snapping and groaning, creaking and cracking, the earth split asunder to reveal three behemoths that were so big, so *huge*, that they dwarfed the others of their kind. Terrible hands of stone began to slowly emerge from the ground.

The Tremen moaned.

And as if to add to their woes, the very skies cracked with thunder.

'Wait,' said Kelko as a glimmer of reason muscled past his anger, 'there are no clouds in the sky.' He turned to shake the Treman next to him. 'Thunder!' he shouted.

'Wot?' muttered the dazed man.

'Thunder!' roared Kelko with unsurpassed joy and pointed towards the smoke rising over Deepforest.

Growls, deep and heavy with the promise of retribution, burst across the battlefield. The sounds startled both the Tremen and the Stomen and sheared through the Stonesong. Unpowered, the three gigantic behemoths sank back into the ground but no one noticed. All eyes were looking towards Sylvaris. They saw a flicker of colour and a sudden spinning of smoke as something powerful sent vortices rushing through the air. There was a tense pause and then, flicking forward on mighty wings, came Winged One after Winged One.

Hundreds of them.

Thousands of them.

48

Brokering the Peace

Charlie watched as long lines of Stomen were engulfed by fire and the behemoths were torn into rubble. Shocked by the turn of events and horrified by the immense power and size of the Winged Ones, the Stoman army fell silent.

Torn Moon flew low over the battlefield. As she passed the ranks her shadow drenched the soldiers in darkness. 'IF YOU WOULD LIVE,' she roared, her voice rich and full of authority, 'DROP YOUR WEAPONS!' Flaring her wings, she landed on top of a behemoth, bringing it crashing down and crushing the unfortunates that were too slow or dumbfounded to get out of the way. She stood amidst the sea of Stomen like a figure of legend, then slowly padded forward, crushing soldiers and Shades between her talons and dripping flames from her teeth. 'OR IF YOU WISH TO TEST THE METTLE OF MY WILL, RAISE YOUR BLADES AND LET US SEE HOW THIS DAY UNFOLDS!'

Those nearest Torn Moon looked up at her and the other dragons flying overhead in dread. Unwilling to face her wrath, they allowed their weapons to drop from numb fingers. As more and more Winged Ones landed amongst the Stoman army the clatter of falling weapons grew until it seemed that the entire Great Plains was awash with the clank and jangle of discarded blades and maces, spears and bludgeons.

'Better,' said Torn Moon in her normal voice. 'Last Laugh! Handino! Dancing Stone! Bitter Sail! Attend me!'

Obeying their summons, Torn Moon's captains flew low to join her. They put their heads together and began to confer. The Stomen stood nervously, unsure how to proceed. The sudden change from proud invaders to shamed warriors was not lost upon them.

'What's happening?' asked Charlie as she and Hotstepper flew lazy circles overhead.

'The end,' said Hotstepper. 'Defeating the Stomen was the easy part but now you get to witness the slow part: deciding what happens with the losers and how best to dispose of the troops.'

'"Dispose"?' squeaked Charlie and although she found herself full of rage every time she looked at the Stoman army she could not stomach the image that that word brought to mind. 'Please, Hotstepper, please tell me that doesn't mean what I think it means!'

'It does not,' replied Hotstepper. 'Fierce and ferocious we might be but we are *not* animals. By "dispose" I mean disarming and transporting the soldiers. Torn Moon and her councillors will judge the defeated and decide who will be punished, who will be imprisoned, who will be made to rebuild what they have broken, and who will be allowed to go free.'

'You would let some of them go?'

'Of course,' said Hotstepper. 'Although some will undoubtedly have come here with evil in their hearts, others will not. Some will have come here for foolish reasons – pride, duty, misplaced belief. These we will allow to depart. The others though . . . they will face sterner judgements.'

As Charlie looked down at the multitude of the defeated and the Winged Ones that stood like sentinels amongst them, dozens of questions came to mind, but she pushed them aside. She had other matters to attend to first.

'Can you take me back to Sylvaris?' she asked. 'I need to check on my friends.'

'Of course.'

Dipping his wings, he banked in a long turn that took them out across the Great Plains, until they slowly righted themselves to face back towards the forest and its city. Charlie stared at the smoke and smouldering fires with tired eyes.

She had done it, or rather *they* – the Winged Ones – had done it. Peace. They had brought about the end of hostilities, the end of the killing, the burning and the destruction. And with this came the promise of rebirth and regeneration.

But for all this she could not prevent herself from staring unhappily at the ruins of Sylvaris and the great swathe of Deepforest that had been ravaged. The tender part of her wanted to cry at the cost, at all the loss of life and pain that had been inflicted to reach this moment, but for some particular reason she found herself thinking of a piece of fruit. To be exact, a Verraverry berry. Rushing out of her heart, pushing past her depression and overcoming her exhaustion, came a sense of *life* that materialized as a smile upon her face.

'Rumbling Hunger,' she chuckled, 'wiser than you seem.'

'What was that?' asked Hotstepper.

'Nothing,' replied Charlie. 'I'm just going fruity.'

As Hotstepper politely chose to ignore her nonsensical answer she grinned happily. No longer did she see the flames and smoke, or the devastation and ruins. What she chose to see instead was Sylvaris as it would look when they started to rebuild. She could picture the Tremen calling forth new trees and using the power of their treesinging to build their towers anew. She could see the Winged Ones flying overhead and bringing peace to all of Bellania. And with those images in her head it did not take her long to picture the Winged Ones crushing Bane and freeing her parents.

Life suddenly seemed sweet.

As they sped back towards Deepforest she caught sight of Nibbler and, unable to stop herself, she held her hands aloft and shouted, 'Dude, I'm flying a dragon!'

Nibbler threw her a cheeky wave and performed an insane-looking loop-the-loop.

'Winged One,' corrected Hotstepper.

'A draaaaaaaaagon!' she hollered, startling nearby Winged Ones and causing Shades and Stomen to look up in wonder. She couldn't have stopped herself even if she wanted to; she was simply too high on life.

Even though he was flying, Hotstepper somehow managed to slap paw to muzzle. 'The sooner I reunite you with your friends,' he said, 'the better.'

'Ssh,' said Charlie, 'don't spoil the moment.' Spurred on by the wonderful feeling of success, she asked Hotstepper to fly lower. Skimming just above the Stoman army she shouted, 'Hey, suuuuuuuckers! We won! We won! Victoooooooory!'

Cackling with delight, she leaned back, closed her eyes and breathed deep. Victory. At last.

An eerie howl sliced through the sky.

It came again, loud and guttural.

Alarmed, Hotstepper wheeled round and almost caused Charlie to lose her grip in his haste.

'What was that?' he growled.

The other Winged Ones, just as concerned, were looking towards the distant horizon.

The scream sounded once more. It slammed across the Great Plains, over the heads of the Stoman army and crashed against Deepforest, causing the birds that had returned to panic and take to the sky. The jubilant Tremen, cheering for all their worth, fell suddenly silent.

49

Dark Wings Over Deepforest

A silhouette appeared in the distant sky. It twisted and coiled through the air with sinuous grace. The gathered crowd watched it with mesmerized eyes. A whisper of wonder arose as it became apparent that the silhouette was not alone. More of the shapes appeared until the sky seemed thick with wriggling forms.

The bitter scream came again. Others' voices joined the first. Shrieking and howling, hissing and clicking, the noises burst across the crowd, so harsh and powerful that they forced several people to step backwards.

Charlie, still riding Hotstepper, felt her earlier joy dissolve to be replaced by an acidic sense of dread. Unlike the people below, she knew what was coming.

'They're Stowyrms,' she said.

'What?'

'They're Stowyrms,' she repeated, louder this time so she could be heard over the howls. 'Bane took the Wyrms and turned them into something new.'

'Stowyrms?' Hotstepper repeated the unfamiliar word. 'I –'

'WINGS!' came Torn Moon's sudden roar. 'UP! UP AND READY YOURSELVES!'

There was a flutter of motion as those who had landed joined their kin patrolling overhead. Eyes wide, talons flexing, the dragons prepared themselves. The Stowyrms drew close, their shrieks growing louder. Closer.

'Get me to Torn Moon!' shouted Charlie. 'I can tell her what to expect. She needs to know that flames won't work!'

But it was too late for that. Growling and snarling, the two sides came together. Horrific sounds cut the air, enraged screams mixed with hisses of agony and deep barks of challenge blended with squeals of shock. Great torrents of flame exploded overhead, claws ripped at wings and teeth tore at muscle. The soldiers below, both Treman and Stoman, looked on with open mouths and wide eyes.

They'd never seen anything like it.

Bellania had never seen anything like it.

The Winged Ones were larger and undoubtedly more powerful than the Stowyrms but their foes were numerous. At this stage in the sudden conflict it was impossible to tell which way the battle would go. One of the Stoman warriors, realizing that the Stowyrms had come from the direction of the Western Mountains, licked his lips uncertainly. Retrieving his bow, he nocked an arrow, aimed at a Winged One and let fly. With the turbulent chaos boiling overhead it was impossible to tell if the arrow had found its mark but the message was clear. With a shout of defiance, the Stomen scrambled for their fallen weapons and, buoyed by the sudden appearance of their mysterious allies, they rampaged forward.

Horrified, the Tremen were forced to defend themselves again.

Pandemonium reigned.

Charlie couldn't believe her eyes. The sound, the sights and the sudden scent of blood were an attack upon her senses. Her shell-shocked mind tried to work out how they had gone from certain victory to this. Uncertain what to do or how to respond, she grabbed hold of her Will and . . . did nothing. What should she do? Try to get to the ground and do her best to find her friends? Or should she try to help the Winged Ones?

The decision was taken from her as a Stowyrm collided with Hotstepper. The force from the blow almost dislodged Charlie. Fighting to regain her seat, she was knocked again as its tail coiled round and thumped against Hotstepper's flank. She acted without thinking and unleashed a whip of Will, striking the beast in the face. It shrieked and fell back. Hotstepper, taking advantage of the moment, ripped its glassy wings from its back but before they could watch it fall to the ground a second and a third slammed into them.

Charlie yelped when a set of teeth snapped inches away from her face. Slashing at the thing with a torrent of Will, she tried to slide further down Hotstepper's back but found herself dislodged and suddenly caught in freefall. Eyes bulging, she windmilled her arms and, unable to stop herself, she screamed and screamed and –

'Oof!' She landed on a passing Stowyrm. Her fingers scrabbled for purchase on its stony skin but failed and once again she found herself dropping. Horror magnified, she screamed as she landed on top of a behemoth, bounced as her Will cushioned her impact, then slipped down its shoulders and landed flat on her back.

Winded, she stared up at the Winged Ones and Stowyrms churning through the sky. A fierce face loomed over her, blocking her view. She glimpsed the flash of a blade and was surprised as her own Will-clad hand snapped upward to catch it with a burst of sparks. Instinct taking over, she flipped to her feet, kneed her opponent in the groin, turned to flee and was shocked to find herself in the middle of the Stoman army.

'What have we got here –'

Charlie didn't plan on hanging around to hear the rest of that sentence. Tearing open a Portal back to the Jade Tower, she jumped through. She caught a glimpse of tired-looking councillors and felt a thrill of delight when she saw Jensen and Lady Dridif.

'Charlie –' began Jensen, but she didn't hear the rest. A strong arm grabbed her by the scruff of the neck and hauled her back through the Portal.

'Going somewhere, little girlie?' scowled a hulking soldier. In his other hand he held a warhammer aloft.

'Lass!' squawked Jensen. 'I'm com–'

His voice was cut short as Charlie was forced to release the Portal and defend herself. Deflecting the warhammer so it slammed into its wielder's foot, she backflicked, only to stumble into a Stonesinger.

'Eep!'

Dancing to the side, she bumped into another.

'Not good,' she mumbled and scrambled back on hands and feet to avoid his flaming hands.

She managed to regain her feet and tried to run the other way but quickly realized that she was completely surrounded. She tried the Portal again but a flung mace put an end to that idea. Heart pounding, Charlie raised her hands and, attempting to look in every direction at once, prepared to defend herself.

'Aw, got nowhere to run to?' sneered a Stonesinger. Pulling a huge club from the ground, he stepped forward . . . and was crushed as a shattered Stowyrm fell out of the sky. Amazed, Charlie and the other Stonesingers looked hesitantly upward, wondering if they should expect anything else to fall from above.

Something did.

There was a flutter of wings and a flash of lightning, then Nibbler was standing next to her, blue eyes blazing and flickers of flame gusting from his nostrils. 'Back off!' he roared. His young voice cracked but his message was clear.

Several of the Stonesingers skittered away, only to be pushed forward by angry comrades.

'There's only one!' shouted a soldier.

'He's only a Hatchling!' goaded another.

Hotstepper landed on them.

A moment of silence followed as those nearby checked the heavens again. When they looked back down they were greeted by a wave of fire from Hotstepper, a jet of lightning from Nibbler and a torrent of Will from Charlie.

There was a scramble as those still capable of running

did so. The three companions suddenly, and thankfully, found themselves in a shallow of calm amidst the battle.

'Get on,' said Hotstepper. Ducking his neck low, he waited for Charlie to clamber on. He looked to Nibbler. 'Ready, little brother?'

'You bet.'

They sprang back into the war-torn sky.

50

Black Orchids

Charlie stared at the battlefield with eyes full of shock. She simply couldn't believe it – everything had gone wrong. Victory had been snatched out of her hands and now she was confronted with an uncertain future. She felt a coil of anger writhe in her heart and beneath this a flicker of fear. She had thought she could count on fate and the Winged Ones to see things through but she should have known better. Clenching her teeth, she wracked her brains to find some way to reclaim her future. After all that she had endured and after all that she had overcome, there was no way she could allow it to end like this. Not when she was so close.

An image of Fo Fum rearing over the city, smoke cascading from his eyes, flashed through her mind. Remembering how she had defeated him, she leaned forward to shout in Hotstepper's ears.

'Take me higher!'

Hotstepper waited until he had dodged past a Stowyrm before replying, 'Why?'

'I know a quick way to take out the Stowyrms!'

Charlie felt touched when he didn't question her. Taking

her at her word, he grunted and flapped his way upward. Nibbler zigzagged after.

They didn't stop until the air grew thin and the temperature plummeted. When Charlie leaned out she could see that Deepforest, Sylvaris and the two battlefields, heavenly and earthly, were laid out beneath them in one breathtaking view. There were layers upon layers of detail. Fire and lightning blossomed in the sky while Winged Ones and Stowyrms wrestled, careened and flew through the carnage. Beneath them, behemoths flung rocks and Stonesingers threw craggy missiles at their adversaries. Shades lashed at Tremen and soldiers rained arrows in all directions.

'What do you have in mind?' asked Hotstepper.

'I'm going to open a Portal to the Western Mountains,' said Charlie.

'What will that achieve?'

'Hopefully a lot,' admitted Charlie. 'I can use Bane's barrier to travelling as a weapon. A really, really impressive weapon.'

'I have not heard of this,' said Hotstepper. 'Is it as powerful as it sounds?'

'It stopped Fo Fum so I figure it should see an end to the Stowyrms,' replied Charlie. 'Let's just find somewhere that I can use it.'

'Why not here?'

'Er . . . no.' Charlie thinned her lips. 'It's not too precise. I don't want to risk hitting any Winged Ones.' She paused as she gave thought to what she was about to unleash. 'Or Stomen,' she said. She didn't want to add war crimes to her list of life's failures.

'How about there?' Hotstepper pointed to the west where a wave of fresh Stowyrms were speeding across the Great Plains to bolster the ranks of their siblings.

'That'll do. Get me over them and I'll do the rest.'

Hotstepper worked his way towards them while Nibbler flitted by his side.

'All right, this'll do,' said Charlie. 'Just watch out, OK? Last time we tried this it wasn't too stable.'

Breathing deeply, Charlie summoned her concentration. She pulled deeply on her Will and, holding her glowing hands aloft, tore open a Portal to the Western Mountains. Almost immediately it began to shake from side to side and Charlie was forced to fight it. Gritting her teeth, she kept it open. A wind picked up and with it came a sharp whooshing noise that grated at their ears.

'What's going on?' hollered Hotstepper. He struggled to keep them aloft. 'Why does it sound so chaotic?'

'Don't worry,' replied Charlie. Her voice was iron-like and crisp with the knowledge that she was doing the right thing. She shouted so Hotstepper could hear her over the commotion, 'THIS IS SUPPOSED TO HAPPEN!'

As she channelled even more power, the whooshing noise reached unbearable levels, the shaking increased and, just as it seemed as though everything was at risk of exploding, an inky torrent of blackness burst from the Portal.

'YES!' hollered Charlie and punched her fist into the air. But as she stared at the dark waterfall her sense of certainty vanished. 'Er . . . OK, so that isn't supposed to happen.'

The Portal was not delivering, as she had expected, a wave of lava but instead was vomiting forth an endless torrent of black flowers. As Hotstepper flew closer she could see that they were orchids. Perfect black orchids. Shocked, she allowed the Portal to iris shut. Nibbler, Hotstepper and Charlie watched the flowers tumble out of sight.

'Not much of a weapon,' grunted Hotstepper, delivering the understatement of the year.

'But-but-but . . .' stammered Charlie – she couldn't believe what had just happened – 'someone changed it.'

Nibbler, pulling close to them, was as shocked as Charlie. 'Looks like Bane got wind of you using his barrier as a weapon.'

'But black flowers?' said Charlie, still dismayed.

'Well, at least we know that evil tyrants have not lost their sense of style,' grunted Hotstepper. 'Charlie of the Keepers, it was a good plan and though it failed to bear fruit I congratulate you on your spirit. But we have wasted enough time. We must return to the fray!'

He prepared to dive only to be stopped when Charlie pounded on his shoulders. 'Stop! Wait a minute, Hotstepper!'

'What is it, Charlie of the Keepers?'

'Look at those!'

Charlie pointed to the line of Stowyrms that continued to pour from the Western Mountains.

'What about them?' asked Hotstepper.

'They're reinforcements,' she explained.

'I can see that,' grumbled Hotstepper. 'All the more reason to return to aid my brethren.'

He tucked his wings in but Charlie protested. Banging on his shoulders yet again, she demanded to be heard. 'Think about it! Are we winning?'

They looked down at the combat. The battlefield was littered with the shattered remains of Stowyrms. As more and more were torn apart they began to form mounds and heaps over which the enraged Stoman armies clambered like a carpet of ants. There were fallen dragons too. Death had robbed them of their majesty; their bodies lay limp, their mouths hung open and the wind tugged mournfully at their wings. And yet for all the dead and the chaos, the battle still raged.

Hotstepper growled and his tail lashed at the sky. 'We might not be winning yet, but we will! By Fire and Realm, we will tear these upstarts from the sky!'

Spitting out a jet of flame, he reared and pawed at the air.

'For Bellania!' he roared. Teeth bared, flames whisking from the sides of his mouth, he tucked his wings in and dived. Nibbler, following the lead of his larger sibling, sped after them.

'Oh, for crying out loud . . .' Charlie groaned to herself. Blocking out the stomach-clenching view of Bellania jumping up to meet them, she slid down Hotstepper's neck and rapped her knuckles on his skull. 'Come on! Stop with that barbarian mentality and use your head for a minute!' Seeing that she wasn't getting through to him, she grabbed his ears and pulled. 'Stop!'

Hotstepper snarled and barrel-rolled through the air, then splayed his wings to bring them to a sudden stop. 'Charlie of the Keepers, your ways are too forthright! My people are dying down there and you wish to talk me out of joining them? Where is your honour?'

'I'm trying to think like a Keeper!' retorted Charlie. The

shard of determination blazed in her chest. 'And you should be trying to think like Rumbling Hunger, so just listen to me for a minute! If you disagree with what I've got to say, then I'll gladly follow you and we'll fight the Stowyrms together. Please, Hotstepper, just a minute, that's all.'

Nibbler, keen to support his friend, looked Hotstepper in the eye. 'Charlie's always worth listening to,' he said.

Hotstepper growled as his blood ran with the urge to battle but his head won out. Allowing his passion to settle, he nodded to show he was willing to talk.

Charlie leaped on the opportunity to get her point across. 'The Stowyrms are new to Bellania, aren't they?'

Too full of passion to speak, Hotstepper merely nodded.

'So it's safe to assume that Bane is manufacturing them,' said Charlie.

Hotstepper nodded a second time.

'One last point,' she added. 'Would you consider that –' she pointed at the carnage unfolding below – 'a stalemate, or are we winning?'

'For now, I would call it a stalemate,' acknowledged Hotstepper. 'But if we can arrange an organized front and a flanking manoeuvre, we can yet win this.'

'Maybe you can,' said Charlie, 'but you've got to remember there's a limited amount of dragons –'

'Will you get it right?' growled Hotstepper. 'We're not dragons, we're Winged Ones!'

'Dragons, Winged Ones, whatever,' snapped Charlie. 'Look! There's only so many of you Winged Ones, but if Bane is using his god like Darkmount used his, then he could produce a limitless number of Stowyrms! Edge Darkmount made tens of thousands of gargorillas! Imagine if Bane does the same! Do you really think you'll be able to stop that many Stowyrms? Do you?'

Hotstepper fell silent as he digested her argument.

'I know not of these "gargorillas",' he said, 'but your logic is valid. Charlie of the Keepers, you have a point.' He was quiet as he studied the turbulent events below. 'It is possible –' he paused as though unable to believe what he was about to admit – 'that we could yet lose this fight. Bane . . . might defeat us.' Suddenly he growled and let loose another burst of fire. 'But win or lose, victory or defeat, I will not sit idly by. So unless you have a better idea we *will* join my brothers and sisters and we *will* make a stand against this new threat.'

Hotstepper and Nibbler waited for Charlie's reply.

51

A Division of Forces

In that moment, riding on Hotstepper's back, with the battle raging beneath them and with the scent of Sylvaris burning in her nostrils, Charlie felt something heave inside her. Something that wanted to rise above her exhaustion, something that wanted to climb above the doubt and soar over her fear and anger. Feeling it lurch inside her chest, Charlie realized it was something that could not be pushed aside or ignored. It was something that had to be listened to, something that had to be obeyed.

Determination.

Rumbling Hunger had been right: it was her one constant, the only thing that had not abandoned her throughout her adventures in Bellania. It had kept her going; it had allowed her to beat Constantina, had pushed her forward to find the secret of the pendant and it had kept her on the path to find her parents. When Stotch, Azariah and Marsila had died and all she had wanted to do was scream and stamp at the heavens, it had been her stubborn resolve that had propelled her forward. And now, right at this moment, she was *determined* not to lose. After all that she had been through, after all she had endured,

she had come too far to give up now. She was going to
succeed no matter what.

'You want to know if I've got a better idea than going
out in a blaze of glory? Too right I've got a better idea!' said
Charlie. 'Let's go and take out the source of all our trouble.
Let's go and take down Bane.'

'What?' squawked Nibbler.

'What?' echoed Hotstepper.

'I'm serious!' retorted Charlie. 'He's the root of the problem. He always has been! But if we don't do it, and do it
soon, we're going to be pinned down. The Winged Ones will
lose and he will win. So let's do it! Let's go squash him once
and for all!'

There was a long moment of silence, broken only by the
sound of the rushing wind and the clamour of battle.

'All right,' agreed Hotstepper, his green eyes ablaze with
purpose. 'Your plan has merit. But we will need reinforcements and Torn Moon must be informed.'

Without waiting for a reply, he descended to a lower
altitude. They found Torn Moon not, as Charlie had thought,
in the thick of things, but flying over the battlefield, looking
down on it with a careful eye. Two large Winged Ones,
acting as guardians, flew by her side. From time to time
others would fly up from below, carrying news or requesting
fresh orders.

'Elder,' cried Hotstepper as he neared her. 'I seek your
counsel.'

Torn Moon glanced briefly at him, noted Charlie on his
back, then returned to watching the events below. 'Make it
quick and make it concise.'

'Charlie of the Keepers suggests that these "Stowyrms" are creations of Bane. She argues that they are not a finite resource but an infinite one.'

Torn Moon stole another quick look at the young Keeper. Charlie stared right back.

Hotstepper continued. 'I have seen more Stowyrms arrive from the west and even though we cull their numbers they are replenished anew. I would –'

Torn Moon silenced him with a wave of her paw. She turned to a freshly arrived messenger. 'Handino is to fall back with his crew. Command him to present a unified front and to attack from the north. Go.' She gestured for another waiting messenger to approach. 'News?'

'Dancing Stone requests reinforcements.'

'There are none,' replied Torn Moon. 'Tell him to hold fast. Go.'

Hotstepper tried to continue. 'I would –'

Torn Moon silenced him again. 'I must see this with my own eyes. Show me.'

Hotstepper and Nibbler led the way back up to higher altitudes. Once there, Hotstepper pointed to the west. 'There, Elder.'

Torn Moon took in the sight of the slow but steady stream of Stowyrms and growled. She looked back at her warring children, then back once more to the enemy's line of reinforcements. With mounting tension, she began to open and shut her talons.

'Bad news never travels in ones or twos but ever arrives in an unwelcome crowd.' She paused to run tricky calculations through her mind. 'It does not look good,' she admitted with a grim shake of her head. She addressed Hotstepper: 'Do you think yourself capable of stemming the flow?'

'Not by myself. I need assistance.'

'Don't we all . . .' Frustrated, she clenched her talons so tightly that her knuckles popped like gun shots. 'Take Last Laugh, Thief Cutter, Rocksteady and their crews.'

Hotstepper blinked. 'Elder, that's only sixty-three.'

'It's all I can afford.' Torn Moon looked over her shoulder to see that a backlog of messengers had arrived and more were spiralling up from the battlefield. Time had expired and she had more than one desperate affair to juggle. 'Hotstepper; little Keeper: get this done.'

52

The Jade Tower

As they left Torn Moon, Charlie's mind raced. 'How long will it take us to fly to the Western Mountains?' she asked.

'Three hours if we push it,' replied Hotstepper.

'That's going to be too long,' grunted Charlie. The battle around them had reached a new intensity. The noise of warfare, the cries of the dying and the wounded, and the clash of blades filled her ears. 'If you can get me to E'Jaaz, I can see to it that we reach the Western Mountains quicker than three hours.'

'You're thinking of opening a Portal, yes?'

'Yeah.'

'That won't work, Charlie of the Keepers. You need a Triad of Keepers to open a Portal large enough for Winged Ones to use. We're going to have to fly.'

'What if you power E'Jaaz and me up with some dragonsblood?' argued Charlie. 'Wouldn't that do the trick?'

Hotstepper frowned. 'It might work but you must remember that our blood is not a gift to use lightly or frequently. The Human body cannot take too much of it and if abused the repercussions can be fatal.'

Charlie heard his warning but she didn't care. She wanted

to finish all of this as swiftly as possible and, besides, she didn't think the Winged Ones would be able to hold back another three hours' worth of Stowyrm reinforcements.

'Hotstepper, look around you. Everyone is taking risks. How can you ask me not to?'

A tangle of Winged Ones and Stowyrms clashed beneath them. The shrieks and snarls sounded harsh and guttural. The air stank with discharged electricity, blood and sweat. Hotstepper could not deny the validity of her point.

'All right, we –'

But Charlie, full of resolve, cut him short. 'Good. Get Last Laugh, Thief Cutter, Rocksteady and their crews and meet me and Nibbler at the Jade Tower. I'll sort out the rest.'

Eyes blazing, she gestured to Nibbler, then clambered from her seat and jumped.

'Charlie, what are you –' she heard Hotstepper call, but his words were cut short as the rushing of wind filled her ears.

Feeling confident in her abilities, Charlie shut her eyes and breathed deep. She could feel the sun on her back, the wind on her face and the flicker of strengthening resolve pulsing in her chest. She flexed her hands and summoned her Will, allowing it to flare around her so that she fell like a blazing comet. Opening her eyes, she saw a layer of brawling Winged Ones and Stowyrms approach from below. She fell through these, narrowly missing the spiked tail of a Stowyrm, then she was past and rushing on towards the ground. The Stomen, wise now to bodies falling from the sky, spotted her coming and hastened out of the way.

She laughed at them.

She opened her arms wide as though ready to embrace

the ground. Her grin grew even wider as she felt her friend's arms close round her.

'I've got you,' grunted Nibbler.

Angling his wings, he pulled them out of their dive. Once they were horizontal, Charlie tore open a Portal. Nibbler tucked his wings in and together the two shot through the glowing circle to find themselves in familiar airspace over the Jade Tower.

The building was in a terrible state. Whole balconies had been sheared clean off, walls had been pierced by projectiles and many of the magnificent windows had been shattered. But the building still stood, its jade- and turquoise-coloured flags and pennants were still flying proudly and people still guarded its gates.

'Think you can drop us by the Jade Circle?'

'No problem,' said Nibbler.

He circled the building once, dropped altitude, then expertly flared his wings so they could both alight on the large viewing balcony. Several councillors and a couple of guards jumped but relaxed when they recognized their guests. Nibbler and Charlie spared them brief nods of greeting, then pushed their way inside.

'Me little Hippotomi!' cried Jensen when he spotted her. Rushing over, he pulled her into a hug. 'Ya nearly gave me a heart attack when that Stoman dragged ya through that Portal.' He pushed her out to arm's length so he could better study her. 'Well, I'm glad ya're safe and . . .' He fell silent as he caught sight of her mangled hand. 'Aw, no, lass. No, no, no.' He grabbed her hand between his. 'How did dis happen? Tell me who did dis ta ya? I'll rip their heart out!'

Charlie couldn't help but grin. Jensen's concern warmed her heart more than the memory of her missing finger pulled her down. 'Forget it,' she said. 'It's nothing I can't sort out by myself. But, Jensen, I can't talk. We're in a world of trouble and I need to move fast to make sure that we succeed. Is E'Jaaz about? And is he awake?'

Upon realizing they had visitors, Lady Dridif had moved closer. 'He's healed and he is awake,' she said, 'but he's weak from blood loss. Wot's the issue, Charlie, and is it something that we can help with? And while I'm being inquisitive, would ya please tell me wot those things with wings are? They look like Wyrms . . .'

Feeling the need for speed, Charlie rushed through her explanation. 'They're Wyrms made from stone and maybe something else, and Marsila wanted to call them Stowyrms so the name has kind of stuck. The other thing is, Bane or his god is making them and even though the Winged Ones can destroy them, they keep coming, so we need to get over to the Western Mountains as quickly as possible so we can stop them. And I need E'Jaaz so we can open a Portal large enough for some of the Winged Ones to get through.'

Dridif's eyes grew wide as she heard Charlie speak. Deciding not to waste time with any more questions, she snapped her fingers at the captain of her guard. 'Bring in E'Jaaz Keeper straight away!'

'Ma'am,' said the captain. He and some of his men hastened from the room.

'How are ya going ta stop these Stowyrms?' asked Jensen.

'We're going to crush Bane and his god,' said Charlie.

Jensen and Dridif stared at her, uncertain if she was telling the truth or trying to spin some type of jest.

'Really?' asked Jensen.

'Really,' said Charlie.

Hearing the certainty in Charlie's voice, Lady Dridif smiled grimly. 'Good,' she said. 'That's the best news I've heard in the last seven years.'

'Ma'am,' said a guard, interrupting their conversation. 'E'Jaaz Keeper.'

Charlie was horrified when she caught sight of him. He was held up, not by Treman guards, who would have been too short, but by two of the Human councillors. His face was ashen, his cheeks gaunt, and his hair, normally well kept, was in a state of disarray.

'I know, I know,' said E'Jaaz. His voice was hoarse and the chuckle that eased between his lips was dry. 'I look like I've been dragged through the briar patch. Truth be told, I've had better days and better hangovers, but at least they got that cursed arrow out my leg.'

'Are you . . . OK?' asked Charlie.

'The docs say I lost a lot of blood but if I rest up I should be fighting fit in a week or two.' He paused to look out the window at the chaotic warfare raging over the grasslands. Making a wry face he added, 'Of course, the way things are going I don't think I'll be getting a chance to rest up. Still, I have your friend Apple Crumble to thank for healing my broken bone. Without his talent for stonesinging, the docs say I'd be limping for the rest of . . . however long I've got left to live.'

'It's Crumble Shard,' said Charlie, automatically correcting her friend's name but all the while unable to believe the state E'Jaaz was in. If he was too weak to help, her plan could fall apart. 'Listen . . . E'Jaaz . . .'

'Spit it out, Charlie. I might not look fit to dance right now but you know I'm always game for mischief, so tell me what's on your mind.'

'We need to put a stop to Bane's Stowyrms and we need to do it now. So what I want to know is can you help me open a Portal big enough to get the Winged Ones to the Western Mountains?'

'What? All of them?'

'No, just sixty-three of them, sixty-four when you add Hotstepper.'

'Sixty-five when you add me,' said Nibbler.

'Right,' agreed Charlie. 'Bane has twisted his barrier against travelling but it's still there so we need to open a Portal just outside the Western Mountains' metropolitan border. Any closer and it won't work. Think you can help with that?'

They all looked at E'Jaaz.

He shrugged one of his arms from the councillor's supporting shoulders and, holding his hand aloft, he summoned his Will. It was feeble and flickered weakly above his fingertips. Frowning, he tried to call more but he had reached his limit. He shook his head with a grimace.

'Sorry, kid, looks like I'm a little low right now.'

Shadows blurred past the window, followed seconds later by the sound of flapping wings and the rush of wind. The tower trembled as Last Laugh, Thief Cutter, Rocksteady and their crews landed on perches and balconies. Hotstepper himself landed right on the balcony that Charlie and Nibbler had only recently used.

Charlie turned to E'Jaaz. 'What would you say to a little pick-me-up?'

53

Goodbyes

The Winged Ones repositioned themselves so that when Lady Dridif stood on the balcony it was Last Laugh who greeted her.

'Hello, old friend,' said Last Laugh. He lowered one of his great paws so Dridif could lay her hand upon his.

'Last Laugh,' said Dridif with a catch in her voice. 'How I've missed ya.'

'It would appear that our Chrysalis cycle has dragged on longer than normal.'

'We have Bane ta thank for that.'

'And thank him we shall,' growled Last Laugh. 'Rock-steady?'

Rocksteady descended to join them on the balcony. A Stoman councillor approached with two large chalices on a tray. Before he could hold these up for Rocksteady, E'Jaaz stopped him.

'We'll only need one of these,' he said.

Charlie looked at him askew. 'What? One? E'Jaaz, what're you doing?'

'You're going to the Western Mountains, right?'

'Of course,' replied Charlie.

328 *www.keeperoftherealms.com*

'Well, you'll need all the Will you can summon so there's no point in wasting any here.' E'Jaaz gave her a wistful smile. 'I'll open the Portal.'

'What? No, you won't. It should take three of us to do it. Two will be a struggle but for one it'll be nearly impossible!' Charlie wanted to smack her head in disbelief but controlled herself. 'And look at the state of you! You're too tired. I felt bad enough asking you to do it with me, but there's no way I'm going to let you do this by yourself. No way, no how.'

Feeling the sun on his face and the wind in his hair, E'Jaaz chuckled. 'Ah, Charlie, you're going to become a legendary Keeper! A Keeper that playwrights will want to write about and bards to sing of . . . but that's when you're older and right now I'm an adult and you're still a young 'un so I'm pulling seniority. Save the dragonsblood for when you need it. *Really* need it. It *is* a restorative but take too much and there can be repercussions. Last Laugh, Rocksteady, you'll back me on this, won't you?'

'It is your choice,' rumbled Last Laugh, 'and your call to make. I concur.'

'Not a wise decision,' said Rocksteady, 'but under our current circumstances I agree.'

With no further ceremony, Rocksteady used a talon to part the flesh on his paw. He allowed his blood to drip into one of the chalices before sealing the wound with a jet of flame.

E'Jaaz pulled Charlie into a hug and whispered into her ear. 'You know this is the best way and if our roles were reversed you would do the same. Now get this done and should you run into the Delightful Brothers or Bane, you give them some solid payback from me and Marsila.' He pulled her even tighter and repeated his entreaty. 'For Marsila!'

Releasing her from his embrace, he grabbed the chalice and held it aloft. 'To victory, to Sylvaris and to missing friends. Bottoms up!' With a flash of his old cheeky grin, he downed the contents of the chalice.

He started screaming almost straight away and it was only the two councillors on either side of him who prevented him from falling. Charlie and the others looked on with horror.

When it was done E'Jaaz pushed the councillors aside and stood upright. His skin glittered, his hair writhed as though unseen fingers were running through it and trickles of golden Will seeped from his eyes to join the halo of gold that flickered over his head.

'If you've got any last goodbyes to say, say them now,' he said with a voice that cracked with barely restrained might.

Charlie grabbed one of Lady Dridif's arms. 'Where's Kelko and Sic Boy?'

'They're on the battle line.'

Charlie grimaced. She had expected as much but wasn't any happier for having her fears confirmed. 'Just . . . just . . .'

'I'll do wot I can to keep them safe,' said Dridif, offering her support without being so foolish as to promise anything.

'And Crumble Shard?'

'He's with all the other healers. He's a good boy and with all the lives he's saved he's worth more than his weight in gold.'

'OK, that's good.' Charlie nodded to herself. Even though

she wouldn't have a chance to say a final goodbye to her friends she at least knew they were where they were supposed to be, doing what they were supposed to be doing. Heroes in their own right.

'At least I can say goodbye to Jensen.'

She turned but he was no longer by her side. Panicked, she went to stick her head back into the Jade Chamber.

'Hey, me little Hippotomi! Up here!'

Charlie's mouth dropped when she saw Jensen astride Rocksteady's back.

'Not much for a chancellor ta do once the fighting starts,' he said with a shrug and a smile. 'Besides, I've given away most of me fortune so there's not really that much left for me ta do. I'm coming with ya. Lady Dridif, do ya best ta keep Salixia safe for me.'

'I'll do wot I can,' agreed Dridif.

Thrilled that Jensen would be accompanying her to the Western Mountains, Charlie gazed around the balcony one last time. 'So that just leaves –'

'Me,' said Dridif. Stepping forward, she pulled Charlie into a surprisingly strong hug. 'Me thanks for freeing the Winged Ones and for all yer've done for me city. Yer've done me and yer parents proud. Now, wotever happens out there, remember yer've always got friends and family waiting for ya back here. Leaf bless ya, Charlie Keeper.'

'Ready?' asked E'Jaaz.

Charlie nodded, took one of his flaming hands and pressed it between her own. 'Thank you, E'Jaaz,' she said. 'Thank you for everything.'

He nodded and Charlie turned to look for Nibbler. To

her shock, she was suddenly plucked from the balcony and plonked between Hotstepper's shoulders.

'You can ride with our little brother another day,' said Last Laugh. 'But today, for battle, you will need a little more power, so ride with Hotstepper you shall.'

One by one the Winged Ones peeled off from the Jade Tower, spread their wings wide and began to circle the building. Faster and faster they went until the wind roared past their ears.

'E'Jaaz Keeper!' roared Last Laugh. 'We are ready!'

Squinting her eyes against the fierce draught, Charlie glanced towards the balcony. She saw E'Jaaz blaze like a volcano, an explosion of warm yellow light and the briefest flash of a large Portal, then they were through and the Jade Tower and her friends disappeared from sight.

54

The Western Mountains

The Winged Ones burst over the mountains with great cracks of thunder. Roaring with delight, they beat their wings with broad thrumming sweeps and sped past craggy peaks, jagged crests and low-lying puffs of scattered cloud. The air was crisp and, even though there was thick cloud at higher altitudes, strong shafts of sunlight lit the landscape.

Charlie, riding upon Hotstepper's back, felt her stomach churn with worry for E'Jaaz. She had concerns that opening such a large Portal by himself, even strengthened by the dragonsblood, could cause complications. She crossed her fingers in the hope that he suffered no permanent damage.

Another wave of nervous excitement washed through her and she gripped Hotstepper's shoulders tighter. This was it. The end. No matter what happened when they reached the Western Mountains, for good or for ill she would see this through. Her time had come.

Doubts, fatigue and concerns aside, she was surprised to find that she felt OK. She breathed in deeply and felt full of life. The bracing wind felt amazing on her skin and when the Winged Ones soared through a shaft of sunlight she was mesmerized by all the colours of their glittering scales. Life, just as Rumbling Hunger had said, could be good.

'Just got to make sure I stay alive long enough to enjoy it,' she whispered as she held her ruined hand aloft. It was a stark reminder of all the things that could go disastrously wrong.

'What was that?' asked Hotstepper.

'Nothing,' she replied.

Jensen turned so he could wave at her from Rocksteady's back. She was just about to mirror the gesture when she caught a flicker of motion out of the corner of her eye. Twisting round, she saw a line of twelve Stowyrms flying east to join the Stoman army and just as she had seen them they had spotted her too. Now they broke formation and sped towards the Winged Ones.

'Hotstepper!'

He followed her outstretched finger.

'Last Laugh!' he hollered. 'Foes to the north!'

After a moment's contemplation, Last Laugh shouted his commands. 'Remember, we're not here to fight these, we're here for the source! Stay low and keep up!'

Whipping his tail, he hurtled down the sheer slope of a mountain, then disappeared into a bank of cloud. The others followed. Still not used to these gut-wrenching dives, Charlie yelped when she felt the unfamiliar acceleration (and was slightly reassured to hear Jensen's shriek of horror), then they were through the cloud and racing alongside the walls of a steep valley. Speeding onward, they churned over ancient glaciers, scraped above razor-sharp mountain passes and whisked through the spray of cascading waterfalls.

Minutes later they passed their first Stoman dwelling. Smooth and organic-looking, like some wonderful seashell, it flashed beneath their feet. Charlie caught a glimpse of startled faces – a young boy trying to herd shirasheer and mountain huffalo, an old woman with a pack of firewood hanging from her back – then they were gone. In the next valley they saw more buildings and more people, then a small hamlet, then a village. Every once in a while they would see statues too, some large, some huge and one so big that it was nearly the same size as the mountains that neighboured it.

Seeing the increase in population density, Charlie knew they must be nearing their destination. With this too came the knowledge that she would soon be facing her adversary. Trying to ignore the sudden surge of stage-fright, she pushed aside the last vestiges of doubt and summoned her Will. It flickered reassuringly around her and left a trail of yellow sparks to flutter from her knuckles as it was caught in the wind.

The Winged Ones felt their approaching destination too. They began to growl and bark and allow streams of flame to seep from their nostrils and the sides of their mouths. Jensen, after giving her one final wave of reassurance, pulled his Bramblesword from its scabbard and began tying it to his fist with a length of green ribbon so it would not fall from his grasp, no matter what.

Gusting around a valley corner, they were greeted by two gigantic peaks that had once been mountains but had since been carved into the likeness of two Stoman warriors armed with sword and spear. Arms outstretched, their weapons

met to form an archway of sorts. The sky above was heavy
with turbulent clouds and the ground beneath thick with
buildings. Beyond the archway lay the city. And in the city
centre there lay a dark maw. Its walls seemed sheer but it
disappeared into the shadows before Charlie could guess at
its depth. And from this sucking pit of darkness a steady
stream of Stowyrms snaked and whirled into the air before
disappearing like bad omens into the roiling clouds overhead.

'Destroy the source first!' cried Last Laugh, repeating his
earlier commands. 'Then we find that upstart Bane and show
him the severity of justice!'

The Winged Ones began to growl in earnest. The sound
of their ferocity rumbled across the cityscape, causing the
startled inhabitants to look up and point in alarm. Tails
lashing, wind roaring around them and flames bursting with
greater frequency from their mouths, the dragons stormed
over the city of the Western Mountains.

They hugged the buildings and swerved beneath the legs
of huge statues. At last they flew out over the dark maw that
lay in the centre and –

Time slowed.

Charlie's eyes widened. The maw was not the bottomless
hole she had imagined but a canyon, wide and deep, and it
was this that held the city proper. With swift realization it
dawned upon Charlie that the buildings above had been
nothing more than suburbs. As Hotstepper's wings spread
wide, she leaned out so she could drink in all the details.
Shapes, statues and dwellings had been carved into the
canyon's walls but these were minor compared to the

gargantuan buildings that reared from the canyon's floor. Twelve and thirteen storeys tall, they loomed like a herd of gigantic beasts that, pressed close to one another, had no space to grow other than upward. But it was the shape of the buildings that really drew Charlie's eyes and caused her to gasp. They had been formed to resemble Stoman faces. Some sneered and posed with lofty expressions; others appeared cold and distant. Smaller buildings, crammed between the larger, had been sculpted into clenched fists. The Stoman metropolis was the very antithesis of Sylvaris. Where the Tremen had celebrated life and growth, this urban cityscape revered and revelled in might and militant power. Heavy with shadows and illuminated weirdly with glowing crystals, it bristled with an uneasy atmosphere.

Charlie blinked and time renewed its normal speed.

'THE SOURCE!' commanded Last Laugh in a voice that rivalled Torn Moon's. 'FIND THE SOURCE!'

Hotstepper followed these hasty instructions with words of his own.

'No matter what, Charlie of the Keepers, you hold tight and do not let go. Do not let go!'

Charlie grunted a non-committal reply. His words were wise but she was unsure how she felt about Last Laugh's directions to destroy Bane's dark god first rather than taking on Bane. Half-composed thoughts of abandoning the Winged Ones to find her parents came to mind, but before she could think these through Last Laugh raced towards a rocky chasm that zigzagged between a row of Stoman monuments. The chasm was dark and forbidding and glowed with a moody red light that suggested the distant presence of lava.

From this unappealing passage a new flight of Stowyrms appeared. Shrieking and hooting, they slalomed between two buildings that looked like a fist and a screaming face before gaining enough height to climb over the canyon's rim and disappear from sight.

Unbelievably, for all the Winged Ones' ferocious growls, the Stowyrms appeared not to have noticed them.

Yet.

Rocksteady and Last Laugh took the lead. Their crews, Hotstepper and Nibbler squeezed close behind them. Faster and faster they flew. Growling with eagerness and pent-up rage that screamed with the need to be released, they fell towards the chasm.

Straight into another wave of Stowyrms.

Last Laugh collided with two of the beasts and, gnashing and rending at each other, they disappeared into the darkness. Rocksteady managed to tear the wings off an adversary, then he too disappeared. The others, unable to check their momentum, also piled into the Stowyrms.

Charlie was blinded for a moment by a wave of fire. As this cleared she swiftly ducked beneath a row of glistening teeth, then ducked the other way to avoid a spiked tail.

Then she too was in the chasm.

Cracks of brilliant blue and white lightning pushed back the shadows. Charlie caught flashes of wrestling figures and nightmare shapes. Fierce growls, shrieks and piercing whistles tore at her ears. Something slammed against her, knocking her part-way down Hotstepper's spine. Fighting to regain her balance, she clawed herself back up to his shoulders. There came yet another flash of lightning; she caught a glimpse of an approaching Stowyrm, all teeth and buzzing wings, then darkness again. The next blow, unseen and violent, was so powerful that it knocked her clean off Hotstepper and, with a yell of surprise, she found herself free-falling.

Through the darkness.

Surrounded by growling beasts.

55

Falling in the Dark

As Charlie fell, fear clenched her throat so tightly that she struggled to breathe.

Something slapped against her. Panicking, she tried to spin round only to feel the thrum of wings brush through her hair.

'Hotstepper!' she yelled at the top of her voice.

Getting no response, she cried, 'Nibbler!'

A fork of lightning momentarily lit the air and Charlie found herself, not as she'd hoped amongst friends, but surrounded by Stowyrms.

Darkness fell again.

Feeling the fear well up to the point where she thought she might explode, Charlie instinctively opened a Portal . . . only to realize that she'd completely forgotten about Bane's barrier to travel. She saw the outline of her Portal and heard a roar, then a whoosh that, constrained within the walls of the chasm, was almost deafening. There came another flicker of lightning, then a flare of flame. Charlie saw Winged Ones battling overhead and, beneath her, a torrent of black orchids jettisoning from her Portal.

Darkness again.

Panicking, and certain that at any minute she would feel the teeth of a Stowyrm closing round her waist, Charlie pulled deeply on her Will and thrust a protective shield beneath her feet. She slammed against something, bounced, slammed again, then came to an abrupt and painful impact that jarred her feet and rattled her bones.

'Ooooff!'

As she lay there, winded and unable to move, she caught a final flicker of light and then nothing. The furious sound of battle receded, leaving her very much alone. Still cocooned in fear, she was hesitant to move her limbs in case she found something broken. Unpleasant memories of the cave beneath the Stubborn Citadel, Lallinda the Daemon Queen, Edge Darkmount, her broken leg and of being buried alive flickered before her eyes. Panting, she felt sweat drip down her spine and pool in her lower back. Then she heard something rustle in the darkness, shrieked and jumped to her feet.

Brandishing waves of yellow Will, she held her hands aloft like blazing torches. The rustle came again and she spun round to find not a Stowyrm or a Shade as she had thought but a teetering pile of black orchids that whispered as they cascaded downward. There were more beneath her feet and with a flash of insight she realized that although the Portal had not acted as a Gateway, or a weapon, it had instead cushioned her fall.

'No broken bones, that's good,' she whispered.

Putting more power into her hands, she studied her surroundings; she seemed to be in a smaller side tunnel that led away from the main chasm. Seeing a subtle red glow, she nervously headed towards it but stopped when she heard more rustling. It was the orchids tumbling over a lip and out of sight. She edged forwards and found herself peering into the throat of the main chasm: one direction led upward to the distant city (she couldn't believe how far she had fallen!) and the other direction led down to some unseen destination. From the glow and the smell of sulphur, Charlie assumed that molten lava was in some way involved.

There was no sign of the Winged Ones.

Grasping a craggy handhold, she leaned a little further out in the hope of locating the end of the chasm, some sign of a suitable destination, or at least some companions.

'Companions would be good,' she muttered.

She screamed and leaped back as a nightmare array of teeth suddenly lunged towards her. Scrambling back into a pile of orchids, she watched in horror as another column of Stowyrms shrieked past her on their way to the surface.

Heart pounding, fingers shaking, she backed even further away from the chasm. A calmer, more sensible part of her brain realized she was close to losing her cool and that panic was setting in.

'What would Rumbling Hunger say about fear?' she whispered. 'Probably something stupid about turning it into a Fluttercarp and eating it . . .'

She knew it was a little odd to be talking to herself but she also knew that it helped to hold back the terror. Squeezing her fingers so the nails dug into her palms, she tried to distract herself with memories of travelling through the Winged Realm. Images of floating islands, indigo skies and riding Hotstepper's back came to mind, as did the sound of Rumbling Hunger's deep laugh.

'No, he wouldn't say anything about Fluttercarp. Hunger would say *Use your fear . . .*' She paused to give some thought to the matter. 'Use it as a tool to help me get out of here.'

Feeling a bit more in control and realizing she still had a job to do, Charlie once again summoned her Will so she could better look around. The chasm's throat lay in *that* direction, so she chose to investigate the other direction. Forcing Will from both hands, she crept forward and was pleasantly surprised to find that the cave was not a dead end but in fact offered another way out.

Using her fear to spur herself on, she decided to see where it would take her.

The flicker of her Will allowed her to see where she was going. Unfortunately it also cast eerie shadows that did little for her confidence. It didn't take much for her imagination to start working against her and she started mistaking stalactites for Rhinospider legs and weird rocks for Shades waiting to pounce. Gritting her teeth, she pushed onward.

The tunnel, not easy to navigate in the first place, began to contract and soon Charlie had to hunch over as she progressed. The roof grew even closer and she was forced to her hands and knees, then on to her stomach, with no choice but to squirm along. Claustrophobia began to kick in and Charlie worried that the tunnel, already pressing against her, might collapse at any moment. Alternating between whimpering and cursing her own shortcomings, she nonetheless pressed onward. After all, what choice did she have?

Suddenly she heard a *click-click* from ahead and froze. The last thing she needed right now was to come face to face with a spitting Shade.

'Going to have to show it who's boss,' she blustered.

Pushing more Will in front of her, she squirmed forward, expecting at any moment her enemy to pounce on her. As she rounded a sharp curve that caused her spine to scrape uncomfortably against the cramped ceiling, she spotted not the Shade she had expected but a fat toad. The sides of its chubby back glowed with a soft orange luminescence.

The toad and Charlie stared at one another.

With a hop and a plop, the toad leaped on her back, jumped along her legs, then disappeared the way she had come. Charlie blinked in astonishment. Not sure what to make of the weird experience but glad it had been nothing more unpleasant, she wriggled onward. As she persevered, the tunnel started to expand and she was once again able to get back on to her hands and knees. Another toad cheerfully hopped past her. Eventually the tunnel widened to the point where she could stand and, rounding another bend, she found herself in a cave.

It was so full of fat toads that it glowed with enough orange light for Charlie to see without the need of her Will. Skirting a pond, she listened to their chirps and ribbets. At the far side of the cavern she was dismayed to find a dead end. Just as she was about to slap her forehead in frustration she noticed a large grille implanted in the wall. Unwilling to go back the way she had come, she put her hands on the lattice and gave it an experimental tug.

It didn't move.

'I'm not going back!' protested Charlie. The thought of returning to the dark chasm and the Stowyrms filled her with dread. 'I'm not!'

She filled herself with Will, grabbed the grille and ripped it from the wall in one effortless motion.

Charlie looked at the grille in astonishment. When she let it drop from her hands it *clank-clunked* with a sound indicative of great weight.

She blinked. 'Well, what do you know?' She was surprised at her own strength. 'Fear does have its uses after all.'

Feeling more confident, she waved goodbye to the cheerful toads and leaped into the vent.

56

Fear

Jensen clung tightly to Rocksteady with one hand and struck out with his Bramblesword whenever there was lightning to see by and a Stowyrm to strike. Regretting his decision not to wear armour, he gritted his teeth and hoped he would escape this chaos and madness with all his limbs intact.

The soft red glow intensified and he was almost blinded as they entered a new cavern complex that was partially submerged under a broad river of lava. Coughing on the unpleasant gases, he squinted over Rocksteady's head to peer in front of them. The red river trailed onward and just before stalactites obscured the view he saw a star glittering in the distance. Instinct told him that this was probably the source they were looking for. He turned to share the news with Charlie, only to find her and Hotstepper missing. Just as he was about to cry out in alarm, Hotstepper plunged from the tunnel with two Stowyrms grappling at his throat. Charlie was not on his back. The sight sent a shiver of panic slamming down Jensen's spine.

'Rocksteady, we're a man down!'

'We're more than a man down,' said Rocksteady. 'We're

missing a good quarter of our number. The fools must have taken a wrong turn in the darkness.'

'I'm not talking about Winged Ones, I'm talking about Charlie. She's missing and Hotstepper needs help!'

Heeding Jensen's call, Rocksteady spun round and went to his sibling's aid. He sank his teeth into a Stowyrm's tail and flung the creature into the lava. Free of one of his antagonists, Hotstepper was able to finish off the other.

'Where's Charlie?' shouted Jensen.

Hotstepper spat the taste of Stowyrm from his mouth and growled. 'Chaos! It is pure chaos up there! The young Keeper was knocked from my back during the ruckus!'

'Well, wot are we waiting for?'

Hotstepper didn't reply but nodded to show his willingness to find their young colleague.

Rocksteady, however, shook his head. 'We cannot go back for one soul. Not when so many are at stake. We must continue!'

'I'm not leaving Charlie!' protested Jensen.

'I cannot afford to divide my numbers any further. I have lost some of my crew in that maze of tunnels and I know not where they are! All I can hope is that those who are lost are causing enough chaos inside the Western Mountains to keep Bane occupied. But as for the rest of us, we must continue with the task at hand. We must!'

'I can't leave her up there,' repeated Jensen. 'I'm sorry but I've got ta go.'

'And how will you find her without wings?' asked Rocksteady.

'I'll take him,' said Hotstepper.

Unwilling to argue but making his displeasure known, Rocksteady allowed Jensen the time to jump to his brethren's back.

'Luck be with us all!' called Rocksteady, then returned to his allotted task.

Hotstepper flailed his wings until he was facing the other way. He waited until the rest of the Winged Ones exited the tunnel and prepared to ascend, but halted when a smaller shape burst from the shadows with a flutter of wings. It was Nibbler.

'Hey, what are you doing on Hotstepper's back?' he asked in confusion. 'Did you swap seats with Charlie?'

'We lost her in the tunnel!' said Jensen.

Nibbler frowned and, without waiting for them, sped back the way he'd come. Hotstepper and Jensen raced to join him.

Kicking out yet another grille, Charlie wriggled free from the vent and dropped to the floor below to find herself in a gloomy tunnel that stank of decaying matter. The walls were rough and craggy, and the floor dry with the dust of ages. There were flickering torches hanging on brackets but they were few and far between and did little to push back the shadows. Both directions looked unappealing so Charlie picked one at random. As she trotted along she heard a soft scrape from behind. She peered back the way she had come but could see nothing. Assuming it was just another of the fat toads, she continued on her way.

Then froze when she realized her mistake. If it had been a toad she would have seen its luminescence.

Gulping, she spun round and pushed a questioning flicker of Will into the darkness. It revealed a Rhinospider that had been stealthily hunting her. As Charlie gazed at its row of beady eyes, bloated body and spindly legs, she felt a surge of arachnophobia rise in her gorge. The thing scuttled forward and pounced. Charlie yelled and, unwilling to touch it with her fists, instead beat it back with a flurry of Will until it crumpled into a heap. Panting heavily, she checked there was no chance of it bothering her again, then turned and ran.

Seconds later, she looked back again at the sound of yet another rustle and a hiss from behind. She raised her flaming hands. She had feared another Rhinospider but was horrified to find herself instead facing a full pack of Shades. Having lost the element of surprise, they howled towards her. Panicked, Charlie slammed a wall of Will across the passageway. She paused to watch as they struck and spat at her glimmering barrier. When she was certain they couldn't get past she fled once more.

Only to stagger to a stop.

Looking ahead, she could see no end to the tunnel. She groaned as she understood the ramifications: the further she travelled from her shield, the harder it became to hold. She wouldn't be able to maintain her barrier long enough for her to escape this subterranean passageway.

That meant she was going to have to face the Shades.

She hesitantly made her way back. They were still there, still slamming and pounding at the constraining layer of gold. She forced herself to look at them. As she stared at their inky flesh, their writhing tendrils and clawed append- ages, she became aware that this was nothing she hadn't seen before. She had fought dozens and dozens of Shades and had survived.

Her fear dwindled and a glimmer of anger took its place.

The Shades were a strong sign of Bane's blight across the land and as long as they roamed free Bellania would strug- gle to bloom.

'Are you sure you want to come and get me?' she asked them.

The Shades didn't answer her but continued to strike the wall.

'Are you sure?' she yelled and struck one of her own fists against the barrier, causing it to spark violently.

The Shades exploded into a frenzy, spitting and hissing as they tried even harder to reach her.

'Right! You want it, you got it!'

Tugging the shield aside, she raised her burning hands and slammed into the pack.

It took her less time than she'd thought.

As the shadowy remnants of the Shades evaporated, she pulled back her lips and howled. She was done with fear. If anyone was to feel a sense of dread it would be her enemies, not her. Growling like a beast, she hurtled down the tunnel.

And if she encountered any more Shades, Rhinospiders or random creepy-crawlies she would make them sorry.

57

Anger

Rocksteady and his crew pushed and fought their way deeper into the tunnel. The light that they assumed to be their destination drew closer but with it came an increase in opposition. More and more Stowyrms appeared in a steady stream that bogged them down. Metre by metre, he and his crew clawed and bit and lashed their way forward, ripping the wings off their opponents or shattering them with great forks of lightning. But it was a slow advance. Too slow for Rocksteady's liking. As another trickle of Stowyrms approached, it was the final nudge that tipped the balance of power against them. Their advance stumbled to a halt.

Stalemate.

The combat intensified and Rocksteady tried to take stock of his forces. It didn't look good: three or four had fallen to the enemy and they were few in number. Too few.

'Thief Cutter!' he cried. 'Where is Last Laugh? Where are the rest of our brethren?'

'We lost him as we descended beneath the Western Mountains. One of my crew thinks they saw him take a wrong turn,' replied Thief Cutter. 'And Last Laugh was not the only one to disappear. Half his crew tried to follow him too! This is a shambles! Should we fall back and regroup?'

'No! If they are lost, they are lost! We must push on!' Rocksteady raised his voice so all the Winged Ones could hear him. 'Keep going, we are almost there! Push! Push!'

After finally finding a way out of the gloomy tunnel Charlie had progressed up a long, rickety set of stairs, thick with cobwebs and discarded bones, to find herself in a huge hallway decorated with imposing statues and illuminated by glowing crystals that hung from the ceiling.

Again uncertain as to which direction to take, Charlie was about to pick one at random when a Winged One burst through a wall, careened through another, then disappeared on its way to wherever it was going in a rumble of destruction and a cloud of dust and debris.

Amazed, Charlie just stood there. She thought the Winged One looked like it belonged to Last Laugh's crew, but what was it doing there? Was it as lost as she was?

She heard shouts of fury and before she could think to hide a crowd of Stonesingers and Stomen appeared, intent on chasing the Winged One. Many of them didn't see her and sped onward. However, those who did notice stopped to stare.

The soldiers looked furious. Hefting heavy cudgels and cruel maces, they glared at her in astonishment. The Stonesingers, in contrast, appeared quite happy to find someone to vent their cruelty upon. Chanting softly, they caused the purple flames of their power to writhe higher around their forearms.

'Keeper,' grunted one when he noticed the flicker of Will surrounding her.

'Young 'un,' sneered another.

They chuckled and shared mocking stares.

Charlie couldn't be bothered to wait for them to make the first move. Still gorged on anger, she summoned her Will and charged forward with it billowing around her.

Fists blurring, she pummelled two, then three, into submission. Blocking a strike with a flurry of sparks, she cartwheeled into a frothing soldier, then punched another in both knees before finishing him with a blow to the head. Using her small stature to her advantage, she spun and twisted, kneed and kicked her adversaries into submission. As she finished the last of them she found herself standing on the broad chest of one of the fallen Stonesingers. She gazed down into his bleary eyes.

'Which way to Bane's Throne Room?' she asked.

'Loyal,' he mumbled, 'I'm still loyal. You won't get that out of me.'

Growling, she raised her hands theatrically overhead.

'If you don't tell me I'll open a Portal to the Winged Ones' Realm and get them to ask the questions instead.

'Keepers can't open Portals to the Winged Realm, only Gateways,' groaned the Stonesinger. 'And we both know that my lord has barred Portals from working in our city.'

'Oh yeah?' bluffed Charlie. 'Try this for size.'

She tore open a Portal.

The Stonesinger's eyes widened in disbelief as her actions

appeared to prove his words wrong. As the rumble and whoosh of something approaching grew louder, his nerve crumbled. 'Th-that way,' he stuttered, unable to bear the thought of being judged in the Winged Realm. He pointed down the hall.

Charlie grinned and held the screaming Portal open anyway. She waited for a small mound of orchids to fall to the floor before allowing it to close. The following silence was a merciful contrast.

'Oops, guess you were right about the Portal, but thanks anyway,' said Charlie. 'Now normally I'd hang around and do my best to say something witty but my brain's a little scrambled at the moment. So what I'm going to do instead is tuck one of these orchids behind your ear –' she pressed the flower into place – 'and leave you looking pretty. After all, even a big bad Stonesinger like yourself shouldn't feel he has to look like a hard man all the time, right?'

The Stonesinger opened his mouth once or twice like a landlocked fish but was too beaten to say anything.

'No reply? Ah, don't worry. I've got to go – people to beat, giants to topple. You know how it is.'

Charlie scampered off.

Last Laugh was lost. More than lost; he had no idea how to rejoin his crew and comrades and finish his allotted task. Rather than bemoan his error, he jumped at the opportunity to wreak as much chaos as possible, reasoning that it would buy his brethren time to finish off Bane's erroneously titled 'god'.

His duty was first and foremost in his mind as he started his new undertaking. With fire and lightning, claws and muscular tail, he began to slam through the subterranean palace, wrecking all that he could find.

Perhaps, if he was lucky, he might even bump into that arrogant Stoman, Bane. If he did, he would teach him a lesson he would never forget.

The thought brought a smile to his face.

58

The Horror

'Oh, come on!' complained Charlie. 'Lost again? Again?'

Thinking that she was perhaps too old to stamp her feet, she instead crossed her arms and frowned. She had made good progress and, having left the utilitarian corridors behind to reach richer passageways, she was sure she was nearing her goal. She had also encountered fewer soldiers and more servants, which she took as a good sign, but now with no one around to ask directions she was stumped.

She strode forward and opened a door at random.

It was a cleaning cupboard.

'Gah!' Completely forgetting her earlier decision, she stomped her foot, the sound of it striking the marble floor carrying off into the distance.

Almost snarling with frustration, and hoping that she would encounter some idiotic Stonesinger so she could release some anger, she ripped a door off its hinges and – to her surprise – found herself staring into a kitchen of daunting proportions.

On one side she could see pastry chefs working at flour-coated benches mixing batter for cakes and piping melted chocolate into intricate shapes. On the other, hotter side of the kitchen she could see more chefs toiling over steaming pots, flaming woks and bubbling vats. Spits of meat roasted over fires, ovens belched out smoke, and kitchen porters hustled and bustled around in search of potatoes to peel and pots to scrub. Strange scents, spices and the wonderful smell of grilled meat filled her nose and caused her stomach to gurgle with hunger. It had been a long time since she had last eaten.

Screaming constantly over the noise of culinary labour was a gigantic head chef, big even by his race's standards. While Stomen were normally clean-shaven, this man had a long beard that had been neatly tied with the help of a black ribbon. One of his ears had been pierced with a long line of rubies while the other was missing completely. A large white hat hung at a rakish angle and a chef's tunic did little to disguise his muscular physique. In his hands were a cleaver and a rolling pin, but both were so large they could easily have been mistaken for weapons of war rather than the tools of his trade.

When she saw that only a very confused kitchen porter had noticed her entrance, Charlie hastily dropped the door and scampered in. Thinking that she could perhaps get past the brigade of chefs without a fight, she took a deep breath, squared her shoulders and walked through the steam, smoke and flour dust as though she belonged there.

It went well until the moment when an overworked commis chef stepped backwards and nearly tripped over her.

'Watch it!' he said. Then, 'Hey, what are you doing here? Chef! Chef! One of the goods got out of the larder!'

Having absolutely no idea what he was talking about, Charlie picked up a pot and cracked him over the head with it.

Ducking low, she scuttled down to the end of the aisle and slinked round the corner, only to bump into a surprised-looking pastry chef.

'How did you get out?' he asked. With a frown, he tried to pick her up but Charlie was having none of it. Kicking him hard in the shin, she brought him down to her height, then rendered him unconscious with a blow from her glowing fist.

'What is going on?' she muttered in confusion. Clearly these chefs had been working too long in the kitchen heat because they were all mad and making no sense whatsoever.

She stood for a moment, rubbing at her forehead, and decided to get through the kitchen as swiftly as possible so she could return to beating Shades and Stonesingers. At least she knew where she stood with them.

SCCKRMPF!

The head chef's cleaver buried itself into a wooden work station mere centimetres away from her head.

Charlie gulped at the near miss, then looked up the blade, along the length of the chef's arm to stare directly into his cold eyes.

'You've got five seconds to crawl back into the pantry before I cut your limbs off and turn you into seasoned broth!'

That was it. Charlie had had enough. The anger that had been simmering inside her suddenly boiled.

'Cut my limbs off? Don't be a fool! Get out of my way

or I'm going to rip that silly ribbon out of your beard and make you eat it!'

When the head chef failed to budge and instead raised his rolling pin in a threatening gesture, she didn't hesitate to strike but he quickly countered her attack with a twist of his cleaver. Surprised by his skill, Charlie chased him back down the aisle, raining blow after blow on him, but he deflected each with casual sweeps of his blade. This was a man who knew how to use his tool of choice with the same precision that a master swordsman would use his. Sparks flew as metal met Will, and the shouts of the two combatants caused the other chefs to look up from their work in alarm.

Growing ever more furious, Charlie pulled deeper on her Will and was about to really let loose when the head chef swung at her with his rolling pin. Swift as ever, she ducked beneath it, and with its momentum unchecked it cracked against a large pot, spilling its contents all across the floor.

Charlie stopped when she saw the ingredients.

Hands. Lots of hands.

Her anger vanished.

Her stomach heaved.

All this time she had heard rumours of Bane's appetites but this was too much. It was the cold slap in the face that really woke her up to the nasty extent of Bane's twisted cruelty.

A young chef, keen to defend his boss, threw a frying pan at her head. She blocked it without thinking.

'How . . .?' she began but was so overcome with horror that she couldn't finish.

Another chef barrelled down the aisle and attempted to

wrestle her to the ground. She knocked him senseless.

'Why . . .?' she tried again but couldn't get the words to come out of her mouth.

Suddenly all the chefs and kitchen porters piled in with knives, pots, pans and meat hooks held in their calloused hands. Charlie was too preoccupied by her unpleasant discovery to fight with any rage so she knocked them back with efficient but lacklustre movements. Ripping a pan from a kitchen porter's hand, she parried a knife thrust and bashed its owner's toes before throwing the pan with such force that it bowled three chefs from their feet. Still in a state of disbelief, Charlie moved stiffly and, with none of her usual grace, from opponent to opponent until all were groaning or lying still on the tiled floor.

Which just left the head chef.

The two adversaries stared at each other.

The head chef sneered and adjusted his grip on cleaver and pin.

Unfortunately Charlie didn't manage to look quite as cool. Horrified at how the kitchen's scents had at first caused her to salivate with hunger, she grabbed the closest pot and emptied her stomach's contents into it. She wiped her mouth with the back of her hand, her face pale with nausea.

'Why, you filthy little Human piece of meat . . .' jeered the head chef, clearly disgusted that she could do such a thing in his kitchen. 'You're good for nothing. I wouldn't even want to turn you into *pâté*! You're going straight into the slops bin!'

He swung his cleaver at her, then followed up with a thunderous blow from his rolling pin. Charlie, still dizzy with disbelief and revulsion, fell back before his onslaught. Tripping over an unconscious pastry chef, she landed on her backside and was forced to scrabble backwards as the head chef repeatedly slammed his rolling pin into the floor. He pursued her down one aisle and into the next, leaving a trail of broken tiles. Charlie was about to spring back to her feet when one of the kitchen porters revived enough to open his eyes, clamp his fingers round Charlie's shin and pin her to the floor.

'Good!' smirked the head chef. 'Hold her fast!'

He brought the cleaver whistling down.

59

Appetite

Time seemed to slow as the blade fell towards her.

The head chef's face was pulled into a grimace, the ribbon in his beard fluttered and clouds of disturbed flour swirled around his feet. Charlie could hear the high-pitched whistle of some unattended kettle, the excited chuckle of the kitchen porter as he held her fast and beneath all of this the *tha-thud*, *tha-thud* of her beating heart.

Time sped up.

The cleaver, edge glinting with reflected light, sheared towards her at terrifying speed.

Grunting with effort, and still trapped by the kitchen porter, Charlie did her best to parry the blade.

K-CHUNKK!

The blade buried itself in the floor, next to her supporting hand and right in the gap where Charlie's little finger used to be.

Kitchen porter, head chef and Charlie stared at the still-quivering cleaver in a shared moment of disbelief.

Charlie's eyes narrowed. She raised her free leg and slammed her heel against the kitchen porter until he slumped into an unconscious heap. The head chef rushed to free his blade but Charlie held it fast with one hand and grabbed his beard with the other. The head chef's eyes bulged when he realized that, as big as he was, he wasn't able to free himself from her grasp. In a final bid for freedom he swiped at her with the rolling pin but she blocked it with her shin.

'No, no,' protested Charlie, 'we won't be having any of that.' To underline her point she tugged his beard. 'Now, if you don't want me to stuff that rolling pin in your ear I'd strongly suggest that you let it go.' He did as he was told. 'And take your fingers off that big knife too.'

'It's a cleaver,' said the head chef, then shrieked as Charlie gave his beard another painful tug.

'Does it look like I care what the correct culinary term is?' said Charlie. 'Let it go and show me where your larder is.'

Disarmed, he pointed past the pastry section. 'That way.'

Charlie grunted and marched over with him in tow.

'Open it.' She thrust her chin towards the door.

The head chef staggered forward and, still bent double, unlocked the door with clumsy fingers.

They were greeted by rows of tear-stained faces. The larder was crowded with Human and Treman children.

'Oh no . . .' muttered Charlie as she felt something shatter inside her heart. 'How could you . . .?' The chef groaned and the small children shied away as Charlie's Will flickered higher and higher, pushing back the shadows and causing the ground beneath her feet to crack and splinter.

'You!' snarled Charlie. She kicked the head chef's feet from beneath him, then dragged him deep into the larder. The room was long, almost a corridor. Children sat on the

floor and several listless adults were held in cages that lined
both sides of the chilly chamber.

'Get those cages open!'

The head chef, daunted by her aura of Will, pulled keys
from his pocket with shaky fingers. He dropped them several
times but did, eventually, manage to free all the adults.

'Get in,' commanded Charlie.

The head chef eyed the cages uncertainly. 'I won't fit,' he
protested.

Charlie fixed him with her blazing eyes. 'You'd better
make sure you fit or else . . .'

The huge Stoman scrambled into one of the cages and
pulled the door shut with a satisfactory clang. Charlie picked
up a dropped padlock and secured his cage. But she wasn't
done. Reaching in, she yanked the ribbon from his beard.
'Open your mouth.'

The head chef stared back at her with a look of incom-
prehension.

'It's not rocket science,' said Charlie. 'Open your mouth.'

He hesitantly did as he was told. Charlie stuck the ribbon
between his teeth. 'Now chew on this.'

Clearly feeling like an idiot, he chewed.

'Good,' said Charlie. 'Now swallow.'

The chef's eyes bulged. Alarmed at the idea, he shook his
head from side to side.

'You better eat that ribbon,' growled Charlie, 'or I'll rip
that beard off your chin and glue it to your eyebrows. Now
eat the ribbon!'

Coughing, gagging and whimpering, the chef did as he
was told.

'Well done. Now stay here and wait for the Winged Ones to arrive. Oh, and if you get bored just think about all the kids that you cooked and count your lucky stars I'm not putting you in one of your own stew pots.'

She turned to look at the people gathered around her. She guessed there were forty to fifty of them, many too shell-shocked or too emotionally broken to display much excitement. A couple of the adults stood out from the rest. They held themselves upright and seemed better equipped at managing their fear.

'What are your names?' asked Charlie.

'I'm Paila of the Low Cedar,' said the Treman woman. She pointed to the Human next to her. 'He's Ottokar from Alavis and we owe ya our thanks.'

'You can earn my thanks by getting these kids out of here,' said Charlie.

'Out?' Ottokar chuckled with dark humour. 'Do you know where we are? It's going to take more than us two to shepherd this lot out of the Western Mountains.'

Charlie gestured for them to follow her into the kitchen; several of the kids, not wanting to be left alone, trailed after them. She pointed towards the entrance with the torn door. 'Go that way, follow the corridor and keep heading down. I've cleared the way and so long as you keep coming across unconscious bodies you'll know you're on the right path and still safe. Take weapons from the bodies and find a place to hold up and hide. Either I or the Winged Ones will come and get you when it's over.'

'The Winged Ones are here?' asked Paila.

'Yes,' said Charlie. 'Listen.'

Paila and Ottokar shared a look, then cocked their heads to one side.

'I can't hear anything,' said Ottokar after a couple of seconds.

'Ssh,' said Charlie and was rewarded moments later by the faint sound of a distant boom.

The smiles on Paila and Ottokar's faces were a welcome sight.

'OK?' asked Charlie.

The two adults nodded.

'Good,' continued Charlie. 'Get those kids out of here and with a bit of luck I'll see you guys later.'

'Which way are you headed?' asked Ottokar.

'I'm finding Bane,' said Charlie. 'And I don't think you want to be around to see that.'

Ottokar sucked in a sharp breath. 'Yeah, yer probably right about that.'

Charlie nodded one last time, then walked off, feeling confident that if she had found Bane's kitchen, then his Throne Room couldn't be too far away.

'Wait!' urged Paila. 'Wot's yer name?'

'Charlie.' And although the gesture wasn't necessary she showed them her still-flaming hands. 'Charlie Keeper.'

As the children crowded round the adults, Paila and Ottokar gave her a grateful nod.

Charlie waved, then made her exit.

60

Fallen Wings

Stones leaned over and gently nudged his brother. Putting finger to lips, he pointed down the corridor. A long scaly tail was disappearing round the corner.

The two brothers shared a predatory glance. It looked like they had made it back to the Western Mountains in time to join the party. They nudged their Stowyrms forward with masterful ease. The beasts slinked quietly down the corridor and, rounding the corner, they found their prey silhouetted against a wide entrance that opened into a vast shaft. Weapons at the ready, the Delightful Brothers moved forward, then stopped. Stix looked to Stones, and Stones nodded back.

'Hey, Winged One!' called Stix. 'We thought about stabbing you in the back but that would have been too easy. If we're going to do this –'

'And we are,' interjected Stones.

'– then we want this to be memorable,' concluded Stix. 'We're hunters, the best at the game, and we want a conquest worthy of our reputation.'

The Winged One shook its tail like an angered tiger, then turned round. It was Last Laugh.

'The Delightful Brothers,' he said. 'Your reputation does precede you. But I will not fight you. I have more pressing concerns. Leave me and I'll pretend you were never so arrogant as to think that you could challenge a Winged One.'

Stones let loose an arrow. Last Laugh burned it to ash. Both parties knew the shot was easy to parry but that was not the point. It raised the stakes and underlined the Delightful Brothers' deadly intent.

'Ancient and beyond your years I might be,' snarled Last Laugh, 'but I'm not impervious to rage! Leave me now or I will turn you to cinder and ash!'

'Good!' cried Stix. 'That's the spirit!'

'Yes!' roared Stones. 'Show us your fire! Let us dance as only the mighty should!'

Last Laugh let loose a mighty howl that eclipsed Stix and Stones's shouts of encouragement. Sucking in a deep lungful of air, he spat out a great wave of crackling fire that engulfed the corridor. The Stowyrms reared and the Delightful Brothers, quick as a flash, ducked beneath their mounts to use their rocky sides as a barrier to Last Laugh's attack.

Realizing that his fire was not up to the task, Last Laugh unleashed a barrage of lightning. The sound of the Delightful Brothers' laughter floated towards him.

'More!' cackled Stix. 'It'll take more than that!'

Last Laugh snarled and lashed his tail against the walls. As the smoke cleared, the first thing he saw was Stix and Stones's strange cat's eyes staring back at him. With an even louder snarl than before, he surged down the tunnel towards his tenacious foes.

Stix and Stones roared with delight and urged their mounts

forward. With bow and sword in hand, they lunged into combat.

It was a fierce, bloody fight. But when it was done, it was Last Laugh who lay still and the Delightful Brothers who stood victorious.

Stix looked to Stones, and Stones looked back.

'We are the best,' said Stix.

'Brothers like none other,' agreed Stones.

'Hunters,' said Stix.

'Predators,' said Stones.

'The most feared.'

'The mightiest.'

The two slapped hands and pulled the other into a hard embrace.

'To success!' shouted Stones.

'Success!' echoed his brother.

Grinning wickedly, Stones peeled back Last Laugh's lips and helped himself to one of his teeth. He would add this to his necklace that carried proof of all his previous victories. Then, smirking like two children locked in a sweet shop, the brothers pushed Last Laugh over the edge to fall like discarded garbage into the shaft.

Mr Crow flinched as he watched Bane's god continue its work. Its long fingers, blackened skin and mouthless face sickened and terrified him in equal measure. Unable to understand how such a thing could exist, he had secretly taken to calling it the 'charcoal monster'. As he continued to watch from a safe distance the charcoal monster dipped its hands into the bridge and, after a few seconds' manipulation, pulled free four more eggs. They squatted there like inanimate objects until the charcoal monster teased them into life with odd stroking motions. Bit by bit the eggs grew, they elongated and stretched into the disgusting maggot shape that Crow was now all too familiar with. And in less than a couple of minutes the job was done and another four of Bane's new Stowyrms lay coiled upon the ground. With an abrupt lurch, they shook free their wings, lifted themselves off the floor and threw themselves from the bridge. Crow rushed to the side to see them briefly hover before disappearing down a lava-laden tunnel.

Rubbing his head to dispel the headache that had been continuously pounding at the inside of his skull, the lawyer returned to his former position only to freeze when he realized that the charcoal monster was looking directly at him.

Mr Crow shivered as he stared at the multifaceted eyes of Bane's god. His shivers turned to spasms as he felt the thing try to dig once more through his thoughts.

'Get out! Get out!' he screamed.

He couldn't stand the sensation of its weird presence inside his head. Covering his eyes with his hands, he huddled into a ball and rolled back and forth until he felt the charcoal monster's presence recede. When he dared to open his eyes he saw it had resumed its work, shaping a new batch of Stowyrms.

Uncertain if he was sobbing out of pain or humiliation, he stumbled to his feet. He was too scared to disobey Bane's command to remain but too frightened to loiter within the charcoal monster's reach, so he chose to wander some distance down the seemingly never-ending bridge.

As he stumbled along on numb feet, his mind tangled itself into a state of flux. Memories of the things he treasured – gold, money, fat bank accounts – got snarled with bitter images of the people he despised the most: Elias and Mya Keeper, that senile grandma and their brat of a girl, Charlie.

'Spoilt, pampered and undeserving good-for-nothings,' he muttered as his brain continued to whirl with what-ifs and what-could-have-beens. 'And that house . . . that house! That whelp of a girl didn't deserve it. No, she didn't! Did she work as hard as me? Pah! Never done a scrap of work in her life. Her life has been all honey and syrup, not like mine. Not like mine at all! Does she have to deal with Bane or the charcoal monster? No, I bet she doesn't. All me! Always poor Crow that has to suffer and . . . what's this?'

The skinny lawyer staggered to a stop. There was a glowing wire, a bit thinner than a hosepipe, lying on the bridge. Blinking in consternation, he bent over to better investigate it. It really was glowing, like a piece of molten silver, and when he picked it up it felt soft, like playdough in his hands. He rocked back on to his heels and rubbed his angular nose in surprise. Looking ahead, he could see that it disappeared into the distance. Looking back the way he had come, he could see that it ended somewhere amidst the glow that surrounded Bane's god.

Eager for a distraction and desperate for any excuse to avoid the god's plucking fingers, Mr Crow stopped rubbing his sore head and made his way down the bridge, keen to see where the wire would lead him.

Charlie knocked the dagger from the footman's hand, then slammed him against the wall. 'Throne Room. Which way?'

The footman lifted a shaking finger. 'Down the corridor, across the courtyard, through the next two doors and you're there.'

Charlie released her grip from round his robes and allowed him to slump to the ground.

As she walked down the corridor and past the paintings, sculptures and beautifully carved doors that lined either side, her mind was awash with turbulent thoughts. She couldn't get over what she had seen in that kitchen. The images of the meat on hooks and the fleshy lumps simmering in pots was something that would stay with her for life. Would *haunt* her for life. That awful evidence and the tragedy of seeing the terrified children forced her to re-evaluate her outlook.

All this time she had been fighting to free her parents with the intention of returning her life to some measure of normality. Sure, she had been fighting on the just side, the *right* side, but in reality she had been fighting for her own selfish reasons. That had to change now and so too did her priorities. There was no way she could put herself first, not any more, not when Bane was about to eclipse thousands upon thousands of people with his shadow. And certainly not when young children were at risk of being eaten.

'Never again,' she muttered.

The jigsaw of her soul revolved and rearranged itself. Gone were the fear and the anger, and in their place pulsed a fist of determination. Her Will changed with it. The gold of its colour intensified and sparks of bright light fizzed and spluttered around her.

Reaching the end of the corridor, she opened a door and stepped into the courtyard beyond. Large moss-covered rocks protruded from the ground and around these was a fine layer of pebbles combed into swirls and circles, which looked to Charlie not unlike a Japanese Zen garden. Glancing overhead, she saw there was no ceiling, only a perfectly square shaft that opened hundreds of metres above to reveal the welcome sight of daylight. Before she looked away she noted that there were windows and passageways that opened above at differing levels, but seeing no movement or threat Charlie disregarded these and made her way to the far side.

THHHHHHHHHHHUDD!

The sudden sound of a heavy impact caused her to jump. Whipping round, she faltered and felt her knees go weak.

'No . . . no, no, no, no, no.'

It was Last Laugh. He stared back at her with unseeing eyes. His mighty wings fluttered slightly, then stilled. He moved no more.

Horrified, she glanced upward but saw no friend, no foe, no other Winged One or Stowyrm. The shaft was empty and other than the churning of distant clouds there was no movement. On weak legs she shuffled towards the fallen Winged One, then stopped when blood began to pool over the pebbles. Grabbing hold of her senses, she staggered over to him with squelching footsteps and rested her hands gently on his muzzle.

The sight of this magnificent creature dead and crumpled before her was not easy to bear and although she hadn't known him well his passing affected her almost as much as the sight of the children, lost and hopeless, in the kitchen.

Her heart lurched as another wave of determination swept through her.

'You were kind to me,' she said as she remembered him in the Winged Realm, standing by Torn Moon's side.

Words failed her and, unable to speak or think any further, she left him and headed for the door opposite the one she had come through. Opening it, she found herself in a large antechamber. Rich red carpet blanketed the floor; treasures and paintings of exceptional beauty graced the marbled walls. Directly in front of her was a broad, spiked door that wouldn't have looked out of place on a castle with a moat and portcullis.

And between her and the door stood three gigantic Stomen dressed in luxurious black robes. Green haloes of power hovered over their heads, flame fluttered down their arms and words of chanted Stonesong echoed from their lips. After her misadventures with Edge Darkmount, Charlie immediately recognized them as Stone Bishops.

Masters of Stone.

As she entered the antechamber, each of the bishops ripped great chunks of stone from the floor and rapidly shaped them into weapons. The first held a brutally large axe, the second a spear and the last a heavy warhammer.

Gritting her teeth and clenching her fists, Charlie drank deep on her Will and stepped forward.

61

Stone Bishops

The fight had not favoured Charlie. Breathing deeply, she wiped the blood from her mouth and jumped back to avoid a sweep of the axe. She felt the wind from its passing on her cheek. Spinning round, she dodged the spear and tried to lash out before the bishop with the warhammer could strike.

But her blow never landed. She was instead knocked across the room as the first bishop kicked her squarely in the back.

Blood dripping a little faster from her torn mouth, she picked herself up, ignored the pain in her body and returned to circling her adversaries. Each of them was insanely powerful. To face one of them alone would have been a desperate challenge; having to deal with three at once was a Herculean task.

But the lump of determination lying in her heart wouldn't allow her to stop.

Flowing from K'Changa stance to K'Changa stance, she twisted through the air . . . only to be slammed back against the wall as two of the bishops countered her blows while the third struck her with his warhammer.

Charlie was wheezing a little as she picked herself up yet again and, ignoring the blood and saliva that dribbled from her chin, smiled at her foes.

'Oh, you're good,' she chuckled. 'I've got to give you that.'

The three didn't reply. The only sound to escape their lips was Stonesong and the occasional grunt and groan of exertion.

'Don't talk much do you?' said Charlie in a casual voice that hid the tempest of emotions boiling inside her chest.

She ran at them again. Lunging for the two on the right, she ducked beneath the axe, jumped over the spear, then rapidly jinked left, rolled and punched the third as hard as she could. She rolled back and was about to kick one of the others but was instead forced to block the spear as it whistled towards her. Before she could move away the third Stone Bishop, now recovered, grabbed her by the forearm, whipped her round and flung her against the wall again. She bounced off in a shower of sparks and landed heavily on the floor.

Laughing to herself as though she had just discovered something wildly amusing, she used the wall to help heave herself back to her feet.

'Yeah, you're good. Powerful too.' Standing straight, she looked each of them in the eye. 'But I'm not too shabby myself and what's more . . .' She raised her flaming hands and looked at them over her knuckles. '. . . I've just learned how you guys like to move.'

With a growl so loud and so ferocious that a Winged One would have stared at her in surprise, she sprinted towards the Stone Bishops.

'Did you think you would stop me?' she cried.

Slamming the heel of her palm against the first, she knocked the axe from his grasp.

'Did you think that after all I've endured I would whimper and give up?'

She kicked the spear from the second's fist.

'Did you think I would be a pushover?'

Grabbing the warhammer, she twisted it from the last's grasp.

'Well, you thought wrong!' she shouted. 'Nothing is going to stop me from reaching Bane. Nothing!'

Still growling, she fell upon the three gigantic Stone Bishops with stubborn resolve in her heart and golden Will churning from her hands.

The footmen who lined the walls of the Throne Room did not show it but they were jittery. Explosions, booms and distant thuds had been shaking the palace for the last hour. Long lines of Shades and mortal messengers had filtered up to the Devouring Throne to deliver messages to their lord and receive fresh orders to carry back to waiting captains, colonels and lieutenants.

From what they could glean, it sounded as though their lord was managing two battles. One that was distant and conducted on Treman soil and apparently going well; the other too close for comfort and seemingly in some state of confusion as conflicting reports kept coming in. There were whispers of Winged Ones too.

But the footmen knew better than to show any doubts.

Although it was considered a position of honour to stand and serve in this inner sanctum, it was not an easy task ... nor a safe one. All of the Stomen that stood in the Throne Room were well aware of their lord's fabled rages and knew that, no matter what, they were never to speak until spoken to.

That discipline was put to the test when shouts and sounds of struggle erupted from just outside. But as the noises carried on and their lord showed no concern they relaxed somewhat.

BOOOOOOM!

The great door to the Throne Room suddenly rocked on its hinges. The hugely muscled men-at-arms who stood amongst the footmen stared in amazement. As their training overcame shock they hastened forward to fall into aggressive formations, facing the besieged door.

BOOOOOOM!

One of the footmen dropped a tray of refreshments. The clash of shattered glass caused the Shades to spike their rubbery flesh in alarm.

BOOOOOOM!

The lord held out a hand to still a messenger's garbled report and turned, curiously, towards the cause of the disturbance.

BRRA-BOOOM!

The door exploded. Striding through the dust and splinters came, not a Winged One, as they had expected, but a Human girl, draped in golden flames. Behind her, in unconscious heaps, lay the Stone Bishops.

62

The Throne Room

Charlie strode into the Throne Room, ignoring the rows of armoured guards. She only had eyes for the giant sitting on the Devouring Throne.

'You chump!' she shouted. 'You and I need to –'

She didn't get a chance to finish her sentence. A large guard swiped at her with his sword. She grabbed it with her hands and scowled at its owner. The Stoman stumbled as he saw how hard her eyes were. Letting the blade drop with a clang, she took a step forward, expecting the others to lose their nerve and move aside.

They did not.

With a bloodthirsty roar, they charged at her in a mass of spiky armour and glittering weapons. Shades, dark and elemental, scampered between them and lashed at her with claws of shadow. And rising from a recess at the back of the room came two Stowyrms.

'Bane!' she snarled. 'I'm coming for you! I'm going to –'

A serrated sword slammed against her shield of Will, cutting her words short yet again. Irritated by the interruption, she knocked the warrior aside only to discover that she was nearly surrounded. It came to her in a flash of unpleasant realization that she had become so focused on Bane that she had failed to appreciate just how fierce and loyal his guards were. Furious at her own lack of foresight and hoping that she didn't fluff it, she was forced to retreat several stumbling paces.

Shades hissed and snapped at her. Men-at-arms bellowed and tried to punch, stab and kick her. She retaliated with whips of flame and a barrage of blows and such was her power that she knocked great clusters of them aside and even managed to reclaim several feet of lost ground. But when the Stowyrms, with a shriek and a hoot, barrelled in and tried to rip her to pieces she was forced to retreat further until she was beneath the arch of the splintered doorway.

She stood, sucking in great lungfuls of air, then began to move far faster than before. Hands blurring, feet racing, she knocked weapons from hands, sent Shades flying and pummelled Stomen backwards, leaving great dents and rips in their armour. Growing more confident, she waited until a Stowyrm wriggled close, loaded up one of her fists with as much Will as possible, then leaped up and brought her hand hammering down.

There was a great crack. Charlie grinned as the Stowyrm slowed but her expression faltered when it started moving again. 'Oh, you've got to be kidding me,' she muttered. All she had to show for her efforts was a spiderweb of cracks across the Stowyrm's rocky skin.

Confidence now dented, she moved back through the arch and into the antechamber. The few Shades and warriors still standing hesitated to follow but the Stowyrms were not as timid. Screaming like something dragged from the abyss, they skated forward and started to squirm through the door frame.

Charlie grabbed the large stone axe that lay next to one of the Stone Bishops, heaved it over her head and brought it down as hard as she could upon the first Stowyrm. There was another thunderous crack, louder than the first. The axe shattered and a great shard fell from the Stowyrm's head. But even that didn't stop it. Shrieking belligerently, it continued to force its way beneath the door frame; the second, just behind it, battered its head against the first's tail as it too struggled to get at her. Charlie, growing desperate, picked up the spear that she had only recently knocked from the Stone Bishop's hands and tried to jam it down the thing's gullet. It thrashed and gurgled and if it had been made of flesh it would have impaled itself upon the weapon. But it wasn't and as it continued to press forward the spear started to bend until it snapped apart, showering Charlie with a cloud of splinters.

She shouted wordlessly as the Stowyrm successfully squeezed through the doorway, slithered forward and reared over her. Drenched in shadow, she summoned all her Will but before she could defend herself the wall behind her shattered.

For a split second her tired mind convinced her that it was Last Laugh, returned from the dead and surging in to defend her, but when she rubbed at her eyes she realized her mistake. Nonetheless, she wasn't disappointed to see that it was Hotstepper, Jensen and Nibbler charging through the rubble. The sight was most welcome; even more so when Hotstepper and Nibbler unleashed crackling jets of lightning to push back then shatter the first Stowyrm that threatened her. Hearing an unusual *snick-snack* noise, she spun round to see Jensen burying his sword in the remaining Stowyrm.

It didn't move.

'How . . .?' she began in shock. There was so much she wanted to know that she mentally tripped. She didn't know what to ask first: how had they succeeded in finding her or how had Jensen managed to destroy a Stowyrm when she couldn't achieve such a thing with all her Will? 'How did . . .?' she began again, only to stutter to a stop.

'Remember me Thornsword? Well, I've gone one better. Say hello ta Bramblesword!' said Jensen, assuming she was asking after his weapon. He pulled it free with an effortless motion.

'I, uh . . .' Still lost for words, Charlie stared at her friends. 'Timing. Good.' She knew she sounded like a caveman but she didn't care. Her friends were awesome.

Hotstepper leaned low so he could peer through the door into the chamber beyond.

'Shall we?' he said.

Charlie grinned.

Marching back into the Throne Room, she slouched into the most insolent stance she could think of. 'Hey, Bane. I'm back and I've brought friends!'

Jensen and Nibbler stood by her side and Hotstepper loomed behind them.

Charlie knew that with the Will boiling from her hands, the flames flickering from Nibbler and Hotstepper's nostrils and the torchlight reflecting off the tip of Jensen's Bramblesword, they were an impressive, even an imposing, sight. But Bane was not moved.

'Childish,' he muttered. 'Scum,' he added as a discordant afterthought.

Grabbing the armrests of his Devouring Throne, he slowly pulled himself upright. A dark nimbus of shadow flickered over his shoulders and head. Growling, deep and low, he slowly clapped his hands together.

Eight maggot-like shapes detached themselves from the ceiling and fluttered downward to reveal themselves as Stowyrms.

'It is time,' said Bane, 'to teach you a lesson.'

Mr Crow stopped with a lurch. The glowing wire he had been following led to a plain brown vase. The sort that wouldn't have looked out of place in a Greek or Roman display in some dusty museum. The sight was so unusual and so unexpected that the lawyer looked over both shoulders to see if anyone was watching him or playing some kind of trick. But he was all alone in this weird environment apart from the Stowyrms and Bane's god, and they were hundreds of metres away.

'Huh,' muttered Crow.

Ignoring the pounding in his head and gathering what measly courage he had left, he reached out and rapped the vase with his knuckle.

It sounded hollow. He picked it up, peered inside and nearly dropped it in shock when he saw what it contained.

'How . . . how can that be?'

Feeling the remnants of sanity threatening to leave him, he looked again, hoping that he had been mistaken.

He had not. The vase contained stars. Hundreds upon hundreds of stars.

A cackle of laughter escaped his lips and with it his final hold upon reality. The madness he had been holding back since he had first encountered Bane slammed past his thin mental barriers and rushed forward to crush his mind beneath a wave of insanity.

'Stars!' he cried. More manic laughter bubbled past his mean lips. 'It's full of stars! Whoever heard of a galaxy in a vase? Ha!'

Finding this uproarious, he grabbed his sides and laughed like he had never laughed before.

When he finally managed to regain some measure of composure, he wiped the tears from his face and held the vase aloft for better inspection. As he turned it from side to side his mind whirred. The glowing wire that he had followed dangled from the vase's side.

'Is this where the charcoal monster lives when it's not making those *things*?' he croaked. He gave the glowing wire an experimental tug. 'Like a shell for a sea mollusc or . . .' He paused as his dazed mind considered further possibilities. '. . . Or a genie in a lamp . . . Or a spirit in a bottle. Could it be . . .?'

Rubbing his nose with his skinny fingers, he smiled uncertainly. If this was indeed the thing that housed Bane's god, then perhaps he had found a way to rid himself of the charcoal monster forever.

His lips peeled back to form a horrible smile. Lurching down the bridge on legs that quivered with fear and uncertain excitement, he made his way back towards the one thing that scared him almost as much as Bane.

His master's god. The charcoal monster.

63

Bane

The Stowyrms charged forward but Charlie was in no mood to tangle with them. All she wanted to do was get to grips with their boss. She burned with the need to confront him. Sprinting forward, she built up enough speed to launch herself on to the closest Stowyrm. She avoided the gnashing teeth and ran between the blur of its wings, down its tail and leapfrogged over it and the others to land at the foot of the dais.

Trusting to her friends to keep the winged beasts occupied, she stared at the menacing figure that had haunted her nightmares. 'Bane.'

'Squishy little maggot.'

The giant cocked his head to one side as though scrutinizing some strange little insect. Charlie stared right back at him, boldness overcoming any trace of fear. She tried to make out some shape, some features beneath his hood that would hint at a face but all she could see was impenetrable shadow.

'I despise you, little fleshy Human. You are weak and soft and yet you are the source of all my woes. You brought the pendant into my world and now you mar my kingdom with the return of those meddling Winged Ones.' His finger stabbed towards Hotstepper and Nibbler. 'I will rip your limbs from their sockets and beat you with them.' He descended a step. 'I will tear open your stomach and feast on your squishy innards.' He descended further. 'And when your corpse lies lifeless I will harvest your skin, your tendons and your cartilage and use these to make a cloak that I will wear once I have crushed the Winged Ones beneath my feet.' His foot thudded on the next step. 'And if any scrap of your meat remains I will impale it upon the spikes of my Devouring Throne and leave it there to fester and rot. What say you to that, Charlie of the Keepers?'

Charlie fought back her fear and forced herself to stare right back at the looming giant.

'I say . . .' she began, but faltered as a thousand possible replies screamed through her mind. This was the man who had ripped her parents from her life; this was the giant who had trampled entire nations beneath his feet and wherever he went had left death and destruction, misery and gut-wrenching sorrow in his wake. There was so much she wanted to say, so much that *needed* to be said, but rather than risk tripping over her own tongue she resorted to instinct and replied as only she could, with all the cheekiness she could muster: 'I say that you're a bully and a chump and that you have the dress sense of a depressed dinosaur, and I also have a sneaky suspicion that you practise your evil poses in front of a mirror when no one's looking, but if you want to give up and surrender right now I might go easier on you. But no promises because, let's face it . . . you really, really need a good beating for everything that you've done.'

There was a moment of disbelief that stretched as the Stoman Lord digested Charlie's words, then –

'Impudence!' roared Bane. His shout was so rich, so powerful, it caused the columns that supported the roof to shake, the bodies of the unconscious guards to tremble on the floor, and the Stowyrms and Charlie's friends to momentarily pause their combat.

Bane began to chant. The shadows around his shoulders rose, flames of power trembled around his fists and with a terrifying growl he pounded down the few remaining steps. Charlie, every bit as determined as Bane was furious, pulled deep on her Will. Deeper than she had ever done before.

The two collided.

Light flared. Shadows reared.

The sound of their meeting cracked around the Throne Room and Charlie was suddenly and painfully forced to confront the reality of what happened when a teenage girl challenged a giant. The force of Bane's inhuman blow knocked her off her feet and sent her whistling through the air. She crashed through several columns and landed in a crumpled heap at the foot of a leering statue.

'Did you think,' whispered Bane in an awful voice that somehow managed to cut through the bedlam, 'that you could best me? That a mere squishy Human could stand against my might? Foolish child, all your fears and nightmares are about to come true.'

He began to slowly, confidently stride across the rubble. Stonesong writhed and cracked around him, pools of shadow collected in his footsteps.

'I'm not done yet,' said Charlie. Pushing herself to her feet, she repeated her words: 'I'm not done yet!'

Standing straight, she faced her foe.

Nibbler sheared the wings off a Stowyrm with a bolt of lightning, then ignited the carpet beneath it with a jet of flames, causing the fibres to melt and stick to the beast, slowing its movements. Growling, he leaped on its back and pounded his claws repeatedly against its stony hide, interlacing his blows with spears of lightning.

The thing shattered.

Nibbler opened his mouth and let loose a wave of victorious flame but his triumph was cut short as another Stowyrm slammed into him in a bundle of crazed teeth and rock-hard scales. He slashed at his adversary, his talons leaving a trail of sparks across its flanks. Grabbing one of its wings in his mouth, he hauled himself on to its back. He caught a brief glimpse of Jensen and Hotstepper wrestling with opponents, then the view was lost to him as the beast he was riding slammed itself through a line of statues in an attempt to dislodge him.

Pushing his concern for Charlie and his friends aside, Nibbler was forced to concentrate on his own survival.

Charlie could not believe how powerful Bane really was. Each of his punches threatened to shatter her Will and when she managed to deflect them or dodge aside, his fists left craters in the floor. She had been fooling herself when she thought that she stood a chance. And now she was suffering for her lack of foresight.

But Charlie was not going to give up. Not now. Not after everything she had endured.

Slipping into a K'Changa stance, she rolled beneath his lunging fingers, sprang to her feet and kicked him as hard as she could. It felt like she had kicked a mountain. Biting back a hiss of pain, she ducked beneath a blow and cartwheeled away.

He thudded after her with no trace of a limp or any sign to indicate that he had felt her kick.

But that wasn't going to stop her. If her attack hadn't worked the first time, then she would simply try again. He had to feel something sooner or later. He *had* to.

Fanning the fire in her heart, she caused her Will to flare around her and, gritting her teeth, she began to move faster and faster. She ducked beneath his lumbering attacks, tumbled over his grasping hands and weaved back and forth just out of his reach. As she moved, images of past pains flashed before her eyes. Eager for any advantage, she used these bitter memories as fuel to feed her aggression. Blocking a blow that sent her sliding, she recalled the first Bellanian friend who had been taken from her.

'For Stotch!' she cried, remembering how the poor Treman had looked after Bane's Wyrms had robbed him of life. Running forward, she slammed her elbow as hard as she could against his thigh.

Twisting away, she slid behind his foot and sliced the hard

edge of her hand against the giant's calf. 'For Marsila!'

Bane tried to grab her but she was too fast for him. She teased him towards one of the statues, then ran up it to somersault over his head. 'For Azariah!' she screamed and lashed out as she flew past.

Breathing deeply and riding a wave of righteous anger, she shouted, 'For my parents!' and leaped straight for him.

But Bane was ready for her and snagged her out of the air with a snort of derision. 'Idiotic child! You are but a puppy before a wolf! A kitten before a lion!' Wrapping his fingers round her arms, he trapped her in his grip. 'Did you really think you would find justice here? You, like all your kind, are fragile, foolish and mistaken!'

He finished the last words with a roar and swung his fist with Charlie in it, slamming it through a statue. Not stopping there, he continued down the line, bursting statue after statue and watching with grim satisfaction as Charlie's Will flared less and less with each successive explosion.

Grazes and cuts began to appear on Charlie's head as her Will grew weak. The wound on her lip that she had received from the Stone Bishops opened up and began to bleed.

Bane grunted at the sight of it.

'Fleshy and weak. How I despise your kind.' He started to walk between rows of columns, heading towards a secluded part of his Throne Room. 'I know not who this Stotch is and I care not to know who this Azariah or Marsila were, but I do know one thing . . . your parents make the perfect decoration.'

He held Charlie aloft so she could better see what lay in front of her.

Bane's Tapestry.

It was a broad ribbon of an amber-like material that stretched from one wall to the other. Flickering torches cast enough light for Charlie to see its contents.

People.

Dozens upon dozens of people.

Humans, Stomen and Tremen. Each displayed in various poses. Some stood alone, others were arranged in groups. Some stood as though lost in thought, others stretched out hands as though pointing to distant objects, and a few had been twisted into classic sporting poses: the discus thrower, the wrestlers, the archer and the sprinters. It was horrendous. A dishonourable and defamatory punishment like none other.

And placed slightly off-centre, like two forlorn pieces of art, were her parents. They stood hand in hand but had been set with their heads cast away from each other, forever denied the opportunity to look their love in the eye.

Charlie's tears mingled with the blood and saliva that were dribbling from her mouth. The red liquid trickled down Bane's fist to drip and puddle on the floor.

'Do you see, little worm? Do you see what happens to those who offend me?' Bane walked up to one end of the Tapestry and thrust her head against its smooth surface. He began to walk down it, rubbing her cheek and forehead against it as he moved. Face after face passed before Charlie's weeping eyes. 'This is where the Stone Bishops and the leaders and the politicians who oppose me end up. Here, forever immortalized in lacklustre glory, lie the freedom fighters, the usurpers, the backstabbers, the traitors and the Keepers.'

Charlie caught a glimpse of her parents, their downturned eyes and held hands, then they were gone and others passed before her. It would have continued but Bane snatched her away and brought her perilously close to the darkness of his hood. 'Think you'll end up in here, maggot? As a treasured foe? Well, you thought wrong! You are a cur, a piece of offal and an offence to my sight. I have other things planned for you. Darker things. Before I ruin your flesh I will take you to my god and have your soul ripped from your body!'

With a cloud of darkness still hanging over him, Bane ignored the sound of combat coming from the Stowyrms and marched towards the tunnel at the rear of the room.

Charlie, arms pinned to her side and nearly broken from physical and mental pain, did the one thing, the only thing, that she could do. She channelled all her heartache and horror, summoned all that remained of her Will, and bit Bane's finger with all her might.

'Graaaah! Wretch!' bellowed Bane. He opened his fingers in reflex and flung her upward. Angered and enraged beyond all measure, he brought his other hand high and smacked her like a sportsman striking a ball.

Charlie went tumbling through the air. Head over heels in a ragdoll motion, she flew into the tunnel and was swallowed by the shadows.

64

Lost

Jensen slammed the hilt of his sword against the guard's armoured chest, then spun round to slice a long line of spikes from the Stowyrm's tail as it tried to club him to the floor. It shrieked and lunged for him but Jensen tumbled out of the way in true K'Changa style, springing from hands to feet and back again. Whirling the sword in intricate patterns, he was about to thrust it at the beast but paused when he saw Hotstepper, already waylaid by three Stowyrms, tackled by a fourth.

He cursed the fates, tripped a footman, sliced a Shade in two and slid beneath the Stowyrm that was chasing him. Regaining his feet and wishing he had a Keeper's speed, he sprinted to aid his winged companion. He clambered up the body of a shattered Stowyrm and ran along it, then – using its height to his advantage – jumped on to one of the beasts that wriggled over Hotstepper. Bringing his sword to bear, he slammed it into the Stowyrm and grinned in satisfaction as he heard the fatal *snap-snap* that heralded its demise.

From the back of the now lifeless Stowyrm he jumped on to Hotstepper's shoulders, intent on aiding him in his moment of need. Drenched by shadow, he looked up to see

Jensen

another Stowyrm. Instinctively, he thrust out his sword and allowed it to impale itself. But that was the last of Jensen's luck. The beast, now dead, fell forward, pinning him to Hotstepper. The Winged One, still battling three others, was suddenly waylaid by the extra weight. The Stowyrms sensed an opportunity and stampeded forward. Banging and butting, they repeatedly pounded into Hotstepper, forcing him back.

Flailing desperately to free himself, Jensen cast his eyes around. He caught sight of Nibbler battling one of the remaining Stowyrms and beyond that glimpsed Charlie just as she was flung into the tunnel. The sight of Bane thundering after her caused his heart to pound.

'Nibbler!' he screamed. 'Nibbler!'

The Hatchling dodged his adversary and looked to Jensen. His eyes widened in disbelief and he took a stuttering couple of steps towards him.

'No!' shrieked Jensen. 'Charlie! Save Charlie! She's in the tunnel! Go! Go –'

The Stowyrms battered Hotstepper through the doorway and into the ruined antechamber, cutting the Throne Room and Nibbler from Jensen's view.

It was dark and gloomy inside the tunnel. The air stank unpleasantly of burnt metal and asphalt. Grunting in agony, Charlie rolled on to her knees and tried to stand. But her calf bore a nasty gash and wouldn't bear her weight.

'My leg,' she cursed, 'why is it always my leg?'

'I can hear you, little worm!' Bane's voice sang out of the darkness. With it came the measured tread of his footsteps.

Biting her lip, Charlie dragged herself forward and allowed herself to roll off the path, to fall in a windmill of legs and arms before slamming to an abrupt and painful stop on top of a ledge. Her eyes, not yet adjusted, were unable to judge how far she had fallen or what lay below, but she didn't care. As long as she was off the path and out of Bane's sight, that was all that mattered.

The sound of Bane's footsteps increased; so too did the sensation of approaching menace. Sweat broke out on Charlie's forehead and she dug her nails into her palms to stop herself from shaking.

'Do you think you can hide from me?' came his voice. It grew loud as he drew level with her, then receded as he passed. 'Do you think that I won't find you? This is my realm, my domain, and it is I who belongs in the darkness and you, my little wretch, so used to the light, are the one who should learn to shiver in fear. I will find you, maggot, have no doubt about that.'

Charlie breathed a little deeper when she heard his foot-steps disappear. Reaching down with questing fingers, she checked the fresh wound on her calf. It was deep but not dangerously so. If she could bind it she should be able to regain her feet and then . . . and then what? She knew now that the power of her Will and the strength of her determination simply weren't enough. She would have to come up with something else. Some other plan.

But what could she do, a teenager before the might of an enraged giant? Desperate for an answer, *any answer*, she did her best to think how her two mentors, Azariah and Marsila, would have approached a problem like this. Surely they would have thought of a suitable tactic by now?

'But what?' she whispered to herself.

'There you are,' chuckled Bane. Singing softly, he allowed the flames of his Stonesong to illuminate himself. He stood quite a distance above her, still on the path but looking down the cliff towards her. Somehow he had managed to creep up on her unawares. 'Talking to yourself, little wench? Whispering to your gods? And trusting to the fates?' His sneering laugh came again. 'Time for pain, little one, time for –'

Charlie didn't wait around to hear the rest of his words. Wrapping herself in the cracked remnants of her Will, she crossed her fingers for luck, rolled off the ledge and dropped into the darkness.

The wind and the sound of Bane's brutal laugh whistled around her as she fell. She hit the side of the cliff in a shower of sparks. She bounced, then slid painfully down a steep incline before coming to a juddering stop. It felt like she'd landed on some cavernous floor but without light to see she could not be sure.

'Think you can run?' The giant's voice echoed down from somewhere far above. 'It will do you no good. I will get you in the end!'

Charlie knew better than to answer him and give away her position. Gritting her teeth, she rolled over and used her elbows to crawl deeper into the gloom. After long minutes and when she could no longer hear the sound of Bane's footsteps, she pulled her jacket from her shoulders and tore strips from it with which to bind her calf. Ignoring the pain, she pulled herself to her feet and, unable to summon her Will for fear that it would act like a beacon, began to blindly walk through the darkness. It was not a comfortable moment and she had to fight the sense of claustrophobia that threatened to overwhelm her. She would have done almost anything for the chance to stand once more beneath Bellanian skies.

A faint whisper of movement caused her to stiffen. Fearing that Bane was approaching, she hastened to find somewhere to hide but without the ability to see she was getting nowhere fast. With her heart pounding in her chest, she hobbled forward, her arms outstretched, certain that at any second she would either stumble face first into a rock or walk straight into Bane's grasp.

'Charlie!' someone hissed.

She almost yelped but relaxed when she recognized the familiar voice.

'Nibbler?' she replied. 'Where are you?'

'Here.'

She felt his paws take her hand and guide it to his shoulder.

'You can see?' she asked.

'Not amazingly well, but I do OK in the dark.'

'Is Bane about?'

'Not that I can see.'

Charlie summoned her Will and grinned at her friend in relief. He returned her smile but it faltered when he noticed her latest collection of wounds.

'Things aren't going as well as we'd hoped, are they?' he said.

'Oh no, I think everything is going to plan.'

'What? Really?' replied Nibbler with naive charm.

'Er, no. I was being sarcastic,' admitted Charlie. 'So far, today has been the worst day of my life.'

'Oh. What happened to you? You were on Hotstepper's back when we arrived in the Western Mountains, then you were gone.'

Charlie, still concerned that Bane might arrive at any moment, glanced anxiously over her shoulder.

'If you can carry me back to Bane's Throne Room,' she said, 'I'll tell you all about it.'

'That sounds like a plan. Get on,' said Nibbler and knelt down so she could scramble on his back. Then he bunched his legs beneath him and took off at a run.

65
Bane's Tapestry

Mr Crow hobbled towards the glowing cloud of light that hid the charcoal monster. Bane's god terrified him and the rocky Stowyrm thingies that it kept creating didn't exactly thrill him either. But all of that was about to change. Half cackling in delight and half whimpering in fear, he moved closer. As close as he dared.

'Charcoal monster,' he whispered.

Bane's god, busy with the task of creating Stowyrms, ignored him.

'Charcoal monster!' snapped the lawyer.

Still the god ignored him.

'Charcoal monster! I'm talking to you!'

The god hissed. Spinning round, it confronted Crow with its wide eyes and grasping hands.

'Eeeep!' blurted Mr Crow and took several steps back.

The god cocked its head at an angle to better study the lawyer. Behind it the latest batch of Stowyrms took flight and disappeared from view. Angered or inquisitive, it was hard to tell which, the god floated towards Crow, its long burnt-looking fingers grasping and pawing at the air with an unquenchable hunger.

'No!' screamed Mr Crow. 'No more! My mind is my own! My own!'

The god moved closer, its eyes glowed brighter and Mr Crow squealed as he felt it attempt to force itself once more into his mind.

'NO!' squealed Crow.

Summoning all of his weird strength, all of his crow powers, he raised the vase high.

The god's eyes widened.

Mr Crow brought his arms flashing down. The vase tumbled through the air and smashed with an anticlimactic tinkle.

He paused. Somehow he had expected more.

A wind rose. It started softly, then grew until the sound of it roared around the chamber. A ball of light appeared amongst the shards of pottery and as the wind increased in power a whirling vortex of stars appeared. Terrified, Mr Crow backed away. The feeling of suction increased and he turned and ran.

A horrific screech caused him to falter. Looking over his shoulder, he saw the halo that surrounded Bane's god stream towards the ball of light, momentarily revealing the charcoal monster in all its ghastly splendour before it too was pulled towards the sphere. Shrieking and howling, it resisted the gravitational pull for as long as it could.

SSSHHHKMPF!

The god, the light, the twinkling stars and the wind disappeared, leaving nothing behind. Not even a shard of pottery.

Mr Crow blinked in astonishment. He moved hesitantly forward and patted at the ground to test for any concealments or traces. There were none.

A wicked smile appeared on the lawyer's face. He capered around and danced a jig.

'Freeeeeeeee! Free! Free at last! No more eyes! No more scrabbling and pawing through my brain! No more charcoal monster! Ha!' Cackling in delight, he continued to dance from side to side in a jaunty rhythm. He stopped abruptly. His smile turned from one of joy to one of malice. 'If I'm free, then it's time to balance the books. Time to wipe the slate clean! Time for the Keeper family to feel a little justice!'

Chuckling to himself, he skipped down the bridge, spread his arms wide, jumped and burst apart into a pack of crows. They flew over the side of the bridge, shrieking and hooting, then headed down one of the many lava-lined tunnels in a mass of inky wings.

As they wheeled round a corner they came face to face with a snarling pack of dragons who were finishing off the last of the Stowyrms. Croaking and hooting, whistling and cawing, the pack of birds fluttered past the combatants and, before anyone could react to their presence, hastened on their way.

The Throne Room was deserted. There were no Shades, footmen or Stowyrms. Nor was there any sign of Hotstepper or Jensen. Charlie and Nibbler stood in front of the Tapestry.

'Are those your parents?' asked Nibbler.

'Yes. Mya –' she pointed to her mother – 'and Elias,' she pointed to her father. 'This is the first time I've seen them in more than seven years.'

Unable to think of a suitable reply, Nibbler stood quietly by her side. After a minute of contemplation, he cleared his throat. 'Think we should be getting out of here?'

'Probably,' admitted Charlie. 'But I won't. I'm going to stay here and defeat Bane once and for all.'

Nibbler looked at her like she was crazy. 'Charlie, look at you. Look at the state of you! If you couldn't defeat Bane when you were fresh, what makes you think you're going to be able to do that now?'

'Because I've got a plan.'

'Yeah? Why didn't you use it the first time?'

'Because I thought I could win through sheer strength and determination. It didn't work so now I'm going to act smart and use Bane's sense of superiority to our advantage. Are you with me?'

'I don't know . . . You'll need to prove to me that you're not going to do anything foolhardy before I get on board. What do you have in mind?'

'Did you see Last Laugh?' asked Charlie.

Nibbler's face twisted. He, Jensen and Hotstepper had passed the fallen Winged One earlier. 'I saw him.'

'I want you to get all the Winged Ones you can find and wait for me in that shaft where Last Laugh is lying now.'

'And then what?'

'I bring Bane to meet his judgement. Now, do you think you can do that for me?'

'Of course, Charlie . . . but I wish you wouldn't do this. Come with me and we'll get the others together. It'll be easier to finish Bane as a group.'

'You know it won't work like that. Bane is too smart, too

cunning, and if he can't beat us with strength then he'll do something else. When we defeated Bane's First we thought Sylvaris was safe but he had another two armies to call on. And when we freed the Winged Ones we thought we'd finally won but then he had the Stowyrms. Don't you see that he's always got something up his sleeve and he's always one step ahead of us? Come on, Nibbler, you know there's too much at stake! It's not just us who will lose if things fall apart but all of Bellania. We've got to defeat him and we've got to do it now. Please, I'm asking you as my dearest friend. Help me with this. Please go and get the Winged Ones and meet me back in that shaft.'

Nibbler didn't appear happy. Nor did he appear ready to agree with her, but he had seen her like this before and knew there would be no arguing with her. 'Charlie, you can be as stubborn as a mule,' he said with a begrudging yet loyal admiration. 'But I'll do it. Just make sure you meet us there.' He grabbed her mangled hand and held it aloft. 'And for the realm's sake, make sure you get there in one piece!'

Charlie gave him a swift hug. 'I'll do my best.'

She walked him through the ruins of the Throne Room, past the antechamber and into the courtyard. Hearing a crash reverberate from somewhere close by in the building, Charlie slapped Nibbler on the rump. 'Go! Get it done and be quick.'

'I'll do it,' promised Nibbler. 'Stay safe until I get back.' Spreading his wings, he beat his way up the shaft.

Charlie shouted at his dwindling back, 'Just make sure you meet me back here as quick as you can!'

He waved at her, then scrabbled his way into one of the broad openings that lined the shaft's interior.

Charlie waited until she was certain that he wouldn't double back, then guiltily made her way to Last Laugh's corpse. She stared at the fallen dragon. Quickly, before her nerve gave up, she whispered, 'I'm sorry.' Knowing that she would need all the strength she could get for the task ahead, she knelt down and dipped her hands in his blood. She smeared a generous amount over her wounded calf and gritted her teeth against the sudden pain that surged through her leg. When the sensation subsided, she pushed her trembling fingers back into the pool of blood and, grabbing hold of her courage, upended another handful between her lips.

'Aaaaaaagh!' she half screamed, half gurgled.

The agony was terrible. Falling backwards, she drummed her heels and flailed her arms. When it was over, she gasped and sucked in great lungfuls of air. She could feel the strength of it, just as she could feel the changes it was rendering in her body. The wounds and aches, the sprains and the knotted stiffness all disappeared and were replaced by a jagged sensation of barely contained power.

But she wasn't done. Not yet. If she was to stand any chance of defeating Bane she would need more. Dipping her hands in the still-warm liquid, she drank again and again until she could stand no more. And when the pain was over, Charlie stood up with a new glimmer in her eye.

She looked a different creature from the young girl who had first set foot in Deepforest. Her finger was missing, her leg bore too many scars to count and her hair was covered with so much ichor and blood that it was impossible to tell its true colour. But the gash in her calf had healed and her Will, so nearly broken by her last encounter with Bane, had returned. More than that, she felt strong. Stronger than she had ever felt before. Last Laugh's blood chased through her stomach and into her heart and raced through her veins.

She was as ready as she would ever be.

Placing one hand upon Last Laugh's muzzle, she leaned low and knowing that it was a pointless gesture nonetheless whispered, 'You lived up to your name and even though you're gone you'll still be inside me when I deliver justice to the Western Menace.'

Swiftly and silently she ghosted back through the door and headed for the Throne Room. She would wait for Bane there.

66

Crow

She was sitting quietly in front of the Tapestry when she heard the sound of footsteps behind her.

'So you came back to finish the job?' She turned round with an expression of certainty on her face that abruptly faltered when she saw the figure behind her. '*You?*'

Mr Crow twitched his head from side to side before peeling his lips open to reveal wickedly sharp teeth. 'Yes, Charlie, it's me. Your old friend and steadfast lawyer.'

'Bu-but –' stammered Charlie, astonished. He was the last person she had expected to see. She cast her eyes frantically around, hoping to find Bane so she could get on with the task at hand, but it was just the two of them.

'What?' screeched Crow. 'Got no time for me? Got no time for the man who worked his fingers to the bone to keep you and your grandmother in house and home?' As he grew more agitated parts of his body split into birds, then reformed seconds later. It was a disconcerting effect and hinted at the madness unfolding inside his head. 'Got no time for the lawyer who put clothes on your back and food on your plate?'

Flabbergasted by the nonsense coming out of his mouth,

Charlie struggled to keep her temper. She had bigger fish to fry but with the dragonsblood rampaging through her veins it was proving hard to master her emotions. 'Look,' she reasoned, 'I know you've . . . changed but you can't be here right now. You can't.'

Crow shrieked. Opening his mouth, he wriggled his long black tongue back and forth. 'Can't? Can't be here? Trying to boss me around, my filly? Oh, that sounds just like your mother and father! That's just the sort of thing they would say. Don't! Can't! Shouldn't! Mustn't! Rules! Laws! Obligations!' He burst apart into a flock of birds, then reassembled closer to her. 'Well, look where that sort of talk got your parents! Look!' He pointed at the Tapestry. 'That's what they deserve for treating me so poorly.'

Charlie suddenly snapped. She couldn't help it. All the buried emotions and hurts of years gone by now resurfaced, demanding to be heard.

'You greedy, spiteful fool! You never did an honest day of work in your life! You did next to nothing for Gran and you're a thief! A low-down, good-for-nothing thief! If I didn't have something else to do I'd pay you back for all the bruises you gave me. Get out of here!'

But Crow wasn't listening to her. He only had ears for the tirade of twisted words screaming inside his own skull. 'You never deserved to live in that house! You never deserved any of it! Someone else should have had the chance to live there! Someone who was worthy of all the opportunities and privileges that came with it!'

'Yeah?' shouted Charlie, every bit as infuriated as Mr Crow was mad. 'Who?'

'Me!' screamed the lawyer. 'Me!'

'Wh-what?' stammered Charlie, shocked by his reply. 'You?'

'Why not? If I'd had your upbringing, then none of this would have happened to me. I'd be rich and I'd be happy!'

'Rich? Happy? Why, you callous chump! With all the furniture and antiques you stole from my parents' house, you're rich already! And as for happiness, you crush any sort of joy each time you see it! You ruined the house, robbed my gran of her health and you used to beat me every day of the week! You're a –'

Charlie's words were cut short as Mr Crow's insanity reached fever pitch. Wriggling his long tongue like a serpent sniffing the air, he let loose an anguished scream.

'You!' he shrieked. 'It's all your fault! None of this would have happened to me. None of it! It's your fault I was turned into crows! Your fault that I look like a ghost! Your fault that the charcoal monster picked through my brain! All your fault!'

Growing even more agitated, he suddenly burst forward and backhanded her across the head. His blow, amplified by his weird strength, sent her teetering back to slam against the Tapestry.

Charlie's eyes flared with barely restrained Will as she glared at the madman. 'You've gone too far, Mr Crow, too far! You need to know that I'm no longer the little girl you used to bully. I'm giving you one last chance to go and if you don't take it I'm going to return all the beatings you gave me . . . with interest.'

'If there's going to be any beatings going on here, little

worm,' said a familiar if unpleasant voice, 'it'll be done by me.'

'Bane!'

The giant strode towards them.

'Crowman, you should not be here. Go back to my god.'

The lawyer's high-pitched cackle caused the giant to pause.

'God?' tittered Mr Crow. 'I won't be returning to that charcoal monster any time soon.'

Bane was unaware of Mr Crow's terrible crime, but was nonetheless displeased with his behaviour. 'Silence your gibberish and stand aside! I will deal with you later.'

The fear Mr Crow felt for his master quelled some of his madness. Subdued, he fluttered out of sight.

Bane returned his attention to Charlie. 'Your turn has come.'

67

Judgement

Charlie raised her chin to Bane. 'I'm not scared of you any more.'

'What was that?' Even with a gap of several metres between the two of them, Charlie could feel the fury pulsating around him. But she did not flinch.

'I said I'm not scared of you any more.'

'We'll see about that.'

Bane marched forward. Charlie, fired up by dragonsblood, went to meet him.

They had tested each other's mettle in their first encounter but this was different. Faster, stronger and healing at a rapid rate, Charlie was more of a match for her gigantic opponent. Running forward, she ducked beneath a hooked punch and unleashed a sequence of vicious kicks against his torso before rolling out of range. Leaping to her feet with a grim smile, she countered another punch with a flash of Will that left a trail of bright sparks. The two collided, roaring furiously, and exchanged blow after heated blow. The display of raw power cast long shadows dancing across the ceiling. Bane, still the more powerful of the two, would from time to time pummel her to the floor and send her cascading through the air, but each time Charlie would bounce back and attack with renewed vigour.

Weaving, bobbing and ducking, she flowed from one K'Changa stance to the next. Jumping over his attacks, she countered with a flurry of blows and whips of flame before somersaulting away. Back and forth they went, leaving a trail of broken statues and splintered columns in their wake.

'What do you think, Bane?' shouted Charlie. 'I'm not so easy to defeat this time, am I?'

'I don't know where you found your new strength from,' he growled, 'but it'll do you no good. I will still exact my revenge upon you!'

'Revenge!' choked Charlie in disbelief. 'You were the one who stole my parents, killed my friends and plunged this realm into war. Since you came into my life I've lost loved ones, parts of my soul and even pieces of my flesh! If there's to be any revenge it won't be you taking it!'

'Writhing flesh-bag!' snarled Bane. He blocked a strike, then stabbed his python-like fingers towards Charlie's face. 'It is time for Bellania to be free of meddling Keepers and overbearing winged reptiles! By force or by manipulation I will stamp my desire upon this realm!'

Charlie hurled a ribbon of Will at the Stoman Lord. 'Your *desire?*' Her screaming voice cracked with disbelief. 'Your desire for a Stoman empire cost me my parents! You turned them into a mantlepiece ornament! I'm going to stuff my foot through your stupid hoodie and out the other side!'

'We will see, squishy maggot!'

Clearly getting more incensed with Charlie's newfound strength and her impudent words, Bane changed his tactics.

Summoning more power and washing the Throne Room with the chant of his Stonesong, he began to dip his hands into the floor to rip free large clumps of rock. One by one, he sent these slamming through the air towards Charlie. She yelped and jumped out of the way at first, but as she grew more confident she began to actually *play* with the projectiles as though they were a zephyr from a K'Changa game. Grabbing one in passing, she allowed it to almost slip past before spinning round and kicking it with the heel of her foot. She grinned when she saw it change direction. Her smile broadened as she began to intercept more of Bane's missiles – and then, in a move that surprised both of them, she sent one flying right back at Bane. It shattered in a cloud of fragments when it struck his chest.

'Yes! Take that, you bandage-swaddled fool!' Charlie taunted Bane with her cheeky grin. 'I told you I wasn't scared of you any more!'

'WHAT?' growled Bane, his rage erupting. 'Not scared of me? Forget being scared! It does not do justice to the sensation that you should be feeling. Mere fear is not enough. You should be terrified of me! I am BANE! The Western Menace, devourer of men and children, killer of legends, breaker of civilization and a plague upon happiness! I am the silent fear in the night, the quiet dread before sunrise. I am the beating of a terrified heart as it looks into the shadow. I am all that causes the great to tremble and the just to shiver in fear! Do not scorn me, little girl, for it is I who shall break your skinny spine across my knee!'

'Promises, promises!' jeered Charlie. She knew it might seem like she was needlessly baiting an angered lion but she had to keep going. She had to keep him enraged, for the angrier he got the less likely he was to consider her a threat and the more likely he was to make mistakes.

'Gah! Enough of your infantile chatter! The time has come for you to see the true measure of my power!'

Spitting his song out like pure venom, he spread his legs and, ignoring the wind that suddenly whipped and whistled around him, raised his fiercely glowing hands. Tensing his muscles, he made a ripping gesture that caused the ground to tremor and shake. Still churning with a fury that demanded to be released, he forced his arms wide, and the floor of his Throne Room split asunder with a thunderous crack.

Charlie, horrified by what she had unleashed, was forced to dance aside as the crack zigzagged towards her. She squeaked as the ground split even further, revealing an abyss that led to a pool of bubbling lava. For a split second she thought she might have overdone it. Maybe Bane was too angry now. If he continued to unleash this sort of power her chances of survival dwindled. But a feverish sense of determination rose within her and forced her to hold her ground. She would defeat him. *She would.* And in order to do that she had to continue to lure him on.

'Foolish child!' hollered Bane. 'How dare you think you could defy me!'

Groaning with power that was of a different magnitude from Charlie's, he reached up to the ceiling and tried to pull it down on her head. With a shriek, she somersaulted out of the way, but Bane was far from finished. He stamped forward, pursuing her across the room, opening chasm after chasm. Stumbling over a fallen statue, Charlie lost her balance and wasn't quick enough to scramble away. A wail of terror escaped her as she rolled over a chasm's lip and fell down its sheer side. Fear gave her the speed and strength to grasp hold of a jagged rock face. Holding tight, she slammed hip first into the wall. Magma boiled and spat mere metres beneath her feet. Moaning with barely contained fear, she hauled herself up the cliff face and back on to safer ground.

Bane's unpleasant laugh welcomed her back into the fight and, without giving her a chance to recuperate, he began to open more and more chasms, forcing her closer and closer towards his waiting grasp. Realizing what he was doing, Charlie summoned her courage and, instead of jumping away, actually ran towards him. But Bane was wise to her tricks and greeted her with a punishing blow from his fist. It sent her flying, shattering what few columns were left, until the far wall stopped her. Groaning in disbelief, she sank to the floor.

Bane laughed yet again. The sound of it was bitter and cruel to Charlie's ears.

'Not healing so fast now, are you, maggot?'

When Bane ripped free yet another section of the ceiling, Charlie heaved herself upright and staggered for the door. She had to get to the courtyard.

'Going somewhere? Pah! This is my palace. My city. There is nowhere to run to. Nowhere left for you to hide. Why not face the inevitable and surrender to your fate?'

But Charlie was definitely not interested in that. She picked up a handful of broken statue shards and flung them at Bane in the hope that they would momentarily blind him. Without waiting to see if her ruse had worked, she hobbled through the antechamber, pulled herself through the hole in the wall and crawled into the courtyard on hands and knees, hoping against hope that Nibbler wouldn't be late, hoping that for once fate wouldn't stack all the odds against her. Hearing the *thud-thud-thud* of Bane's pursuing footsteps, she crawled faster. For good or ill, for life or death, the moment of truth was fast approaching.

The giant grunted when he caught sight of Last Laugh's corpse.

'Ahhh . . . so that's where you got your new strength from. But you are a fool to think that more blood will help you now.' He forced his way through the wall into the courtyard. He flicked her over with a negligent nudge from his foot so that he could stare down at her for one last time. 'Humans. Squishy little Humans. I hate you all.'

Charlie stared back at him and although fear flickered across her face, it also glistened with determination. 'After all I've endured, after all I've had to fight through, I've never given up. I've never stopped moving forward. My parents have always been in my mind and so too has the thought of defeating you. And at last, at long last, today is my day. Today I am victorious.'

'Are you mad?' sneered Bane. 'Disgusting maggot, it is you who lie beneath my boot, not the other way round. It is you who face defeat.'

Charlie gazed up at him. The fear had left her face now and all that remained was confidence and certainty. 'Oh, I wouldn't be too sure about that. But before you go, I've got one last question that I'm dying to ask.'

Puzzled by her words, Bane actually paused to humour her. 'And what question is that?'

'Well . . . is there any chance you'd let me see what's under that hood?'

'What?'

'No? Oh well, I didn't think you would.' Charlie looked past him and waved at the heavens.

Bane looked up.

Rocksteady, Thief Cutter and their crews clung to the sides of the shaft. Jensen sat astride Hotstepper and at his side was Nibbler. Seeing the tyrant who had imprisoned them in the Winged Realm, the Winged Ones began to howl, their combined voices rising to a thunderous explosion of noise that whipped and echoed around the courtyard. Releasing their grip upon the shaft, they spread their wings, splayed their talons and dropped like stones.

Bane bellowed and lifted his shadow-wreathed fists. The dark halo covering his shoulders spiked and flared. Bunching his legs beneath him, he sprang towards his adversaries.

But it was a futile act of defiance. There was no stopping this avalanche of judgement, no means of stemming the tide of glittering scales and razor-sharp teeth. Winged One after Winged One collided with him and soon he was lost beneath a rustling mass of snarling, growling dragons. 'NO!' he roared and punched a fist free. 'I WILL NOT –'

The Winged Ones shouted wordlessly and pulled him back into their embrace.

'– MY LAND! MY EMPIRE! MY –'

Again he surged free from the mass, flailing at the pack of Winged Ones, and, ignoring the teeth clamped round his limbs, he lurched towards Charlie.

'YOU! MAGGOT! ALL YOUR FAULT –'

Somehow he managed to free an arm from his executioners. Lashing out, he tried to grab at Charlie. But once again his efforts were foiled as the Winged Ones pulled him back.

'– FILTH! I HATE –'

Then he rose no more. The dragons enveloped him and smothered him with their bodies.

Charlie watched with grim eyes. As the mass of winged beasts rolled over Bellania's greatest enemy there were flickers of bright colour as lightning was released and sombre blooms of darkness as Bane's powers ebbed away. It was not a pleasant sight but she had to be sure. She had to be certain that he was gone. She waited until it seemed to be finished.

'I've done it,' she whispered to herself. 'It's over.'

She felt a weight fall from her shoulders. Her back straightened and her eyes glistened not with tears but with hope. After all she had been through – the Wyrms, Lady Narcissa, Stix and Stones, Constantina, the Daemon Kindred, Edge Darkmount, the broken bones, the lost friends and mentors – she had finally succeeded in accomplishing all her ambitions. The Winged Ones had returned (dragons, real dragons, she still couldn't believe it!), Bane was dead (she'd defeated an actual giant!) and Bellania was free. She had suffered dark cruelties and horrors but now at last she could enjoy her fairy-tale moment.

Charlie, still covered in all sorts of dirt and wearing little more than rags, smiled broadly up at the heavens. Life felt sweet.

'Hey!' she said to Rocksteady, who had paused to oversee his brethren. 'Did you guys sort out that god?'

'It wasn't us who attended to the matter,' he replied, 'but that problem has been fixed.'

'So I can Portal?' she asked.

'You can Portal.'

Charlie grinned at that. Summoning her Will, she tore open a rift. As she jumped through the glimmering opening, the last she ever saw of Bane were wisps of his bandages fluttering beneath the Winged Ones' talons.

68

Crow's Revenge

Charlie's Portal deposited her in the ruins of Bane's Throne Room. Breathing freely and feeling more relaxed than she had in a long time, she padded past the chasms and crevices that now marred the marble floor and headed towards Bane's Tapestry . . .

Then staggered to a stop when she realized that something was dreadfully wrong. Where her parents should have been there was nothing but a gaping hole.

'Over here, Charlie,' chuckled a cold voice.

Feeling her stomach lurch, Charlie took her time in turning round. She really didn't want to see what came next.

Mr Crow stood at the edge of one of the crevices. The smile on his face and the nasty gleam of victory in his dead eyes said it all. On either side of him, still encased in lumps of the amber-like substance, were her parents.

Elias and Mya Keeper.

And they were uncomfortably close to the chasm's edge with nothing but a long fall between them and the fires below.

'You –' began Charlie, but was cut short by the lawyer.

'Oh no, no, no,' he tut-tutted. 'We won't be having any

Mr Crow the Lawyer

of that, my filly. It is my time to speak. Yes, it is.' He paused to twitch and twitter, then waited for a wayward crow to return to his body before carrying on. 'I'm a lawyer so I can accept that other people will always have different views. But let me tell you this, my pretty filly, in my humble opinion *all of this is your fault!* Yes, you, Charlie, have caused all of these mishaps to happen to poor Mr Crow. So it is only fitting that you suffer some hardship by way of recompense. But I'm not an unnecessarily cruel man; I'm a lawyer, not a thug, so I present to you a choice. Who shall pay for your sins? Elias Keeper?' He gave the casing that housed her father a little nudge that carried him closer to the edge. 'Or Mya Keeper?' He gave her mother's casing a similar nudge. 'So who is it to be, my filly? Make your choice.'

'I'm not playing your game.'

'Oh yes, you will, Charlie. You will! For if you do not, both parties will take the plunge!' Reaching out, he pushed the casings further until they were teetering right on the edge. 'Choose!'

'Neither.'

'Oh, how very spineless of you. Choose one so that at least the other will live. Show some of that courage I've always been hearing about. Come on, little filly, it really isn't all that hard. Just pick the parent who you love the least.'

Charlie scowled at that. 'You're more twisted than I ever remember.'

'Yes!' shrieked Mr Crow, abruptly furious. He briefly split into birds before assuming his original shape. 'And who do we have to thank for that? You, little miss perfect. You! Now make your choice before I grow weary and make it for you.'

'No,' repeated Charlie firmly. 'You don't get it, do you? I'm not making a choice and I'm not playing your game. And you must have been reading too many bad books or watching too many cheesy movies to think that a thing like this would work in real life. Only an idiot would allow themselves to get sucked into a decision where one of their parents had to die. Forget it.'

'Last chance, Charlie Keeper.'

'No! This is *your* last chance. If you leave now I'll give you six months' head start before I come for you, and that's the only offer you'll get from me. Now or ever.'

Mr Crow looked at her like she was a fool. 'You don't seem to grasp the principle of my offer, do you, my little filly? I hold all the cards and you have none.'

'Oh, I wouldn't know about that. My friends are just behind you. I'd say that gives me a slight edge to my bargaining power.'

'I'm not falling for that old trick,' sneered the lawyer, and instead of looking round he kept his eyes fixed firmly on Charlie.

'It's no trick,' said Jensen.

Hotstepper was too dignified to say anything and merely growled loud enough for echoes to bounce around the once great room.

Nibbler, on the other hand, couldn't have kept his mouth closed for all the money in the world. 'You pack of feather-less birds! You big-nosed chump! You'd better step back nice and quiet or I'm going to finish the job I started in Sylvaris. Next time I open my mouth –'

'Thanks, Nibbler,' said Charlie, interrupting his flow. 'I've got this.'

He blushed and waved at her.

Mr Crow screeched, more than ever like a bird. Twisting his head round, he stared at Charlie's companions. He was somewhat reassured to see that they still stood on the far side of the room and that several crevices lay between him and them. There was still an opportunity for him to come out on top.

'So what's it going to be, Mr Crow?' asked Charlie. 'I come for you now or in six months' time?'

Rapidly growing more and more unstable, Crow jerked back and forth from bird form to lawyer. Pretending he'd never heard her words, he shouted at her, 'Choose!'

'No.'

A stillness settled on Mr Crow. 'Very well. I'll choose for you. Both.'

Screeching, he pushed both parents from the ledge. With a final hop and a skip, he leaped into the air and – with that peculiar sound of breaking glass – split apart into hundreds of crows.

'Nibbler!' screamed Charlie.

'On it!' he replied and burst into motion.

'Hotstepper!' cried Charlie. 'Keep those birds in this room!'

He nodded and spread his wings wide.

Charlie raised her arms and tore open two Portals. Seconds later, her parents, still encased in the fabric of the Tapestry, appeared through the Portals in front of her. They plummeted back down the chasm only to reappear seconds later, falling in a non-stop loop much like she had done with Jensen on top of Narcissa's tower.

Nibbler appeared above the chasm's edge with Charlie's mother in his grasp. He gently deposited her casing at Charlie's feet, then disappeared back over the edge. Long moments later he returned with her father.

'Thank you, Nibbler.'

'You got it, Charlie.'

The two of them paused to watch Hotstepper hurl himself around the Throne Room in complicated manoeuvres. Every once in a while he would unleash a jet of flame, shepherding the crows away from the exit.

'Want to help Hotstepper push Mr Crow towards me?'

Nibbler grinned. 'It'll be a pleasure.'

Jumping in the air, he joined his elder brother in harassing the birds.

'Hey, Mr Crow!' shouted Charlie. 'If you don't want to get eaten by dragons or burned to a crisp, I'd suggest you get out of here.'

The birds shrieked angrily at her.

'What? Nowhere to go?' She pulled open a large Portal. 'I know you like choices,' she hollered, 'so how about this? You've got five seconds to get out of here and then I'm going to let Nibbler and Hotstepper indulge in their passion for roast chicken. Sorry, roast crow!'

The two Winged Ones growled accommodatingly for her and even breathed out an extra flare of flame. Jensen, looking on, smiled in amusement.

'One! Two! Three! Four!'

The birds didn't wait for the count of five. With a nasty shriek, they spat towards Charlie's Portal. She waited for them to grow closer, then tensed and twisted both her Will and the

Portal in an unusual motion. When the last crow had disappeared she allowed the golden circle to shimmer shut.

'So where did the other end of the Portal open?' asked Jensen with an appreciative grin.

'In the lava?' suggested Nibbler.

'Did you send him to the Tangerine Isles so the crocophiles could have an afternoon snack?' said Hotstepper.

'None of those,' said Charlie.

'So where did ya send him?' asked Jensen. 'Back ta Earth?'

'No, I sent him to as many different places as possible and to as many different destinations as I could think of. I've scattered those birds up and down Bellania, across Earth and even sent some to the Patchwork Realm. There's no way he's coming back from that.'

'So he's not dead?' asked Nibbler.

'No,' replied Charlie, 'but he's not exactly whole either. And at least this way we can rest assured that he's never going to hurt anyone ever again.'

'Well, I'm not sure about that,' said Hotstepper, taking the part of devil's advocate. 'We're talking about hundreds of evil birds haunting the realms. There could be a whole lot of people out there getting pecked on the hand right about now.'

'Yeah, maybe,' admitted Charlie, then chuckled at the foolish image his words conjured. 'But sooner or later any bird that angry is going to get swatted to the ground and turned into mincemeat. No . . . it's the best solution I could think of. Besides, what's the worst that could happen?'

'Grumpy, black-feathered birds try and take over the world?' said Nibbler.

'A sharp increase in unwelcome bird poop falling on people's heads?' suggested Hotstepper.

'Courts of law constantly get interrupted by crows pretending ta be injury lawyers?' said Jensen with a sly wink.

Charlie paused to shake her head at her friends. 'I gave you guys the perfect opening for bird puns and that's the best you can deliver? It's a sad day in Bellania when the only heroes we have to offer are you three.'

'I like the taking-over-the-world idea,' admitted Hotstepper. 'Maybe we should come up with a name for potential bird threats? How does this grab you? Doctor Crow and his army of Feathered Commandos.'

'Nice,' agreed Jensen. 'Wot about the Dark Crowman and his Peckmeister Minions?'

'Oh, my days, are you trying to kill me with pure cheesiness? Enough already,' insisted Charlie. 'Stop trying to drop one-liners and help me with my parents.'

Charlie used what was left of her Will to open a large Portal back to the Jade Circle. The others lifted her parents with as much reverence as possible and together they left the ruined shambles of Bane's Throne Room behind.

Minutes later, Charlie and Nibbler returned through another Portal. They scampered over to the dais with cheeky expressions plastered across their faces. Grunting and groaning, they strained against the Devouring Throne until it toppled into one of the chasms to plunge into the lava with a satisfactory splash. Job done, the two exchanged a high five then departed, to return no more.

69

The Day After

E'Jaaz strode by Charlie's side as they wandered along Deepforest's floor. The dragonsblood had not been as kind to him as it had to Charlie. Perhaps he had taken too much or maybe he had tried to use too much Will while physically weakened. Whatever the cause, it had left grey streaks in his hair and dark shadows beneath his eyes, his face looked gaunt and it was clear that he had lost a lot of weight. But for all the physical changes he had undergone, his roguish spirit still remained, he still stepped with a swagger and each time he smiled his white teeth flashed merrily in the sunlight.

The pleasant sound of Treesong carried through the air and with it the scent of fresh sap and blooming lilies. As the two followed the gently curving path it flowed around several of Deepforest's gigantic tree trunks to reveal a panoramic view of Sylvaris.

Sadly, the city was not what it had once been. But the people of Sylvaris would not be allowing the city to remain in such a sorry state for long. As soon as Bane's forces had been defeated and the last of the Stowyrms torn from the skies, the inhabitants had set to work rebuilding the city from its ashes. Stoman soldiers and Stonesingers judged guilty of their crimes were working in supervised chain gangs clearing the land of detritus and waste. Tremen, Humans and free Stomen were planting new saplings and measuring foundations so that the fabled towers of Sylvaris could rise up once more. Clustered in scattered groups were the true architects of the city's revival, the Treesingers. Their song teased saplings into spurts of rapid growth, sending the young trees climbing into the air, their bark thickening and their branches dividing into fresh limbs heavy with green leaves. Those who weren't intent on replenishing Deepforest's trees were busy using their powers to grow fresh towers. Floor by floor, new buildings began to take shape, growing right before Charlie's delighted eyes.

'I . . . I can't believe it,' she said. 'The speed of it still amazes me.'

'It'll take long months before Sylvaris reclaims its former splendour,' said E'Jaaz. 'But you're right, it's a sight to behold, is it not? A sight like none other! And Lady Dridif is keen to take advantage of this rebuilding – she aims to make the city more than it was before. There will be new bridges, wider boulevards, better organized marketplaces, more schools and, of course, a new K'Changa amphitheatre.'

Charlie grinned and was about to reply when a massive bundle of fur knocked her from her feet and proceeded to lick her face like it was going out of fashion.

'Sic Boy! Good to see you . . . but hey, enough with the licking! Let me up, you big oaf!' She struggled to her feet and gave the large dog a disapproving look, then, unable to resist, gave him a hug. 'It's good to see you, boy. I'm glad you made it through everything in one piece.'

'Groof!'

'Hey, blossom!' called a familiar voice.

'Kelko!' Charlie grinned. Her day kept getting better. 'What are you doing here? I thought you were supposed to be helping the Jade Circle?'

'I was but I figured that after all me hard work as a general I deserved some time off for good behaviour,' he said with a shrug, then went on to add, 'The Jade Circle has been so busy with governing the lands that they haven't got around ta removing me honorary title. I figure I've got another couple of days of abusing me position before they demote me so I'm going ta enjoy it while I can.'

'You're a bad man,' said E'Jaaz with an approving smile.

'I do me best,' said Kelko, smirking.

'Kelko?' began Charlie.

'Wot is it, blossom?'

'I . . . Well, is there any news about my parents? I mean . . .'

'Ah . . . Charlie, freeing yer parents is going ta take the Winged Ones a while. It's not an easy process, and ta ensure yer parents their safety the Winged Ones are going ta have ta take their time. However, if yer've got a minute or two, Jensen and I have a little something for ya that might take yer mind off the waiting . . .'

'What is it?'

'Pfft. I'm not going ta tell ya now, am I? That'd spoil the surprise. Now if ya would, how about following old General Kelko dis way?'

'Hold up,' said E'Jaaz. 'I think this would be the perfect moment for me to say my goodbyes.'

'Goodbyes?' asked Charlie, a little shocked.

'Don't worry,' chuckled E'Jaaz. 'It's not a *you'll never see me again* goodbye. It's more of a *I'll be gone for a couple of months but promise to come back later* kind of goodbye.'

'Where are you going?' asked Charlie.

'Brazil.'

'Brazil? You mean Brazil on Earth?'

'Yes. It's where Marsila's house and Gateway is. With things settling down over here someone is going to have to take on the duty of watching her patch and I figure it should be me.'

'Wot are ya going ta do over there?' asked Kelko.

'Honestly? I'm going to relax. I want a chance to get my strength back before I'm sent off on my next Keeper's mission. Besides, it'll be great to see where Marsila lived. I've also persuaded some Stonesingers to craft a statue of her; I'm not sure where to put it, here or in Brazil. But there's no rush and I like the idea of having a chance to think things through. Charlie?'

'Huh? What?' said Charlie, clearly lost in the thought of maybe one day visiting Marsila's old home herself.

'Hug, please.'

'Oops.' Charlie went over and pulled him into a warm embrace. 'Will I be able to reach you?'

'Of course. You're a Keeper. Travel is always going to be quick and easy for you so if you feel like you need some sun and a Brazilian breakfast, drop by any time. The Bellanian entrance to Marsila's Gateway is near the southern fishing village of Pherose. Lady Dridif will give you directions if you can't get there through Earth.'

He gave Charlie another hug, flashed both her and Kelko

a brilliant smile, then pulled open a Portal and disappeared.

Sic Boy nudged Charlie in the side and with a *groof* indicated with his head that she should follow Kelko. The three of them weaved through the outskirts of Sylvaris, allowing them a further chance to admire the new growth and rising buildings before heading back into the forest proper. There they found Jensen, Nibbler and several other Tremen in a grassy clearing. A wide circle had been burned into the grass and off to one side a barbecue smouldered.

'Me little Hippotomi!' called Jensen with an easy smile. 'Are ya ready?'

'Ready for what?'

Jensen pulled a brightly coloured zephyr from a bag and tossed it teasingly from hand to hand. 'Why, for a game of K'Changa, of course. From wot I've heard it's been a while since yer last game so it only makes sense that we take the opportunity ta beat ya while ya're not at yer best.'

'What?' snorted Charlie. 'What kind of sportsmanship is that?'

'Cheeky sportsmanship!' replied Jensen with an even larger smile. 'Drums, please!'

A fiery rhythm filled the clearing as the Tremen began to pound upon their drums.

'Right!' said Kelko, jumping into the circle. 'Winner gets first dibs on lunch and the loser has ta treat everyone else ta drinks and dinner!'

'Ha!' retorted Charlie. She slid into the ring and began to slink from stance to flowing stance. 'You're on!'

The Delightful Brothers and their mounts perched on top of one of the southernmost peaks that rose from the Western Mountains. To the north of them lay the city of the Western Mountains. Winged Ones flew in the skies, patrolling the land and ensuring that the new Stoman council would heed their demands for peace. To the south lay the Slumbering Hills and beyond that lay the glitter of the Chiming Grounds. Past the Chiming Grounds lay lands that neither brother had visited.

'What now, brother?' asked Stix.

Stones hefted his necklace with delight. A new tooth, far larger than any of the others, glinted in the afternoon sunlight. 'I think we have outstayed our welcome. Perhaps it is time to move on?'

'What about Charlie Keeper?'

'I think the pain we have caused her will haunt her for life. There is no need to do more.'

'But she's a legend now. She's the girl that took down Bane. Think what it would do for our reputation if we –'

Stones lifted a hand to cut his brother short. 'Forget Charlie Keeper. That little rabbit is old news. Let us look to the future. We are the Delightful Brothers! Let us forget Charlie Keeper's legend and build our own!'

'Build our own legend?' Stix paused to rub one of his sword hilts. 'I like that idea.' Shielding his eyes from the sun, he looked north to the distant silhouettes of flying Winged Ones. 'Those beasties might put a crimp on our style, though. I'm not a fan of waiting until their next Chrysalis Period for us to make our move.'

'So let's go somewhere else,' said Stones. 'Somewhere that the Winged Ones can't reach us.'

'A different realm?'

'I was thinking about the hidden south. Now that Fo Fum has gone, there's a power vacuum down there waiting to be filled. The Delightful Brothers would fill that void perfectly. Let us head past the Chiming Grounds, let us travel past the Great Deserts and part the Great Veil to reach the lands beyond. With Fo Fum out of the way we could defeat the Blind Monks and rule the Dark Temple of the Whispering Wind! We would be as kings! Our names would be shouted across the lands!'

'I like it, brother!' agreed Stix. His yellow eyes glinted with imagined glories. 'A fitting future indeed.'

Grinning contentedly, the two waited until the skies were clear of Winged Ones. Then, guiding their Stowyrms over the mountain crest, they disappeared from sight.

The reputation of the Delightful Brothers would live on.

70

Nibbler

After playing K'Changa for most of the afternoon and having enjoyed a succulent barbecued feast, the companions strolled back through the forest towards Sylvaris.

'How did I lose?' asked Charlie. 'How?'

Jensen and Kelko cracked up laughing.

'Ah, lass, ya might be the legendary slayer of giants but ya still got a thing or two ta learn about K'Changa,' said Jensen with a twinkle in his eye.

Charlie mock-pouted. 'I knew it was a mistake to agree not to use my Will. Of course, you know I won't be able to buy you guys any dinner, right?'

'Huh?' said Kelko. 'Why not?'

'I've got no money.' She turned the pockets of her trousers inside out to prove her point.

'Maybe Jensen can lend you some?' suggested Nibbler.

Before Jensen could offer a suitably cheeky reply, they were interrupted by the flutter of wings. It was Hotstepper and Thief Cutter.

'Apologies for interrupting you,' said Hotstepper. 'But Torn Moon and the Elders request that Charlie of the Keepers and our little brother meet with them.'

'What? Now?' asked Nibbler.

'Now, little brother,' said Thief Cutter.

Charlie and Nibbler said their goodbyes to their friends. Climbing on Nibbler's back, the two of them joined Hotstepper and Thief Cutter in the skies. As they circled the recuperating city they could see that a large crowd of Winged Ones had gathered near the Jade Tower. The four of them landed and made their way over to Torn Moon and Rocksteady's side.

'Child,' said Torn Moon, addressing Nibbler. 'My thanks for attending.'

'Um, no problem,' said Nibbler. 'What's this all about?'

'We have asked you here today to help rebalance the scales. We need you to help swell the numbers of Keepers in this land. Will you aid us in this endeavour?'

Nibbler looked to Charlie, then back to his elders. 'Sure.'

'And so it shall be done.' Torn Moon raised her voice to address all of the Winged Ones gathered around her. 'Our little brother has agreed to help us in Bellania's time of need. Pay him tribute for his sacrifice.'

All the Winged Ones reared back on to their hind legs and let loose a wave of flame that crackled into the skies.

'Sacrifice?' said Nibbler, more curious than alarmed.

Torn Moon padded over and rested one of her great paws upon Nibbler's head. In a quieter voice she said, 'Child, remember that whatever happens here today, we will always love you.'

Charlie, growing slightly anxious, tried to make her way to her friend's side but found she couldn't slip past the Winged Ones who crowded around Nibbler.

'Charlie?' he called in a hesitant voice.

'Nibbler!' shouted Charlie, feeling a surge of panic.

'Ssh,' said Hotstepper. 'Worry not. We will not harm our little brother.'

'What's going on?' asked Charlie.

'Remember when Rumbling Hunger said that one day soon you might get to see what you call "magic"?'

'Yes.'

'Well, today is that day. Stand back and watch.'

The Winged Ones pressed forward, hiding Nibbler from sight with the bulk of their bodies. With the background sound of treesinging washing over them, the Winged Ones opened their mouths wide and spat forth great tides of light.

Charlie blinked at the phenomenon. She had seen the dragons use flame and lightning before but never pure light. She blinked again when she realized the light was the same colour as her Will. Purest gold.

The moment stretched, then one by one the Winged Ones closed their mouths. Standing back, they shuffled out of the way so Charlie could enter the circle.

'Huh?' said Charlie. She was more confused than she had ever been in her life. A very naked teenage boy crouched where Nibbler should have been. 'What's going on? Where's . . . where's Nibbler?'

The Winged Ones didn't speak. They only had eyes for the teenager. The boy stood hesitantly, then staggered as though unused to standing on his own feet. Regaining his balance, he looked down at his body. One of the adult Winged Ones, sensitive to the ways of Humans, tied a cape taken from a Jade councillor around the boy's waist in an effort to preserve his dignity.

'What?' repeated Charlie. While a small part of her was quick enough to work out what had happened, the rest of her mind struggled to come to terms with the enormity of the occurrence. 'I don't get it. What did you guys do with Nibbler?'

At the sound of the name, the boy started. He twisted round so he could look at her.

'Charlie?' he said in a voice that was instantly recognizable.

'Nibbler?'

She couldn't believe it – how could a dragon be turned into a Human?

The teenager seemed a little older than her, maybe fifteen or sixteen years of age. His body was layered with unbelievable muscle, giving him the appearance of an athlete or disciplined gymnast. But if his body was a work of finely chiselled art created by master sculptors, it looked as though apprentices had been allowed to work on his face. It was ridged and formed with hard, unforgiving lines. His jaw was too large, his cheeks too sharp and his nose surely too wide, but Charlie realized it was her friend the moment she saw his eyes. They were the same intense solid orbs of blue that she knew so well. She remembered the day when he had first appeared, flying over Narcissa's tower to send gusts of flame at the Alavisian Watchmen who threatened her, and his eyes blazed with as much life now as they had then.

As Charlie looked at her friend, now made mortal, she felt something melt in her heart.

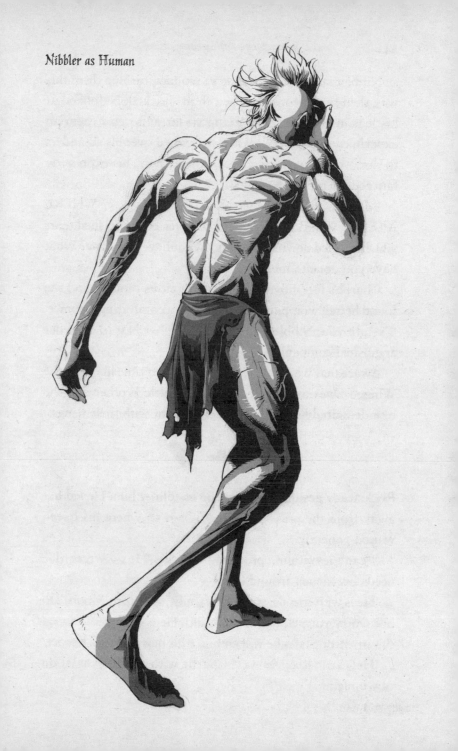

Nibbler as Human

Nibbler stared at his hands in wonder, turning them this way then that. More bemused than shocked, he looked at his legs in surprise, even going so far as to give them an experimental pinch. But when he looked over his shoulders to discover an unexpected lack of feathers, his expression faltered, then grew horrified.

'My w-wings . . .' he garbled. 'Where are . . .? WHERE ARE MY WINGS?' His large blue eyes began to shed tears which trickled down his cheeks. 'What have you done? What have you done to me?'

Charlie's feet moved without conscious thought and she found herself wrapping her friend into a comforting embrace. 'I've got you, Nibbler,' she said, doing her best to calm her anguished companion. 'I've got you.'

Aware that words were insufficient at a time like this, the Winged Ones moved closer to their little brother and the blonde-haired Keeper and covered them with their wings.

Rocksteady gestured for Charlie to follow him. He led her away from the press of Winged Ones to where his queen waited patiently.

'I can't leave him,' protested Charlie. 'He's a wreck! He needs his friends around him.'

'He is with friends; we're his family,' said Torn Moon. 'Do not worry yourself about our child. He is strong and when this moment passes he will embrace his new role as a Keeper.'

'He's a . . . Keeper?' said Charlie with a long exhalation of wonder.

'Hmmm, E'Jaaz of the Keepers did mention you could be a little slow on the uptake.'

'Slow on the uptake?' Charlie was too shocked to squawk but the words still came out a little high-pitched. 'I . . . look, it's not every day you get to have a dragon for a best friend, then see him turned into a Human.'

'It's Winged One, not dragon,' remonstrated Torn Moon. 'And he could better be described as Humanish.'

'Human-*ish*?' repeated Charlie. 'But you said he's a Keeper? Does that mean he can open Portals and hold the Will and the Way?'

'He will retain some of his Winged One's abilities while he will gain some of the Keeper's abilities too.'

Charlie's mind, quick as a silverfish, was leaping ahead. 'Waaaaaaait. Wait a minute. Everyone's been telling me that Keepers share Winged Ones' blood. Is this . . .? Did this . . .? Is this where my family came from? Am I related to a dragon?'

'Winged One,' corrected Torn Moon automatically. 'Listen, little Charlie of the Keepers, I am a queen to my people and I have many tasks to complete before day's end. So as much as I would enjoy listening to you bumble through the history and etiquette of Keepers and Winged Ones, I must attend to my children. I did, however, pull you aside as a courtesy to inform you that our healers have nearly removed the Tapestry fabric that constrained your parents. If all goes well you will be able to see them tomorrow morning.'

Charlie's face flushed and she felt her palms tingle with excitement.

'Charlie of the Keepers?'

'Yes, Torn Moon?'

'My thanks for saving the realm.'

Lost for words, Charlie merely nodded. Torn Moon's wings eclipsed the sun, then with rapid beats she took to the skies.

Charlie made to return to Nibbler's side but paused when Rocksteady stretched out a paw to bar her way. 'Lady Dridif wishes a word with you.'

Charlie looked to the Jade Tower, then back to the huddle of Winged Ones that surrounded her best friend. 'What about Nibbler?'

'Nibbler will survive,' said Rocksteady. 'And as much as we appreciate your loyalty to our brother, we require some time with him alone.'

'Why?'

'Before we send him into the world of mortals we must share some last words of wisdom with him. Knowledge and words intended only for the ears of Winged Ones.'

Charlie pulled a sour face but felt unable to offer a compelling argument that would allow her to butt into a private matter. 'I . . . OK. I'll go talk to Dridif but tell Nibbler I'll be back as soon as I'm done.'

'I shall,' said Rocksteady, then stopped Charlie as she turned to depart. 'Charlie of the Keepers, your loyalty is to be commended. Our little brother is lucky to have you as a friend.'

Charlie blushed. 'I'm sure it's the other way around but, er, thanks.'

Rocksteady smiled.

'Will he be OK?' asked Charlie.

'Yes. He is not the first of our kind to make the change. He will always bemoan the loss of his wings but the joys of being a Keeper do offer advantages that will, with time, bring a smile to his face.' Rocksteady took several steps, then paused. 'I look forward to seeing you tonight.'

'Why?' asked Charlie. 'What's happening tonight?'

'Ha! If you do not know then I will not tell you. I'm not one for spoiling surprises so I will wait for Lady Dridif to inform you.'

Having said all that he would, Rocksteady left her and returned to his brethren.

Charlie jumped through a Portal to land lightly in the Keepers' Room of Travel at the top of the Jade Tower. Curious as to what Lady Dridif had to say, she jogged down the spiralling stairs and tugged open a door, only to slip across a freshly mopped floor. A hand flashed out and grabbed her by the forearm, preventing her from falling flat on her face. Once she regained her feet Charlie smiled, then faltered when she saw that her assistant was none other than Constantina, Lady Narcissa's daughter. She was dressed in a maid's uniform, a mop in her free hand and a bucket of suds at her feet. It appeared that the First Maid was still putting her newest assistant to work cleaning the stairs to the Keepers' Room of Travel, a poetic justice of sorts.

Charlie didn't know what to say. The older girl had been a real thorn in her side and had always seemed to act with malicious intent. She also couldn't help but notice that Constantina had not relinquished her grip upon her sleeve.

'Thank you,' said Constantina, breaking the awkward silence. The words were so heartfelt and at such odds with how Charlie remembered the girl that her mouth dropped open in astonishment. Seeing Charlie's expression, Narcissa's daughter grimaced. 'Look, I know things are never going to be right between you and me. You killed my mother, though from what I hear I understand it might have been an accident. I also know now that Bane was in some way involved. Still, that doesn't change the fact that my mother died at your hand.'

'Constantina –' began Charlie.

'Let me finish,' insisted Constantina. 'That act is always going to hang over our heads and I promise you this: you and I will *never* be friends. But I've learned a lot recently and I've been forced to look at myself too. To say it's been a steep learning curve would be an understatement.' She paused to take a big breath. 'Look, I was wrong to challenge you and I was wrong to try and take the pendant from you. You were the one meant to carry it and I'm glad you did. It was you who saved Sylvaris and it was you who returned the Winged Ones to Bellania . . . so thank you. Really.'

Having said her piece, Constantina pushed her hand into Charlie's and gripped it in some kind of handshake. Then, blushing furiously, she picked up her mop and returned to scrubbing the floor. Charlie scratched her head in wonder. She didn't know what to say to that or even how to start making a reply.

'Ya weren't bothering Charlie Keeper, were ya, Constantina?' called a voice from further down the hallway. It was the First Maid, a well-padded lady with a crisply ironed uniform. Charlie noticed that Constantina gritted her teeth as the First Maid approached and her cheeks blushed an even deeper shade of red.

'Uh, no,' said Charlie. 'She was being very helpful . . . and, er, she was doing a good job.'

She was surprised to find herself coming to the rescue of her old foe. So too was Constantina, if her face was anything to go by. But Charlie shrugged it off; it had been one of those days and she had long since learned that life spun in funny circles.

71

Celebrations

As Charlie trotted towards the chamber of the Jade Circle the Treman guards opened the large doors and waved her through with cheerful smiles.

The chamber was empty apart from Lady Dridif and the two strangers who stood by her side. The woman on Dridif's left was tall and graceful, with the darkest of skins. She was attired in green and brown clothing that in Charlie's mind was reminiscent of the sort of thing that Robin Hood or his companions would have worn. The man on Dridif's right was Asian-looking with grey dreadlocks bundled into a mound atop his head, a wild-looking grey beard, saffron-coloured robes and an apparent fondness for beaded jewellery.

'I asked the councillors ta give us some privacy,' explained Dridif with a welcome smile and a gesture that Charlie should join them. 'Dis is Tosin Keeper –' she introduced the woman, who gave Charlie a polite nod – 'and dis is Haiku Keeper.' The man smiled brightly and bobbed his head in a move that sent his dreadlocks swaying.

'We have heard of all your accomplishments,' said Tosin in a dulcet voice. 'As Keepers, you have done us proud.'

'You do your parents much honour,' added Haiku,

underlining Tosin's compliment. 'And we have you to thank for our freedom.'

'Tosin and Haiku were imprisoned in one of the lower dominions,' said Dridif by way of explanation. 'With the return of the Winged Ones and the demise of Bane's guardians, they were able ta escape. I have asked them here today not only ta meet ya but ta tie up loose ends.'

Lady Dridif crossed over to the Jade Table. Summoning her powers as First Speaker, she placed her hands upon the turquoise surface of the table. The colours shifted, revealing the entombed body of Azariah Keeper lying within the very table. With his arms folded across his chest and a serene expression on his face, he looked the very embodiment of a buried knight.

'Our friend has lain here throughout the battles that have struck at our city and we have taken comfort from his presence,' said Dridif. She stroked the table over Azariah's face with fondness. 'But the time has come for him ta find his true resting ground.'

'With the two of us,' said Tosin, 'and you, we can form a Triad. Together we can send Azariah through to the Nether Realm where he can find solace amongst the other heroes of our land.'

Charlie's heart fluttered at the thought. The idea had first been mentioned to her at the time of his death but without other Keepers present it had not been a possibility. Now that it was, it certainly seemed a suitable undertaking for her fallen mentor.

'Or,' said Dridif, 'ya can wait for yer parents ta awake and do it with them.'

Charlie's mouth dropped. Although the Winged Ones had promised that her parents would awake soon, the possibility of forming a Triad with them was something that had never occurred to her.

'I . . . if you don't mind, I'd like to wait for my parents,' said Charlie. It seemed more fitting to send Azariah on his way with the aid of Elias and Mya Keeper, more personal.

'Good,' said Haiku with a beaming smile. 'If Azariah were with us now I'm sure he would take comfort from knowing it is his friends who will send him through to the Nether Realm.'

'We will leave you now,' said Tosin, 'but we look forward to seeing you tonight.'

'Er . . . wait, what's happening tonight?' asked Charlie.

'I'm sure Lady Dridif will tell you,' said Tosin with a smile.

'Wait!' urged Charlie. 'Before you go, my friend Nibbler was a dragon but –'

'We have heard,' said Haiku. And surprised Charlie by not remonstrating with her for calling Nibbler a dragon. 'And do not worry. He is not the first to have been changed, nor will he be the last. Although young Nibbler might take a while to adjust to his new form, adjust he will.' He graced her with another big smile. 'See you tonight, Charlie.'

The two exited from the chamber, leaving Charlie with Dridif.

'So what *is* happening tonight?' asked Charlie.

'Can't ya guess?'

Charlie squirmed uncomfortably. 'A celebration parade?'

'Ya got it in one,' said Dridif. 'I know ya're not one ta enjoy being the centre of attention but Kelko and Jensen, not ta

mention all the councillors, were most insistent . . . come ta
think of it, so were Torn Moon and Hotstepper. So there will
be a celebration parade tonight and ya, Charlie Keeper,
will be our guest of honour. Now, we can't be sending ya out
dressed like that so if ya would, please come this way.'

Dridif led her to a side room where a selection of clothes
had been laid out.

'I had our seamstresses put these together using measurements from yer old clothes so they should fit. Pick wot ya
want, then meet me back in the Jade Chamber.'

Charlie couldn't help but grin as she stared at the selection of clothes. She wasn't normally swayed by the ebb and
flow of fashion but this was different. There were baggy
trousers with discreet dragon motifs, shimmering shirts with
seams of silver, dark-hued jackets with scrollwork across
the shoulders and rows of boots and shoes, some made from
a fabric that seemed to suck at the light and others tailored
from a material that was as tough as stone but as light as a
feather and as comfortable as silk. Arranged on a table was
a selection of jewellery – bracelets made from lionbark, rings
of idlefire, necklaces hammered from strange metals – and
of course, in true Treman fashion, a further selection of
bright feathers with which to secure her topknot in place.

Feeling as though she could get used to this life after all
the hardship she had endured, Charlie pulled on the funki-
est clothes that she could find, wrapped a silver bracelet
round one wrist, a leather bangle round the other, then fixed
her hair with a verdant green feather. Leaving the rings and
necklaces behind, she checked her reflection in a large mirror,
grinned, then headed back into the Jade Chamber.

'Surprise!' shouted Kelko, followed moments later by everyone else.

Charlie gaped in astonishment. All her friends were there: Crumble Shard, Jensen, Kelko, Sic Boy, Nibbler (looking uncomfortable in his new skin), Salixia and, arranged behind them in two rows, all the Jade councillors. A generous spread of foods and drinks had been laid across side tables and footmen dressed in their finest were waiting with trays of delicacies.

'I, er . . .' stuttered Charlie, not sure where or how to begin.

Lady Dridif stilled her tongue with a waved hand. 'We have one more surprise for ya, Charlie.'

The councillors parted to reveal –

'Grandma!' Charlie ran across the room and pulled her gran into a fat hug.

'Sweetness,' said her gran, 'you've grown.'

Trying to decide whether to continue holding her grandmother or to stand back so she could better admire her, Charlie asked, 'Are you OK? Is everything . . .? I mean, I've been worrying about you for –'

'I'm fine, Charlie!' said her gran with a laugh that tinkled delightfully across the room. 'Really I am. After that horrid Mr Crow disappeared I got a little bit lost but the neighbours took me in and they were wonderful. I got my medicine back too.'

Charlie peeked over her gran's shoulder at Lady Dridif; the wise councillor nodded back to verify everything that her gran had said.

'Wow . . . awesome!' said Charlie, still a little breathless.

'Are you going to tell me what you've been up to?' asked Charlie's gran.

'Sure, Grandma, and . . . wait a minute. You're OK with being here in Bellania? It's not a shock to you?'

'No, sweetie, of course it isn't. I've been here many times with Mya.'

Bits and pieces of the jigsaw of Charlie's life began to fit into place. It did, after all, make sense for her gran to know about Bellania; you didn't live in a house like theirs without learning about both realms.

'How did you get here, Grandma?'

'Ya have Tosin and Haiku ta thank for that,' said Dridif. 'I sent them round ta check yer house. They cleared it of a couple of Shades that had been lurking in wait, then found yer gran. After all yer family have done I wanted ta make sure ya were reunited before yer parents are woken.'

'And do I have you to thank for this gathering?'

'I thought ya'd appreciate a more private party before tonight's parade,' said Dridif with a gentle smile. 'So, shall we get ta it?'

'Yes!' hollered Kelko. 'Party!'

'Paaaaaarty!' echoed Jensen in their time-honoured fashion.

'Paaaaaaaaarty!' shouted Nibbler, getting carried away with the moment enough to forget his lack of wings.

'Grrrroof!' barked Sic Boy.

'Party?' said Charlie's gran. 'Ooh, yes please! Who's for a dance?'

Charlie grinned.

During a lull in the party Nibbler gestured for Charlie to follow him out on to one of the balconies that lined the Jade Tower. Still laughing at one of Jensen's outrageous jokes, she joined him. Her grin faltered when she saw him looking nervously at her with his piercing blue eyes.

'What is it, Nibbler?' she asked with sudden concern.

'I . . . uh, well . . .'

'It's not like you to be shy with words. What's the matter?'

'Well . . . it's just that we haven't really had a chance to talk since I changed. Since I became Human.'

'I know, it's been crazy, hasn't it? There's been so much going on that –' She stopped talking when she realized how anxious he appeared. 'Nibbler? Are you OK?'

'I wanted to know if you and me are still good?' he blurted, his unusual face looking anguished. 'Do you think, well . . . has being Human changed our friendship?'

Charlie's jaw dropped open.

'What? No, how can that have changed anything? You're still you . . .' She faltered as she realized that wasn't exactly true. 'OK, you might not have your wings any more and you might be walking around on two legs instead of four but you're still Nibbler. You're still my boy.'

It was such a simple thing to say but she said it with such heartfelt honesty that it instantly silenced any of Nibbler's doubts. He released a big breath and grinned unreservedly at Charlie.

'Whew, that's good to know. I'd been getting more and more worried about that as the day drew on. So does this mean you're going to help me out with learning to become a Keeper?'

Charlie laughed in delight. After all the physical changes he had undergone his personality hadn't changed at all. 'Help you become a Keeper? Well, I'm not sure if I'm even halfway there myself but, yes, of course I'll help you become a Keeper.'

'Awesome! And do you think we'll get the chance to travel around Bellania together? You know, see all the sights and places that we haven't visited yet? Like the Scented Mountains and the Dream Isles?'

'That would be amazing. We should ask my parents when . . .' Her voice trailed off. She still wasn't certain how things were ultimately going to work out with her parents' wellbeing.

'They'll be fine,' said Nibbler. His eyes blazed with certainty. 'Torn Moon has already got the Elders working on reviving them. Who knows? In a couple of months, when everything has calmed down, we might get the chance to see some of the places with them as guides.'

Charlie smiled gratefully at her friend.

'Hey!' said Jensen, poking his head through the door that led back into the tower. 'Will ya two stop flirting and come help me with Kelko? He's teamed up with some of the councillors and they're challenging me ta a K'Changa match. I need some skills on me side and I figure ya two likely suspects would fit the bill. Wotcha say? Are ya coming ta help Jensen the Willow in his hour of need?'

'Hour of need?' said Nibbler with a cheeky shake of his head. 'You mean hour of desperation.'

'Wot? How could ya say such a thing?'

'Well, you've got to be desperate to ask someone who's never played K'Changa to help you out.'

Jensen narrowed his party-fuelled eyes as his overwhelmed wits struggled to catch up with the words coming from his mouth. 'That's right, yer've never played before, have ya? Ha! Well, there's a first time for everything. Look, if the worst comes ta the worst and ya think ya're gonna fall flat on yer face, just make sure ya fall on top of one of the opposition. Got it?'

'Got it!' said Nibbler with wild enthusiasm.

As Jensen lurched back into the building Nibbler went to follow but was pulled up short.

'Huh?' he said. He looked down at Charlie's restraining hand upon his forearm, then looked into her eyes.

'You don't get off that easily,' she said.

'What? But I haven't even had a chance to get into trouble yet!' he protested.

'No, not that,' said Charlie with a ferocious shake of her head. 'You've still got something to say.'

'I do?'

'Yes!'

Realizing that it could be all night before Nibbler understood what she was hinting at, Charlie repeated her earlier words.

'You're my boy . . .'

'Uh . . .?'

'Nibbler!'

'What?' he said with feigned innocence.

Charlie stared accusingly back at him.

'Ha! Just winding you up!' The sound of his chuckle carried off into the night sky. 'Charlie, I'm your boy and you're my girl.'

Grinning so widely that his lips threatened to split his cheeks, he pulled her into a big hug, let loose a huge whoop, then tugged her inside so they could help Jensen out in his hour of need.

Their K'Changa game, as wild and as raucous as it was, was interrupted some time later when Hotstepper alighted upon the side of the Jade Tower. Bidding Charlie to clamber upon his back, he spread his wings and took flight. The two of them did not go far, and to Charlie's growing curiosity landed some few miles distant from the trees of Deepforest amidst the grasslands of the Great Plains.

'Rumbling Hunger,' said Hotstepper as Charlie slid from his back, 'has sent a message from the Winged Realm. He has instructed us to bestow upon you one last gift.'

Eyes twinkling Charlie looked around expectantly.

'No, Charlie,' chuckled Hotstepper, 'this is not a physical gift but a spiritual one.' Raising a paw he pointed up into the sky and there, flying towards them, was a wide formation of Winged Ones. Their scales twinkled and glittered in the light of the late-afternoon sun so that they looked like bejewelled toys made miniature by the distance. As she squinted, Charlie could just about make out some familiar shapes. She could spy Torn Moon, Thief Cutter, Handino and Dancing Moon leading from the front, and a good number more that she did not know by name but recognized from recent events.

'Oh, wow!' gushed Charlie, suddenly feeling like royalty. 'They're doing a fly-by!'

'Not quite,' murmured Hotstepper with a wry smile. 'Allow me to recount my grandfather's words.' When he spoke next it was in a deep voice, reminiscent of Rumbling Hunger's. 'Charlie of the Keepers, you have done us and Bellania proud, but do not forget that we are the *true* Keepers of the Realms and that we are familiar with all the races that populate all the many realms. We know you and we know what the Humans of Earth are like. Thus we know that a seed of disharmony lies buried in your soul, that deep within you lies a fear that Bane, although dead, will one day arise to haunt you and all you hold dear.'

Charlie's face paled. How did he know that? After all the books and comics and movies and games that she had enjoyed on Earth, a part of her always believed in the age-old plot of the return of the nemesis. How could Bane be any different?

A shadow fluttered over her. Startled, she raised her eyes to see that the Winged Ones had drawn near.

'How . . .' began Charlie, but fell silent as objects dropped from the majestic beasts. She watched with dazed eyes as the shapes plummeted then landed with a splat some metres distant. At Hotstepper's indication, she hesitantly moved closer until she could see what it was . . .

'Poop? Dragon poop?' she blurted in amazement, once again forgetting to call them Winged Ones.

Hotstepper bellowed with laughter. 'Yes, Charlie of the Keepers! Poop!'

'Wh-what?' Charlie's jaw fell, not knowing what to make of this bizarre incident.

'Poop,' chuckled her winged friend, 'is our final gift to you.'

'Er . . . I don't get it.'

'Well, as crude as this gesture is,' explained Hotstepper, 'and surely one you should have expected from my grandfather, this gift to you is peace of mind. This, Charlie of the Keepers, is all that remains of Bane. And, Charlie, let me tell you that there is no coming back from that. Bane, the so-called Western Menace, is well and truly gone.'

Charlie gazed first at the splattered mess, then at the Winged Ones wheeling and rolling acrobatically through the sky, then back at the amused face of her companion.

'So what do you think of your present?' he asked.

'What do I think?' asked Charlie, remembering the cruel giant that had haunted her and her family for so long. Her eyes glinted with merriment. 'I think that this is what I call poetic justice.'

'So you approve?'

'Of course! This is the best ending to an adventure and the best payback for an evil, flesh-eating chump ever! Hotstepper?'

'Yes, Charlie?'

'You and Rumbling Hunger are stars!'

'Ha!' roared Hotstepper. 'Well, we try, Charlie, we do try. Now hop on my shoulders and let's see about getting you back to the party.'

The day blurred into night. The Sylvarisians, in true spirit, partied like only they could. There were impromptu games of K'Changa held on half-finished bridges, hastily assembled restaurants cooked sweets and served pastries on the boulevards, fireworks gusted from towers, and the Winged Ones, not to be outdone, lit the sky with lightning and crazed displays of aerial acrobatics.

Stonesingers shaped the rocky remains of Stowyrms into heroic sculptures to honour the fallen, Treesingers encouraged trees into wondrous shapes, circus performers tumbled back and forth and tiptoed across tightropes. And weaving back and forth across streets and bridges was the long line of floats and dancing troupes that formed the celebration parade. The people cheered and whistled as Charlie, in pride of place, rode on Hotstepper's back.

The party continued long into the night and was still going strong when the first rays of dawn broke the horizon. The Winged Ones that led the procession spread their wings and took to the skies. They carried Charlie and her friends back to the Jade Tower where a phalanx of guards in ceremonial armour pulled their swords from scabbards to form a sabre arch. Lady Dridif waited for Charlie to dismount. Nibbler jumped down from where he had perched on Rocksteady's back, then pushed his way forward to stand by Charlie's side. Reaching out, he took his friend's hand in his own.

Dridif gave him a thoughtful nod, then turned to Sylvaris's saviour. 'Are ya ready?'

Charlie nodded.

'Then let's go and greet yer parents.'

Bright and shiny and sizzling with fun stuff . . .

puffin.co.uk

WEB CHAT

Discover something new
EVERY month – books, competitions
and treats galore

WEB NEWS

The **Puffin Blog** is packed with posts and photos from
Puffin HQ and special guest bloggers. You can also sign up
to our monthly newsletter **Puffin Beak Speak**

WEB FUN

Take a sneaky peek around your favourite **author's studio**,
tune in to the **podcast, download activities** and much more

WEBBED FEET

(Puffins have funny little feet and
brightly coloured beaks)

Point your mouse our way today!

It all started with a Scarecrow.

Puffin is seventy years old.
Sounds ancient, doesn't it? But Puffin has never been
so lively. We're always on the lookout for the next big
idea, which is how it began all those years ago.

Penguin Books was a big idea from the mind of
a man called Allen Lane, who in 1935 invented
the quality paperback and changed the world.
**And from great Penguins, great Puffins grew,
changing the face of children's books forever.**

The first four Puffin Picture Books were hatched in 1940 and the
first Puffin story book featured a man with broomstick arms called
Worzel Gummidge. In 1967 Kaye Webb, Puffin Editor, started the
Puffin Club, promising to **'make children into readers'**.
She kept that promise and over 200,000 children became
devoted Puffineers through their quarterly instalments of
Puffin Post, which is now back for a new generation.

Many years from now, we hope you'll look back and
remember Puffin with a smile. **No matter what your age
or what you're into, there's a Puffin for everyone.**
The possibilities are endless, but one thing is for sure:
whether it's a picture book or a paperback, a sticker book
or a hardback, **if it's got that little Puffin
on it – it's bound to be good.**